Dark, brooding and ruthless…
These fiercely attractive Italians
will claim what (or who)
they want…

The
Italian's

BABY BARGAIN

Three exciting, intense novels by three
powerful writers: Kim Lawrence,
Kate Walker & Trish Morey

the *Italian's*

BABY BARGAIN

KIM LAWRENCE
KATE WALKER
TRISH MOREY

All the characters in this book have no existence outside the imagination
of the author, and have no relation whatsoever to anyone bearing the
same name or names. They are not even distantly inspired by any
individual known or unknown to the author, and all the incidents are
pure invention.

THE ITALIAN'S BABY BARGAIN
© Harlequin Enterprises II B.V./S.à.r.l. 2010

The Italian's Wedding Ultimatum, The Italian's Forced Bride and *The
Mancini Marriage Bargain* were first published in Great Britain by
Harlequin Mills & Boon Limited in separate, single volumes.

The Italian's Wedding Ultimatum © Kim Lawrence 2006
The Italian's Forced Bride © Kate Walker 2006
The Mancini Marriage Bargain © Trish Morey 2005

ISBN: 978 0 263 87463 1

010-1010

Harlequin Mills & Boon policy is to use papers that are
natural, renewable and recyclable products and made from
wood grown in sustainable forests. The logging and
manufacturing processes conform to the legal environmental
regulations of the country of origin.

Printed and bound in Spain
by Litografia Rosés S.A., Barcelona

The Italian's Wedding Ultimatum

KIM LAWRENCE

Kim Lawrence lives on a farm in rural Anglesey. She runs two miles daily and finds this an excellent opportunity to unwind and seek inspiration for her writing! It also helps her keep up with her husband, two active sons and the various stray animals which have adopted them. Always a fanatical consumer of fiction, she is now equally enthusiastic about writing. She loves a happy ending!

Look for Kim Lawrence's latest exciting novels, *Unworldly Secretary*, *Untamed Greek* and *Sophie's Seduction*, which are available in September 2010 from Mills & Boon© Modern™ romance and October 2010 from M&B™.

CHAPTER ONE

SAM identified the person who had come to stand behind her chair long before his hands came to rest lightly on her shoulders. Her heart rate quickened a little before she forced herself to relax. As she turned her head her smile stayed in place. It wasn't easy, but Sam had reached the point where she felt pretty well qualified to give a master class in hiding her true feelings.

She firmly steered her thoughts from the self-pitying direction they were drifting. Reality check, Samantha Maguire—you weren't singled out for any particular cruelty from fate. Hearts get broken most days of the week!

So live with it, girl, she told herself sternly.

She was living; in fact she was living *proof* that there was life after a broken heart! Not that she was ever in danger of downplaying the disaster that was unrequited love—when the only person you had ever imagined spending the rest of your life with married someone else you didn't become indifferent overnight, or even after two years. But you did develop a protective shell; you had to.

There were days now when Sam could go an entire morning without thinking about Jonny Trelevan. Admittedly on those occasions she hadn't had a glass of champagne and he didn't have his hand on her shoulder!

Sam suspected that getting on with her life and not brooding on what might have been would probably have been easier if she could have erased him from her life, but that had never been a serious option. There were just too many connections. Not only were the Trelevan and Maguire families friends and neighbours in the small Cornish seaside town where she had been born and brought up, but Jonny's twin, Emma, was one of her best friends. And now, after the christening that morning, they were both godparents to Emma's first daughter, Laurie.

'So this is where you've been hiding, Sam.' Jonny bent down and his lips brushed gently against her cheek.

She was surprised by the unexpected gesture. Jonny wasn't normally a wildly tactile person—at least not with her—and, for a brief moment unable to shield her feelings, Sam dropped her chin and fixed her attention on the baby in her lap while she fought to regain her composure.

Her god-daughter looked back at her and gave a gummy smile. Sam felt a stab of wistful envy for the childlike innocence.

Why are you worrying? she asked herself as she grinned back at the baby and tweaked her button nose. 'Are you laughing at silly Aunty Sam…?' *See—even a ten-month-old knows Jonny wouldn't notice if you stripped naked.*

Or if he did it would only be to ask if she was warm enough! The bottom line was that to Jonny she was always going to be good old Sam—the slightly odd, skinny redhead from next door.

As she lifted her chin a moment later, her serene just-good-friends smile firmly pinned in place, Sam's unwary gaze connected head-on with the enigmatic hooded stare of Alessandro Di Livio, who was standing a little apart from a laughing group of guests on the other side of the room.

She stiffened, and her smile guttered.

A little apart just about described the man who, in Sam's opinion, carried 'aloof' to the point of plain rudeness.

With some men she might have suspected that the entire

dark, brooding man-of-mystery thing was cultivated for effect, just to make people notice him. But Alessandro Di Livio didn't need to make the effort.

He got noticed!

Of course he got noticed. He was tall, lean, and rampantly male, and if his body looked *half* as good without clothes as it did—Sam lost the thread momentarily as she thought about him naked. Face rosily tinged, she reined in her wayward imagination and concentrated on his face. Individually, his strong, dark features were memorable; collectively, they were nothing short of perfect. And that was before you even touched on the subject of the forcefield of raw sexuality that preceded him into any room!

Even from this distance the unnerving intensity of his stare had her stomach muscles behaving unpredictably. Without dropping her eyes she rested her chin on the top of the baby's silky head; his eyes really *were* the darkest she had ever seen—not dark warm, but dark *hard.* That man, she thought, repressing a shudder, wasn't chocolate. Not even the dark, bitter variety. He was cold, hard steel!

Despite the familiar wave of antipathy she always experienced when around the Italian financier, Sam forced her lips into a polite smile—while thinking, God, but there's just something about you that sets my teeth on edge.

Actually, not something, she admitted. *Everything!*

From the way he walked into a room as if he owned it to the ability of his deep voice with its tactile quality and intriguing accent to make her skin prickle. Even the fact that his incredibly well-cut suit didn't have a crease in it got under her skin. She knew it was totally irrational, and it probably made her a freak, considering that just about every other female she had ever met drooled when his name was mentioned, but she found his brand of arrogance and raw, in-your-face sexuality a total turn-off.

When she had said as much to Emma, during Jonny and

Kat's belated wedding party, her best friend, who had a pretty warped sense of humour, had grinned slyly and suggested innocently that maybe all this hostility was because Sam was secretly attracted to the Italian.

Well aware that if she showed how repugnant she found the joking suggestion Emma was going to take the *she protests too much* route, she had rolled her eyes and joked, 'Sure I am—I dream about him every night.' Trying not to think about that one shameful occasion she had almost successfully blanked from her mind—the one when she had woken with her entire body bathed in sweat and her heart pumping so fast she'd felt as if she was choking.

Fortunately a girl couldn't be held accountable for what her subconscious got up to.

'I think we'll make a lovely couple,' she'd added.

Disregarding the irony heavily lacing this prognosis, Emma grinned. 'So, you think you're the woman to get our famously commitment-phobic Italian stud to the altar? You do realise that the only time his name has ever been linked with marriage was with that woman...the lawyer...messy divorce, husband a junior minister or something.' Her smooth brow furrowed as she failed to retrieve the name. 'What was her name...?'

'Marisa Sinclair.' When the ring everyone had expected to see appear on her finger hadn't materialised Marisa Sinclair had responded to prying questions by saying that Alessandro was and always would be one of the most important people in her life.

'That's the one. Stunning-looking—half-Scottish, half-Italian, and super smart. But she didn't get her man in the end. You fancy taking a shot, Sam...?'

'You don't think I'm his type?'

Emma ran a mock critical eye over her friend. 'You scrub up pretty well when you make the effort, Sam, but...'

Sam held up a hand. 'I'm no Marisa Sinclair. All right, stop right there, while I still have some self-esteem left,' she pleaded.

'Don't fret, Sam. You're too deep for him. I think he goes for superficial and obvious. You want to know what my theory is about our enigmatic Italian?' Taking Sam's silence as assent—wrongly, as it happened—she went on to explain. 'When they were handing out the pheremones he got a treble dose. Have you seen the way women act when he walks into a room? Honest to God, an expert in body language would have a field-day!'

Thinking about the uncomfortable all over tingle she had personal experience of, Sam nodded.

'All that and money too.' Emma sighed. 'They do say that the *palazzo* on his Tuscan estate is out of this world—though I don't see how anyone knows, because nobody ever gets to go there except a few really close friends.'

'I'm surprised he has any.'

From Emma's amused expression Sam could tell that there were more comments about hostility masking attraction heading her way, so she added quickly. 'Well, maybe now you're related you'll get to see it in person.'

'I hope so. I could do with a couple of weeks in Tuscany this summer. However, if my brother's connections don't get me an invite, I'll just have to rely on my best friend to remember when she lands her dream man.'

Nightmare man, Sam thought, maintaining a long-suffering, smiling silence as her friend dissolved into fits of helpless laughter once more.

Sam sighed and pushed aside the recollections as across the room the man who had been the subject of that long-ago conversation carried on staring, with that same unnerving intensity.

Damn the man, she fumed. He has no manners at all!

It was childish, she knew, and maybe the challenge she thought she read in his eyes was all in her imagination, but

Sam was determined that she wasn't going to be the one to look away first. Consciously allowing her own smile to fade, because making an effort to be polite was clearly wasted on him, she picked up her glass of orange juice and raised it to him in a mocking salute.

The defiant gesture fell rather flat when he didn't respond. His enigmatic dark eyes, with their heavy fringe of curling lashes, just continued to drill into her from across the room.

Sam's resolve was wilting fast, but she was saved a humiliating climb-down when an attractive blonde sidled up to him…sidled so close that her breasts were almost touching his chest. Actually, they *were* touching.

Sam recognised the blonde, who had come with one of Emma's cousins. The girl had been stalking Alessandro with single-minded determination all day. Sam saw her catch hold of his sleeve and thought viciously, Serve you right! It wasn't until he turned his head away that she realised she had been literally holding her breath.

Gasping a little, to draw air into her oxygen-deprived lungs, she put her glass down on a table. What a conceited bore the man is, she thought, her lips thinning contemptuously.

A conceited bore with the ability to make your hands shake just by looking at you.

The warm fingers on her shoulder tightened and Sam's eyes widened. It was kind of shocking to realise that, far from struggling to keep a lid on her feelings for Jonny, she had forgotten he was there! And it was utterly irrational—considering he was not only another woman's husband, but oblivious to the fact she adored him—that Sam felt a pang of guilt.

As if I've been unfaithful! Now, how crazy is that?

'And how are you, my gorgeous one?'

Sam relaxed a little and felt wistful. Jonny's voice was exactly like him. Warm, solid, uncomplicated and reliable. Everything, in fact, that the Italian was not, she thought, unable to repress a tiny shudder as an image of those dark, lean, impossibly symmetrical features formed in her head.

Feeling irritated with herself for allowing Alessandro Di Livio to intrude once more into her thoughts, she angled a warm smile at Jonny. And of course she hadn't for a second made the mistake of thinking that his crooning question had been addressed to *her*.

She'd known it never would be.

It hadn't always been that way, and it was deeply embarrassing to recall that for a long time she had firmly believed that one day the scales would fall from Jonny's eyes and he would finally realise that little Sam Maguire was the only woman he could love.

A rich fantasy life was one thing, Sam mused, but her fantasy had become so firmly embedded that she had believed totally that it was going to happen—to the extent where it had affected the decisions she'd made. This belief had persisted right up to the moment Jonny had arrived home with a stunning girl whom he had proudly introduced to his family as 'my wife.'

'She's pretty much perfect,' Jonny observed now, awkwardly stroking the smooth cheek of his baby niece with a finger.

Much like yourself.

Sam guiltily lowered her eyes and turned her attention back to the baby on her lap, who gave a contented gurgle and captured the pendant around Sam's slim neck.

'She looks just like Emma, doesn't she?'

'Kat thinks she looks like me,' Jonny mused.

'The same thing, really,' Sam pointed out.

The twins, though poles apart personality-wise, had always been very alike in looks. And now that Jonny had given up surfing competitively to run first one and then several more stores across the country selling surf gear, his sun-bleached blond hair had darkened to the same honey-brown as his sister's, so the likeness between the siblings was even more pronounced.

'What's up, Sam…?'

'Up?'

'You sound… I don't know…' He studied her profile. 'Cranky,' he decided.

'I was just thinking about your brother-in-law.'

'Alessandro!' Jonny's eyes automatically sought out the tall figure standing across the room. Their eyes connected and Jonny smiled tensely before looking away. He never had been able to rid himself of the feeling that the older man could read his mind…always an uncomfortable experience, but with the cheque burning a hole in his pocket at that moment particularly so.

She nodded. 'He may have a perfect face, but his manners could do with some major work.' Seeing Jonny's brows lift at the spitting vehemence of her declaration, Sam cautioned herself to downplay her dislike. 'You have to admit,' she challenged in a milder tone, 'he makes no effort whatsoever.'

'Effort to do what?'

She pursed her lips into a disapproving line. 'Mingle.'

'*Mingle!*' Jonny echoed, and laughed.

'He always gives the impression that he's looking down his nose at me…at everyone…but then I suppose he thinks he doesn't need to be polite to ordinary people like us,' she observed contemptuously.

Jonny gave a shrug, still looking amused. 'Oh, you know Alessandro.'

For once Sam found Jonny's laid-back attitude irritating. 'Happily, no, I don't. We don't exactly move in the same circles.'

'He's actually a pretty private person, Sam, and with the paparazzi on his case all the time, sniffing for a scandal, you can't really blame him for being a bit cautious.'

'He's not cautious. He's stuck up and snobbish. Still, at least he's safe from the paparazzi today.' Nobody was going to expect to see Alessandro Di Livio at a christening in a Cornish seaside village.

Jonny looked at her curiously. 'God, you really don't like him, do you, Sam?'

'He doesn't like me,' she countered.

Jonny looked startled by the suggestion. 'Oh, I doubt that.' His eyes moved from her bright copper head and slid over her trim but slight figure. 'He's probably not even noticed you, Sam.'

From his expression it was obvious that Jonny thought she'd be pleased to realise that she was actually too insignificant even to register on Alessandro Di Livio's radar.

Sam forced a smile. 'You mean I'm mistaking indifference for rudeness?'

The ironic inflection in her voice sailed over Jonny's head. 'He can be a bit stand-offish,' he admitted. 'And he's not a great talker—at least not with me. But then he still thinks I'm not good enough for Kat.' He lowered his voice and recalled, 'You know, the night we told him we'd got married I was expecting an explosion, but the guy didn't turn a hair. Then later, when Kat wasn't in the room, he told me that if I ever hurt her he would make me wish I'd never been born.' The recollection made him shudder.

'He threatened you?' Sam bristled with indignation. The man was nothing but a thug!

'It was more in the nature of a promise.'

'I hope you told him where he could put his threats.'

Jonny looked amused. 'Yeah, that's *really* likely.'

'You have to stand up to bullies,' Sam contended angrily.

'He wasn't being a bully, he was looking out for his sister—and I don't really blame him. He's been fine with me since, but I've never forgotten, and he…' Jonny shrugged. 'Alessandro doesn't forget anything,' he admitted.

'Well, I think you and Kat were made for each other!' Sam declared, meaning it.

It *should* have been easy to dislike Kat. She had it all—pots of money, beauty and Jonny. But it wasn't! It was impossible not to like Jonny's wife, who was as warm, spontaneous and sweet-natured as her brother was revolting, cold and conceited.

'But he's right.' Jonny sighed gloomily. 'I'm not good enough for her.'

'Rubbish. Since when is Alessandro Di Livio the expert on relationships? The only person he's likely to form a loving and long relationship with is his own reflection!'

Jonny chuckled. 'Don't let Kat hear you say that,' he warned, flashing a guilty look towards his wife. 'As far as she is concerned, Alessandro can do no wrong. But then,' he added, a note of defence creeping into his voice, 'he did virtually bring her up single-handed after their parents were killed in that crash.'

Sam felt a cold shiver running down her spine and gave the baby a sudden hug, closing her eyes and burying her face deeper in the comforting warmth of her sweet-smelling soft hair.

The crash Jonny referred to had killed two members of the famous aristocratic Italian family and left a third fighting for his life. It must have had saturation media coverage at the time, but Sam, who had only been in her teens, had only a vague recollection of the story. Coincidentally, she had caught a TV programme only the previous night, in which it had featured prominently.

In asking *Are Some People Born Lucky?*, the programme-makers had presented a pretty compelling argument that some people *did* lead a charmed existence, surviving situations which logically they should not have.

The programme had made compulsive viewing, but it had had the sort of voyeuristic qualities that made Sam feel uncomfortable. She had been about to vote with her feet and switch off when a computer simulation had shown the route the Di Livio car had taken when it had gone over the cliff-edge, and she had literally held her breath as she watched the action replay.

Sam hadn't been surprised to hear emergency workers

comment that it had been the first time they had ever taken anyone out of a wreck alive on that treacherous mountainside.

When the commentator's voice had posed in thrilling accents the question 'Was this man born lucky?' the screen had been filled with the image of a young-looking Alessandro, his dark hair whitened with dust, his bruised face leeched of all colour, strapped to a stretcher about to be air lifted away from the twisted, mangled remains of the car.

Sam had then switched off the TV and muttered angrily to the cat, '*Lucky?* Very lucky, if your version of lucky happens to involve nearly dying and losing both your parents… *Idiots!*'

She had caught sight of her scowling reflection in the mirror and stopped dead, her eyes widening. I'm getting all protective and indignant on behalf of Alessandro Di Livio…now, how bizarre is that? One thing was for sure, she'd thought, flashing a wry smile at her mirror image. The recipient of her caring concern would not have been grateful!

The programme had preyed on her mind. She just hadn't been able to get the image of his tragic, blood-stained face out of her head, no matter how hard she'd tried. Then this morning at the church, as she'd sat alone and waited for everyone else to arrive, in he'd walked!

It had really spooked her—think about him and he appears… That will teach me to be more careful about who and what I think about in the future, she had reflected, shrinking back into her seat.

Unobserved, she'd had the luxury of being able to stare at him. People would probably pay for that privilege. But, no matter how hard she'd looked, she hadn't found any trace of the vulnerability she had seen in the face of that young man with the bleak, empty eyes, clinging to life.

Same classical profile, same aquiline nose, same razor-sharp prominent cheekbones, and his mouth was still sexy enough to cause a sharp intake of breath in the unprepared observer, but the man exuded an air of unstudied confidence and control.

If she had glimpsed even a shadow of that younger man Sam thought her attitude to him might have softened, but she hadn't, and when a few moments later she'd knocked a hymn book to the floor and alerted him to her presence she had looked away quickly.

'I saw a programme about the accident last night,' she said now.

Jonny nodded. 'Yeah, Alessandro phoned Kat and told her not to watch it. He said it was sensationalist rubbish and would only upset her.'

'And did she watch it?'

'After he'd told her not to?' Jonny laughed at the notion of Kat not following her brother's suggestion.

'Well, he may be a control freak, but in this instance,' Sam admitted, 'he was right. It *would* have upset her. It was a bit graphic.' A chilly shiver traced a path down her spine as she recalled the bleak devastation in the eyes of the man they had called lucky.

'I suppose he's afraid it will resurrect the story.'

'How old was Kat at the time?' Jonny's wife had only been nineteen when they'd married, after a whirlwind romance.

'She was eleven. She would have been with them on the trip, but she spiked a fever at the last minute…turned out she had mumps.'

'Lucky mumps,' Sam said thinking about the moment that morning in church, when her eyes had brushed Alessandro's. Her smooth brow furrowed. Jonny's wrong. He *doesn't* like me. Her chin came up to a belligerent angle.

Which suits me fine!

Her grim expression lightened as Laurie's fingers closed over the beaten silver pendant she wore around her neck and she tried to draw it to her rosebud mouth. Sam, grateful to be distracted from her thoughts, disentangled the tenacious chubby fingers and shook her head.

'No, Laurie, it wouldn't taste good,' she reproached.

Jonny's fingers tightened on her shoulder. 'Feeling broody, Sam?'

The question sounded teasing and light, but something in his voice made Sam lift her head and study his face. 'Broody—*me*…?' Jonny smiled, but she noticed it didn't reach his eyes. 'I prefer babies when you can hand them back at the end of the day.' Not true, but it sounded like a suitable response. She could hardly go with the other option, which was to say *If I can't have your babies I don't want any!*

'You think that now, but all women start talking babies.'

Sam received a jolt as his meaning sank in. Jonny a father… It would happen one day, so get used to it. 'Are congratulations in order?'

Jonny didn't respond to her question. Following the direction of his distracted gaze, Sam saw his eyes had come to rest on Kat.

Feeling like an intruder, Sam quickly averted her gaze, trying and failing to imagine a man looking at *her* with the kind of suppressed longing she had read in Jonny's face. She caught a glimpse of herself reflected in the enormous gilt-framed mirror that covered the wall to her right and thought, *Sure—that's really going to happen.* It was a fact of life that freckles, red hair and a body that was never going to be curvy did not inspire dumbstruck lust and longing.

'Congratulations?' Jonny dragged his attention back to Sam.

'I thought you and Kat might be starting a family.'

Her innocuous remark caused Jonny's good-looking features to freeze. 'I'm not ready to start a family.'

Meaning Kat was…? Sam speculated, puzzling over his expression. 'I thought you loved children…'

Not that she could for a second imagine Jonny as a hands-on father. Though he had many good points, Jonny did have some pretty old-fashioned ideas.

'This isn't a good time.'

'Is there ever a good time?'

Dark colour flooded Jonny's face as he bent closer. 'For God's sake, Sam,' he hissed. 'Do I have to spell it out? You of all people should realise that I can't *afford* to be thinking of babies. And I can't tell Kat…' He swallowed, drew a deep breath and shook his head. The strained smile he gave her was ruefully apologetic. 'Sorry, Sam. I shouldn't take it out on you.' Absently he patted her shoulder. 'Could I have a word, Sam?'

He looked so apologetic that she immediately forgave his outburst. 'Isn't that what we *are* doing?'

Jonny cleared his throat and nodded towards the closed French doors. *'In private.'*

You can have anything you want.

Her colour slightly heightened by her traitorous thought, Sam nodded placidly and reminded herself for the tenth time that afternoon that she was a strong, independent woman who didn't need a man—and, anyway, she wasn't the sort of person who would settle for second best.

In the alcove, where he had retreated to watch them, Alessandro Di Livio tightened his long fingers around the stem of his untouched glass of champagne as he observed his brother-in-law's head move closer to the glossy copper one of the seated woman.

They were so close they looked like lovers about to embrace. He couldn't give the man his sister had chosen a backbone, but he could make damned sure that he didn't cheat and break his besotted little sister's heart!

God knew what either woman saw in him. Maybe it was the surfing thing? He presumed, from the cabinet of trophies ostentatiously on show in his sister's apartment, that the younger man had been more successful riding the waves than he was at business. Perhaps the younger man could have coped with one store, he conceded, but his rapid and reckless expansion over the past eighteen months had been nothing short of suicidal. The only thing that surprised Alessandro, who had been set to bail him out for the past year, was that he was still financially afloat.

His sensually sculpted lips formed a twisted, cynical smile as the Maguire woman lifted her hand in a fluttery gesture to her slender, pale throat. The action was as revealing as he had come to expect of her, but he couldn't quite decide if she was as transparent as she appeared, or if it was all part of some sort of act.

Alessandro's nostrils flared. If Jonny Trelevan didn't know she was his for the asking the younger man was an even bigger fool than he'd taken him for. His eyes slid towards his sister, who had been talking too loudly and brightly all afternoon, and found she too was watching the couple. As he watched she turned her head, and he was sure he caught the glitter of tears in her eyes.

Whatever was wrong with his sister's marriage, he would have laid odds that the red-headed little witch was responsible. What was her game? Alessandro wondered as he angled his dark head a little to one side and studied the slim figure.

If asked to classify her look he would have called it sexy, yet demure. Not to his taste, but he knew a lot of men went for the perennial virgin look. She was the sort of female who simultaneously aroused predatory and protective instincts in the opposite sex.

No wonder men got confused around her. They didn't know whether to kiss her or protect her from a light breeze! He, on the other hand, knew what he wanted to do—namely shake her and tell her to display a little more discretion when she looked at Trelevan with those big hungry eyes!

Of course her dress sense was nothing short of a total disaster, but colour co-ordination wasn't going to be high on your average male's list of priorities when he heard her laugh—that low, husky, wicked chuckle.

It was the sort of laugh a man imagined hearing behind a closed bedroom door. *Or is that just me…?*

He had known from the beginning, of course, that she was in love with Jonny Trelevan—though astonishingly, as far as he could tell, he was the only person who did! Her friends and relations seemed uniformly oblivious to the intense misery behind the brave smile. He had suspected at that time that if you had taken away that smile and the screaming tension in every fibre of her slender body she would probably have collapsed.

He was neither a relation or a friend, but an objective observer, so her unrequited love was none of his concern so long as she represented no danger to his sister's happiness.

He had decided to give her the benefit of the doubt.

For starters, Trelevan had seemed to view her as one of the boys, and the only time he got physical was when he punched her playfully on the arm.

As for the girl herself... His eyes narrowed as once again they fell on Samantha Maguire, face buried in the hair of the baby on her lap, so that all he could see was the top of her copper head. If he had thought she represented a threat to his sister's happiness he would have taken whatever action he deemed necessary. But two years ago he had decided that she did not possess the tempestuous nature that was meant to accompany her vibrant colouring.

She would look, but not touch. And there was no law against looking. He had done some of that himself. On every occasion since, when their paths had crossed, he had kept a watchful eye on her.

Of course he'd been glad that Katerina did not have the added complication of a jealous would-be lover in the background, trying to sabotage her marriage, but he'd felt a stab of contempt when he considered the Maguire girl's passive acceptance of the hand fate had dealt her. It was incomprehensible to him, but maybe, he mused, it had something to do with British stoicism—something which Alessandro with his more volatile Latin temperament had never been able to get a handle on. But then he never had understood people taking pride in being a good loser.

Now, though, he wasn't so sure about his earlier assessment. Had he been mistaken in her? Had Samantha Maguire been playing the long game and waiting for her chance? Alessandro was not the sort of man who left things to chance, and this was a possibility he had to consider.

Jonny Trelevan wasn't the husband he would have chosen for his sister—he was too weak and ineffectual to Alessandro's mind—but Alessandro had accepted that his wishes were not the ones that counted. The younger man was the husband Kat wanted, and as her brother he would do anything in his power to give Katerina, deprived of the parental love and support he himself had enjoyed, what she wanted.

He stood listening to the inane prattle of the young woman at his side, catching only one word in three of what she was saying, and plunged headlong into one of the flashbacks which had been part of his life for the last ten years.

CHAPTER TWO

A FLASHBACK implied that you'd lost sense of your surroundings, but for Alessandro it was more a sense of dislocation, of being in two places at the same time.

Like today—in the here and now he was saying something that made the plastic blonde girl giggle, while simultaneously he was back on the dark road of that night, pressing the brakes and feeling no response.

The only outward evidence of what was happening to him was the sheen of sweat across his brow.

He could hear the blonde listing her favourite haunts. The flickering images always followed the same rigid sequence. He knew that the next one involved being pretty sure he was going to die.

'I don't go to nightclubs,' he replied, when she finally asked his own preference.

She could have looked no more shocked had he confided a predilection for women's underwear. Alessandro might have laughed had he not been calling on every skill he had, and then some he didn't, in a futile attempt to control the car. Knowing as he did so that nothing he could do would affect the outcome.

Looking at the card scrawled with a number, he nodded and murmured an ironic, 'You're very kind,' as his guts tightened in anticipation of the car launching itself into space.

Then the blonde was gone, and so was the car, and they

were falling on and on. He could hear the high-pitched female scream that seemed to go on for ever, and then the screech of metal as it ripped and tore. The foul stench of petrol filled his flared nostrils.

Wiping a hand across his damp brow, he looked across the room and saw Samantha Maguire on the point of stepping through the French windows with his brother-in-law. Watching the couple slip outside, Alessandro narrowed his eyes in speculative anger. Did they think nobody had noticed?

Maybe conducting their illicit relationship under the very nose of Katerina added spice? Or maybe the redhead *wanted* to be discovered?

In his head there was silence, an eerie silence broken finally by his own voice calling to his parents, asking, 'Are you all right?'

Imprisoned in his seat, he could only imagine why there was no reply to the question he kept repeating, and all the time he had the knowledge that it would take only one spark and the car and its contents would become a raging inferno.

Dawn had been breaking before the first rescuers had arrived.

Alessandro had still been in hospital when the inquest was held. And, thanks to the irritating intransigence of the surgeon responsible for uniting the shattered fragments of bone in his right leg, he had been banned from attending.

His personality was such that going against expert opinion did not normally present him with an obstacle. Alessandro's problem on that occasion was that the expert advice he wanted to flout came from the man who had saved his leg when the general consensus of medical opinion had been that the mangled limb was beyond saving. He figured that following his advice was the least he owed the man who had operated not once but three times to give him back his mobility.

The inquest had gone ahead in his absence, and had resulted in the total recall of a series of high-performance

cars, all of which had shared the faulty braking system discovered in the one that had plunged off the side of the moun-
tain with him at the wheel. The fact that no blame for the
fatal accident had been assigned to him personally, that in
fact the crash investigators had said nothing he could have
done would have prevented the car going over, did not lessen
the responsibility that Alessandro felt for the death of his
parents.

He had relived the disastrous moments innumerable times
since, sure that if he had done something differently his parents would still be alive. Not that it was in his nature to waste
time indulging his survivor guilt. He'd had a sister to bring
up—a sister who, thanks to him, had no parents.

His chiselled jaw tightened as, without waiting for his
heart-rate to return to normal, he made his way towards the
terrace doors. The expression on his face made several people get out of his way.

It was time to issue a warning—a warning that was long
overdue. And if Miss Maguire knew what was good for her
she would take notice. If not? Well, that was her decision. For
his part, Alessandro had no doubts concerning his ability to
make her see things his way.

The terrace was empty because, despite the brilliant April sunshine, the fluffy white clouds and the expanse of daffodils on
the wide green lawns, the wind held a bone-biting chill.

Sam shivered as the wind cut through the beige linen suit
she wore. The skirt length and A-line cut didn't do her petite,
narrow-hipped and high-bosomed frame any favours. As her
mother had pointed out earlier, she should never, *ever* wear
beige as it made her look drained and haggard.

Sam had agreed. And of course since then she had *felt*
drained and haggard.

'God, I'm going to get hypothermia,' she said, hugging her
arms around herself as a particularly harsh gust of wind cut

through the fabric. 'Couldn't you say what you needed to say inside?'

'Here.'

Sam looked from the envelope he had thrust into her hand to Jonny's solemn face. 'What's this?' she asked, making no attempt to open it. She knew what it was.

He ran a hand through his disordered fair curls, and the familiar gesture made Sam's heart ache. 'I said I'd repay the loan, Sam,' he reminded her.

'And I said there was no hurry, Jonny,' she returned quietly, hating the way his eyes slid from hers. 'I don't need the money. It's just sitting there in the bank.' The amount of money that worldwide sales of the *Angela's Cat* series made was shockingly large, and Sam's tastes were pretty simple. And in a funny way she owed her success to Jonny.

Without Jonny she would never have felt the need to escape, and she might never have discovered that writing was the perfect way to do so. In which case the chances were her children's story might never have been anything more than a few pages lying forgotten in the back of a drawer. And she might still be working as a supply teacher.

'You helped me out of a sticky spot, and for that, Sam, I'll be eternally grateful. But,' he said, closing her fingers around the envelope, 'this is yours. And thanks to you Kat isn't going to know how close to bankrupt I was.'

Sam gave a worried frown and hoped Jonny's male pride wasn't making him repay the loan before he could afford to. But, aware she couldn't do much about it, she reluctantly shoved the envelope into her pocket. 'Well, you know what I think, Jonny.'

'That I should have told Kat I was on the verge of bankruptcy.' He shook his fair head and gave a grim laugh. 'Leave it, Sam. You don't know what you're talking about. I *had* to borrow that money.'

'But your grandmother's legacy—' Sam protested.

'Paid for the initial investment,' he slotted in. 'And I needed money to expand.'

'Why expand?'

Jonny's features settled into obstinate lines. 'I couldn't expect Kat to be a shopkeeper's wife.'

Sam shook her head in exasperation. 'For the record, I think you're a total idiot. Your wife is rich, and her brother is—'

Jonny ran an unsteady hand over his cleanshaven jaw and interrupted. 'Her brother is *Alessandro Di Livio*. That's the whole point, Sam. He's worth billions, and I—'

'Kat knew you weren't a billionaire when she married you,' she interrupted impatiently.

His blue eyes slid from hers. 'How could I tell a girl like Kat that I was taking less out of the shop in a year than she spends on shoes in a month? Her brother has always given her everything she wants before she even asks. She worships him,' he gritted, unable to conceal the envy in his voice as he added dourly, 'And, let's face it, Alessandro is perfect.'

An image of a dark, patrician face flashed into her head, and Sam was unable to voice the denial she would have liked. Physically at least he was about as close to perfect as you could get. If your idea of perfect happened to be six feet five of lean, toned muscle, flashing dark eyes, a sinfully sensual mouth, cheekbones that you could cut yourself on and an aristocratic profile. His gorgeous Mediterranean colouring presumably went all over...

She stopped, alarm filtering into her expression. Mentally undressing the man twice within the space of half an hour was not a good development.

Well, gorgeous body or not, he wasn't Sam's idea of perfect. But she accepted that on this she was in the minority. However, it didn't take a great leap to see how a creature like that could make other men feel inadequate.

'Tell me, Jonny, what's the most important thing in your life?' she asked him quietly.

'Kat, of course.'

Sam heard the indignation in his voice that she should need to ask, and wondered bleakly if the other woman knew how lucky she was. 'Exactly.' Her lips twitched into a contemptuous smile. 'Can you imagine a woman being the most important thing in Alessandro Di Livio's life?'

She watched Jonny struggle to do so, and gave a triumphant *I told you so* smile. 'Of course you can't. Because the only person important to Alessandro Di Livio is Alessandro.'

'He cares about Kat!' Jonny protested.

Too much, Sam thought. 'Fair enough,' she conceded. 'But if Kat had wanted another version of her brother she'd have found one. She didn't, because she's a hell of a lot brighter than you are. What she wanted was a decent bloke who puts her first. She wanted you, Jonny.'

'You really think so?'

'How would you like it if Kat was in trouble and she didn't come to you? Just stop being a stiff-necked idiot, tell your wife the truth, and give her what she wants…which presumably is you, Jonny.' There's a lot of it about, she thought, before adding, 'And maybe a baby…?'

The anger died from Jonny's face and he clutched his head in his hands. 'God, Sam, you're right!' he cried. 'I've been a total idiot. I know I should have told her. But I didn't want her to think she'd married a total loser!'

Sam had got into the habit of avoiding physical contact with Jonny—it was a self-protective thing—but if ever there was an occasion for a hug this was it. 'God,' she said, wrapping her arms around him, 'but men are stupid.'

Jonny, who had rested his chin on her glossy hair, lifted his head. 'Especially me.'

'Especially you,' she agreed with a watery grin as she drew back from the embrace.

'One thing, Sam…?'

'Anything.'

'Don't say anything about this to Alessandro. Like I said, he never did think I was good enough for Kat, and if he found out about my cashflow problems he'd…Well…'

Sam nodded. 'I understand.'

She understood, all right. She understood that the only way Jonny's marriage was going to work out was if Kat managed to escape her brother's overpowering influence.

'My lips are sealed,' she promised, miming a zipping motion along the generous curve of her mouth.

About to turn away, Jonny swung back and took her by the shoulders. 'Sam, I may not say so very often, but I do know that you're the best friend in the world!' he said, planting a light kiss on her lips.

'Sure I am. Now, go and talk to your wife.'

Oblivious to the husky catch in her voice, Jonny responded to her urging, pausing only to blow a kiss back to her from the doorway as he dived back indoors, his expression determined.

Sam forgot her desire to escape the cold wind and closed her eyes, lifting a hand to her lips. Her smooth brow puckered into a frown. No tingling…no wild surge of uncontrollable lust! In fact, no lust at all. Could it be that her under-used sex drive had simply died?

'That was a very *touching* scene.'

CHAPTER THREE

THE air was expelled from her lungs in one startled gasp as Sam spun around, thinking, *It can't be…?*

Of course it was. Nobody else had a voice like that.

'Oh, it's you…' she said stupidly, then flushed.

Alessandro watched as she pushed the strands of hair that had come free from the loose knot on her head from her face with both hands. It was an almost child-like gesture. The vibrant copper, he noticed, glowed against her pale skin. Actually, now that he thought about it, her skin glowed too, with an almost opalescent sheen.

It was the sort of skin a man would find difficult to look at and not think about touching…the silky softness was a tactile invitation. His brother-in-law had clearly decided it was an invitation, he thought, his angular jaw tightening as he looked at the lips the younger man had found so irresistible.

Sam's expression grew defensive as she returned the silent, hostile stare of the person responsible for a tingling that extended to the soles of her feet. Inside her chest her heart was banging against her ribcage like a trapped wild animal.

Actually, her trapped wild animal instincts were kicking in pretty hard right now. It was only the fact that he stood between her and the door that stopped her from fleeing.

When she had asked Emma earlier why on *earth* she had invited the wretched man, her friend had reminded Sam that she'd invited all her own family, and he was Kat's brother and she didn't have any other family, poor thing.

'Besides,' she had admitted with a rueful grin, 'I never expected him to actually accept.'

Now, looking up into that lean, arresting face, Sam, who if she was honest had been exasperated by Jonny's inability to stand up for himself where his brother-in-law was concerned, felt a strong surge of sympathy for him. Small wonder he felt nervous and inadequate around the man—and as for confiding his problems…! Dear God, banana skins probably got out of the way when they saw his hand-made Italian shoes coming!

His was certainly the very last shoulder *she'd* choose to cry on, she thought as her glance brushed the broad, well-developed area in question. How many women had made use of those manly shoulders? Or even sunk their teeth into that smooth golden flesh during a moment of heightened passion…?

You didn't look at Alessandro Di Livio and think, Here's a man with empathy. You thought, Here's a man who's never put a foot wrong in his life… *Or a man who inspired women to bite his shoulders?* You thought, Here's a man who has no insight and even less sympathy for the failings of lesser mortals… *And maybe the ability to make a woman lose control…?*

A flurry of alarm filtered into her guarded expression as she wondered where those maverick thoughts had come from.

Had he heard any of her conversation with Jonny?

Her alarm lessened as she realised that unless he'd been lurking in the shadows for a long time, which didn't seem likely, he couldn't know about the cheque burning a hole in her pocket. The most he could have witnessed was a quick hug between friends and a peck on the cheek—so nothing incriminating there.

Sam released a tiny sigh of relief. Jonny's secret was safe.

'I'm sorry—I didn't see you there.' Her normally sunny smile was on the stiff side, but she quietly congratulated herself for making the effort—even though all she wanted to do was escape from his oppressive presence.

'*Obviously.*'

'Is there a problem?'

Considering the degree of hostility emanating from his lean body, it now seemed laughable that on the occasions when Sam had previously encountered the man she had considered him to have a glacially cold disposition. A man with the coldest eyes she had ever seen. A man totally incapable of spontaneous emotion, or for that matter *any* emotion that wasn't clinically calculated.

The nerve jumping erratically alongside his sinfully sexy mouth and the combustible air of barely suppressed fury that was emanating from him now rather suggested that he was capable of doing a lot more than raising his voice. He was certainly raising the hairs on the nape of her neck. She refused point-blank to analyse the things his proximity was doing to any points south of her neck!

His dark eyes meshed with hers. '*You* are the problem.' And one he was going to sort once and for all.

Sam stared, totally bemused by his aggressive response. 'Have you been drinking?'

'No, I have not been drinking. I saw you throw yourself at him.'

Sam shook her head at this harsh addition. 'Throw…? Who…?'

His dark eyes flicked across her slightly parted lips and his own moved in a moue of distaste. 'Kiss him…' He smiled cynically as he watched the guilty colour fly to her pale cheeks. 'There is a name for women who do that to married men.'

This last contemptuous observation and that horrid smile snuffed out the guilt Sam had nursed for the secret she carried in her heart and loosened the firm grip she normally kept on her Celtic redhead's temper. She trembled with the force of the surge of anger that washed over her as she read the superior condemnation in his face.

If she hadn't been in the grip of strong emotions—namely

the desire to physically remove the nasty smile from his smug face—she might have remembered that it probably wasn't a good idea to antagonise someone who was in a position to make Jonny's life uncomfortable. But caution wasn't part of her plan as, head flung back, she took a step towards him.

The sheer, unmitigated nerve of the man—looking down his nose at her like that. Especially when you considered this was the same person who had refused to deny or confirm the rumours that he was the *real* reason a high-profile politician and his lawyer wife had split up. He was obviously as guilty as sin! Sam chose to ignore the fact that at the time she had argued with a friend that silence did not equate to guilt.

'You have something against kissing…?' she asked, injecting sarcasm into her voice and being rewarded by the expression on his face.

Clean up your own act before you criticise other people, she thought grimly.

'Is that kissing generally…?' A finger pressed to the soft indentation in her firmly rounded chin, she pretended to consider this possibility. 'No,' she said, shaking her head from side to side. 'That can't be right. Because you appeared to have nothing against kissing at that film premiere, when that girl was eating your face.' The tasteless pictures had been plastered over every tabloid's front page the next day.

Sam almost laughed. He couldn't have looked more astonished if one of the pieces of furniture had spoken up for itself. She was dimly aware, somewhere in the recesses of her mind, that the adrenaline rush she was experiencing was responsible for half the things coming out of her mouth. Her inability to back down in the face of warning signs you'd have to be blind not to see was down to her own stupidity.

Her breath coming in short, shallow bursts, she studied his proud, patrician features. Hard disdain and anger was implicit in every intriguing hollow and strong plane. His nostrils were flared and his firm jaw tight, and his golden skin was drawn taut across the angles of his jutting cheekbones.

'The lady in question was not married.'

That made a change, then. 'Nor very fussy, it would seem.'

She sniffed, and smiled sweetly in response to his hoarsely ejaculated, 'Dio mio!'

'But then some people will endure almost anything to advance their careers. I suppose I'm just lucky that I didn't need to sleep my way to the top.'

Sam registered the dark glitter visible through the mesh of his long lashes and her stomach took a lurching dive. It was only sheer bloody-minded obstinacy—of which her nearest and dearest said she had been gifted an extra portion—that enabled Sam to maintain eye contact.

'You are at the top, then, are you…?' His smile said more clearly than any words that he thought she was lying.

The comment made Sam, normally the most self-deprecating of creatures, who would have been the first to play down her success, stick out her chin and boast boldly, 'I will be.' Her long-suffering editor, who was often heard to despair over her lack of drive and ambition, would have stared to hear that. 'And wherever I am,' she added, with the confidence of someone who knew a company wanted her to write a TV serialisation of the accident-prone feline she had created, 'at least I won't have to rely on my looks to stay there.'

There was a pause as his dark glance moved down her reed-slender figure. 'That is indeed fortunate.' Actually, she had the sort of delicate bone structure that would enable her to grow old gracefully. And lily-pale flawless skin. His eyes slid over the graceful length of her slender neck and the line between his brows deepened.

Two can play at that game, mate, she thought, smiling at him through gritted teeth. 'Nor do I have to worry that people want to be my friend just because of what I can do for them.'

'I consider myself an excellent judge of character.'

Sam's malicious smile widened. In a rather perverse way she was almost enjoying this exchange of smiling insults. Of course she would have enjoyed kicking his shins even more, but as she was no longer six the option wasn't open. 'Of course you do. But this time you have got it so wrong you're going to feel very stupid.'

'I doubt that.'

'Being able to admit when you're wrong is a sign of maturity.'

'A subject *you* would not know one hell of a lot about.'

Great—so now I'm childish, and I go around kissing married men! Sam, who didn't like the way his dark eyes were lingering on her mouth, decided enough was enough—even if the verbal tussle *was* exhilarating. 'Look, you've got it wrong—'

'I know what I saw.'

His sheer bloody-minded intransigence made her want to scream. 'And even if I *did* kiss him, what business would it be of yours?' Even before she saw his expression she knew that he'd interpret her angry retort as an admission of guilt. Frankly, she was past caring.

'Katerina is my sister, and I will protect her.'

She gave up trying to prove her innocence and asked, 'How are you going to stop me sleeping with Jonny?'

'I think telling him you are mine will have the desired effect.'

He said it so matter of factly that Sam thought at first she had misunderstood him. The uncertainty only lasted a moment. There was no room for misinterpretation in his ruthless smile. Honestly, this man belonged in a different century! *Mine,* he had said... As though *owning* someone body and soul was perfectly acceptable.

The idea of surrendering control to a man like Alessandro Di Livio was a concept that made her shudder with horror... *Are you so sure it's horror?*

Sam swallowed. 'I take it you're not an advocate of political correctness?' she observed, moistening her dry lips with her tongue. She inhaled and raised her eyes, only to discover his burning gaze was fixed on her mouth. As their eyes connected the blaze of raw hunger in his nailed her to the spot.

Paralysed by a stab of lust so strong she couldn't breathe, Sam stared up at him. He reminded her of a sleek jungle cat—beautiful, and totally ruthless. She had always considered the claim that danger was attractive a particularly stupid one. Now she knew that she had been very wrong. The fear she had denied feeling moments earlier was now coursing through her veins, along with some primitive stuff she had no intention of *ever* analysing.

There was no point. None of this was real, she told herself. It was all the result of some freak chain of events—events that were *never* going to happen again. She was never going to feel this way again. She was going to go home and close the door and everything would go back to the way it had been before Alessandro Di Livio had looked at her as if he wanted to rip off her clothes.

Sam closed her eyes, thought about closing that door, and felt slightly calmer. She might get a new safety bolt fitted… She opened her eyes and pointed out the obvious flaw in his manipulative plan.

'Jonny wouldn't believe it…' She thought about it, and added. '*Nobody* would believe you.'

'Why not?'

Was he serious? Her eyes travelled up the long, lean, gorgeous length of him before settling on his dark, fallen angel features. 'Because you're…' She just stopped short of saying *incredibly beautiful,* and substituted a husky, 'I don't like you. *Everyone* knows that.'

One dark brow lifted at *everyone*, and he looked amused. 'Liking is not a prerequisite to…' he slotted in.

'Ownership…?' she suggested sweetly. 'Look, this conversation is going nowhere—but *I* am.'

She edged towards the door, but he blocked her way with his body.

Lips pursed and eyes narrowed, she glared up at him. 'You're in my way.'

'Before you go I want to make very sure that you know it would be unwise for you to continue your pursuit of Trelevan.'

A whistling sound of frustration escaped her clenched teeth. My God, the man was fixated! 'Where do you get off, making a judgement about me?' she demanded, indignation making her voice shrill. 'How many times have we met…? Five…? How dare you? You don't even know me!'

'Eight. Not including today.'

The smooth correction made her stare. 'You were counting…?' Her brows lifted and she laughed nervously. 'Should I be flattered?' Her expression hardened. 'Or afraid…? You'd like that, wouldn't you? But then bullies always do,' she contended grimly. 'Only I'm not afraid of you, Mr Di Livio. Not at all,' she stressed shakily, before she was forced to pause to gasp for breath.

'There is nothing preventing us getting to know one another better, if that is what you would like.'

Sam rubbed her damp palms against her skirt and didn't even let herself *think* about what he meant by that. 'Other than mutual dislike. And I *wouldn't* like.'

'Dislike…?' he mused contemplatively. After a moment he shook his dark head and a predatory smile split his lean features. 'Dislike is such a mild word. I think it goes much deeper with us than mere *dislike*.'

The tactile quality she had noticed before in his deep, darkly textured voice was stronger than ever. Sam swallowed. This man really did have the market in enigmatic and disturbing cornered!

'You lack caution and judgement.'

'I was just thinking the same thing.' Her response had worryingly little to do with caution and a lot to do with the excitement that was tying her stomach in knots! 'Now, if you'll excuse me, it's a bit cold out here.' Actually, she no longer felt the cold—her skin was burning.

Instead of moving out of her way, he leaned against the ajar door, causing it to close with a loud click.

Sam's voice was flat, even though inside she was panicking. 'Excuse me…'

His dark eyes slid down her slim figure before returning to her face. The overt contempt in his expression brought a sparkle of anger to Sam's wide-spaced eyes.

'No, I will not excuse you.'

Taken aback by the overt provocation in his response Sam blinked.

A long silence followed, which he showed no signs of filling until he suddenly said accusingly, 'Your eyes have turned green.'

'Pardon me…?' It was possible she had misheard him. It was equally possible her aquamarine eyes *had* turned green. This happened when she was in the grip of strong emotions. Chameleon eyes, her father called them. Though the colour-change did not disguise but reveal the depth of her feelings.

'No, I will not do that either.' Without warning he reached out and took her chin in between long brown fingers and carried on looking into her eyes, which were still green. 'You would not want me for an enemy, *cara.*'

Gazing up into the dark mesmeric depth of his astounding eyes, Sam felt the breath leave her body in one long, shuddering sigh. Her knees began to give, and she closed her eyes while she tried to tap into her reserves of wilting composure.

She opened her eyes and gave a contemptuous smile. 'Almost as little as I'd want you as a friend.'

One corner of his mouth lifted in a sneer. 'Friendship is not possible between men and women.'

That he held this chauvinistic viewpoint did not surprise Sam at all. 'You *would* think that. It just so happens that one of my best friends is a male.'

'And sex has never got in the way…?'

He said it as calmly as if he was asking her how she liked her steak. Sam was less then comfortable about discussing sex in the same *county* as this man, let alone while he was touching her. She looked away, aware of the flush that had mounted her cheeks. 'I'm talking about Jonny.'

'So am I.'

Sam's horrified gaze flew to his face. 'All I am to Jonny is a s…supportive friend. I'm getting tired of telling you— there's never been anything like that between us!' she protested shrilly.

'And you wouldn't *want* there to be? Do not play the innocent with me. I have been watching you.'

'The all-knowing, all-seeing Alessandro Di Livio?' Sam cut in, her voice a successful marriage of boredom and amusement. Inside, however, she was struggling to control her rising panic. She lifted her chin, carefully focusing her gaze somewhere over his right shoulder to avoid contact with those hateful *knowing* eyes. 'In case you've forgotten,' she reminded him, 'Jonny is married.'

Alessandro arched an ironic brow and wondered if the copper hair felt as silky as it looked. 'I haven't forgotten.' His voice dropped to a low, threatening purr as he pushed his point home. 'And I suggest *you* don't.'

Sam felt the humiliating colour in her cheeks deepen.

Of course it wouldn't occur to him that she might have the odd principle or two. 'I've told you—Jonny and I are just good friends.'

A quiver of irritation crossed his olive-skinned face and he gritted something soft and angry in his native tongue.

'Well, let's just say your mouth says one thing…' He paused, a slightly distracted expression drifting across his face as his glance zeroed in on the soft full curves of her lips. 'And,' he continued, anger hardening his voice, 'those big, hungry eyes say another thing entirely. Have you been waiting for him to notice that you're a woman?' He released a low, scornful laugh as his eyes raked her stricken face. 'Of course it is entirely possible you wouldn't like it if he had,' he mused, half to himself.

'I wouldn't know—he never has!' Sam was pushed into yelling.

A moment later she connected with his eyes and wanted to curl up and die from sheer humiliation. But pride, and the scorn in his eyes, made her stick out her chin and pronounce in a low, but clear voice, 'But I'm not the type to give up at the first hurdle.'

His dark brows twitched into a disapproving straight line above his masterful nose. 'Are you totally without conscience?'

The irony made her laugh. *'Gosh!'* she sighed, holding up her hands in mock surrender. 'You've seen right through me. I'm your original scarlet woman. Your sons are not safe while I'm around.' Her lips twisted into a derisive grimace. 'For goodness' sake, you silly man, I don't represent a danger to anyone.'

He stiffened, and from where she stood she could distinctly hear the sound of his startled inhalation. Sam studied his face and thought, I'm guessing that nobody has ever called him a *silly man* before. More's the pity. If they had he might have learnt not to take himself so desperately seriously.

His dark eyes narrowed to slits, but the startled annoyance glittering in the dark depths was mingled with reluctant admiration as he registered the mockery shining in her eyes. 'You are a very aggravating female.'

She glared back up at him, torn between exhilaration and exasperation and wishing that he'd yelled—not used that purring tone which made more places than the soles of her feet tingle. 'And you,' she declared, dumping diplomacy in favour of bluntness, 'are much more likely to be the cause of the break-up of your sister's marriage than I am!'

His lips curled. *'Me…?'* He dismissed her words with a

shrug of his magnificent shoulders. 'You think you can shift the blame that easily?' A suspicious expression slid into his deep-set eyes. 'You are talking as though a break-up is inevitable…?'

When Sam turned her head away, her lips tight, Alessandro placed a finger under her chin and drew her face round to him. His narrowed eyes scanned her angry face.

'*What do you know…?*' he demanded, his voice dropping in volume in direct proportion to the degree of threat in his tone.

'Like I'd tell *you* if I did know anything,' she retorted, pulling her chin free.

Her breath coming in short, angry gasps that made her chest rise and fall in tune with her rapid respirations, Sam planted her hands on her hips and angled an angry glare up at him, her eyes flashing green fire.

'Oh, you *will* tell me…'

At that moment Sam was willing to do just about anything to wipe that confident smirk off his impossibly good-looking face. 'Brought your thumbscrews with you, did you?'

Before he could confirm or deny this a giggling couple carrying glasses of wine came around the corner. They saw Alessandro and Sam and stopped dead.

'Oops—pretend we're not here!' said the girl, grabbing her partner's hand and winking at Sam before she dragged him away.

'Oh, God!' groaned Sam, burying her face in her hands. 'Just what I need.' Pam Sullivan was the sort of gossip who could make the most innocent incident sound salacious.

'You're right—we need some privacy.'

Sam's head came up, her expression horrorstruck. She needed privacy with Alessandro Di Livio the same way she needed cellulite!

'That place over there—what is it?' He nodded towards a section of tiled roof just visible beyond a large shrubbery.

'It's the gazebo, I think.' The original intention had been for a band to be situated there, so that the guests could listen while they sat or strolled around the lovely grounds. Then the weather had intervened and things had been hastily transferred indoors.

'It will suit our purposes,' he announced.

God, if Pam had heard that it would have made her year. 'Look,' Sam said, deciding it was time to inject a little reality into the conversation, 'the only place I'm going is back indoors. I'm freezing cold, and this conversation—such as it is—is over.'

She froze and looked at the hand on her arm. A strong, shapely hand, with long, tapering fingers. Having it touching her without any sort of warning switched her brain into mush mode.

'Yes, you are cold,' he agreed, sliding one brown finger under the neck of her blouse. It slid slowly across the bony prominence of her collarbone before moving back to the hollow at the base of her throat. The blue-veined pulse there was throbbing so hard that he couldn't fail to feel it.

Had her brain not already been mush, she might have noticed that his fingers lingered there a lot longer than was strictly necessary—not that it mattered. The damage was done in the first micro-second of contact.

It had an electric effect—almost literally! It was, Sam mused, as she tried to focus her hazy thoughts, like being plugged into the mains. It took the space of a heartbeat for the shock to travel all the way to her curling toes.

'I don't want your jacket.' Actually, there were other things she wanted less—things like the surge of lustful longing that was making her ache in every cell of her body. But a lifetime of focusing on good things enabled her to look on the bright side: now that he was no longer touching her, her paralysed vocal cords had started working.

Acting as if she hadn't spoken—*no change there*—he carried on shrugging off the beautifully tailored pale grey jacket he wore. Draping it over her shoulders, he placed a hand in the small of her back and propelled her in the direction of the gazebo.

'You don't take no for an answer, do you?' His jacket retained the warmth of his body and held the faint, elusive fragrance that was exclusively him—a mingling of the masculine fragrance he favoured, soap, and warm male.

Standing there in his silk shirt, he appeared not to notice the cold—even though the fabric was fine enough for her almost to see through. She could definitely see the strategic drift of dark body hair on his chest, and the suggestion of muscle definition on his taut washboard belly.

Ashamed of what amounted to a fascination with his body, Sam—painfully aware that her cheeks were burning—turned her head to one side. Well, as far as she was concerned he could freeze to death—and good riddance!

'This is ridiculous,' she muttered under her breath, thinking, *He's not a man, he's a darned force of nature.* Despite the fact that saying no to him had as much impact as saying no to a hurricane, she was uneasily aware that she ought to have at least tried. The casual observer might have been forgiven for jumping to the conclusion that she actually wanted to prolong their time together.

A comment Emma had made not long after she'd met the man she was eventually to marry popped into Sam's head. 'You know, Sam, I have more fun fighting with Paul than having sex with any other man. Makes me wonder what the sex will be like… Actually, I started wondering *that* about five seconds after I met him.'

When Sam had admitted with a touch of envy that she'd never met a stranger who had that effect on her, Emma had laughed and said with total conviction that she would one day.

Though exposed on one side, the gazebo did offer some protection from the elements. Once inside, Alessandro took her by the shoulders and spun her to face him. Leaving his hands where they were, he looked down into her face.

CHAPTER FOUR

OH, GOD, did today have to be the day? And did he have to be this stranger?

'Why are you looking at me like that?' he asked.

I was trying to imagine what it would be like having sex with you, was clearly out, and she wasn't sure if her voice even worked, so Sam shook her head, and inside his jacket carried on trembling. She had no intention of surrendering to her darkest urges even had the opportunity arisen. And she supposed to some people the gazebo, tucked away from prying eyes, might represent that opportunity.

Actually, the fact she *had* dark urges at all was a bit of shock-horror revelation. The urges she felt for Jonny could not be described as dark, she mused. Those feelings were a lot more wholesome and easier to handle. Also, there was a certain safety in fantasising about a man who had never noticed you had breasts.

While Alessandro didn't like her, and actually seemed pretty much to despise her, Sam *did* get the impression he knew…

'This situation is easily resolved. Just tell me what you know.'

Shamefully aware of the ache and burning tingle in her shamelessly engorged breasts, Sam crossed her hands across her chest in a protective gesture. 'This is getting beyond ridiculous.'

'What is ridiculous is you thinking I'm going to let you go before you tell what you know about the problems in my sister's marriage. And don't tell me you don't know anything, because you look as guilty as hell.'

'And you look—!' She watched as his lashes dipped, casting a shadow across the slashing curve of his strong cheekbones, and the breath suddenly snagged in her throat. *You look perfect, damn you!*

She stepped back, and his hands fell from her shoulders. Still feeling the imprint of his light touch on her skin, she squinted angrily up at him. 'This isn't guilt,' she said pointing at her face. 'This is fear for my safety. You are obviously a total lunatic.'

'Then I suggest you humour me.'

Sam swung away, her hands gripping the lapels of his jacket. Her low heels clicked on the wooden floor as she walked to the opposite side of the octagonal enclosure to put as much space as was humanly possible between them. A faintly pointless exercise, as the sound of footsteps behind her indicated the wretched man had followed her.

'Fine!' she cried, throwing her hands up and turning to face him. 'The problem with Kat's marriage? Yes, there's a problem.' She jabbed a finger in the direction of his chest. 'Like I said—you.'

Alessandro looked at the small finger and felt a sudden distracting desire to lift it to his lips. 'I warn you, I *will* have an answer.'

'And I'm giving you one. Has Kat *asked* you to intervene in her marriage?'

In the act of dragging a hand through his dark and tousled hair, Alessandro stopped and slung her an exasperated look. 'What sort of question is that?'

Sam ignored the interjection. 'Well, has she?'

'Of course she hasn't.'

'And would she feel able to come to you if she needed to?'

He looked indignant. 'Of course she would.'

'Then don't you think it might be a good idea to wait until

then before you jump in with your…' she glanced at his feet and added, '…size twelves? Kat is twenty-one,' she reminded him.

'She was *nineteen* when she got married. At nineteen she should have been—'

Sam actually felt a twinge of sympathy as he clamped his lips together and inhaled deeply through flared nostrils.

'You thought she was too young to get married?'

'Do you think at nineteen you should be deciding to commit yourself to one person?' he demanded scathingly. 'What were *you* doing at nineteen?'

She responded unthinkingly to the curious question. 'I was training to be a teacher.'

'And would your parents have been happy if you'd turned up at home married to some beach bum?'

'Jonny was *not* a beach bum—he was a champion surfer.'

'I stand corrected,' he inserted drily. 'Married to an ex-champion surfer.'

'My parents would have flipped,' she admitted. 'But it happened, so you just have to live with it. You know, *I* think Kat is pretty resourceful—and *quite* capable of sorting out her own life. It might be easier for her to do that if you weren't always there, hovering in the background like a bad smell.' Actually, he smelt pretty wonderful—but she felt the occasion called for a little poetic licence. 'Don't you think,' she asked him gently, 'that it's time you let go? Doesn't Kat deserve the chance to make her own mistakes?'

An expression of blank astonishment spread across Alessandro's face. 'You think *you* are qualified to offer *me* advice?'

'Not qualified, maybe,' she conceded, flushing at his sneering tone. 'But you asked. I know you have a close relationship with your sister—'

'You know nothing about it.'

'I used to wish I wasn't an only child, but meeting you has made me realise what a lucky escape I've had. Let me spell it out. The fact is you are no longer the person she's meant to turn to for support. Couldn't you settle for being emergency back-up rather than the main man? Have you any idea,' she wondered out loud, 'how intimidating you must be to a younger man?'

'Intimidating…?' he echoed, looking bewildered by her contention.

'What man could compete with the marvellous Alessandro Di Livio?' she asked, rolling her eyes.

His mobile lips thinned with displeasure. 'Don't be ridiculous.' Looking thoughtful despite his terse tone, he added, 'It isn't a competition.'

'Not to you maybe…' she inserted drily.

'I have never interfered in my sister's marriage.'

Sam stared at him, wondering how on earth he could say that with a straight face. 'Oh, pardon me. I must have imagined the past…' she glanced at her watch, her eyes widening '…half an hour.'

'It has felt like longer,' he gritted.

Under the capacious folds of his jacket, Sam folded her arms across her chest. 'You're being nasty because you know I'm right. You really shouldn't grind your teeth like that.'

She stood and listened in silent admiration as he loosed a flood of very angry-sounding Italian. If tone was anything to go by he seemed to have an extensive knowledge of expletives in his native tongue.

'If you're in love with Trelevan surely it would be in your best interests to see his marriage fail?'

The angry colour in Sam's cheeks deepened. 'Caring for someone obviously doesn't mean the same thing to you as it does to me. When you care for someone you want them to be happy.'

'Care…?' His lips twisted derisively as he spat the word. 'I am not talking about caring. I am talking about passion…lust…'

And I so wish you wouldn't! 'I think you're talking about sleazy sex.'

'And you? What are *you* talking about? Holding hands?' he suggested, reaching out and capturing one of hers. 'Picking out matching china and deciding on the new garden furniture?'

Angrily Sam tore her hand from his, praying that his no doubt well-developed predatory instincts had not told him what the contact had done to her. 'You're obsessed with sex!' *And it's catching.*

The claim made him laugh. 'Well, at least I don't have a problem with it.'

The taunt made her cheeks burn. 'I don't have a problem with sex—just you!'

'It makes you blush just to say the word…' he discovered, sounding astonished. 'I don't believe you have ever wanted someone so much that you would do anything to have them.' He angled a speculative look at her flushed face. 'When was it you decided he was the love of your life?'

'I'm not going to discuss Jonny with you.'

He gave a grimace of distaste. 'Give me honest lust rather than mawkish sentimentality any day.' His expressive upper lip curled. *'Look at me—I've got a broken heart, but what a little trouper I am…'* He gave a snort of disgust and shook his head. 'Heaven preserve me from women who fancy themselves as martyrs.'

Scenting a certain inconsistency in his criticism, she held up her hands. 'Hang on—I thought I was some sort of calculating, husband-stealing—'

'Frankly,' he said, dragging his hand through his dark hair in an exasperated manner, 'I'm not quite sure *what* you are.'

The way he was looking at her made Sam's throat grow dry. She pressed a hand to her throat, where her heart was trying to climb out of her chest.

'You have been generous with your advice…so let me give you some in exchange.'

She folded her arms across her chest and looked bored. 'This should be good…'

'Stop weaving your sexual fantasies around somebody else's husband and go out and get yourself a lover.'

This recommendation drew an inarticulate gurgle from Sam's throat. 'Jonny does *not* feature in my sexual fantasies!'

His eyes stayed hard and hostile while he bared his teeth in a wolfish leer. 'Then he definitely isn't the man for you.'

'I do not have sexual fantasies!' she choked.

'Then you really are as repressed as you look.'

Sam regarded him with loathing and prayed that one day he would tell a woman he loved her and she would laugh in his face. That such a woman existed was somewhat doubtful, but if there was any justice at all one day he would crash and burn—and she would be there to see it!

'Then you don't have to worry, do you? I'm too repressed to seduce your sister's husband. And, just for the record, I do not fancy myself a martyr,' she added, in a voice that shook with the strength of her outraged feelings. 'And I doubt if *you're* capable of anything deeper than lust—with anyone other than yourself, that is.'

The only response she got to her biting condemnation was a quirk of one dark brow. 'Are you surprised he has never noticed you are a woman when you dress like—? On every occasion I have seen you, you dress to hide your femininity, not celebrate it.'

'You mean flaunt?' Sam suggested, and gave a scornful laugh. Actually, she didn't find being thought dowdy and unattractive by a man who had to be about the most attractive creature on the planet nearly so amusing as she made out. 'I don't enjoy being leered at.'

One ebony brow lifted as he affected amazement. 'I'm amazed you have any experience of leering.'

Ashamed of the weakness which brought the hot sting of tears to her eyes, Sam gritted her teeth and glared up at him. 'Not all men are as shallow as you!'

'I think you'll find they are, *cara*.'

'Well, I wouldn't want the sort of man I have to tart myself up for and pretend to be something I'm not.'

'I think the idea is that the man should make you feel sexy and attractive. Hasn't any man done that for you?'

Sam pressed her hands to her ears and shook her head in a childish gesture of denial. 'If you don't shut up, I'll…I'll…!'

Her frustrated threat ignited a look of astonishment in his heavy-lidded eyes, and then, as he appeared ready to reward her audacity with a killer retort, he saw the telltale glitter in her eyes. 'You're crying…?'

Sam bit her lip and shook her head. 'You'd like that, wouldn't you?' she accused.

Without warning he reached across and took the hand she held clenched against her chest, raising it towards his mouth. 'I have no desire to see you weep. But that red-headed temper…it will get you into trouble if you don't learn to tame it.'

Fighting clear of the paralysis which held her a pliant spectator, Sam snatched her hand from his grasp and backed away. Her eyes trained unblinkingly on his face, she carried on backing up until the backs of her legs made contact with a wooden chair. She let out a small shriek and stumbled, and would have fallen if a strong arm hadn't snaked around her waist.

'You should be more careful,' he cautioned.

A shaky laugh squeezed its way past the emotional congestion in her aching throat. 'That sounds like excellent advice,' she said, fixing her eyes on a point mid-way up his chest.

His dark, autocratic features were hard and remote as he posed his question. 'You love him…?'

Very aware of the arm still encircling her waist, she cleared her throat. 'I'm not about to discuss my feelings with you.' *So what have you been doing for the past half an hour?*

'What I don't understand is why you stood back and let her take him?'

Sam felt something inside her snap. Her head came up. *Let*

her…? He made it sound as though she'd had some sort of option.

'What would you have had me do?' she demanded, stabbing a finger within a whisper of his broad chest.

'*Do…?*' he said, watching the accusing finger with an expression of fascination.

'Well, you seem to be the expert.' She angled her head, directing her resentful glare into his lean face and stepping backwards. The fact that she wanted to protest when his hand fell away only made her angrier.

'How would *you* go about making someone notice you?' She recognised the total stupidity of her question the moment the words had left her lips.

As if anyone was not going to notice him!

Let's face it, the man was a total hunk—with more rampant maleness in his little finger than most men had in their entire bodies. He was the perfect male specimen—from the top of his sleek, glossy head to his highly polished shoes. Her resentful glare slid from his bronzed, beautifully sculpted features and skidded over his lean, lithe frame. Some men might wear a suit to disguise a few unwanted inches around the middle, but not him. Even sheathed in perfect tailoring there was no disguising that Alessandro's body was in perfect condition.

'I thought such things came naturally to a woman,' he offered suggestively.

Sam sucked in a furious breath through her clenched teeth. 'There's nothing *natural*,' she sneered, 'about push-up bras.' Glaring at him, she clamped her hands over her not terribly impressive breasts. 'Or, for that matter, comfortable—and besides, this has nothing whatever to do with underwear.'

'You were the one who introduced the subject,' he pointed out mildly.

'What would *you* have suggested? That I flaunt a bit of leg?' she asked, extending one slender appendage in his direction. A snort of disgust escaped her lips as she shook her hair back from her hot face. 'Take up pole-dancing?' she challenged.

His dark eyes travelled up the slender curve of her calf. 'An interesting thought,' he murmured, swallowing. 'But it probably wouldn't have done you any good if there was no chemistry to begin with.'

'For your information, I wouldn't *demean* myself just to get a man,' she declared hotly. Then aware that his eyes were fixed on her hands and what they covered, she dropped them and added, 'I suppose that's the sort of thing you like? Women who make fools of themselves to get your attention?'

His dark brows lifted to a quizzical angle. 'You consider it demeaning to seduce a man?'

'*Seduce…?*' she echoed, as an image of herself astride the prone figure of a man, running her fingers down his lean, hard torso flashed through her mind. The image itself was deeply disconcerting. The fact that the man in question was Alessandro was utterly shocking.

'It is what a women who is worthy of the name would do to get the man she loves,' he contended calmly. 'It is certainly a more healthy option than clinging to a juvenile infatuation.'

'I'm not infatuated with anyone,' she choked, thinking that if she could curse anyone with unrequited love it would be this man.

Continuing to scan her upturned features, his only response to her protest was a smile that made her want to hit him.

'You spend too many evenings alone with your romantic dreams. Sex isn't about soft focus and sweet music,' he derided scornfully. 'Sex is visceral. It's about smells and texture…' Without warning he reached out and ran a long brown finger down the inner aspect of her wrist. Sam gasped as the light contact sent an electric shock through her body.

When she finally got her paralysed vocal cords to respond, her voice seemed to be coming from a long way away. 'Thank you for the lesson…' She had no doubt at all that he was a master of the subject.

His mesmerising eyes locked onto hers and Sam felt her knees shake.

'It's about sweat.' His low, throaty purr had an almost narcotic quality, and Sam, aware of the danger it presented, was seduced by it anyway.

She might not like the man, she might loathe what he was and what he stood for, but she wasn't crazy enough to imagine she had been granted some sort of immunity to the raw sexuality he exuded.

Painfully conscious of her wildly quivering stomach muscles, and aware that she was quite literally panting—which could give the wrong impression—Sam fought to control her breathing, perfectly aware that there was nothing mutual about the chemical reaction she was suffering. How could there be? Compared to the sexy, in-control women he dated, she must seem like a sexless reject…an oddity.

Sam sniffed and lifted her chin to an aggressive angle. At that moment if she had been granted any wish she would have blown it without a second thought for that special X factor that made some women totally irresistible to the opposite sex—or at least *one* of the opposite sex.

Well, let's face it, Sam, the only place you're going to be able to say no when he begs you to be with him is in your dreams.

'If I want sweat I'll go to a gym,' she retorted, just managing to sound derisive even though her knees were shaking.

The longer this confrontation went on the stronger the feeling became that she was a voyeur rather than a participant in the scene. She shivered and released a scared gasp as his half-closed eyes moved over her slender body.

'What you need is some reality,' he concluded.

His thickened accent nailed her to the spot. Was there anything short of a Lotto win that was *less* real than discussing sweaty sex with Alessandro Di Livio? *'Reality...?'* A shaky laugh emerged from her lips, sounding reckless when in reality she had never felt less reckless in her life.

'What I don't need,' she panted hoarsely, 'is advice from *you!*'

'What you need is some...' his heavy-lidded eyes touched her mouth and his own lips quirked '...*substance.*'

'Next you'll be telling me that what I need is you...' Her scornful laugh faded as he took her face between his big hands, and she thought, *Did I invite this...?*

As he looked at her wide, soft pink mouth, a sound that was close to a growl vibrated in his throat. Sam felt the vibration and opened her own mouth to say something frosty and ascerbically cutting, which would awaken him to the fact that he wasn't dealing with one of his simpering push-overs, but encountered his glittering eyes. All her life her cutting one-liners had saved her from uncomfortable situations, yet now, of all times, her ability to deliver a slick comeback had failed her!

The last time she had seen that much barely restrained heat had been in a disaster movie about a volcano. She became aware of the fact that she was no longer cold—no longer cold to the point where she was burning up.

'If you kiss me I'll sleep with Jonny,' she hissed.

CHAPTER FIVE

OF COURSE she realised too late that this wasn't the sort of man who responded well to threats—even empty ones. Only he didn't know it was empty, because he clearly considered her a trollop when he wasn't thinking she was frigid. His entire attitude towards her was decidedly schizophrenic.

Alessandro cupped the back of her head in one hand and drew her face up to his. This was one of those moments that definitely required a verbal bucket of cold water to stop a bad situation getting worse.

A moment where Sam knew she had to send him a very strong, unambiguous message.

Moaning and grabbing his jacket while she gasped, 'Oh, God!' was not the message she had intended to send! But it was either that or fall down at his feet, so she chose the option which was on balance marginally less humiliating.

His long fingers moved through the strands of hair, grazing her scalp and causing several million nerve-endings to sigh as she inhaled the warm male scent of his hard, lean body. There was an expression of fierce fascination in his face as he let the silky strands fall through his fingers, making Sam's senses spin.

'Your hair should be hot,' he rasped throatily.

Why not? The rest of me is. She was burning up from the inside out. Common sense told her that there were no flames burning in his utterly spectacular eyes, but knowing it was a mirage didn't stop her stomach dropping to somewhere below her knees.

'I really think… Oh, God…' She sucked in her breath sharply as he moved his thumb across her trembling lips. 'The thing is, you don't have to do this…'

It didn't take a genius to work out his sudden interest. He thought if he kissed her she would forget about Jonny and start lusting after *him*. An inconvenience he was no doubt prepared to put up with for his sister's sake!

Her heavy lids lifted when he stopped what he was doing—something which Sam was dismayed to discover she had mixed feelings about. Blinking, her passion-glazed eyes wide and wary, she glimpsed for a split second his expression. She thought he looked shocked, then a short, strange laugh was wrenched from his throat and he bent his head towards her.

'The thing is, though, I find I do.' His expression suggested that the discovery didn't make him overwhelmingly happy.

'But I'm not going to seduce Jonny,' she protested weakly. 'And if I did,' she confessed, 'he probably wouldn't notice. He doesn't think of me as a girl…'

Alessandro focused on the curve of her lower lip, which was hard to do without biting into the luscious pink softness. 'Not even *he* is that much of an idiot…' he said, thinking he probably was.

'He is… That is, no, Jonny's not an idiot!' Sam protested. 'You just don't understand—'

Alessandro's angry voice cut across her faltering defence of the man she was clearly infatuated with. 'I don't want to understand,' he informed her tautly.

'But you…' The raw, driven intensity of the way he was looking at her made the words dry as her aching throat closed over.

'The only thing I want to do is taste you,' he confided, in

a rough velvet drawl that made every individual cell of her body ache with a deeply disturbing nameless need. 'And I'd prefer you didn't talk about another man while I do it.'

'Don't I have any say in the matter?'

She stopped, her expression freezing as she realised that she wanted to kiss him. She wanted him so much that she could feel it in her bones. And, actually, what harm could it do?

My God, am I even considering letting this man kiss me? Could I stop him? And, more to the point, do I want to stop him?

Well, it might be interesting. Actually being kissed by a man who was hard and lean, who smelt delicious and male and… Sucking in a horrified breath, she brought her private debate to an abrupt halt. *Interesting…!* God, I'm going insane—stark, staring mad!

Alessandro gave a fierce smile and ran a brown finger along the moist inner curve of her lower lip. 'I don't generally ask permission before I kiss a woman,' he confessed, before reaching up and calmly unfastening the clip that held her hair in a careless topknot on her head.

Too astounded by his action to do anything, including breathe, she stood there, her shocked gaze trained on his face, while her hair tumbled around her shoulders. He reached out and lifted a hank of shiny coppery hair, winding the tendril around his finger before he released it. 'You should always wear your hair loose. Why would I ask for permission to kiss you when it is obvious that you want me to?'

'You're insane!' And he's not the only one, she thought as she grabbed her hair in both hands before pushing it ruthlessly behind her ears. 'If you go around doing this sort of thing I'm amazed you've not been arrested yet.'

He looked amused by the accusation. 'It's the signals you're sending out. Though you're probably not even aware of doing so,' he conceded. 'Your pupils are dilated and your skin is flushed.'

'So is yours.' There was a faint sheen to his glorious olive-toned skin, and bands of colour accentuated the sculpted elegance of his prominent cheekbones.

'You look like you'll taste…sweet,' he observed, his breathing quickening perceptibly as he stared at her lips in a way that made Sam's sensitive stomach flip and quiver.

'That would be the strawberry cheescake…' she responded, faint, but holding it together in a pulse-racing, knee-shaking sort of way—until she made the mistake of allowing her darting gaze to linger on the sensually moulded curve of his mouth. 'Cheesecake,' she echoed, getting hot inside as she carried on staring at his mouth and thought about how it would feel on her skin. 'Do I have some on my mouth…?' She touched the tip of her tongue to her lips, very aware of and mortified by the heat spreading through her body.

Alessandro sucked in his breath through flared nostrils, and the reckless, predatory gleam in his hooded dark eyes made Sam's already stressed pulse kick up another notch. She brought her eyelashes down in a protective shield and plucked fretfully at the neck of her shirt, to loosen the fabric that was clinging to her damp, hot skin.

'The only thing you need on your mouth is mine…' he claimed, with the sort of macho arrogance that should in theory have brought a scornful laugh to her lips.

But this wasn't theory, and it was no theoretical tongue that slowly traced the outline of her quivering lips and tilted her face up to his. Paralysed with lust, she literally ached for the taste of him. The man didn't have many things right, but in this particular instance, as she felt the first movement of his lips against her own, Sam could find no fault with his conclusion. She *did* need his mouth on hers.

Oh, God, did she need it!

Her lashes lifted from her flushed cheeks when his head lifted. *'Oh, God!'* she moaned, meeting his hot, glittering eyes. 'I suppose you think that proves something? Other than the fact you can kiss quite well.' Which had always been pretty much a given. Nobody with a mouth like his could be a bad kisser.

One corner of his fascinating mouth lifted. 'Let's see if I can improve on *quite well…*' he rasped, placing one hand on the back of her head and the other on her bottom. He put his lips to hers and jerked her towards him in one smooth motion.

Sam felt something inside her explode as the erotic pressure increased until she could bear it no more, and with a groan she opened her mouth and moaned into his mouth. As they kissed with a wild, frenzied hunger that Sam had never experienced or dreamt existed she pressed her body into his, drawing herself up onto her toes to slide her fingers into his hair.

When his head lifted it was small comfort that he looked almost as dazed as she felt. She stared at him, her eyes big and shocked, and rubbed the back of her hand across her swollen lips. On legs that felt like cotton wool she took a shaky step backwards.

'Why did you do that…?'

Good question. 'If you kiss Trelevan—no,' he corrected. 'If you go near him, I will wring his pathetic neck,' Alessandro promised grimly, knowing that she cared for the other man's safety and comfort a lot more than she did her own.

Well, now she knew why he had done it. Her own motivation was much less clear-cut. 'You are a manipulative bastard.' *And I am a total push-over.* 'And if you lay one finger on me ever again—'

'You'll say, *Don't stop*,' he inserted smoothly.

A wave of mortified colour washed over her milk-pale skin as she stared up at him with loathing. 'I'll sell my story to the tabloids.' As empty threats went, this one was pathetic. He obviously thought so, because she could hear the sound of his laughter as she walked away.

Sam kept her back rigid and her head disdainfully high until she shut herself in a booth in the powder room. She was in there half an hour all told, what with crying and then fixing the damage to her face.

When she emerged she had concluded that it would be a mistake to get hung up over a kiss… It was nothing major—just a wrinkle.

She almost believed it.

CHAPTER SIX

'LISTEN, Em, I should be making a move.'

'Now! But it's still early,' Emma protested, raising her voice above the gentle buzz of conversation and the music supplied by a string quartet from the local music college. 'What have you done to your hair?' she added, looking at the skewed knot on the top of her friend's head.

Sam, whose efforts to repair the damage had been severely hampered by shaking hands and a need to mouth *You idiot* at her reflection in the powder room mirror every two seconds, ignored the question.

'I want to get back before it gets dark.' Sam felt guilty when her friend's face dropped, but stuck to her guns. She was pretty sure that if called upon to make polite small talk with Alessandro she might make a total fool of herself. Whether this would involve slapping him or begging him to kiss her was a matter she didn't want to think too hard about!

'I thought you were staying with your mum and dad tonight?'

That was before one of your guests kissed me and I kissed him back. 'Change of plan.' She flashed a smile. Her guilt injected a couple of extra million volts into it.

Emma took in the brilliance and grinned back. 'What's his name? Do I know him? Are we talking husband material?'

An image of Alessandro's dark, devastating features flashed into Sam's head. Anything *less* like husband material would be hard to find. Some women would just look, but there would always be those ready and willing to lead him astray.

She wasn't saying being totally gorgeous to look at automatically made a man incapable of fidelity, but it would take a woman who was supremely confident in herself to be able to take the covetous stares of other women in her stride.

The woman who married Alessandro would have to be a supremely confident creature or totally gorgeous—probably both. In short the female equivalent of him.

'I had a phone call...publisher...' She shrugged.

Emma looked dissatisfied by her response, but beyond subjecting her friend to an uncomfortably searching look made no further protests beyond, 'Well, you definitely can't go without saying goodbye to Paul. When last seen,' she revealed with a smile, 'he had retreated with half the other men to the Orangerie. I think they're talking cricket.' She rolled her eyes.

'Lead on,' Sam said, picking up her handbag and following her friend down the plush carpeted corridor that led to the Orangerie. Emma's husband, Paul, and half a dozen of the other male guests were indeed there, but they weren't talking cricket. They were huddled in one corner displaying varying degrees of horror and discomfort as they watched the object responsible for the ear-splitting din that Sam had heard halfway down the corridor.

When Sam had last seen the blond-haired three-year-old he had been enchanting the adults with his sunny smile and a lisping rendition of a nursery rhyme. Now he was lying in the middle of the floor, his red tear-stained face contorted with fury, as he screeched and drummed his heels on the floor.

On seeing his wife, Paul Metcalf hurried across. 'Thank God you're here, Emma. It's Harry. Simon got a call, and he asked me to keep an eye on Harry for a minute.'

'How long,' Emma asked, wincing as the toddler hit a high note, 'has he been like that?'

'It feels like hours,' her harassed husband responded dourly.

Emma exchanged glances with Sam. 'I think he needs his mum. Do you know where Rachel is, Sam?'

Sam shook her head. 'Shall I go and look for her?'

Despite the fact that Rachel, whose father was the local vicar, was a couple of years older than both herself and Emma, the three girls had always been inseparable. And, unlike many childhood alliances, theirs had not fizzled out when they reached adulthood and went their separate ways. Rachel, who combined a career in banking with being wife to a very dishy NewYorker, had asked Sam to be godmother to Harry, her firstborn. When she had uprooted and followed her husband to the States the previous year both Sam and Emma had visited, but had been delighted when Simon's firm had decided to resettle them in London.

Paul caught Sam's arm. 'No, you stay here. I'll go,' he offered eagerly, before his wife told him very firmly to stay put.

Sam paused before going to console her godson, her amused glance sliding around the group of men. 'Didn't it occur to any of you lot to *do* anything for the poor little mite?'

'Have you seen the state of him?' her indignant host demanded, speaking on behalf of the other men present. 'There is enough chocolate cake on that kid to feed the five thousand, and I'm wearing my best suit. And,' he added, eyeing the flailing legs, 'the "poor little mite" has a kick like a mule.'

'Wimp!' his wife retorted scornfully.

'This situation obviously calls for the female touch,' Paul observed with dignity. 'Either that or a good child psychologist,' he added under his breath.

Emma caught his arm. 'You think so?' she said. 'Look at that,' she invited, venting a loud, incredulous laugh as she nodded towards the prone toddler. '*He* doesn't seem too bothered about getting *his* suit dirty. My God—this is marvellous!'

Along with Paul, Sam turned in time to see a tall, elegant figure squat down beside the screaming youngster. She watched in total amazement as Alessandro, balancing on his heels and appearing totally unfazed by the pandemonium or the risk to his designer suit, began to talk casually to the screaming toddler.

'The man has guts—I'll give him that.' Paul's brows knitted as an expression of horror spread across his face. 'Our sweet little Laurie is never going to do anything like that, is she…?'

Ignoring her husband's worried enquiry, her fascinated gaze trained on the man and baby, Emma said knowledgeably to Sam, 'It's a cultural thing. Mediterranean men have no problem showing affection to babies and children—unlike our homegrown variety…' she added, directing a scornful sniff towards her spouse.

Alessandro carried on talking as he loosened the knot on his tie. Sam was too far away to make out what he was saying, but the child obviously could, and it appeared to have an immediate and nothing short of magical effect on the distraught youngster.

'*My God!*' Emma breathed, as the child's cries became noticeably less strident, then faded totally. 'What is he saying, do you suppose?' she wondered in an awed undertone.

The child lifted his tear-stained face towards Alessandro and chuckled.

Sam didn't respond. For some insane reason, when she saw Alessandro respond to the child with a smile that made him look relaxed and at least ten years younger, she got an empty, aching feeling in the pit of her stomach.

'Come!'

Responding to Alessandro's imperious command and to his open arms, the toddler climbed into them without a moment's hesitation and wound his grubby hands around the man's neck.

There were several gruff murmurs of appreciation as Alessandro got to his feet.

The genuine quality of Alessandro's smile became—to Sam's mind, at least—forced when he noticed her. Sam, the lapel of her criminally unattractive suit clasped in one hand, expelled a gusty breath and tried to act as if every nerve in her body wasn't screaming.

Beautiful man…baby…the whole thing was so painfully clichéd she would have to be a total idiot to fall for it. But falling she was… *Oh, what is wrong with me? I must be one of those women who are only attracted when there's no chance of their feelings being returned,* she decided. *Even if in this case they were shallow and lustful. A shrink would have a field-day dissecting my twisted psyche.*

'That,' declared Emma, walking up to Alessandro and ruffling the toddler's blond hair, 'was very impressive. I'm glad I invited you now.'

Alessandro's dark eyes creased at the corners as his smile warmed the dark depths. Sam, whose nerve-endings were twanging like an overstrung guitar, knew that if he ever smiled at her that way she was in deep trouble. *And you're not now?*

'You weren't glad before?'

'You were welcome as Kat's big brother before, and now you're welcome because you are a brave and resourceful man who laughs in the face of danger.'

'It's always nice to feel welcome,' Alessandro responded, his dark, heavy-lidded eyes briefly flickering in Sam's direction.

Sam, her heart thudding wildly in her chest, pretended not to notice.

'Shall I take Harry?'

Emma didn't argue when he shook his head and said, 'Harry would like to find his mum, and if the route should take us anywhere near ice cream this would not be a bad thing.'

Sam looked at the smear of chocolate down his cheek, at the sleek hair ruffled by childish fingers, and her indignation escalated. Alessandro looked so damned relaxed and at ease with a grubby, cranky kid on his hip…How *dared* he slip out of the hedonistic playboy role she had assigned him?

'No idea where Rachel is,' Emma admitted. 'But as for the ice cream, I'll get that for you myself…'

At that moment Rachel, wrapped in her habitual air of unruffled serenity, walked into the room. She took in the situation at one glance.

'I take it from the glazed looks that you have been treated to one of Harry's grade A tantrums? Goodness, Harry,' she reproached, as her son wrapped his arms limpet-like around her neck, 'you'll put Aunty Sam totally off having children,' she observed, flashing Alessandro a warm smile as the transfer of grubby child was smoothly completed. She arched an enquiring brow as she lifted her eyes to the tall Italian. 'It looks like I have you to thank Mr Di Livio…'

Alessandro gave a self-deprecating shrug. 'Not at all. Harry and I were just becoming acquainted and discovering a mutual fondness for ice cream. Now, if you'll excuse me… Oh, and ladies…' the voltage of his smile switched up several notches as he added firmly '…it's Alessandro.'

'If you don't have children,' Emma called after him, 'it will be a total…no, a *criminal* waste!'

Without breaking stride Alessandro flung her an attractive grin over his shoulder. 'I am not married.'

'Where were you three years ago?'

'Being cited in a divorce case,' Sam muttered. Did Marisa Sinclair, who had lost both her husband and her lover, regret her affair? Sam wondered. Or did she consider it a price worth paying?

'Sam, how could you? I'm sure he heard you,' Emma remonstrated as the tall, dark-headed Italian vanished from view.

Sam gave a defensive shrug. 'What if he did? And what do you mean, *how could I*? *You* don't like him.'

Rachel stood looking bewildered by this uncharacteristic display of childish venom. 'Did I miss something?'

'Sam doesn't like the gorgeous Alessandro,' Emma explained. Rachel laughed as she expertly wiped excess chocolate from around her son's mouth. 'That much I *had* gathered. Well,' she conceded, 'he's not the sort of man who inspires *liking*, is he?' She gave a naughty grin and added, 'Personally, I think he's rather sweet.'

'*Sweet?*' Sam echoed, staring at her friends as though they'd lost their minds. 'He's not sweet,' she hissed. 'He's a snake!'

Emma and Rachel looked at their normally good-natured friend in amazement. 'What has the poor guy done to you?' Emma asked.

Goaded, Sam yelled, 'The *poor guy* kissed me!'

Sam registered the identical looks of shock closely followed by delight that spread across her friends' faces, and with a groan closed her eyes. 'Pretend I didn't say that,' she begged, knowing there was little to no chance of her plea being heeded.

'You and Alessandro…' Emma drew a shuddering breath. '*Wow!*' she gasped enviously. 'I'm assuming that he is a *very* good kisser. How could a man who looks like *that* not be…?' she concluded logically.

'He,' snipped Sam crossly, 'would be the *first* person to agree with you.'

Emma looked totally unperturbed by the loathing in Sam's retort. 'I sort of thought he would be…I bet he's something in bed.'

'Don't look at me!' cried a pink-cheeked Sam, flinging up her hands in exasperation as she gazed balefully at her best friends. 'I've no intention of finding out.'

Rachel grinned. 'Well, I call that mean. You're a free agent, and what have Emma and I got left except enjoying a sex life vicariously through our friends? And, let's face it, Sam, so far your love life has not exactly been any compensation.'

'So sorry,' Sam drawled. 'Look, you two,' she added uneasily, 'you're not going to make a big thing out of this, are you? It was nothing…absolutely nothing.'

'Nothing that's got you pretty hot under the collar… Oh, all right,' Rachel placated as Sam gave a frustrated groan. 'We'll be the souls of discretion,' she promised, miming a zipping motion across her lips, as she winked at Emma.

By the time Sam had extracted the spare tyre from her boot she had been supplied with ample evidence that the age of chivalry was dead and buried. The only attention her plight had gained so far had been honks on the horn from several lorries. She had been trying to figure out which way up the jack went for five minutes when a car actually pulled up. Her knowledge and interest in cars was, to put it mildly, limited. The one that had drawn up was big and black and to her uneducated eye looked expensive.

Brushing her drenched hair from her eyes, she peered through a sheet of rain which was falling horizontally… If it wasn't a man behind the wheel it was a very large female.

Just my luck!

A woman would have been much less likely to dish out patronising stuff about clueless female drivers in this situation, and with a woman she wouldn't have had to worry about the sleaze factor. Oh, well, she thought, giving a stoical shrug. This was a situation that called for a lot of smiling and teeth-gritting, and if necessary the defending of her virtue…that was if she wanted to get back to town before she drowned—and she did.

And when you thought about it, it was her own fault. If she didn't want to be treated like a stereotypical helpless female she should have picked the car maintenance evening class and given Italian Summer Cooking a miss.

Knowing your way around a risotto is *not* going to get you home, Sam…so smile nicely and book in to the next car maintenance class.

'Hello, there—' Sam broke off, her jaw dropping as she identified her rescuer. 'You!' she ejaculated in disgust.

It was definite. Fate was having a laugh at her expense!

'This is your spare wheel…?' Alessandro pulled up the collar of his jacket and with his toe nudged the tyre, where it lay on the ground.

'Go away!' Sam snarled from between gritted teeth.

The broad shoulders lifted in one of his inimical shrugs. 'As you wish.'

Sam watched as he turned and began to walk back to his car. Almost bursting with indignation, she ran after him. 'You're just going to leave me like this?' she yelled.

He stopped and turned. 'Was that not what you wanted?'

Her eyes narrowed. 'You're such a creep!' she declared forcefully, then added, 'And don't think I'm not perfectly capable of putting on my own tyre.'

'Not *that* tyre.'

'Yes, that tyre.'

He shook his head and looked so smug that she wanted to scream. 'That tyre has no tread.'

She looked at him blankly.

'It is illegal.'

A flicker of uncertainty crossed her face. 'It looks fine to me,' she muttered mutinously.

'It is useless—actually, worse than useless. Because in this weather the only place it will get you for sure is the nearest casualty department.'

'You're exaggerating,' she charged.

He gave another of his magnificently expressive shrugs. 'It's your neck.' Halfway through turning, he swung back. His eyes slid down the pale column of her throat before he added harshly, 'I suggest, if you feel unable to accept my help, that you ring the nearest garage.'

Sam bit her lip. She knew the admission was going to make her look even more of an idiot than she already did as she fished her phone from her pocket and grunted, 'My battery is low.'

He released a long hiss of irritation and wrenched open the door of his own car. 'Get in—I will give you a lift.'

Sam, who had been looking wistfully at the luxuriously upholstered interior, stiffened at the terse invitation. There was a militant glitter in her aquamarine eyes as she released a scornful laugh. 'You think I'd get into a car with *you*…?'

'Don't you think it is a little late to display caution?' His nostrils flared as his eyes swept across her upturned features. 'I find it staggering,' he revealed, in a voice that suggested he was trying *very* hard not to yell, 'that an apparently *intelligent* female should act with such wanton disregard for her personal safety.'

'What do you mean?' No man had a right to look that good with his hair plastered to his skull…but she was forgetting it wasn't just *any* skull—it was the *perfect* variety. God, she thought, it would be so much easier not to loathe the wretched man if you could discover one minor imperfection.

'*Dio*…!' he gritted. Muttering under his breath in angry Italian, he let his head fall back, revealing the strong lines of his supple brown throat. Then, as she stared through the rain and the mesh of her spiky lashes, he dug both hands into his drenched sable hair and pulled it back in a way that sent water streaming down his olive-skinned face and neck.

Sam, unable to tear her eyes from the spectacle—which oughtn't to have been erotic but was—felt things move deep inside her. Unspecified, but deeply disturbing things. She reluctantly recognised that something far more worrying than the rain was responsible for the drowning, breathless sensation she was experiencing as she watched the water glide over his smooth brown skin.

Alessandro's head came up, and guiltily her eyes dropped.

Jaw clenched, he glared at her downbent head. 'You have been standing at the side of a lonely road, fluttering your eyelashes…'

The injustice of this harsh accusation brought her head up. The first thing her distracted gaze lighted on was the silvered drops of rain trembling on the tips of his own preposterously long eyelashes.

Eyelash-fluttering would get *him* further than it would me, she thought.

'I haven't…' Her voice faded away as her eyes connected with his.

'And,' he continued, once she had lapsed into silence, 'inviting the attention of any psychopathic lunatic who happens to drive by. You either have an unhealthy addiction to danger or you have no sense of self-preservation whatever. I suspect both,' he concluded grimly.

The awful part was, he had a point. 'Well, I'd prefer to get into a car with a psychopath than you!' she blurted out childishly. Then, lowering her eyes, she added in a small voice, 'Could I use your phone?'

At that moment another articulated truck went by and blasted its horn.

Alessandro followed the vehicle with his eyes until it vanished from view over the brow of the hill. When he turned his attention back to her his jaw was set and his eyes held a steely look of determination.

'Get in!'

His attitude did not suggest compromise, but she'd try anyway. She looked at his mouth, and her defences slipped just enough to let through one forbidden thought. *I kissed that.*

If she got into that car who was to say she wouldn't repeat the performance? *Chance would be a fine thing.* She took a deep breath and told herself sternly that thinking that way was going to get her into trouble.

'If you would just let me use your ph—'

'Get in, or I will *put* you in,' he interrupted, not sounding like a man with kissing on his mind. 'I have no intention of being interviewed by the police as the last person who saw you alive.'

Sam paled a little at the image his brutal words conjured. 'There's no need to be so dramatic.'

Ignoring her scornful complaint, he swivelled his eyes significantly towards the door of the car. 'I do not have all day.'

Sam hesitated. 'You wouldn't…?' Their eyes met and she gulped. He would.

I need therapy, she decided, appalled by the gut-tightening excitement in her belly. When did I turn into the sort of woman who gets turned on at the idea of being man-handled? Her eyes ran up the long, lean length of the man who stood there radiating impatience, and she thought, Not *any* man.

With as much dignity as a person who was literally dripping could muster, she arranged herself in the front seat as he stood and watched. His expression suggested that the outcome had never been in question.

Did people always do what he wanted? she wondered as she snuggled down into the cream leather upholstery. She looked blankly at the hand he'd inserted.

'Keys…I need to lock up your car. Not that it would be the car of choice for most self-respecting car thieves,' he said, sliding a contemptuous look towards her ancient Morris Traveller.

'It's a classic,' she said, dropping the keys into his palm. 'And it has character.'

'It's a heap. And it doesn't go,' he contradicted, before slamming the door.

Cocooned from the rain and wind, the quiet interior of the car felt like the eye of a storm. Despite the relative warmth, she shivered as she became conscious of the clammy coldness of layers of drenched clothes against her skin.

She tried to wring some of the excess moisture from her hair while she examined her surroundings. Nice—but then you'd expect Alessandro to travel first class—and big too, she thought, stretching her legs out. Big, but not nearly big enough. Her heart started to beat out an erratic tattoo against her breastbone as she thought about spending any time in such close proximity with him.

It stood to reason there must have been an alternative solution to her dilemma, that didn't involve being touched by Alessandro or locking herself into a confined space with him. Quashing the growing sense of panic she felt as she looked around the interior of the car, she closed her eyes and reflected on the unfortunate fact that around him she acted like someone suffering from oxygen deprivation.

She was wondering whether it might not be better to brave the elements and any passing bad guys when the door was wrenched open. She stiffened as the interior of the car was for a moment filled with cold wet air, followed by the elusive male scent of the exclusive fragrance he favoured.

'Here,' he said, handing her the keys.

'Thanks,' she said, fumbling as she tried not to touch his fingers. She lifted her head in time to see him shrug off his drenched jacket.

A sigh shuddered through her body. *Oh, my God!*

His white shirt had been rendered totally transparent by the rain, and clung like a second skin, revealing every individual muscle and hard contour of his lean, bronzed torso. Her breathing quickened as she tore her fascinated gaze away from the tantalising shadows created by drifts of dark body hair.

'Take your coat off,' he suggested, casually slinging his own jacket into the back seat.

She shook her head and clutched at the lapels of her knee-length pink trench coat. 'No, thanks,' she croaked. 'You could drop me at the first service station. There's one in the next village along, I think.'

He slung her an impatient look before pulling off the grass verge. 'Two petrol pumps and a tin hut, as I recall. Even if they *did* happen to be open for business at nearly eight p.m. I doubt if they'd retrieve your car until the morning.'

'Eight...?' Her expression shocked, she glanced at the watch on her wrist. She hadn't realised until that point how long she had been standing there. Lips pursed, she slid him a belligerent look. 'I suppose you think I should say thank you?'

'Not if it's too painful.'

'The tyre *was* bald…?' She looked at his hands on the steering wheel, then looked quickly away as she felt the muscles in her abdomen tighten. Her sensitised nostrils quivered. The car was heating, intensifying the disturbing scent of warm, wet male mingled with the subtle fragrance Alessandro favoured. Short of not breathing, it was impossibile not to inhale the heady concoction.

'Totally.'

Looking out of the window, her posture rigid, Sam missed the amused sideways glance he slid her.

'Why would I lie about such a thing?' he asked. 'Unless, of course, you think this is all part of a plot to have you at my mercy?'

'Very funny.'

'You are cold?'

Sam, who was very conscious of the trickles of sweat running down her back, shook her head.

'Then why are you shaking?'

'I'm not,' she lied. Then, because she clearly was, she added gruffly, 'My clothes are wet.'

'How long were you standing in the rain?'

'I'll be fine. I'll have a nice bath when I get home.' Anticipating the luxuriant soak that lay ahead, she sighed— and missed the flare of heat in his eyes as they swerved briefly from the road ahead.

The silence between them, which wasn't anything close to cosy or comfortable, stayed unbroken until he drove straight past the turn-off for the motorway a couple of miles farther down the road.

'This isn't the right road.'

'It is for where we are going,' he responded, with aggravating calm.

Sam glared at him, bristling with suspicion. Just as she was about to demand an explanation he slowed, and with a display of fast reflexes avoided a cat that darted across the road. The action made her think of the accident which had killed his parents. Had it been difficult for him to get in the driver's seat again? If it had you certainly couldn't tell from his calm, competent manner at the wheel of the big powerful car.

'I saw that programme last night,' she confessed, without thinking.

He slanted her a quick sideways look.

'About the accident…' she added, when he didn't respond.

'It was exploitative rubbish.'

For once she was in total agreement with him. 'Yes, I know.' She looked at his flawless profile and added, 'I'm glad you don't have any scars…physical ones, that is. Not that I'm implying that you have mental scars, but anyone would… Oh, God, if I was writing this I'd delete those last few lines of dialogue.'

To her amazement he laughed, and said, 'I do.'

'You do what?'

'I do have physical scars. You just haven't seen them…*yet.*'

Threat or promise—whichever it was, the result was the same. Desire clutched low on her belly as she struggled to lock the whimper that fought to escape in her throat.

Do not go there! Sam told herself. The sexual tension crackling in the air was too strong to ignore, but maybe if she didn't react to it, it might go away…? She turned and stared out of the window, and wondered how much more of this her nervous system could take before she burst into flames!

A few moments later the probability of spontaneous combustion became all the more probable when he observed casually, 'We need to get a room.'

CHAPTER SEVEN

Now, this she couldn't let ride.

'You need your head examined,' she rebutted huskily. 'If you assumed that just because I kissed you—' she gave a mocking laugh and was grateful he had no idea of the images playing in her head '—I'm going to *sleep* with you!'

'I suggest you wait until you're asked before you say no.'

The humiliating colour flew to Sam's cheeks as she turned her head back to the window, cursing her unruly tongue.

'I'm not saying it won't happen—'

'I really couldn't be that lucky…' she drawled sarcastically.

Alessandro grinned, but didn't turn his head. 'I like to prioritise.'

'You sweet, spontaneous romantic, you.'

Again he grinned. 'I had no idea you wanted me to be romantic. I assumed you just wanted me for my body. Seriously.' He slanted a quick sideways glance at her huddled figure. 'You urgently need to get into some dry clothes. There's a place a mile or so down here where I sometimes stay. You can take a hot bath while they dry your things.'

Sam released an incredulous laugh. This high-handed behaviour was clearly par for the course for him. 'It didn't occur to you to ask me if I *want* to go there?'

He looked mildly surprised by the question. 'Not really.'

'Do people always do what you tell them?' she wondered out loud.

'You would prefer to be wet and uncomfortable?'

Sam, very aware that her saturated clothes were chafing in several places, gritted her teeth. 'That's not the point…'

'On the contrary—it is very much the point. I realise that you would prefer to walk barefoot over hot coals than fall in with any suggestion *I* make…'

'It wasn't a suggestion, it was a *fait accompli!*' she snapped.

He angled a dark brow. 'You noticed?' He congratulated her. '*Fait accompli* rather makes this conversation pointless, wouldn't you say? Why don't you give in gracefully? We can even pretend that it was your idea, if you like.'

Glaring at his smug, patrician profile, Sam lapsed into seething silence as he turned through a pair of big wrought-iron gates. The hotel's impressive driveway was a mile long, and led through some charming parkland where deer grazed in the fading light.

When Alessandro opened the passenger door Sam, who was staring at the big sprawling half-timbered building they had pulled up in front of, shook her head. 'You can't walk into somewhere like this and demand a room for an hour. They'll think…'

Alessandro gave a sardonic smile. 'They'll think what…?' The malicious amusement glittering in his dark eyes made it impossible for her to maintain eye contact. 'That we could not contain our mutual lust until we got back to London?'

'Don't be disgusting!' she choked.

'This display of puritanical outrage might carry more weight with me if you hadn't tried to rip off my clothes once already today. Perhaps it is *me* who should be concerned about *my* reputation?' he suggested, the gleam in his eyes becoming more pronounced as a fresh wave of mortified colour rushed to her cheeks.

'Reputation!' Sam yelled, leaping soggily from the car. Feet crunching on the gravel, she advanced, her small fists clenched. 'I think *your* reputation is beyond further blackening,' she sneered. 'What has it taken…? Ten years…? Still, I'm sure the effort was worthwhile. I think everyone knows by now that you're a sleazy, womanising loser! And as for ripping off c…clothes…' A distracted expression slid into her eyes as the memory of her hands sliding under his shirt and over hard, satiny-smooth skin flashed into her head. It was the wrong time to recall how warm and solid and male… She inhaled and shook her head, reminding him angrily, '*I'm* the one missing two buttons.'

It wasn't until she saw the direction of his gaze that Sam realised that in pulling open her jacket to reveal the gaping section of her shirt she had also unintentionally revealed a section of smooth, pale midriff. With an indignant squeak she dragged the fabric of her jacket together.

His smouldering eyes locked onto hers, and the simmering silence that stretched between them tore her already traumatised nerves to shreds.

'Relax—they don't rent rooms by the hour here. And besides, I keep a suite,' he revealed casually.

Relax? After what he had just said! Sam almost laughed. 'You keep a suite…?' she echoed incredulously. 'You live in a hotel?'

'Not live, obviously, but it is useful.'

Sam, who didn't see how a hotel off the beaten track in rural Cornwall could possibly be useful to a man who spent his time flitting from one European capital to another, looked sceptical. 'How often do you actually use it?'

'It varies. Twice…maybe three times…' He began to look impatient with her interrogation.

'A month…?' It seemed shockingly extravagant and wasteful to Sam. But then she wasn't a millionaire—or was that a billionaire…?

'A year,' he corrected, and her jaw dropped.

'*A year!*' She shook her head, unable to disguise her disapproval. 'That must cost a fortune.'

'You are lecturing me on fiscal imprudence…?' His expression suggested the idea amused him.

'It's nothing to me how you choose to spend your money. You can burn it for all I care.'

'If it makes you feel any better, I am joint owner of the hotel…a silent partner.'

Sam looked at his hand, extended in a silent invitation for her to climb the shallow flight of steps that led to the porticoed entrance where a tall figure had emerged from the building. The woman, her grey hair tied back in a smooth knot at the nape of her neck, was wearing a silk shirt and tweed skirt.

'What are you doing standing there?' She peered over the top of her half-moon spectacles, subjecting Alessandro to a critical glare. 'This poor child looks perished.'

To Sam's astonishment, far from going into one of his haughty freeze-you-with-a-glance routines, Alessandro smiled—the sort of heart-flipping smile that he probably reserved for the select few he genuinely gave a damn about.

The possibility that her own heart was utterly susceptible to the warmth of that smile brought a ferocious scowl to Sam's face.

She felt a hand in her back, propelling her up the steps, and heard him say, 'Sorry, Smithie.'

Smithie?

Inside the wood-panelled hallway, which didn't boast the usual reception desk, it was blissfully warm. The moment she stepped in, even before she had had an opportunity to register that the décor was 'lived-in country house', Sam was conscious of the warm, comfortable laid-back atmosphere. Despite the fact that her stress levels were off the scale, she felt some of the tension slip from her shoulders.

While Alessandro warmly embraced the older woman Sam

examined her surroundings curiously, conscious as she did so of the loud ticking of a grandfather clock set against the wall and of the distant murmur of conversation interspersed by the occasional laugh somewhere close.

'You look marvellous, Smithie. Like a fine wine, you improve with age.'

'One of the advantages of being an ugly young woman is that your face becomes more acceptably interesting as you get older.' Pushing Alessandro away with a sharp admonition not to drip on the carpet, she turned her attention to Sam. 'And who is this you have brought to see me?'

Sam, still bemused at seeing Alessandro spoken to as though he were a grubby schoolboy, blinked as the interrogative blue eyes swept over her. The woman personified her mental image of a girls' school headmistress—the sort that probably didn't exist outside a film-maker's imagination. She had the smallest and sharpest eyes she had ever seen. But I bet you don't miss much, Sam thought as she endured the searching scrutiny.

As Alessandro placed a hand lightly on her shoulder and drew her forward Sam caught sight of the crackling flames of an open fire through the open double doors to the right. 'This is Miss Samantha Maguire.'

Very conscious of the fingers on her shoulder, Sam nodded and flashing Alessandro a sideways glance, corrected him. 'Sam.'

'Well, hello, Sam Maguire. I'm Dorothy Smith—I manage the place.'

'Smithie is the non-sleeping half of the partnership,' Alessandro explained.

Considering the amount of energy the older woman exuded, Sam wouldn't have been surprised to learn she didn't sleep at all!

'My mother's family have lived in this house for centuries. When she died—' She broke off and sighed, adding, 'If it hadn't been for Alessandro's intervention it would have had to be sold to pay the death duties.'

'I know a sound investment when I see one.'

The older woman lifted her brows and laughed before turning to Sam. 'He had to sink a small fortune into it just to stop it from falling down,' she confided, slanting him a challenging look that dared him to contradict her. 'On present performance it will be another ten years before our hard-headed business tycoon even breaks even. Sound investment! Huh!' She snorted.

'I'm in for the long haul,' Alessandro said, looking as close to uncomfortable as Sam had ever seen him.

'Of course you are, dear,' the older woman agreed. 'Now, introductions over. What you need is a hot bath and a brandy, Sam,' Dorothy announced briskly. 'No, Alessandro,' she said, accompanying her sharp words with a dismissive wave of her hand as he began to follow them, 'we don't need you.'

Now, *that* was something he couldn't hear very often, thought Sam, torn between outright shock and amusement as she turned her head to see how he was taking the rejection.

Alessandro inclined his dark head, accepting the prohibition with an uncharacteristic meekness that made Sam's jaw drop. He intercepted her astonished stare and an ironic glitter entered his eyes.

'Come along, Sam…'

It amused Sam that the older woman's words were an order, thinly disguised as a request.

'I will see you later,' Alessandro said as she approached the broad sweep of the stairs.

'Now, there's something to look forward to.'

Her muttered response drew a quizzical look from the older woman, but she made no comment beyond recommending Sam to watch her step. Deciding to take this ambiguous comment literally, Sam lowered her eyes and clasped the curved banister.

She was eaten up with curiosity as to how this most un-likely of partnerships had come into being, but couldn't work out a way of asking without coming across as nosy. 'Are you very busy at the moment?' she asked, as a couple emerged from a room along the hallway.

Her hostess gave a nod, before asking Sam. 'Have you known Alessandro long?'

Obviously the other woman did not share her concern about appearing nosy. 'Not really. Actually, I don't really know him at all. I've been aware of him, of course…' She stopped, a dark blush spreading over her fair skin. 'Not aware in *that* way—just…' Lowering her eyes from the other woman's amused, knowing glance, she bit her lip. 'My car broke down—hence the drowned rat look.' She laughed. 'And he picked me up.' That, she decided, could have been phrased better.

'Oh, yes—he would,' the other woman said immediately. 'Alessandro is very chivalrous.'

Are we talking about the same man? Sam wondered, re-sponding to this affectionate confidence with a non-commit-tal grunt.

'I have known him since he was a child. I was his nanny.'

'Oh, that explains it!' Sam exclaimed without thinking.

'His mother was still travelling a lot with her work then…' The sharp little blackcurrant eyes scanned Sam's face. 'You did know that she was an opera singer…?'

Sam shook her head. 'No, I didn't know that.' It occurred to her that she didn't know much at all about Alessandro. But then, she asked herself, why should I? Bottom line was, he was the next best thing to a total stranger.

'Oh, yes, she had a very successful career. But after little Katerina was born she decided to become a full-time mother, and I was not needed.'

'That must have been hard for you.' Sam, who imagined that a nanny would become very attached to her charges, sympathised.

'Yes,' admitted Dorothy Smith. 'It was.'

'And for the child too…?'

The observation brought a flicker of approval to the older woman's eyes. 'It was,' she admitted. 'But he always kept in touch. Alessandro was always a punctiliously polite boy, and he wrote me delightful letters. I have kept them all. One day,' she promised, sending Sam a warm glance, 'I will let you read them.'

Embarrassed that the other woman persisted in misinterpreting her relationship with Alessandro, Sam bit her lip. Before she had a chance to set matters straight once and for all, the other woman continued.

'When the accident happened I had retired.' She shook her head, her expression sombre as she thought about those dark days. 'Of course I came back to help—though the first task was convincing Alessandro he needed help.' She stopped outside a door and smiled warmly at Sam. 'But I'm sure I don't need to tell *you* that.'

Sam just smiled. She suspected anything she said was not going to alter the other woman's determination to see a relationship where there was none. Hopefully, Alessandro would put her right. What was she thinking? *Of course* he'd put her right. It would do his reputation no good at all for people to think he was sleeping with a ginger-headed frump who wore beige.

'Alessandro usually uses that one, but the bedrooms are identical and of course they are adjoining,' Dorothy was saying when Sam tuned back into the conversation.

'*Bedrooms…?*'

'Yes, they're adjoining—see,' she said, pushing open a door. She saw Sam's expression and frowned. 'You could have a room of your own, of course, but with the Food Festival and the fishing tournament falling in the same week this year we're totally full.'

'Goodness, no—I just meant to say, I'm not staying. I'm going back to London tonight.'

'Really?' Her barely discernible brows rose. 'I must have misunderstood. I thought Alessandro said he was staying over.'

'Maybe he is—he's a free agent—but I'm not… Staying, that is—not not a free agent. Which I am—' She broke off, lifted a hand to her head and sighed.

The other woman observed her pale, drawn face and looked remorseful. 'Look at me, chattering on when what you need is some peace and quiet. I'll send you up some brandy. Now, off you go and get out of those wet things. The bathrooms here are really marvelous—when I think what the plumbing was like when I was a girl…' Shaking her head she lifted a hand in farewell and left Sam alone…finally.

Lying in the deep bath, her senses soothed by the decadent oils she had added to the water, Sam's thoughts turned to the day's extraordinary events. Her mind, pleasantly blurry from the shot of brandy she ought to have refused—though it would have taken a very strong person to say no to the redoubtable Dorothy—kept returning again and again to that bone-melting kiss.

She had not known that kisses like that one existed! Let alone realised what she had been missing!

Now she knew, and it had been Alessandro who had been the catalyst—the man who had been in the right place at the right time and pressed all the right buttons.

'It could have been anyone.' The room was empty, so the only voice of dissent to this defiant statement was in her own head. *Are you sure about that…?*

She sat upright, her expression mutinous and set. 'Too right I'm sure. There's nothing special about Alessandro Di Livio.'

The sheer ludicrousness of this contention drew a pained laugh from her throat as she slid back into the water. Alessandro was a lot of things, but commonplace was *not* one of them…!

Approaching twenty-four and she had never lost control…now, that was worrying. Even more worrying was the fact that she had not seen the appeal of such a loss until now! A part of her wished that the searing kiss had never happened, that she was still walking around in blissful ignorance, but another part of her was inclined to relive the moment again and again…!

Recalling once more those initial moments of boneless, melting submission made her heart-rate quicken. As Alessandro had plundered her mouth the submission had given way to something equally outside her experience: a frantic, inarticulate need to touch and taste…to fuse with his male heat and hardness. Thinking about the primitive response made her breathing quicken and her pale, translucent skin turn a rosy pink.

Sighing she sank beneath the water. Surfacing moments later, she brushed the fronds of water-darkened hair from her face. She *knew* she loved Jonny. It had been a given in her life for so long that she just hadn't questioned it—not until Alessandro had put doubts in her head with his sneers.

'I *do* love Jonny!' she announced defiantly to the steamy bathroom.

Just because you couldn't imagine yourself having steamy head-banging sex with someone it didn't mean you didn't love them! And, by the same token, just because you could imagine it, it didn't mean you did!

No, the stuff with Alessandro was just about sex. Maybe, she thought, lifting her head as the depressing possibility struck her, you couldn't have love *and* sex. You had to settle for one or the other. Now, that was a depressing thought.

CHAPTER EIGHT

SHE was belting a big fluffy robe when there was a tap on the interconnecting door. Without waiting for her to respond, the door opened and Alessandro walked in.

'*What—?*' she said, her voice accusing, because his presence sent her hard-won composure straight out of the window.

'I did knock,' he observed, dropping the jacket he was carrying on the bed and walking towards her.

'The idea of knocking is that you wait for someone to invite you in…or tell you go away.'

'You don't want me to go away.'

His calm assurance made her want to hit him. Lips pursed, she lowered her eyes. He had changed into a pale cashmere sweater and dark, close-fitting jeans, he smelt of soap and himself, and he looked sexy enough to cause mass hysteria in the female population of a small planet!

'Believe that if it makes you feel happy.' Tightening the belt on her robe, she was reminded of the fact she didn't have a stitch on underneath.

'I didn't come here to fight with you,' he said, sounding weary. 'I came to ask what you want to do about dinner. Do you want to eat here, or with the other guests? Though I must warn you up-front that a quiet dinner downstairs isn't an option. Smithie favours dining dinner-party-style.'

'I don't want to eat full-stop. I'm going home.'

'Don't be stupid—you must be hungry.'

Sam's eyes narrowed. 'Don't call me stupid.' She glared into his eyes and lost the plot. He had such gorgeous eyes— dark and deep and so, *so*...sexy...they made you want... Gasping sharply, she pulled herself up before she lost it completely. 'So you know,' she said, 'what I'd really like...?'

'What?' he asked, thinking she looked so pale and brittle that she might break if handled roughly. But he knew she wasn't that fragile. She hadn't felt breakable when he had held her in his arms. She had been supple, strong, and so very, *very* hot.

'I'd like you to leave right now.' *Before I do something very stupid.* 'Walk out of that door and never come back.' Her problem was she was in danger of believing there was something between them. *The only thing between us is two years of not liking one another.*

While they had been talking he had been moving towards her and she had been retreating, matching him step for step. Of course his steps were bigger than hers, and by the time her shoulders made contact with the wall and she could retreat no farther he was so close she could see the fine lines radiating from the corners of his eyes.

'You don't mean that.'

'I do,' she said, putting as much conviction into the lie as she could.

Alessandro, the strong bones of his face drawn taut against his golden skin, regarded her pale face in silence before his eyes dropped. 'If you tell me you're not interested I'll walk away.' His eyes lifted, and she was pinned beneath a taut, combustible stare that made the muscles in her abdomen quiver.

Sam blinked to clear the rash of red dots that danced across her vision, conscious as she did so of the heavy thrum of blood as it beat through her body. Chirpy, she told herself. You need to aim for chirpy, but firm.

Fingers crossed, she scrunched up her face in a mask of determination as she told herself over and over… *You can do it; you can do it…!*

She opened her eyes, and he looked so damned gorgeous standing there, so dark and lean and excitingly dangerous, that her will-power almost crumbled. My God, but being virtuous and sensible was not all it was cracked up to be, she thought dully.

'I'm not…interested.' She failed miserably with chirpy, but by some freaky accident she hit bored and couldn't-give-a-damn dead centre!

Other than a slight clenching of his muscles no visible re-action to her reply registered on his strong-boned, autocratic features. When he responded a moment later his tone was col-oured only with an easy come, easy go quality.

At least I know I definitely made the right call, she thought.

Just because she'd decided that it was time she moved on with her life and stopped being faithful to a relationship that had never existed outside her imagination, it didn't mean her personality and values had changed beyond recognition.

She was realistic. She hadn't been walking around with her eyes and ears closed. She knew that for a lot of men—and, for that matter, women—sex had the same emotional content as a trip to the gym or a game of squash! A lover, yes. She recognised that she did have needs that weren't being fulfilled. But casual sex—no.

Am I expecting too much? It's not as if I'm asking for a life-long commitment!

It wasn't too much to ask to expect the man you went to bed with to at least remember your name the next day. She didn't want him to sleep with her because it was a rainy af-ternoon and he had a couple of hours in his diary to kill. Or, even worse, because he wanted to make sure she wasn't climbing into his brother-in-law's bed!

Alessandro scanned her heart-shaped face for a moment, his expression inscrutable, then after a slight hesitation in-clined his dark head. 'As you wish.'

Sam nodded back and thought, *Wish…!* If this was about wishes I'd be underneath you now…or maybe on top…

'You've been very kind,' she heard herself say stupidly.

That she could say anything at all with the sort of erotic images that were jostling for position in her head was nothing short of a miracle.

He flashed her a hawkish glare that was not at all kind. As he proceeded to consult the metal-banded watch on his wrist Sam's attention was drawn to the contrast of the cold dull metal to his warm, bronzed, satiny skin. Her stomach did a painful flip as she looked at the light dusting of dark body hair on his sinewed forearm and, appalled by the strength and primitive quality of the urge that made her want to touch him, she turned her head.

You just have to step back, she told herself. *Be objective…!* Great advice—pity there's not a chance in hell of me taking it, she thought, swallowing the bubble of hysterical laughter in her throat.

Inhaling a deep, sustaining breath, she made herself focus on his face. The line between his strong dark brows deepened, as though his thoughts had already moved on to more pressing issues. Of course it was good that he'd accepted her decision and not tried to dissuade her, but she would have felt a little better if he had looked as though it cost him *some* effort!

Obviously not sleeping with me ranks alongside other minor inconveniences—such as missing the last post!

It was just beginning to dawn on her that he'd been standing there looking at his watch for a strangely long space of time when he lifted his head and looked at her.

'If you do want to go back to London tonight speak to Smithie. She will arrange transport.'

'You're not going back…?' His eyes narrowed fractionally and she added quickly, anxious to dispel any impression that she was trying to invite herself along for the ride, 'Not that I expect a lift or anything.'

His hand on the door, Alessandro turned slowly back. Sam gave a sharp intake of breath and shrank back from the molten ferocity of the expression that drew the flesh taut across the sharp angles of his lean face. *'A lift? Madre di Dio!'*

'No, it's fine. I'll probably give my mum a ring and stay at home until my car is sorted.'

His narrowed obsidian gaze moved across her face. 'You stand there looking like that and talk about getting your car fixed!' He closed his eyes, pressed his fingers to the bridge of his patrician nose and released a wrathful flood of fluid Italian.

Italian, Sam decided, listening in awestruck silence to the outpouring, was a very expressive language to get mad in. Though for the life of her she couldn't figure out what she had said or done to trigger this from a man who was legendary for his reserve and control. When he opened his eyes again she realised that she wasn't seeing the polite regret she had felt was being expressed moments earlier. In his searing stare she was seeing overt raw hunger and rampant frustration... Not an *I missed my game of squash* expression at all.

As Sam's stomach muscles clenched she suddenly wasn't so sure about her assessment of the situation. Alessandro wasn't acting like a man who was going to forget her name by tomorrow. He was acting like a man who was pretty near to losing it!

As she studied him through the spiky sweep of her dark lashes she saw him rake a hand viciously through his hair. As he padded across the room, as sleek and dangerous as any jungle cat, she could hear him muttering under his breath in his native tongue. Having put several feet between them, he turned his head and looked at her.

My God, but he really is magnificent! The tightness in her chest became a physical pain as she watched him.

'You think I could trust myself to be alone in a car with you?' The frustration emanating from him was an almost palpable entity in the room.

Sam, not knowing what else she could do or say, shook her head.

His sensual upper lip curled in a grimace of self-derision. *'Dio,'* he rasped thickly. 'I can't trust myself to be in the same *room* as you!'

It wasn't until after the door had slammed, hard enough to rattle the hinges and several pieces of artwork on the walls, that Sam, her emotion-whacked body limp, literally crumbled. Tears streaming down her face, she slowly slid down the wall until she sat in a hunched heap of misery on the floor. A sob of titanic proportions rocked her body as her head fell forward into her hands.

Why on earth did you tell him to go?

Sam had no idea how long she sat there. The next thing she registered was strong hands tilting her face upwards and dark eyes filled with concern examining her tear-drenched features.

Alessandro had dropped down onto his knees beside her.

'Tell me,' he demanded, his velvet voice roughly imperative. 'What is wrong?'

'Nothing…' she claimed, with tears still streaming down her face. 'What are you doing here?' *Other than driving me totally out of my mind.*

'Clearly *nothing* is a lie. I left my jacket.' His eyes didn't leave her face as he nodded towards the bed. 'Now, tell me,' he coaxed. 'No, I know,' he added harshly. 'And the man is not worth it. I know it seems hard now, but if you can forget…'

'Forget?' she shrilled, pulling her face angrily from the protective circle of his fingers with a loud sniff. 'How the hell am I meant to forget when *you're* here.'

He pressed a hand to his chest and looked confused. *'Me…?'*

'Who else?' she demanded, rubbing her teary eyes with her balled fists.

'You were crying before I returned.'

'Of course I was. You left!' Her lips started to quiver as a fat tear slid slowly down her cheek. *I never cry.*

Alessandro dragged a not quite steady hand through his hair and looked mystified. 'Because that is what you wanted.'

'My God, are you *stupid?*' she yelled, glaring up at him through a shimmer of tears. With both fists she scrubbed the dampness from her cheeks and then, as her eyes slid from his, admitted huskily, 'I lied.'

'*You lied…?*'

She nodded and sniffed. 'About not wanting you to stay.'

He tensed and leaned back on his heels, his eyes fixed on her downbent head.

'I didn't want you to go…' With a groan, Sam lifted her head, pushing her still damp copper hair back from her smooth forehead as she met his eyes. 'Well, I *did*—but I didn't…'

A muscle in his lean cheek clenched and then clenched again as he fought the impulse to crush her to him. *Per amor di Dio!* A man would have to be lacking every red blood cell not to respond to the sultry half-scared invitation in those wide-spaced eyes. Despite the fact that his body ached he held himself in check…*just.*

His seething frustration concealed behind a languid façade, he smiled sardonically. 'Well, that makes everything as clear as mud.'

Female mood swings were something he had a healthy masculine respect for, but this woman was in a class of her own! He had always prided himself on his self-control, but if she changed her mind again he feared that his control—already tested to the limit—would prove inadequate to the task of walking away. The women he had mutually beneficial arrangements with knew the score; there were no emotional scenes. By contrast, the red-headed Samantha Maguire was a walking three-act drama!

His ironic drawl ignited a flare of anger in Sam. *What does he want me to do…? Beg…?*

Alessandro watched her white teeth sink into the trembling

curve of her full lower lip. He swallowed. *Dio mio,* it was more than flesh could bear! He had been thinking about that mouth all day, and what he would like to do with it.

Hands clenched at his sides, his thoughts abruptly reversed to the moment earlier that day, when he had witnessed Trevelan kissing her. His primitive desire to choke the life out of the younger man had, he reasoned, been a perfectly legitimate response when the honour of his sister was concerned.

The only problem with that was that Alessandro hadn't been thinking of Katerina—at least not at that moment. He had seen the other man kissing Sam and his first thought had been, *That should be me.* His thoughts were running along the same lines at that moment.

Lifting her chin to a belligerent angle, Sam choked bitterly. 'I thought you were supposed to have a brilliant brain? Do I have to spell it out?' She heaved an exasperated sigh.

He angled a dark brow as his smoky gaze moved across her face, lingering longest on her pink parted lips, before he produced one of his inimitable shrugs and said, 'Maybe…'

'Maybe you'd like me to put it in writing?' Then there would be permanent proof that she was such a push-over where he was concerned that she was totally shameless. That she was ready to beg and he hadn't even touched her. *If he did touch me…* Gulping, she tore her gaze from his long brown fingers. But it was too late. Every nerve-ending in her body was already screaming for attention.

'Then why did you tell me to go?'

For a bright man, she thought, he could be dense at times.

'Because you put me on the spot,' she told him accusingly. 'Because you made *me* the one to make the decision when all I wanted you to do was…'

'What did you want me to do?'

She shrugged and her eyes slid from his. 'Kiss me, I suppose.'

'If you wanted to be kissed, telling me you weren't interested probably wasn't the best clue.'

'Well, I didn't actually know how much I wanted you until you walked away.'

The dark colour scoring his chiselled cheekbones deepened as he inhaled sharply. 'And do you still want me?'

She swallowed and lifted her eyes. The smouldering heat in his made her dizzy, and totally, utterly reckless. 'Only slightly more than I want to breathe,' she confessed huskily.

Alessandro took her face between his hands, allowing his thumbs to move across the smooth contours of her cheeks. 'I think we can arrange for you to do both.'

Breathing hard, Sam turned her head and kissed the open palm of his hand. 'You do know that you've got everything a perfect lover should have…?'

Alessandro stopped what he was doing and studied her flushed face with a fascinated expression. 'Are you going to tell me what those qualities are?'

'You're beautiful—not that you being ugly would be a deal-breaker, exactly,' she conceded. 'Because you've got bucket loads of sex appeal. And you're not going to insult my intelligence by pretending to be in love with me or anything…'

'You don't want love?'

She was suggesting the sort of mutually beneficial relationship that he favoured—so why did he not feel pleasure, even relief…? Actually, he couldn't quite pin down the cause for his perverse gut response, and now was not the moment for deep soul-searching. Alessandro, in the grip of a blind, relentless hunger unlike anything he had felt since adolescence, had more urgent matters to consider—like the very real possibility he might go insane if he didn't bury himself deep inside her in the near future!

'I thought I did, but you've made me look hard at myself.'

He looked startled by the confidence and framed a cautious question. *'I have…?'*

'You know what I do on Saturday nights?' He shook his head, but Sam's head was too filled with images of her unsatisfactory life to notice the strangeness of his expression. 'What I want,' she told him, 'is to be more like you. I have needs,' she told him, 'and I want to have sex without feeling guilty.'

'With anyone in particular?'

She stuck out her chin and thought, If he laughs, I'll die. 'You, for starters.'

He didn't laugh, or even contest the 'for starters'. Instead he grabbed her by the shoulders and yanked her towards him. Then, teasing her lips with his mouth and tongue, he took her face between his hands. His mouth came down hard on hers and Sam melted bonelessly in his arms.

CHAPTER NINE

As HE sat on the edge of the bed, slipping off his shoes, Sam reached out and touched his dark hair. The thick, lustrous texture fascinated her. Raising herself up onto her knees, she pulled his head round towards her and pressed her lips to his in a long, lingering kiss.

'You taste incredible,' she sighed against his mouth, and ran her finger down the stubble that darkened his strong jaw. 'Rough…'

'I need to shave twice a day.'

The smoky glow in her eyes deepened as she caught her tongue between her teeth and sucked in a long sultry sigh. 'Not on my account. I like it.'

'Madre di Dio!' groaned Alessandro, breathing hard as the dark lashes lifted from her flushed cheeks to reveal her passion-glazed eyes. 'Hold that thought,' he instructed imperatively.

Sam smiled and plastered her shaking body to his back. The heat and hardness of him through the robe was shocking, and more exciting than she could have imagined was possible. She felt his lean body tense and he inhaled sharply.

'You are impatient.'

Who wouldn't be? She'd been waiting twenty-four years for this moment. She just hadn't realised it until now.

Sam let out a tiny startled shriek as his hands closed around her wrists, and a breathless moment later she found herself sitting, or rather lying, across his lap. His head bent towards her and she closed her eyes and moaned low in her throat as she opened her mouth to the skilful incursions of his tongue.

'God!' she groaned, suffocating with desire as he kissed his way down the curve of her neck. 'I must have been mad to say no to this.'

Alessandro stopped what he was doing long enough to look at her with hot, hungry eyes and insert huskily, 'I didn't go very far.'

'And you came back,' she whispered, sliding her hands under the thin cashmere sweater he was wearing. A jerky little sigh was snatched from her throat as she made contact with the smooth, warm, hard flesh of his belly. 'You're so…' She sighed as, eyes half closed, breath coming in short shallow gasps interspersed by little moans, she let her hands glide palms flat over his satiny skin.

Sam felt the contraction of his stomach muscles as he sucked in a sharp breath, his hands tightening over her bottom as he gave a deep moan of pleasure.

'I'm awfully glad you came back.' His skin felt like oiled silk, and it was deliciously warm.

There was a long dragging silence before he confided, 'So am I.' Taking both her wrists in his, he drew them from his body and brought them to his mouth.

'I want…'

He stilled her protest by the simple expedient of kissing her, a deep, drugging kiss that left her weak and wanting more…*much more.*

'You shall have what you want. You shall have everything you want,' he promised huskily.

As their gazes locked, the dark promise in his heated stare made Sam's heart thud even harder against her ribcage. Alessandro released her wrists and then, still holding her gaze, lifted his jumper over his head in one smooth motion and flung it across the room, revealing the sleek, hard contours of his bronzed upper body.

Sam's rapt gaze dropped, desire clutching like a tight fist low in her belly, and she thought, *You're the most beautiful thing ever—flawless.* The academic interest she had decided she was going to adopt towards her first real sexual experience became a dim and distant memory as she started to shake from head to toe, and she didn't even realise she had voiced her thought until he said, 'Thank you, but I am not without flaws.'

Not understanding the odd inflection in his voice, Sam felt a frown form between her brows. She reached for him, but to her frustration he levered himself off the bed in a fluid motion. Taking two steps away, he turned back to face her.

'What's wrong…?' The tension that had begun to build between her shoulderblades seeped away as he began to unbuckle the belt on the jeans that clung to his long, muscular thighs, only to be replaced by another sort of tension.

Touching her tongue to the beads of sweat that had broken out across the curve of her upper lip, she felt the feelings that he had aroused in her coalesce into a sexual desire so raw and primitive it pushed every other consideration from her head.

As he kicked aside his trousers he held her eyes.

The lustful surge that slammed through her body was so all-consuming that it was a few moments before Sam registered the scars that ran the length of his thigh. Unable to stop herself, she gasped. 'From the accident?'

Sam had watched the programme, had seen him looking barely alive on the stretcher, but until that point she hadn't considered his injuries. Those scars spoke of many weeks and months of pain and suffering. They spoke of a long and difficult period of rehabilitation.

Her throat closed over as she thought of him going through that alone. Her hands tightened into fists. *Dear God, let there have been someone there for him.*

His flat voice was totally devoid of emotion as he asked, 'You find the scars repulsive…?'

The dry question brought a rush of furious colour to her cheeks. 'Do I look shallow and stupid?' she demanded.

He studied her face for a moment in silence, and then, although his expression didn't alter, she sensed he relaxed. 'You look…' His eyes darkened as they slid slowly over her recumbent form. 'You look incredibly desirable and sexy.'

'*Oh…!* So do you, actually.'

His eyes glittered. 'How well suited we are.'

That, she thought, sucking in a breath as he lowered his long, lean frame beside her on the bed, remains to be seen. *It could be that I'm going to be really awful at this.* Was it really wise to begin with someone who must have pretty high standards? Of their own volition her eyes dropped to the bulging evidence of his arousal, barely contained by the boxers he wore.

'Still my fiercest critic…?'

Sam's eyes lifted. 'I'm not finding fault,' she confessed huskily. 'And how can I be your fiercest critic—we've hardly spoken?' *Hardly spoken…and today you're in his bed!*

'You don't need to speak—you have very eloquent eyes. You have been hating me silently for two years. When I woke up this morning the last person I expected to end up in bed with was Samantha Maguire.' *Except in my dreams.* But a man wasn't responsible for what his subconscious got up to. 'Who did *you* expect to end up in bed with?'

His wicked grin flashed out, and Sam realised that she didn't want to do this with anyone else. It was a revelation she had to share. 'I only want you.'

He laced his long brown fingers into her damp hair and pressed his lips to the pulse-point at the base of her neck. By the time he reached her mouth she was writhing with pleasure. 'I like a woman who knows what she wants.'

As they lay side by side on the bed she slowly ran her fingers over the long white scar that ran the length of his flank, and then over the network of smaller scars above his knee. 'I had no idea you were hurt so badly, Alessandro,' she said huskily.

'It looks worse than it was,' he lied, catching her hand and bringing it to his mouth.

Accepting that he didn't want to talk about it, she sighed with pleasure as his hand curved over her bottom. Lifting her mouth from his some time later, she touched a finger to the scar just below the hem of the silk boxers he wore. 'Does it go all the way?'

He smiled that stunning, wicked smile that made her heart flip and husked, 'No, *cara*, but I do.' Laughing at her blushes, he tipped her onto her back with masterful expertise and reached for the tie of her robe.

Before he slid the knot, she grabbed his hand in both of hers. 'I'm not very…'

Gently but firmly he took her hands, one by one, curving her fingers around the metal bedframe. 'I think we should have no secrets, *cara*.'

Sam held onto the bedframe for dear life and closed her eyes, sure that the moment he unwrapped her he might change his mind. 'No…' he cautioned, kissing her eyelids. 'Open your eyes.'

Her breath coming in short, painful bursts, Sam did as he requested. 'I…can't…'

'Relax…'

Relax! She was in bed with the most beautiful man she had ever seen, who happened to be half naked and about to undress her. In other circumstances she might have laughed. At that moment holding her breath seemed a more appropriate response.

Slowly, his eyes holding hers, he unslid the knot on her robe and parted the fabric. Alessandro swallowed before his eyes dropped.

A reverent cry of, '*Dio*, but you are perfect!' was torn from his lips.

Sam sagged with relief, then tensed again as his hand closed over first one taut tender breast and then the other, stroking her skin, teasing the straining, prominent peaks to new heights of quivering pleasure with his fingers and then his lips.

She snaked her fingers into his dark hair and said his name, her voice aching with the same inarticulate longing that drenched her body. To see his dark head against her pale skin was so unbelievably erotic that Sam writhed and arched her back, pushing up against him, gasping a little as their naked bodies touched, and then a lot more when his hand slid down the length of her smooth pale thigh.

Levering himself up until his face was level with hers, he looked deep into her eyes before he kissed her, and Sam clutched at him, her fingers digging into the taut golden flesh of his back as she moaned, 'Please...' into his mouth.

She had no idea what she needed, but Alessandro was not similarly inhibited. He seemed to know where she wanted to be touched before she did! As his skilful mouth and hands moved over her body she gave a fractured groan and called out his name again, almost sobbing with the strength of her desire.

Sam had no idea how long he touched her any more than she had any idea of at what point she lost her inhibitions about him exploring every intimate part of her. Or being bold about doing the same to him. But when Alessandro finally pulled her beneath him and moved over her she was ready for the next step.

Actually, she was begging for his sensual invasion!

Her body tensed for a moment as he slid into her. Above her she was aware of his doing the same thing. For a moment neither of them moved.

Sam closed her eyes and heard his shocked inhalation, felt his breath warm on her cheek and neck. 'Just go with it, *cara*.' The sensual rasp of his thickened voice was like a caress. 'I will look after you. You don't have to stay in control. Trust me…just let go…' he urged, sliding his hands under her bottom.

Of all the unexpected things that had happened to her that day, this was perhaps the most unexpected. Sam found she did. She *did* trust him. *Totally.* He was the most dangerous thing that had ever happened to her, but she trusted him to keep her safe. It made no sense, but it was incredibly liberating.

As the tension slid from Sam an exultant sigh shuddered through her stretched body.

'You feel incredible,' she moaned, grabbing his tight buttocks because she felt as if she was falling. 'I can feel all of…' A fractured moan was wrenched from her throat.

'So good at this…so beautiful…so tight…' As he moved slowly, hot and hard inside her, sliding deeper and deeper, she was aware of him in every individual tingling nerve-ending. And as he moved he wasn't just inside her body, he was inside her head. With each thrust and stroke he seeped into her senses.

Alessandro was part of her.

As the rhythm inside her built Sam said some wild things that she shouldn't have—things concerning his complete and total perfection, things about wanting him to do this to her for ever and ever—but he said some pretty crazy things too.

'Now, just let go…!'

She did.

As her heart-rate returned to something approaching normal she gave a languid sigh. Alessandro's leg remained thrown across her, pinning her to the bed—not that she felt any urge to move from where she was. Her body was still rocked with tiny golden aftershocks.

She stroked his dark head where it lay on the pillow and smiled a sleepy, smugly contented smile. Her back arched a little as he stroked a brown finger down the valley between her pink-tipped breasts.

His dark lashes lifted from the sharp angle of his cheekbones. 'Why didn't you tell me…?'

Sam, who knew exactly what he was saying, closed her eyes and feigned innocence. 'Tell you what?'

'You have never been with a man, *cara*.'

'I was hoping you wouldn't notice.' She opened her eyes and saw no answering smile on his face. 'Sorry if I was totally clueless, but…' She reached up and stroked his lean cheek, feeling the first stirrings of reawakened sexual interest as she recalled the abrasive sensation of his stubble on her burning skin as he worked his way down her body. 'If you're willing to bear with me, I think I could be a very fast learner.' Then, realising that she was making a lot of assumptions she had no right to make she added quickly, 'Always supposing we ever…you…we decide…' Maybe he was already regretting it? Maybe he was wondering how to tell her she'd have to find someone else for lesson two?

'Perhaps we should get out our diaries and see if we have a spare afternoon?' he inserted, sounding unaccountably angry.

'I don't have a diary.' She held her breath, thinking, That's his cue to say, *And I don't have a spare afternoon.*

He didn't.

'You should have told me…'

'Are you angry?' She looked at his face, memorising each plane and angle. 'About the virgin stuff?'

The awkward addition made his lips quiver. 'I'm not angry. I'm…I would have been gentler…'

'That would have been a pity.' She laid her head on his chest and felt the vibration of his surprised laugh.

'Today was a first for us both.'

She lifted her head. 'It was?'

'I've never slept with a virgin before. The women I—'

'I know,' she said quickly. 'They're like you. That's the way *I* want to be,' she told him, thinking, *I can do this!* 'If you want me, that is…' She swallowed, trying and failing to read his expression.

'*If I want you…?*' he echoed, sounding really strange. He

rolled onto his back. She watched as he lifted a hand and then just lay there.

Sam stared at his chest, rising and falling. His hand fell away, and as he turned his head towards her she held her breath.

'Oh, I want you,' he said thickly, and as he reached for her with a sigh of relief she went to him.

Much later, when the room had grown dark, Alessandro got up from the bed to throw a log the dying embers of the fire. His tall, lean body was silhouetted against the dancing flames as he walked back to the bed.

My God, he's so beautiful!

'A fire in the bedroom is very…decadent,' she murmured as she snuggled up to him.

Alessandro ran a finger down the supple curve of her spine, and in the dark she smiled.

Her smile guttered when he asked quietly, 'Should we be worried?'

Sam knew immediately what he was talking about. The second time they had made love she had not known what he was apologising for until he had explained that the condom had broken. Still floating on a blissful cloud after their slow, sensuous, mind-blowing lovemaking, the implications of his explanation had not hit her. Now they did.

She did some speedy mental calculations and shook her head. 'No, it'll be fine,' she said, with more confidence than she actually felt.

'Well, you would tell me if…?'

Sam frowned. 'I told you—it'll be fine. I'm so glad I settled…'

His finger stopped stroking, but stayed where it was.

'Settled…?'

'Uh-huh,' she confirmed sleepily. Passion expended an awful lot of energy. 'My mum is always saying there's no point waiting for Mr Perfect because he doesn't exist…you should settle…'

'But he *does* exist, doesn't he?'

Bewildered by the edgy note that had entered his deep voice, Sam turned her head on the pillow, and in the shadows found his taut expression inexplicably hostile. 'What do you mean?'

'I mean Jonny was your Mr Perfect, and as he was unavailable you *settled* for me. It is not flattering for a man to realise the woman in his arms was thinking of another man while he made love to her. *Madre di Dio,* do you think I will tolerate being someone you *settle* for?'

'Thinking about someone else…?' she parroted, as though the words had no meaning. Which, of course, they didn't. With her body and mind drenched down to cellular level with awareness of Alessandro, Sam was having understandable trouble getting her head around this idea.

She met his suspicious, angry eyes and experienced a blinding flash of comprehension and anger.

'For goodness' sake, I couldn't even remember my own name—couldn't figure out where you ended and I started. *Think about someone else?*' she ejaculated with a bitter laugh. 'You're the last man in the world I'd have thought needed his ego massaging. Surely someone has mentioned before now the fact that you're really very, *very* good at this?'

'*Dio!*' he breathed as, overcome by embarrassment, she buried her face in his chest. 'I really never know what you're going to say next.'

She slid her hands over the soft whirls of dark hair on his chest and ran a finger across his masculine nipple. 'Neither do I.'

The husky admission drew a short laugh from Alessandro, who placed a hand underneath her bottom and scooped her towards him.

'When my mum was saying all that stuff about Mr Perfect I was still thinking in terms of a life partner. Now I realise I'm not actually suited to marriage.'

'You're not…?'

She shook her head emphatically. The last thing Alessandro wanted was a clingy, needy woman. 'No—definitely not. I'm too selfish. I like my life the way it is…' Her eyelashes swept downwards as she added huskily, 'With certain additions.'

He rolled over until he was looking down into her face and her body was pinioned by his long, lean length. 'A lover being one of those *certain additions…*?'

Not just *any* lover. Her perfect lover.

She nodded. 'Nobody needs to know—I mean, it's not as if we would be dating, or a couple or anything. We'd just be…' She felt the heat run up under her skin as, trying to sound nonchalant, she finished, *'This.'*

'You want this to be a secret affair?'

He looked shocked—or was that relieved? 'Not secret, exactly, but…'

'You don't want to broadcast it?'

'It'll be a lot simpler that way,' she observed, saying what she thought he wanted to hear. If giving him space was the only way to keep him, she could do it, she told herself.

There was a long pause before he said, 'I'm all for a simple life.'

'I thought you would be.'

CHAPTER TEN

ALESSANDRO had been ripping off his clothes with flattering speed when she'd run, laughing, into the bathroom. She had called his name and got no response, and then waited, her heart pounding with anticipation. But when after several minutes the door to the shower cubicle remained closed Sam didn't linger. After shampooing her hair with unnecessary vigour she stepped out.

'Obviously I'm not as irresistible as I think,' she told her image in the steamy mirror. 'Oh, my, do I have a problem.'

Of course there was a problem—and it wasn't restricted to talking to herself! Casual she could do—casual was fine—but casual *wasn't* living for the brief moments they shared. It simply wasn't healthy when for most of the time she was just going through the motions, waiting for him to call or like tonight, ring her doorbell.

The fact was she wanted more, and more was something Alessandro didn't want to give. If he knew how she felt Sam suspected he would run a mile. There was a choice, of course. There was always a choice. She could come clean, tell him how she felt and watch him walk away. Or she could accept what she had.

What was called a lose-lose situation.

Wrapping a towel sarong-wise around her still damp body, Sam stalked back into the bedroom. The first thing she saw was Alessandro. He was actually pretty hard to miss, standing in the middle of the room doing his dark, brooding stare thing into the middle distance.

Well, at least he hasn't fallen asleep, she thought as she walked straight past him and sat herself down at the dressing table. Maintaining a stony silence, she ostentatiously removed his jacket from the back of the chair and dropped it in an untidy heap on the floor. The provocation provoked no reaction. He just stood there, in the same state of semi-undress as he had been when she left.

But something had obviously occurred to put him in such a vile mood, since he had walked into the room looking at her as though she was water and he was a man who'd spent the last ten days walking through a desert.

She lifted a brush and then with a sigh set it down. 'Are you going to tell me what I'm supposed to have done now…?'

In the mirror their eyes clashed, stormy green with cold, implacable brown.

'Why do you assume you have done something?'

'Maybe something to do with the fact you could cut the atmosphere in here with a knife, but mostly because you've got your judge, jury and executioner face on,' she told him sweetly. 'You know, this makes me really sick,' she observed. 'I've waited an entire week for you to contact me.' *Which makes me the sort of pathetic idiot I swore I'd never be.* 'And now you are here all you can do is look at me as though I'm…'

'*Dio mio*, do not take that tone with me!' His unbuttoned shirt billowed as he strode across the room, revealing the sleek, toned lines of his bronzed torso. Taking hold of the back of her swivel chair, he stood there, glaring at her in the mirror.

Sam, who didn't have the faintest idea what was going on, glared right back.

'If you don't like it you know what you can do!' The least a part-time lover could do was be civil when he did deign to put in an appearance. This no-strings, no-explanation thing sounded great in theory, and maybe it worked for some people, but Sam had come to appreciate that she wasn't one of them.

If I had an ounce of guts I'd tell him it's over. Only where Alessandro was concerned she had the backbone and moral fibre of an invertebrate. How many times had she seen and silently sneered at friends who were willing to make concession after concession for their boyfriends? I'd never do that, she had thought, from her position of moral superiority. *And look at me now!*

'Don't think I won't.'

Empty threats…is this what I've been reduced to…?

'Good!' she snapped, thinking, I might be able to do better than 'good' if I had the faintest idea what we were fighting about.

'I suppose you have a perfectly reasonable explanation for this?'

As he bent across her the scent of his warm body caused Sam's nostrils to flare. 'What…?' she said, picking up the creased piece of paper he had slammed down on the dressing table. Her eyes widened as she recognised Jonny's cheque, which she had shoved in her bag and forgotten about.

'What is that?'

'A cheque.'

A harsh expletive was torn from Alessandro's throat. 'I know it's a cheque,' he growled. 'Do not be evasive.' His dark, angry eyes glared back at her from the mirror.

Sam, who had Jonny's secret to guard, had every intention of being evasive for as long as she could—although the expression on Alessandro's face suggested that wouldn't be very long.

She shrugged. 'If you know, why ask?'

His lean face was drawn into savage lines of anger as he spun her chair around and, curving his big body towards her, planted a hand on either arm.

Sam's eyes lifted as his shadow fell across her.

'A cheque for a large amount of money, made out to you,

from my sister's husband. What is Jonny doing, giving you money?' he demanded in a low, driven voice.

'Are you trying to intimidate me…?' If I had any sense at all, she thought, he'd be succeeding. It was pretty obvious from the scorching anger etched into every glorious line of his incredible face that he was just about combustible!

'I am trying to extract a straight answer from you,' he gritted back grimly.

'What were you doing going through my bag?'

He looked outraged at the suggestion. 'I wasn't. The damned thing was sitting there on the bedside table. It fell on the floor, I picked it up and…' He stopped, the muscles of his brown throat visibly working as he recalled the moment when he had realised what he held in his hand. 'What is Jonny doing giving you money, Samantha?'

Sam shrugged, his judgemental attitude causing her to respond with more provocation than was probably sensible. But actually she didn't feel sensible. She felt absolutely fed up that he so obviously didn't trust her. The injustice of it made her want to scream.

'I don't owe you any explanations, Alessandro.' He had certainly never offered *her* any, she thought resentfully. 'You're my lover, not my keeper, and that,' she warned him, 'could change at any moment. And anyway,' she added, 'it wasn't a gift, it was a loan.'

The semantics caused his lips to spasm derisively. 'You will not take money from another man.'

'I did n—' She stopped, her eyes narrowing. 'Another man? Does that mean *you're* offering?'

'Would that not smack of payment for services rendered?'

There was no pause for thought between the intention and the action. Her arm went back in a curve, released, and her hand made contact with his cheek. Alessandro, a look of stark incredulity on his face, straightened up, breathing hard.

Shaking, Sam too scrambled to her feet, pushing her chair

backwards against the dressing table. 'Look what you made me do!' she accused, appalled by her own actions.

'I *made* you?'

'Yes, you made me!' she yelled back. 'You, with your nasty insinuations and always believing the worst.'

'Are you going to tell me what that money is for?'

Sam shook her head, her expression blank. 'No, I'm not.'

'No problem. I will ask Jonny.'

Panic flared in Sam's eyes. 'You can't do that!' she protested.

'You leave me no choice.'

Sam closed her eyes and shook her head. 'My God, but I hate you!'

His lips curled into a sardonic half-smile. 'At this moment,' he confided, 'I'm not particularly fond of you.' But he still wanted to unwind that towel and throw her on the bed. He wanted it so badly he could taste it.

Slinging him a look of loathing, Sam walked across to the bed and sat down before her shaking legs gave way. 'I haven't cashed the cheque, and if you'd bothered to read the date you'd have noticed that's it's almost two months old.'

Alessandro's dark brows drew together in a straight line. 'So why haven't you cashed it?'

'I couldn't stop him giving it to me, but I didn't have to cash it.'

'Do men often feel driven to give you large amounts of money?' At that moment *he* felt driven—*very* driven. The fact that even at this moment all he could think of was burying himself deep inside her and hearing her say, *Yes, Alessandro,* in that breathy little voice that killed his much vaunted self-control stone-dead, was some measure of the spell she exerted over him.

Face facts, Alessandro, his inner voice goaded contemptuously. While you're desperately trying to act as if nothing has changed, the fact is *everything* has changed. You're *so* in control you felt it necessary to sweat for twenty-four hours just to prove that you didn't have to get off the plane and rush to the side of a woman who hasn't made any effort to contact you.

Sam, realising that she had no option but to tell him the truth and hope he kept it to himself, sighed and said, 'Jonny wasn't giving it to me. He was paying me back.' She looked at Alessandro, who just stood there, giving the impression he wasn't even listening. 'Did you hear what I said?'

Alessandro released a long pent-up breath and looked at her. 'No…yes.' A frown formed on his lean face. *'Paying you back…?'*

'Jonny had some cashflow problems and I lent him a little to tide him over until he sorted himself out.'

One dark brow elevated. 'A *little*…?' he said, picking up the cheque and waving it under her nose. 'You think that is a little…?'

Sam flushed under his ironic gaze. 'Well, it was only sitting in my account.'

'I'm all for making your money work for you, but you didn't choose the safest form of investment, did you? At least I know now why he hasn't been to me…'

'You're the last person he'd go to.'

Alessandro's dark lashes lifted from the high angle of his cheekbones. 'And you are the first, it seems,' he slotted in drily.

'Well, at least I don't make him feel inadequate,' she retorted. 'I think you enjoy intimidating people,' she accused.

Alessandro raised an arm to drag a frustrated hand through his dark hair. The rippling this action set in motion over his lean torso caused her to lose the thread of her argument.

'He should have gone to his wife, not to another woman,' Alessandro condemned. 'And the fact is lending him money is only delaying the inevitable.'

Sam, her colour heightened, wrenched her fascinated gaze from his body and said angrily, 'I am not *another* woman.'

'You are not *his* woman.' *You're mine!*

'But I am his friend, and with a brother-in-law like you, boy, does he need one! For God's sake, Alessandro, why can't you give the man a chance? So he's no financial genius…' She lifted her shoulders in an expressive shrug. 'So what? He's doing his best. And no man could love your sister more than he does.'

Alessandro's eyes dropped to where her heaving bosom was on the point of escaping the confines of the towel. 'Would you defend *me* with so much passion?' he wondered, lifting his gaze to her face .

'Defend you…?' she parroted, and laughed. 'What do you need defending against?' she wondered. 'You're so tough you're virtually bullet-proof,' she accused.

The streaks of colour emphasising the strong, carved contours of his cheekbones deepened as he responded in a voice that leaked derisive scorn, 'I would certainly not beg money from a woman.'

'He didn't beg!' Sam protested. 'I found out by accident.'

'*Accident…?*'

'Yes, *accident.*'

'You mean he was drunk?'

Sam read the contemptuous condemnation in the lean, starkly beautiful contours of his face and her lips tightened. 'Small wonder Jonny didn't want to come to *you* for help.'

'I imagine he knew that I would not hand him a blank cheque and offer him tea and sympathy.' He flashed her a cold smile. 'Or was it hugs and kisses?'

'He doesn't want my hugs and kisses.'

Alessandro looked at her mouth, so soft, lush and inviting, and wondered how any man worthy of the name could not want to enjoy them. If Jonny wanted to keep his teeth intact he'd better carry on *not* wanting, he mused grimly. If he had suspected for one second that Jonny harboured any inappropriate feelings for Samantha he would already have taken action.

'Presumably if he did you would not be in my bed.'

She looked at his mouth, thought about it on her skin, and thought, I would be in your bed if I had to crawl there! 'I'm not in *your* bed.'

Alessandro's eyes slid from hers as Sam followed the direction of his gaze to the tumbled quilt she had hastily pulled across the bed when she had realised who was ringing the doorbell. The colour flew to her cheeks.

His voice dropped to a sexy rasp. 'That could easily be fixed.' He accompanied this with the sort of raw, hungry look that stripped her nerve-endings bare and caused goosebumps to break out like a rash on her overheated skin.

Making contact with the sizzling heat in his sensational eyes, she felt her anger and resistance melting faster than snow in July. Gritting her teeth, she clung to the last shreds of her resentment, reminding herself that this relationship was too one-sided.

'That's *my* bed.'

'Does it matter whose bed it is?' Alessandro responded impatiently—because he could think of very little else but her legs wrapped around him as she lay soft and warm beneath him…or maybe on top…?

'I've never been in *your* bed.' Sam's voice went cold as she added bitterly, 'I've never been in your bedroom, or even in your home.'

Alessandro had been scrupulously careful to keep her well away from anyone who knew him. She didn't even know the location of his London home.

'Which is fine by me,' she assured him breezily. 'I wouldn't want to meet any of your friends.' And it was painfully obvious he didn't want any of them meeting his *bit on the side*.

Alessandro looked disconcerted by the acrid observation. 'What are you talking about?'

Meet his friends…? Their casual arrangement, which he was finding increasingly unsatisfactory, meant they spent precious little time together as it was. Having his friends monopolise her time? Sure, he was *really* going to do that!

'I'd probably have as little in common with them as I do you.'

The stubborn, tight-lipped contention caused his taut jaw to tighten another notch. 'You have met Smithie.'

Sam's expression softened slightly as she thought of Alessandro's ex-nanny. 'But she's not like your other friends.'

He raised an eloquent brow. 'As you have never met them, how would you know what my friends are like?'

Sam's eyes narrowed with dislike on his lean face. 'Not *everyone* considers me such a social liability.'

'*Social liability…!*' he echoed. 'Why do you insist on putting words in my mouth?'

'I don't!' she protested mutinously. 'It's *obviously* what you're thinking.'

A hissing sound of frustration escaped through his clenched teeth. '*Fine!*' he said, flinging up his hands in a very Latin gesture of irritation. 'I will arrange a dinner…no, I will arrange a *reception,* and introduce you to everyone I know. Will you be happy then? Or would you like me to invite a camera crew from one of those magazines that specialise in glossy spreads of such things into my home? We can be pictured lounging beside the pool and gush about how inseparable we are…will *that* make you happy?'

His biting sarcasm stung. 'It would make me sick.'

'Then, you see, we *do* have something in common after all. I value my privacy, and I thought you felt the same way.'

What he valued was his freedom. 'Don't glower at me that way. I'm not Jonny.'

His expression darkened. 'You know, I am sick of the sound of that name.' An expression of brooding discontent settled on his lean features as he thought about the younger man. 'I still don't understand why, if he needed money, he didn't come to me?'

'You are Kat's brother—the poor, deluded girl thinks

you're perfect… Jonny is afraid he'll look a wimp by comparison with her *marvellous* brother.' Her expression left no doubt that she didn't share the younger girl's opinion.

'Nonsense!'

The way he brushed aside her explanation made Sam's general crankiness morph into genuine anger. 'That's *so* typical of you. If you don't want to hear something you just pretend it isn't so. But ignoring it doesn't make it any less the truth. The truth is you make Jonny feel incompetent and second best.'

'He *is* incompetent, and also boring—I have no wish to talk about him any longer.' If he didn't get her into bed some time in the next ten seconds he was going to lose his mind…although it was always possible he had already lost it. A swift mental review of his recent behaviour brought a self-derisive twist to Alessandro's lips.

Sam flung up her hands. 'See—you can't help yourself!' she exclaimed.

Alessandro remained unmoved by her dramatic hand-waving. 'I thought you set great store by honesty?' But then I used to think the same about myself, he thought, considering his recent self-deception.

Damn the man—he always had an answer. 'So, if he *had* come to you, what would you have done…?'

'That depends. But I certainly wouldn't have thrown good money after bad.'

'You'd have let him go under?' she accused, shocked by his unapologetic admission. 'But that amount of money is absolutely nothing to you!' she protested, clicking her fingers to underline her point. 'My God, Alessandro, you're so callous.'

'I'd have told him to cut his losses and find something he wants to do. He is clearly doing something he neither enjoys or is suited to. I would have told him to find something he can be passionate about.'

'You make it sound so easy, but Jonny isn't like you…'

His jaw clenched. 'You wish me to emulate your hero…?'

'There's no need to be stupid. Jonny is not my hero.'

Something flickered at the back of his dark eyes. There was a short, dense silence before he added huskily, 'And am I?'

The question threw Sam totally off her stride. 'Stupid? Or my hero…?' She angled an uncertain look at his face and discovered nothing from his shuttered expression. Did he want to be her hero? It seemed pretty unlikely.

'My hero would display a little bit of faith in me—not to mention have some respect for my views,' she retorted, avoiding a direct answer. 'But actually I don't think I need a hero. Actually, I don't think I need a lover.'

If the moment of shocked silence that followed her announcement had lasted another micro-second longer Sam would have retracted it. Only it didn't.

'You wish me to leave?'

Of course it might have been possible to retract her reckless words even then, if he had acted for a moment as if he gave a damn one way or the other. But he just stood there, looking remote in the way only he could, so she dug herself a little deeper and said, 'Well, there doesn't seem much point in you staying, does there?'

'I will not impose on you any longer,' he said, looking so stiff and starchy she almost expected him to click his heels!

She felt numb with shock and disbelief as he walked out of the door, but still managed to scream a defiant, 'Good riddance!' at the top of her lungs, before bursting into noisy, emotional sobs.

She eventually convinced herself that she was better off without him.

It took her twelve hours of intermittent weeping and numerous attempts to trivialise her feelings for Alessandro to arrive at this conclusion, but when she got there she knew it was a plateau—a point from which her life could move on in an infinitely saner and more productive direction. It was, she told herself, good that things had come to a head when they had. It wasn't as if she had ever thought the relationship had staying power.

After all, she was far too old to believe in fairy tales, and if the last few weeks had taught her anything they had taught her that she didn't want a life fraught with dramatic ups and downs. It might suit some people, but she liked an ordered, organised existence, and she was looking forward to things getting back to normal.

Of course at that point Sam didn't realize that *normal* had vanished for ever. That happened a week later.

CHAPTER ELEVEN

DOOR keys held in her teeth, one bag balanced on her hip, a sheaf of property leaflets under her arm and two bags of groceries gradually cutting off the circulation to her fingers, Sam climbed the stairs to her second-floor flat. There were many plus points about living on the second floor of this tasteful Edwardian conversion, including a lovely view of the park, but carrying her weekly groceries upstairs was not one of them.

The impossibility of ferrying groceries, a buggy and a baby was one of the reasons she had done a trawl of the local estate agents after she'd waved goodbye to her mother.

God knew how her mother had guessed, but at least she had been spared finding the right moment to tell her parents. She was pretty sure that, despite her mother's solemn promise not to tell her father yet, it wouldn't be long before he also knew.

Her mother always meant it when she said conspiratorially, *We won't tell your father about this, Sam.* But it didn't really matter if *this* was the price of a new pair of shoes or a dent in the new car, the moment George Maguire walked through the door she blurted out the truth. Not only was she incapable of keeping a secret from her husband, she appeared blind to this defect in her character.

Sam had dropped the bags and retrieved the keys from her mouth before she realised she had a visitor.

'I have been waiting for an hour.'

The breath left her lungs in one gasp as she spun around. Stunned to silence, she just stared. Alessandro, minus his suit but complete with the restless vitality she would always associate with him, stood there. His long legs sheathed in a pair of faded denims, he slouched elegantly, one ankle crossed over the other and his broad shoulders wedged against the wall of the hallway she shared with the other top floor flat.

As she stared, her emotions a turbulent cocktail of longing and loathing, he levered himself off the wall. The black designer T-shirt he wore was fitted enough to allow her to see the tightening of the muscles in his flat belly... She blinked hard to banish the image and bit down on her lower lip.

It had been three weeks since she had last seen him, and she had counted every second.

'You...here...' As if there was any doubt about it! The touch of his dark compelling eyes, the scent of his body... God, who else *but* Alessandro could reduce her to a mindless bundle of hormonal craving by his mere presence?

What was more to the point was *why*?

He arched a brow and looked her up and down. 'You were expecting someone else?'

Failing miserably to adopt the desired attitude of defiance to mask her real feelings, Sam mutely shook her head. Hands clenched into tight balls, she didn't even notice the pain as her nails dug into the flesh of her palms. This, she decided, was the substance of nightmares. Thinking of nightmares turned her thoughts to the frequent occasions when he had featured in her more torrid nocturnal dreams. A rush of shamed heat slammed through her body.

'You're here...'

'We have covered that,' he said, making no attempt to conceal his growing impatience.

'Well, why...?'

'Yes, I am here...for an hour I have been here.' His narrow-eyed, disapproving glance roamed hungrily over her slender body. His manner was terse and impatient as he looked down his patrician nose and demanded, 'Where the hell have you been?'

The flight back from New York had begun productively enough. He had been working his way through the pile of paperwork he had brought with him with his usual methodical speed. Then, somewhere mid-Atlantic, he had allowed the infuriating redhead to creep insidiously into his head. She was on another continent, she was a distraction—yet his body had responded to the imaginary scent of her warm body in his nostrils.

Suddenly not being the one to make the first move had seemed less a matter of principle and more an action of wilful stupidity. What was he trying to prove anyway? It wasn't as if he had any illusions about the nature of his true feelings. The realisation hadn't been a bolt from the blue, but gradually it had crept up on him—he didn't want a casual relationship!

He didn't want some secret little affair.

He wanted Samantha. And he wanted the world, and especially anyone called Jonny Trelevan, to know that she was his.

Putting aside the papers, he'd pulled out the small box secreted in his inside pocket. His expression distant and unfocused, he'd been staring at the square-cut emerald when a passing flight attendant, who had been about to ask him if he required anything, had released a soft, awed cry.

Alessandro had lifted his head.

The girl had flushed a little and given an apologetic shrug. 'Sorry—it's just beautiful. The colour is so intense,' she'd observed, her envious glance drifting to the ring lying on its ruched bed of velvet. Unable to hide her curiosity, she'd added. 'She must be someone very special…?'

Alessandro, his eyes trained on the ring, had nodded. 'She is. But she is also as stubborn as hell. But you know something…? I wouldn't have her any other way.'

The reflective smile that had curved his sensual lips upwards had dimmed as he became aware of the attendant's amazed stare. Shoving the box back into his pocket, he'd announced that he did not require anything.

And why wouldn't she stare…? he'd mused as she left—no doubt to spread the story. A man famed for his ability to cut dead anyone unwise enough to delve into his personal life had gushed on like something straight out of a women's magazine.

He had played out various versions of this scene, where she'd open the door and find him standing there, during the remainder of the journey—while the paperwork had lain untouched. She would, of course, regret her previous unreasonable behaviour, and he in his turn would magnanimously forgive her before he proposed.

In none of those versions had there been no response. In none of those versions had there been three day's worth of newspapers protruding from her letterbox.

A rush of anger enabled Sam to regain the power of speech. 'And that would be any of your business because…?' She angled an ironic brow and, looking at his face, felt a wave of longing so intense, so *visceral*, that for a moment she stopped breathing. 'Of course if I'd known I was meant to be on twenty-four-hour call just in case you decided to *honour* me with your presence I would naturally have stayed home.'

'There were three days' newspapers stuck in the door.' He brandished the offending items, which were barely recognisable as such now, after being slapped repeatedly against his thigh as he paced up and down.

'An open invitation to burglars and one would have thought a cause of concern for your neighbours…' His lips twisted contemptuously as he added drily, 'Though apparently not.' The shifty-looking type in the flat across the corridor had shrugged and looked uninterested when Alessandro had asked him if he knew when Miss Maguire would be home.

'Not the faintest, mate.'

'You are aware that there are three days' newspapers in the door?'

'If you say so… I wouldn't know.'

'And you wouldn't know or, I suppose, care if she was lying ill inside, would you?'

'I keep myself to myself. I don't want any trouble.'

Sam tucked her hair behind her ears and gave a shrug. 'I must have forgotten to cancel them.'

This casual admission caused his jaw to tighten. 'You could have been inside…' The muscles in his brown throat worked as his eyes slid from hers. *'Hurt…'*

'If you were so worried I'm surprised you didn't call the police,' she countered, unable to believe he had been genuinely concerned for her safety. Much more likely he resented being kept waiting—which brought her back to the puzzling question of why he was here at all.

'I considered that, but I decided on reflection that it would be quicker to take a look…'

Sam shook her head, her smooth brow puckered. 'Take a look? What do you mean—?' She stopped, an expression of horror crossing her face as she looked from him to her front door. Ignoring the key in her hand, she pushed the door. It immediately swung inwards.

'I don't believe it—you broke into my flat…you broke in! How could you…?'

'It was not difficult. The security in this building is appalling.'

She swung back, her eyes flashing. 'Don't get smart with me!' she recommended grimly.

Alessandro picked up the grocery bag she had dropped on the floor and walked past her into the flat. 'I think you are making too much of this. I was concerned…'

'Concerned! Nosy, more like. How would *you* like your privacy being invaded? How would you like someone going through your drawers?'

'Relax—your secrets are safe. I prefer your underwear with you in it.'

Sam drew a startled breath as her aquamarine eyes lifted to his. A shock of white-hot excitement washed over her, infiltrating every individual Alessandro-deprived cell of her body as their glances connected.

'Save the smouldering looks, Alessandro,' she growled angrily. 'They don't do a thing for me,' she lied.

'You are a terrible liar, *cara*.'

'Oh, God!' she groaned, lifting a hand to her cheek. 'Don't do this to me, Alessandro.'

'What am I doing to you, *tesoro mio*?'

Appalled, because his chest was the only place her head wanted to be, Sam walked over to the window and lifted the casement. Ducking her head outside, she took several restorative gulps. She tensed and closed her eyes as she sensed him come up behind her. When his hands came to rest on her hips instinct took over and she leaned back into him with a sigh.

It was the sound of crunching metal that broke the spell.

'What was that?' Alessandro, his expression curious, but at that point unalarmed, leaned past her to see through the window. 'That woman has driven straight into my car.'

'"That woman" is my mother.'

'Your mother!' He winced, as there was a further agonised crunching of metal as the Volvo reversed away from the rear of his gleaming Mercedes.

'She says that's what bumpers are for,' Sam explained, as her parents emerged from the Volvo and her mother's voice drifted upwards.

'I thought there was plenty of space, George.'

'Let me do the talking…'

Sam closed her eyes and covered her face with her hands. She had long ago come to the conclusion that her parents' main objective in life was to embarrass her as much as was possible. But today they were surpassing themselves.

'My car…'

Sam's hands fell away from her face. 'Never mind your stupid car,' she hissed. If dented cars were the worst thing to come out of this she would consider herself very lucky indeed. Being a realist, she knew this was unlikely.

This slight made him look offended. 'My *stupid* car…?'

'Well, it's only a car, and I'm sure you have dozens of others. My parents are coming up…'

'And you want me not to mention your mother's driving?'

'I want you not to be here.' Her sinking heart reached rock bottom. Short of making him climb down the drainpipe, she was going to have to explain him being in her flat to her parents. Even *her* fertile imagination wasn't that creative. 'They can't find you here.'

He arched a sardonic brow, a frown forming on his face as he recognised the extent of her agitation. 'Why can't they find me here?'

'Because they might think—' She stopped, her eyes sliding away from his. What was she meant to say? *They might think you're the father of my baby, and they'd be right.*

'That we are lovers?' Sam was unable to tear her eyes from the nerve that had begun to throb in his lean cheek. 'You are ashamed to have your parents know of our relationship?'

'And you on the other hand are ready to shout it from the rooftops…I *don't* think,' she drawled. 'We can't exactly say you just dropped by for a chat, can we?'

'Why not?'

She looked at him, exasperated. 'Because they know I can't stand you.'

'Do you often have sex with men you can't stand?'

'You were the first.'

'In more ways than one,' he observed soberly.

'Oh, for heaven's sake—I don't know why you're so hung up about this virginity thing!' she groaned in exasperation. 'It's not like I was waiting for you specifically or anything.'

'Maybe…' One dark brow arched as he scoured her resentful features. 'But I seem to recall you saying you were glad you *had* waited, and that it was me.'

'And I,' she countered flushing deeply, 'recall you saying a lot of things not to be taken literally either.'

His eyes narrowed as he folded his arms across his chest. 'Such as…?'

'Such as I'm beautiful and sexy and…' Her eyes slid from his bold, provocative stare. 'Stuff,' she added gruffly, 'like that.'

'And you do not feel sexy or beautiful?'

As if he didn't know he had the ability to make any woman feel that way. 'I am a realist.'

'Realist!' he flared. 'You are the most irrational, contradictory female I have ever encountered.'

'Don't you dare start with that *you're an irrational female* guff!' she warned.

He looked from her angry pink cheeks to her tightly clenched fists and heaving bosom and smiled. 'You're the soul of reason, *cara*—' He stopped suddenly, his frowning gaze lingering on her soft features. 'You know, you look different…'

First Mum, now Alessandro…What is it with me? Did someone stick an 'I'm pregnant' sticker on my forehead when I wasn't looking?

'Nobody could stay reasonable around you. And the way I recall it you weren't too anxious to have your precious friends know about our *relationship*.'

A spasm of annoyance crossed his lean features. 'It was you who seemed to get some sort of thrill from our relationship being illicit. I just went along with it.'

Sam stared at him. '*Me…?* You're suggesting…?' Feeling pushed into a corner, she gritted defensively, 'You don't care about me. We didn't have a relationship—we had sex!' she blurted, thinking, *Please say it meant more.*

Only he didn't. In fact nothing in his manner suggested it had meant more—apart from a strong desire to throttle her.

The anger that had flared in his dark eyes faded as he recognised the glitter of unshed tears in her eyes. 'Not enough sex.'

Sam fought the surge of debilitating weakness that followed his seductively soft complaint.

'I came here this evening to rectify that.'

She stared at him, unable to think. Her body was literally thrumming with desire. And then there was a loud knock on the door.

'Don't answer it.'

His compelling glance locked with hers.

If he had touched her then Sam knew she would have gone along with his suggestion... Heck, she'd have gone along with just about any suggestion he cared to make! But he didn't. He just stood there, looking explosive and impossibly sexy, while he waited for her to give in.

Someone outside leaned on the doorbell and didn't let go.

Sam shook her head and tried to think...but every attempt at rational thought got as far as Alessandro naked. 'God, what am I going to do with you...?' She thought of some things she could do with him and her focus slipped another fatal notch.

'You want me to hide under the bed, perhaps...?'

Sam greeted this sarcastic interjection with a genuine sigh of relief. 'Of course!' she exclaimed. 'Why didn't I think of that?'

Outrage and disbelief stamped on his patrician features, Alessandro stared at her. 'You are suggesting I hide under your bed?'

'Not *under* the bed, obviously.' A grin formed on her lips as she looked him up and down. 'You wouldn't fit.' *But with me he fits perfectly.*

In response to the hands she laid flat against his chest, and without taking his fascinated gaze from her face, Alessandro began to back towards the closed door of her bedroom.

'You wish me to hide from your parents?' he said, as if he couldn't quite believe that was what she was suggesting.

'That's the general idea.' When he didn't respond she opened the door and gave him a push. 'And whatever you do,' she added, pressing a finger to her lips, 'don't make a sound. I'll get rid of them as quickly as I can.'

Just as she closed the door the doorbell rang again. Sam took a deep breath and straightened her shoulders. Chin up, she walked to the door and opened it. *If that doorbell hadn't rung when it did I could be doing something very stupid.*

A certain lack of appreciation for her narrow escape was responsible for the cranky expression on her face when she pulled open the door.

'Where's the fire? Mum and Dad—what are you doing here?' She looked from one to the other, pretending surprise, as she added under her breath, 'As if I didn't know. I suppose you'd better come in,' she added ungraciously.

'Sorry, darling, but it just slipped out,' her mother murmured contritely as they stepped past her into the sunny room.

'And just as well it did,' her father observed. 'I'm only disappointed my daughter didn't feel able to tell me herself.'

Sam accepted this parental chastisement with a rueful, apologetic grimace.

'Am I such a terrible father?'

Sam repressed a groan. Her father yelling she could take; it was infinitely preferable to Dad taking the blame. 'Of course not, Dad. I just…'

'Now, what is this nonsense about the father not wanting to know? *Not wanting to know!*' he repeated, his face reddening. 'What sort of irresponsible loser would not want to know about his own child?' he demanded.

'Dad, no matter what I say, you're not going to like it.'

'You tell me who he is, Samantha, and I'll change his mind,' he predicted rubbing his hands in anticipation.

Sam's eyes flickered towards the bedroom door—her father's gruff voice had a penetrating quality and the walls of the flat were paper-thin. She guided them towards the kitchen area, which was farthest from the bedroom. 'Will you calm down, Dad?' she begged. 'It's not the end of the world,' she soothed.

'Calm!' George echoed in an incensed bellow that made Sam wince. 'My little girl gets pregnant by some loser,' he choked, 'and you expect me to stay calm!'

'Shall I open the window?' Sam enquired bitterly. 'I think that deaf lady in number three might not have heard you.'

Her father's eyes narrowed. 'This is no laughing matter. I'll wring the irresponsible bastard's neck. This guy is going to learn you don't mess with a Maguire.'

Sam rolled her eyes. 'You've been reading those Westerns again, haven't you, Dad?' She sighed. 'Say after me,' she suggested. 'I am not Wyatt Earp, I am a middle-aged GP who hates paperwork.' Her father did not return her coaxing smile, so with a rueful shrug she eased herself onto the countertop and began to swing her legs. Regressive behaviour she thought, and stopped swinging like the kid her father obviously considered her to be.

'You think this is some sort of joke, young lady?'

'No, Dad, I do not think this is some sort of joke. But I do think this is my life,' she said quietly. 'You have to let me do this my way.'

'Which is how?'

'I don't know yet,' she admitted.

Her father responded to this confession by pulling at his thinning sandy hair and groaning.

'I *knew* this was the way you'd react—which is why I asked Mum not to tell you. I'm not your little girl, Dad.'

'You'll always be my little girl.'

Sam, who was a whisker away from crying like a baby, sniffed loudly.

'Shall I make a nice cup of tea?'

Her husband and daughter turned to look at Ruth Maguire, their expressions both incredulous.

'*A nice cup of tea* isn't going to solve this, Ruth,' her husband informed her with withering scorn.

'Neither will wringing anyone's neck,' Sam pointed out. 'Actually, Mum,' she said, glancing at her watch, 'I need to be somewhere…'

'Well, if Sam needs to be somewhere, George—' Ruth began hopefully.

'I'm not going anywhere until I get some straight answers,' her husband announced bullishly. 'And neither are you, young…'

'You should have woken me, *cara*.' Rich and sleepily intimate, the deep voice cut across her father's irate rant.

CHAPTER TWELVE

Watching her father's jaw drop, Sam closed her eyes and felt her body flood with dread. Of course in hindsight she could see that this had been inevitable. You didn't shove a man with an ego like Alessandro's in a dark cupboard, or in this instance your bedroom, and *not* expect him to exact some sort of retribution.

Only he had not the faintest idea what he was walking into.

When she opened her eyes and turned her head she saw that Alessandro had pulled out all the stops. *I suppose*, she thought, swallowing past the aching constriction in her dry throat as her glance roamed hungrily across the expanse of rippling golden torso on show, *I should be grateful he kept his pants on!* Though the unbuckled belt that hung around his narrow hips and the unfastened top two buttons of his jeans were a nice touch, all geared to cause her the maximum embarrassment... My God, she thought, you have absolutely no idea of how embarrassing this is likely to get.

Barefooted, he padded into the room, moving with the inimitable sexy animal elegance that even at this moment she found totally riveting. 'Is that coffee I smell?'

No, it's fear, she thought.

Their eyes touched, and the malicious gleam in his told her that her reading of his motives had been bang on target. Still holding her eyes, he stretched lazily and lifted a hand to his artfully tousled sable hair. He stopped, and appeared to notice they were not alone.

An Oscar-winning performance, she mused, watching self-consciousness register on his face as he looked at her parents. *Self-conscious?* Sure, that was really likely, she thought struggling to contain her indignation. She was pretty sure that Alessandro could walk stark naked into a Women's Institute meeting and not blush!

'Mum, Dad—you know Alessandro, I believe?'

'What does this mean, Samantha?' demanded her father, looking from the tall, half-naked Italian to her daughter.

Her mother, who had been staring as the splendid bronzed figure emerged with a stunned expression, suddenly released a long sigh and smiled as things clicked into place.

'For goodness' sake, George, what do you think it means?' Sounding exasperated, she flashed her husband a look loaded with meaning. The smile she then bestowed on Alessandro was so warm and approving that he in his turn looked taken aback.

In response to the questioning glance he flashed Sam, she shrugged. He'll look even more taken aback once he realises that Mum is measuring him up as potential son-in-law material, Sam thought, swallowing the bubble of hysterical laughter that rose to her throat.

'You've been having an affair with this man?'

Sam flushed.

'Well?'

'Answer the man, *cara.*'

'Not an affair,' she snapped.

'He has just come out of your bedroom naked! What was he doing?'

'Well, why ask if you already know?'

Alessandro's dark brows drew together as he bared his teeth. 'Not an affair? Then what would your definition be?'

'The biggest mistake of my life!'

George, forgotten by the two combatants, went a shade

deeper and his barrel chest swelled with wrath as his glare moved from one to the other. 'You're not going to deny that you're sleeping with my daughter?'

'Of course he isn't. Now, please don't get excited, dear. It's bad for your blood pressure,' Ruth said, patting her husband's shoulder.

'I don't need you to tell me about my blood pressure—I'm a doctor!' George Maguire drew a deep breath and turned his narrowed gaze on the younger man. 'I want to know what you intend to do.'

'Putting on some clothes would be a good start—' Sam inserted drily, before Alessandro could respond to the challenge.

'Never mind that,' her father interrupted impatiently. 'What I want know is are you going to marry her?'

'*Marry!*' Alessandro exclaimed, looking shaken for the first time during this interchange.

'It hasn't even occurred to you, has it?' A look of contempt contorted the older man's face.

Sam closed her eyes and missed the revealing expression on Alessandro's face. She accepted that the point where she could avert disaster had passed, and held her breath and waited in a fatalistic fashion for the truth to emerge.

'Men like you are contemptible!' her father declared, looking at the younger man as though he was something unpleasant on his shoe. 'The scum of the earth.'

Alessandro's nostrils flared, his darkly defined brows lifted and his breathing quickened. But his expression remained politely enquiring, if slightly wooden. Sam thought that under the circumstances he was taking the scathing denouncement of his character quite well.

'I don't suppose this is the first time.'

'I am thirty-two, Dr Maguire.' Thirty-two, and I thought I would never find a woman I wanted to spend the rest of my life with. I finally do, and she is ashamed to acknowledge our relationship... Irony glittering in the dark depths, his eyes slid towards Sam as her father yelled.

'Is that meant to be funny? You obviously have no concept of decency whatsoever. Sam is right. She and the baby are better off without you.' Oblivious to the bombshell he had just delivered, George turned his attention to his daughter. 'I demand, Samantha, that you promise me here and now that you will never see this man again.'

'I'd not planned to,' she said, leaden as she looked into a future that held no Alessandro.

'Baby...?' The heel of his hand pressed to his forehead, Alessandro took his first breath for a full sixty seconds. His stunned dark glance swivelled back towards Sam.

Sam, thinking, *Here it comes,* watched the muscles in his brown throat working as he swallowed convulsively.

'Baby...?'

'This innocent act is all very well—' George began.

'Dad,' Sam interrupted, her eyes fixed on Alessandro's lean face. 'He didn't know.'

Her father gaped at her incredulously. 'You haven't told the man you're pregnant?'

Alessandro drew a deep, shuddering breath. *'Dio!'* His searing glance moved over Sam's flushed and defensive face before dropping to her stomach. 'You are pregnant?'

The focus of all eyes, Sam shrugged and pushed out her chin. 'Looks like it!'

'And I am the father...?' There were two slashes of dark colour along Alessandro's cheekbones as his eyes lifted to hers.

Sam took a deep, offended breath. 'It's possible,' she admitted between gritted teeth. 'But when double numbers are involved the maths get tricky.'

'Sam!' her mother reproached. 'She always gets flippant when she's embarrassed,' she explained in an aside to Alessandro.

Sam blinked furiously before the tears that filled her eyes

could fall. 'Thanks for the support, Mum, but I'm not embarrassed,' she muttered bitterly, before turning to the sink. She turned both taps on full blast and began to mechanically pile clean cups into the water.

'If you will excuse me, I need to have a private conversation with your daughter.'

Hands wet, Sam spun around. '*You* don't tell my parents to leave!' she snapped. 'The only person leaving here is you.'

'No, he's right, Sam. We should go. You have things to discuss.'

Sam stared at her father in amazement. 'What happened to *Promise me you'll never see this man again?*' she demanded.

'I didn't have the full facts,' her father retorted. He nodded towards Alessandro and cleared his throat. 'I might,' he conceded, 'have spoken out of turn.'

'You are a father. I would have reacted the same way in your place,' Alessandro said, taking the hand that was extended towards him.

Men...! Sam, watching the man-to-man handshake, was feeling nauseous. 'Sorry to interrupt this male bonding,' she gritted between clenched teeth. 'But actually you can *all* go!'

'Really, Sam,' her father reproved. 'Under the circumstances I think it's about time that you started showing a little maturity.' He turned to Alessandro. 'I can rely on you to do the right thing...?'

Alessandro, looking pale but composed, nodded. 'You can.'

Sam stood there in open-mouthed amazement as George guided his wife from the flat, pausing only to nod in a stomach-turning man-to-man way to Alessandro, who had apparently been transformed in his eyes from a defiler of innocence to a decent sort.

'Enjoy the warm approval while it lasts,' Sam suggested as the door closed. 'He won't be so keen on you once he realises that you're not about to marry me.'

Alessandro opened his mouth, then stopped and appeared

to change his mind about what he had been about to say. 'When were you going to tell me?' His lips twisted as their eyes connected. 'Or were you?'

Sam felt a guilty flush over her fair skin. 'Don't take that tone with me,' she snapped, reinserting her hands up to the elbows into soapy water.

Alessandro's narrowed eyes stayed on her slender back as she hunched over her diversionary chore. 'Well, were you?'

'Yes… No…' She drew a deep breath. 'Eventually, I suppose. I really don't see why you're making such a big thing of this.'

'You don't…?'

She flashed him an exasperated look over her shoulder and saw that his normally animated features were set in a stone-like mask. 'It's not like I'm asking you to support me or anything,' she pointed out reasonably. Maybe, she thought suddenly, he imagined she had ideas of using the baby to get her hands on some of his enormous fortune? Maybe, she speculated, going cold at the thought, it had crossed his mind that she'd got pregnant on purpose with that view in mind…?

'By most people's standards I make a pretty good living—very good, actually. There's no way I'll need any help financially… If you like, I'll sign something.'

'Sign…?'

Wiping her dripping hands on the legs of her jeans, she turned around, her expression earnest. 'To say I've got no claim whatsoever to your money just because of the baby. Honestly, I don't want a penny from you.' Her reassuring smile wobbled in the face of the murderous glare she got in response.

She found his response puzzling. He had a lot of money, by all accounts, but even very rich men, and it sometimes seemed to Sam even *especially* rich men, were notoriously reluctant to be parted from any of their cash. Maybe he hadn't understood what she was saying? She decided to spell it out.

'I'm not looking for any financial hand-outs.'

'You will sign something…?' A muscle in his jaw clenched as his eyes sealed with hers. 'You are talking about *money*?'

She nodded her head vigorously, to confirm the fact she had no avaricious expectations. 'That's right. You really shouldn't bother your head about this—it'll work out fine.' Sam wished that she was half as confident as she sounded. The truth was that, even putting to one side her concerns about the actual physical process of giving birth, the idea of having sole responsibility for another human being made her feel totally inadequate.

'So you have everything sorted?'

His tone made her flush. Did he think she didn't know that her life was about to change for ever?

'I'm aware that I'll have to make some adjustments—of course I am. And obviously I've not worked out all the details yet,' she admitted, skimming a defensive frown up at him. 'But I've only known a few weeks.'

The inarticulate sound that emerged from between Alessandro's clenched teeth stopped her dead.

'You have known a few weeks longer than I have.'

Observing for the first time the pallor that lent a grey tinge to his naturally vibrant skin tones, and the white line around his sensually sculpted lips, Sam's over-developed empathy sprang into painful life.

'I'm so sorry,' she said, her earnest tone filled with self-recrimination as she recalled the mind-numbing shock *she* had experienced when she had realised she was pregnant.

Alessandro looked startled. 'You are *sorry*?'

Not understanding the odd inflection in his voice, she nodded. Even a man as pragmatic and in control as Alessandro had a right to fall apart at a time like this. And Alessandro probably was the most in control sort of guy she had ever met. Except in bed. He was not always in control in bed. Without meaning to, she thought of skin against skin—which was a mistake, because wave after wave of scalding heat spilled through her body while the muscles in her abdomen went into painful spasm.

'Is something wrong?'

Tilting her head up to his, she lied smoothly through her fixed smile. 'I'm fine,' she said, rubbing her goosebump-covered forearms.

His narrowed eyes scanned her face. 'Well, you don't look it.'

'I don't enjoy scenes.'

'Then perhaps,' he counselled, 'you should not invite dramas.'

Sam took a deep, wrathful breath. 'Invite! I didn't invite anything—including you or my parents.' Her lower lip quivered. 'All I want is to be left alone.'

'Grow up, Sam.'

This piece of bracing advice brought a militant sparkle to her eyes. To be told twice in the space of an hour that she was being immature, and by men both times, was too much to take. '*You're* calling *me* childish…!' she exclaimed. 'And I suppose it was sophisticated and mature to strip off and come out of my bedroom that way?'

'I did not appreciate being treated like an embarrassment.'

'You were never keen to broadcast the fact we were lovers before.'

'I only ever went along with what *you* wanted…which was my first mistake,' he observed heavily.

What she wanted? That was rich. 'While you wanted to shout it from the rooftops, I suppose…?'

'Well, I did not want to creep around as though we were doing something to be ashamed of.'

'I wasn't ashamed. I knew you were—'

'I was what?' he prompted.

Sam shook her head. 'It doesn't matter.' Finding out he was going to be a father the way he had must, she realised with a fresh wave of empathy, have been like being hit over the head with a large blunt object.

'You're probably in denial…' The cat from next door jumped in at the open window and absently she reached out to stroke it.

'Denial?' His eyes flickered down as the cat brushed against his legs before disappearing under the sofa.

Her slender shoulders lifted. 'I was,' she admitted. But having your body change on an almost hourly basis was kind of hard to ignore even if you wanted to, and pretty quickly she had become fascinated with what was happening. How could she not? It was all a bit of a miracle…a scary miracle, maybe, but still a miracle.

Alessandro's head jerked up. Sam found his expression unsettling, but then she found most things about Alessandro unsettling. And on the bright side he had stopped looking at her as though she was demented—though she suspected this situation was temporary.

'When did you realise you were pregnant?'

Unconsciously she pressed a hand to her stomach and admitted huskily, 'I think I sort of knew straight off… When I couldn't put it off any longer I did a test…four tests, actually,' she corrected, recollecting with a wry smile her inability to believe the proof of her own eyes. 'This wasn't the way I intended to tell you… Not,' she added with a rueful burst of honesty, 'that I knew *what* I intended. I hadn't told anyone yet. My mother,' she added, anticipating his protest, 'guessed.'

'So I am not the last to know? I suppose that is something,' he conceded heavily.

'God,' she said, pushing the wispy curls of copper-coloured hair from her brow with the crook of her elbow, 'I could do with a cup of tea. Would you like one?' She motioned him to the sofa, and after a pause he lowered his tall, rangy frame onto the squashy cushions.

'I do not want tea.'

'I don't have anything stronger—except the cooking sherry I bought for trifle. I don't suppose you—?'

'No, I do not,' he confirmed. 'Why,' he wondered as she

began to dry the wet cups, 'do the British act as if a cup of tea is the answer to everything?'

'I presume the Italian way is to act as if sex is the answer to everything?' she countered crankily.

'There is certainly more room for creativity in making love than there is in dropping a teabag in a mug. And,' he added giving a wolfish grin, 'it lasts longer than tea.'

'If you do it properly,' she sniffed, feeling that familiar hot liquid quiver low in her belly.

A dark brow angled as he searched her face. 'Are you saying I don't...?'

The flush that she had so far kept at bay by sheer willpower spread up Sam's neck until her face was burning. 'You do it better than properly,' she admitted huskily. An image formed in her head and she added wistfully, 'You do it perfectly.' An impossible act to follow.

Without waiting to see how he'd reacted to this ill-judged piece of honesty, she reached into the fridge for milk.

'Leave that and come and talk to me.'

Sam straightened up. 'There's nothing to talk about. I have everything sorted.'

'You can't seriously believe that?'

'Would you prefer coffee—?'

'Sam!' His warning voice cut through her delaying tactics. Heaving a sigh, and displaying reluctance in every sinew of her body, she responded and took the window seat—now occupied by next door's opportunist cat.

'Your parents—'

'Oh, God,' she interrupted, shaking her head. 'You really shouldn't have said what you did to Dad. He can,' she explained with a grimace, 'take things a little literally.'

'What did I say that I should not have?'

'That he can rely on you to do the right thing. Your idea of the right thing and my dad's are not going to be the same,' she explained.

'And what does Dr Maguire mean by *the right thing*?'

'Marriage. I know,' she inserted, before he had an opportunity to laugh or look horrified, 'he does come over as a bit old-fashioned. But I'm his only daughter and—well, I suppose he *is* old-fashioned,' she admitted.

'I do not consider your father old-fashioned.'

She stared at him. 'You don't?'

Alessandro shook his head. 'Your father feels that a man must take responsibility for his own actions. He believes that a child needs and deserves the security of two parents.'

'Well, obviously—in an *ideal* world—'

'The world,' he cut in, his expression severe, 'is what we make of it. We should not use society's imperfections as an excuse to shirk doing the right thing.'

'Perhaps you should marry my father,' she joked with a thin smile. 'You sound like a match made in heaven.'

'I think a successful relationship requires a little friction to keep it lively, and given the circumstances it would be more appropriate for me to marry your father's daughter.'

Sam, her expression wary but still totally confident he had misspoken, corrected him.

'*I'm* my father's daughter.'

His eyes remained trained on her face, his expression aggravatingly enigmatic as he shrugged and said, 'Your point being…?'

'My point being that even as tasteless jokes go, that one is more tasteless than most.'

'You think me proposing is a joke?'

'You're not proposing,' she told him.

A muscle along his jaw clenched, and then clenched again harder as his eyes captured Sam's. 'I would be interested to know what you think I am doing.'

Her mouth opened as she searched his face. 'You want us to get married…sorry, you think we *should* get married.' Clearly *wanting* did not enter into this.

'There is no other option.'

'This is a knee-jerk reaction,' she explained, thinking there could not be a worse time to learn that her lover had a very strongly developed sense of duty. 'Understandably, you're not thinking straight right now. But fortunately for you I am. Tomorrow,' she predicted, 'you're going to realise that you had a narrow escape. Less scrupulous women would have said yes and got it in writing.'

'You are not scrupulous—you are an idiot!'

'I would be if I married you... God, Alessandro, it would be a total disaster. People don't get married because they're pregnant.'

'They do—every day of the week.'

'Well, *I* don't. The only reason I'd get married is if I was in love with a man.' She spread her hands, inviting him to see that she was right.

His expression like granite, he locked his dark eyes onto hers. 'And you don't love me?' His shrug suggested to Sam that he was indifferent to the fact. 'Well, that may be so, but the man you love is not the father of your baby.' A nerve clenched in his lean cheek as he added, 'I am.'

It took several seconds before it clicked and Sam realised he was talking about Jonny. She opened her mouth to put him straight, then almost immediately realised that it might be easier to let him carry on thinking she still carried a torch for the younger man.

'Yes, Alessandro, you're the father. But that doesn't alter the fact that we don't have a blessed thing in common. We weren't even going out; we were staying in. The only thing we had going for us was...' Her eyes slid from his as she swallowed and added hoarsely, 'Sex. And now I'm pregnant we don't even have that!'

A spasm of anxiety crossed his lean features as he rose impetuously to his feet. 'Why? Is there a problem, medically speaking?'

She shook her head. 'No, I'm fine.'

'Your doctor has not advised you not to—?'

'No, nothing like that,' she inserted hastily. 'Actually, I haven't seen the doctor yet. There's not much point—I'm only—'

'Not seen a doctor…?'

Reading the shocked outrage in his taut features, Sam groaned. 'There's no point, Alessandro. Not until…'

'I think there is every point.'

'Fine…fine… Have it your way.' On this she was willing to humour him. 'I'll arrange something.'

'I will come with you.'

Sam shook her head. 'That isn't going to happen.'

The flat pronouncement caused his eyes to darken. 'I will not be delegated some peripheral role here…'

'Unless you want to give birth, you've not much option,' she rebutted, with a calm she was far from feeling.

Married to Alessandro… It was so tempting—but she knew that she couldn't agree, no matter how much she wanted to. She hadn't been able to cope with the stresses of a loveless affair. It stood to reason that a loveless marriage would be about a million times worse!

Concealing her true feelings had become next to impossible by the end, and Sam doubted she would be able to keep up the façade for five minutes if they were living together.

Alessandro got to his feet and stalked towards her. Laying his hands on the sill at either side of her, he leaned forward. 'You *will* marry me. My child will not be denied his father.'

She looked into his dark eyes. He was close enough for her to see the faint white line that ran along his temple. An image of him lying on the stretcher, with blood seeping from the gaping wound in his forehead, flashed into her head and she went pale.

His hand came up to cup her face. 'What's wrong?'

'Nothing,' she denied, jerking her chin from his grasp. 'I'm not trying to deny the baby a father. You're the father, and nothing can change that,' she admitted, rubbing a finger across the bridge of her nose and avoiding his eyes. 'But I'm afraid that for once in your life, Alessandro, you have to accept that yours isn't the final word on this. Mine is.'

'That has been the case from the start.'

'What?' she said, utterly astounded at his angry, brooding claim.

'You have laid down the rules and I,' he observed grimly, 'have meekly fallen in line. That is going to stop.'

She stopped rubbing her nose and gaped at him. *Alessandro...? Meek...?*

'Is that a fact?'

'You don't know what you are taking on. Being a single parent is not easy.'

If she could cope with loving a man who didn't love her back, Sam felt she could cope with almost anything. 'And you would know all about that, I suppose?'

'Katerina was eleven when I became her guardian.'

The reminder made Sam flush.

'You know that what I'm saying makes sense,' he added.

Sam shook her head mutely. Sense didn't enter into it. She loved him, and that made no sense, but she could no more change the situation than she could her own fingerprints!

'You *will* marry me,' he said, fastening the buttons on his shirt. 'When you see sense,' he added, 'you know where to find me.' Striding to the door, his back stiff and unyielding, he didn't look back once.

If he had, the tears spilling down her white face might have made him reconsider his exit.

CHAPTER THIRTEEN

THE building had incredible views over the river, a startling glass frontage, and bore no identifying logo.

Sam paid the cab driver and eyed the modern edifice with an uncertain frown. 'This *is* the Di Livio Building…?'

'It is, love,' he promised. 'For my money you can't beat Georgian architecture. But what do I know…? This won all sorts of awards, apparently.'

Sam, her thoughts a long way from the merits of modern architecture, handed the man a tip and straightened her shoulders before approaching the building. She paused, briefly succumbing to panic, before she stepped into the revolving doors. Catching sight of her image in the large glass panels and realising she was dressed for going round the supermarket, she carried on walking and ended up where she'd started—outside looking in.

This has to stop, she told herself. Alessandro isn't going to notice what you're wearing.

Actually, they were the same clothes she'd been wearing when he'd proposed. Not really the sort of outfit a girl should wear when the man in her life asked her to marry him. But then it hadn't been that sort of proposal… To her mind it had been more in the nature of an ultimatum.

But then Alessandro was an ultimatum sort of man.

It had been less than twenty-four hours since Alessandro,

not a man accustomed to hearing no, had stormed off, saying that when she came to her senses she knew where to find him. She had never known a man so prone to slinging around ultimatums… The problem was, Sam reflected dully, he generally didn't have to wait long—at least where she was concerned!

He said, *You will,* she responded with an equally determined, *Never,* and five minutes later she was panting to fall in with his plans. It was not a good precedent to set, but she was very aware after the last twelve hours' events that there were more important things at stake than her pride or proving a point.

It wasn't until she had walked out of the hospital that morning and the taxi driver had asked her where she wanted to go that Sam had found the flaw in Alessandro's parting shot— she *didn't* know where to find him!

She didn't have the faintest idea where he lived, worked, or for that matter if he was still in the country. In the faint hope that her taxi driver would not be as ignorant as she was, she had said, 'The Di Livio offices…' and got a cheery, 'Right you are, love,' in return.

As for coming to her senses—that sort of depended on your definition. As far as Sam was concerned coming to her senses involved waking up one morning and not being in love with her Italian lover.

That hadn't happened. She suspected that it probably never would—not that she'd actually been to bed yet.

The phone had rung a bare two hours after Alessandro had stormed off, and Sam still hadn't cooled down.

It obviously hadn't even crossed his mind that she wouldn't come crawling. Well, if he was waiting for her, he'd wait a damned long time. A person would have to be totally insane to marry such a pompous, opinionated, dyed-in-the wool male chauvinist. Of course he was also the man who could make her skin tingle, who could make her feel sassy, sexy and generally irresistible. Never seeing him again might mean she would never have those feelings again. No *might* about it.

I want to feel that way again!

Pushing aside the intrusive thought, Sam had concentrated on all the things she wouldn't miss about him. For a start he was always prepared to think the worst of her—the cheque situation being a perfect example. And not only was he infuriatingly stubborn, he was congenitally incapable of admitting when he was wrong.

He'd had the cheek to say she had no idea of what she was letting herself in for! She'd taught a class of thirty, for heaven's sake!

Taking a certain grim satisfaction from the fact that she was going to show him—even if it *killed* her—that she was perfectly capable of bringing up their child, she had picked up the receiver still on an angry, defiant high. She would be such a perfect single mother that one day even he would be forced to eat his words. Hopefully he would choke on them.

She had nursed her anger until the moment when she had picked up the phone and heard Rachel's voice.

'Sam—thank God you're there! I d…don't know what to do…'

'Rachel…?' Her friend's voice was hardly recognisable.

It took some time, but Sam eventually got the bones of the story out of her friend. It transpired that Rachel had received a call when she'd got to work that morning from the nanny, who'd said she was concerned about Harry. Rachel had left work immediately, and by the time she'd reached home the nanny had already called for an ambulance. Rachel was ringing Sam from the hospital, where the staff had uttered a word guaranteed to make any parent's blood run cold—*meningitis*.

Sam called a cab and rushed to the hospital. The young nanny who was trying to cope with Rachel greeted her arrival with relief. Rachel greeted her with a tear-stained face and a stream of bitter self-recrimination.

'He's got meningitis, Sam, and it's all my fault! I should have stayed at home. A *good* mother would have stayed at home. What sort of mother puts a meeting before her child? I just thought he had a cold...he did say his head was hurting...'

'Rachel, there's no way you could have known...'

'That's what I've been telling her,' said the young nanny. 'Anybody would have thought he had a cold. *I* thought he had a cold. It wasn't until his mum had gone that he really went off,' she explained to Sam. 'The doctors say that it happens that way sometimes. But they all say we got him here very quickly, and that's good.'

Between them, Sam and the young nanny, who both felt pretty inadequate to the task, tried their best to support the distraught young mother through the evening and interminable night.

This morning the doctors were cautiously optimistic—although they were making no promises.

Sam and the nanny persuaded Rachel, who had barely left her child's side since she'd been allowed in the ITU, to come and get a drink.

Rachel, her face waxen with fear and exhaustion, sat and sipped her tea. 'I wish Simon was here. I don't even know if he got my message. New York...' she said, her voice wobbling. 'So f...far away. I just don't know what to do. Simon would know what to do. You two have been great, of course, but...'

'We're not Simon.' Sam nodded understandingly. 'He'll be here soon, Rachel,' she promised, hoping like hell he wouldn't make her a liar.

It was ten minutes later when Simon, who *had* got the message, walked into the small lounge where the three women were sitting.

Sam just knew that she would never forget the look on Rachel's face when she saw her husband. She had seen another side of being a single parent, and quite frankly she no longer thought she was up to the task.

The disaster that had torn apart Rachel's perfect life last night had had the effect of putting her own concerns in perspective, and now gave Sam the strength to walk boldly into the lobby.

'Hang in there, Rachel,' she murmured, crossing her fingers.

The interior of the cutting-edge building had so many reflective surfaces that Sam blinked, momentarily blinded as she entered under the watchful eyes of two uniformed but discreet security guards. The woman seated in a reception area flanked by two metal sculptures was blonde, and groomed to within an inch of her life. Her nails ruled out a lifestyle that involved strenuous tasks like taking the lid off a jar. Women who looked like her were the reason Sam never shopped for clothes in certain smart designer shops.

Now, however, was not a time to be intimidated by a snooty expression and killer nails. Deciding on the direct approach, Sam marched up and with a confident smile announced, 'I'd like to see Mr Di Livio.' She'd reserve the bolshiness in case the direct approach didn't work.

The pencilled brows of the woman behind the desk rose and she looked faintly amused. 'You have an appointment…?'

Sam felt a flush travel up her neck. 'No, but—'

'I'm afraid that Mr Di Livio doesn't see people without appointments.' She served up another professional smile and a look of pitying condescension before turning her attention to the computer screen in front of her.

About to turn and leave, Sam stopped. *You're acting like a wimp.* Lifting her chin, she said firmly, 'He'll see me.'

The other woman's sleek head lifted. There was a slight hint of exasperation in her professional smile as she addressed Sam. 'There are no exceptions.'

'I'm not going anywhere until I see him.' Even as she made this brave claim, on the periphery of her vision Sam was conscious of a security guard who clearly had other ideas approaching. 'Tell him Sam is here. He'll see me,' she told the other woman. 'Tell him I've changed my mind.'

'Miss, if you'll just…?' The security guard's hand hovered above the sleeve of her denim jacket.

'Tell him I *will* marry him.'

The women's rather protuberant eyes widened to their fullest extent. *'Marry…?'*

Sam was suddenly too mad to be intimidated. 'Be very, *very* sure before you laugh,' she suggested quietly to the other woman, who was tottering on the verge of laughter.

Something in her manner brought a flicker of uncertainty to the other woman's eyes.

'Why don't you just ring upstairs?' Sam suggested.

Before the woman had come to a decision a door behind Sam silently slid open and out stepped Alessandro. He froze mid-stride, his dark brows drawing together as he saw her.

'Sam!'

Deaf to the startled note of pleasure in his deep voice, Sam spun around. The breath left her body as she saw him standing there. Until that point she had not realised how badly she had missed looking at him. *Not even twenty-four hours… Dear God, girl, do you have it bad!*

The pleasure had been replaced by caution as he asked, 'What are you doing here?'

She wanted to say, *I've just realised that I can't bring up our baby on my own. I've realised that if anything bad happens I want you there to hold my hand. And I want you there to share the good things too. The first steps, first words…* Feeling her eyes fill, she blinked and said none of those things—which was just as well, because they would undoubtedly have sent Alessandro running for cover. 'I was passing…'

'I'm assuming that means you have come to your senses?'

She loosed a dry laugh. 'Or lost them,' she retorted.

His feet were silent on the polished Italian limestone floor as he walked towards her. 'I must admit I thought you'd make me wait longer.'

The mocking quality in his voice was something Sam told

herself she had to expect under the circumstances. 'What can I say…?' she asked, lifting her slender shoulders in a shrug. 'I can't imagine my life without you in it?' she suggested, rolling her eyes sarcastically.

When he realised how true this was, as he inevitably would, because Alessandro was far too perceptive not to, she wasn't going to be able to shrug it off. But right now she couldn't think that far ahead.

As he scanned her upturned features the taunting quality left his face. The freckles on her nose stood out starkly against the dramatic pallor of her skin. The purple smudges under her eyes had not been there yesterday.

It was only the presence of others that stopped Alessandro demanding on the spot what she had been doing to herself. The anger that caused his dark eyes to flare was aimed almost entirely at himself. How could he be angry with someone who looked one step away from total collapse. If he'd stuck around, instead of walking out, she wouldn't be in this state… But he hadn't stuck around, and in his eyes the fact that Samantha was stubborn and irrational enough to drive the most tolerant of men crazy was no excuse for his behaviour.

He put his hand under her elbow. 'Cancel my meetings for the rest of the day, Edward,' he said, without taking his eyes from Sam's face.

A younger man, whom Sam hadn't been aware of until that moment, blinked, opened his mouth—presumably to protest—and changed his mind.

'I can come back later if you're busy,' Sam said, thinking, *If you say yes, I'll kill you.*

The fingers around her elbow tightened. 'Actually, you can cancel my meetings until Monday.'

In the car, Alessandro got straight to the point. 'Am I to take it that you will marry me?'

'Am I to take it that you had any doubts?' Without waiting for a response to her quip, she tilted her head to look up at him. 'You do know that it would be easier to get to see the Prime Minister than you?' And definitely easier on her traumatised nervous system, she decided, unable to tear her eyes from his face.

'Why didn't you ring to tell me you were coming?'

Her eyes slid from his. A little creativity, if not outright lying was called for. She could hardly say, *I ripped up your number because I didn't trust myself not to ring you every five seconds.* 'I lost your mobile number. Where are we going?' she added shrilly.

'Somewhere we can talk without interruptions.'

Sam's face scrunched up in dismay. 'God,' she groaned. 'Do we *have* to talk?'

He angled an impatient look at her face. 'We are going to get married. I think you should resign yourself to the inescapable fact that we will of necessity spend some of the next forty years talking.' *But most of it in bed.*

'*Forty years!*' Sam exclaimed.

'If you want to talk statistics, the average life expectancy of—'

'I don't want to talk...statistics, that is. You're not trying to tell me you expect us to *stay* married, are you?'

'That's what the contract says.'

Sam shot a resentful glance up at his patrician profile. 'We always end up arguing.'

'Only on the occasions we don't end up making love.'

This silky observation reduced her to silence, which lasted until the chauffeur-driven car he had bundled her into drew up outside a row of Georgian terraces. Not that her silence seemed to have bothered Alessandro, who had spent most of the journey hitting keys on a laptop while simultaneously taking calls in several languages. She had heard of multitasking but this was ridiculous... Pressing a hand to her stomach, she wondered if the baby would inherit his IQ.

It was only when she had preceded him up a shallow flight

of stairs that led to an impressive door that Sam realised this wasn't a terrace, but one house. 'You live here?'

'Some of the time.'

'So nursery space is not going to be a problem, then?' she said drily as she entered the marble-floored hallway. 'Good God!'

Alessandro watched, his expression amused, as she did a wide-eyed three-hundred-and-sixty-degree rotation.

'You approve…?'

'I've always wanted to live in a museum—or failing that a really swish mausoleum. You live here *alone*…?' This much space for one man seemed bizarre to someone who had been brought up in an Edwardian semi.

'There are the staff.' As he spoke, one of their number appeared. Alessandro spoke in Italian and the thick-set figure replied in the same language. He nodded in a respectful way towards Sam before vanishing.

'Did you say something to him about me?' she demanded suspiciously.

Alessandro looked amused. 'I said you were thirsty and would like a cup of tea.'

A cup of tea was the very least she needed. 'Who did you say I was? You didn't say anything about us getting married, did you?'

'I am not required to identify my guests, and I do not discuss my private business with my staff. Now, sit down before you fall down and tell me what has happened.'

The addition made Sam blink. Once more his powers of perception were unnerving. 'How do you know something has?'

'It does not take a genius. You are as pale as a ghost and you look as though you haven't been to bed.'

He too had spent a sleepless night. It wasn't every day a man discovered he was about to become a father and had a marriage proposal rejected. For hours he had silently seethed over what he considered her unreasonable behaviour.

'I haven't.' She lifted her hand to her mouth to stifle a yawn. 'I was in hospital all night.'

At her side, Alessandro froze.

'*Hospital…?*' There was screaming tension in every line of his long, lean body as he scanned her face.

'Yes, I've just come from St Jude's—'

He stared at her, disbelief etched into every line of his taut features. Behind the disbelief lurked fear. 'And you did not contact me?' he cut in, dragging both hands through his hair.

'Contact you? Why should I have?'

'*Dio mio,* I don't believe you… How can you ask?' He stopped abruptly and, exerting obvious self-control, tempered his tone as he said tersely, 'Sit down.' Sam found herself being urged into a chair. Alessandro squatted down beside her, the strain in his face. 'They let you leave?' His voice suggested he disapproved of the decision. 'You are all right…? The baby…?''

Sam, realising his mistake, shook her head. 'No, it wasn't me—I was there with Rachel. You remember? Harry's mum?' Her voice became suspended by tears as an image of the little boy looking so frail and vulnerable flashed into her head. 'Sorry…'

'*Sorry…?*'

Her mind still filled with images of the terribly ill toddler who, when she had previously seen him had been so fit and well, she didn't pick up on his tense tone.

'Well, it would have solved your problem, wouldn't it?' It wasn't that she thought he wished their child harm, but any man in his situation would find it tough not to do a bit of *if only*.

Her unthinking reflection caused the remaining colour to leave Alessandro's face. Eyes blazing in a stony set face, he took her by the shoulders.

'You will never ever say such a thing to me again.'

His tone made her flinch. She met his eyes, registered the molten fury in his taut face and realised belatedly how much her throwaway comment had offended him. She knew that it wasn't reasonable to be mad with him for not wanting this baby as much as she did, any more than it was reasonable to be angry with him because he didn't love her back, but Sam couldn't help herself.

She was dismayed to feel her eyes fill up again with weak tears. 'Well, it's true,' she gulped. 'You may not want to hear it, but the fact is it would have made life a lot simpler for you if I *had* been the patient.' She pressed her hands protectively to her belly and swallowed. 'It's not as if you *want* the baby to be here,' she reminded him thickly. 'You'd like it to go away, so that you can get your life back to normal.'

Seeing the single tear rolling down her cheek, he felt some of the icy hauteur fade from his face. 'Have I ever said that?'

Her eyes slid from his. 'You didn't have to. It's obvious,' she countered with a loud, unhappy sniff. 'Any man in your situation would feel that way.'

'I am not any man.'

Sam lifted her eyes to his face and thought, *Tell me something I don't already know!*

A nerve along his strong jaw began to throb. 'Do *you* wish our baby would go away?'

'That's not the same.'

He arched a dark brow. 'You think not?' Sam released a startled gasp as he moved her hands and laid one of his own across her belly. She looked at the big hand, resting warm and firm on her, and her throat closed over with some unidentifiable emotion. 'You are carrying this child, but this baby is half you, half me—a part of both of us. You would lay down your life to save him.'

An overwhelmed Sam blinked up at him and realised that it was a statement, not a question.

'And so,' he added simply, 'would I. Now,' he said, placing a finger under her chin and tilting her face up to his. 'No more crying…'

'Sorry—I don't know what's wrong with me. I suppose,' she said, blowing her nose on the tissue he handed her, 'it's my hormones…. Oh, dear.' She grimaced. 'I swore I wouldn't use that excuse.'

'What happened at the hospital?' He removed his hand from her stomach—a situation Sam viewed with some ambivalence—and sat on the arm of her chair. 'Your friend is ill?'

'No, it's Harry. He's three, Alessandro, just three. It's not fair, is it…?' Sam swallowed, dropped her head, and felt his hand on her hair.

'No, *cara mia*, it is not fair.' As his fingers moved in a strong, sweeping motion down her tense spine she expelled a shuddering sigh and lifted her head.

'He's got meningitis.'

'Dio mio!' Alessandro exclaimed. While of course he felt sympathy for the unfortunate innocent and his parents, his first concern was for Samantha and their unborn child. 'You had contact…?'

She shook her head. 'No, he was in Intensive Care, and they wouldn't let me go in. But I could see him through the glass and he looked so small…and there were tubes…and Rachel kept saying it was her fault…and I couldn't do anything.' Her voice suspended by tears, Sam covered her face with both hands. 'I felt so useless,' she confessed in a muffled voice.

With a muttered imprecation he slid into the chair beside her, pulling her bodily into his arms. Lifting her hair off her neck, he cradled her head in one hand while looking tenderly into her tear-drenched eyes, before pressing her face into his shoulder. 'You were there for your friend when she needed you, Sam. You did what you could.'

Her entire body shook while she wept. Alessandro, judging that the release was what she needed, let her cry herself out.

When the sobs began to subside he stopped stroking her head and urged gently, 'Tell me about it.'

The sobs stopped completely and she lifted her head, turning a tear-stained face to his. 'You don't mean that.'

'I do not say things I do not mean.'

'That makes you a pretty unusual person,' she observed. 'I'm not normally a crying person,' she added with an apologetic grimace. 'Sorry…' she said again, trying to get up from his lap.

His hands tightened around her waist. 'Stay put.'

It was so tempting to obey his casual command. There was something awfully comforting about being in his arms. 'I'm heavy.' She was actually deeply mortified by her emotional outburst, but amazingly he didn't appear half as dismayed as most men she knew would have been in similar circumstances.

He shook his head. 'Heavy! You are like a small bird,' he observed, running a finger along the elegant curve of her collarbone. 'Though mostly you remind me of a sleek, elegant feline. Delicate to look at, but not someone you'd like to face in a fight. You even have the eyes of a Siamese.'

'My being *delicate* doesn't seem to stop you fighting with me,' she muttered.

'With us, fighting is foreplay.' He angled a teasing eyebrow, wicked amusement registering in his dark gaze as she flushed.

'Well, I've not much room for comparison.' When she got up he didn't try and stop her. Sam immediately wished he had.

'I have,' he slotted in, watching her walk towards the baby grand piano that stood in the corner. 'So you must take my word on this. Let me rephrase that. I *suggest* that you take my word on this. I have already learned that issuing a prohibition does not have the desired effect with you. You really are a natural-born rebel.'

This extraordinary analysis of her behaviour made Sam, whose finger was poised above the keys, stare. 'It's not me, it's you. I'd never broken a rule in my life before I met you.'

'Then I must be good for you.' In one flowing motion that

made her stomach flip, he rose and walked to her side. Leaning across her, he pressed a key. 'You play?'

'Not well,' she said, trying hard to disguise what having his brown finger casually skim over her cheek did to her.

'Now, tell me, how is little Harry?'

Sam sighed. 'The doctors weren't giving anything away, but Rachel's nanny was brilliant. She called an ambulance, and apparently in a situation like that minutes can make all the difference. This morning the doctors seemed a little bit more positive, and Simon—Rachel's husband—had arrived, so I was surplus to requirements.'

'You didn't sleep all night?' he observed, scanning her pale upturned features with a frown. 'I know you wanted to offer support to your friend, but in your condition—'

'Rachel doesn't know I'm pregnant,' Sam cut in. 'And I had to go. Simon was in New York, and her parents are in Cornwall. Her dad is pretty frail since his heart attack last year.'

Alessandro pinned the strand of gleaming copper hair that had lain across her cheek behind her ear. 'Her husband arrived this morning…?'

Sam nodded and, unable to resist any longer, rubbed her cheek against his hand, which remained close to her face. 'Apparently,' she said, closing her eyes and smiling weakly, 'he paid a small fortune for a seat on the next flight out. You know, just seeing him this morning seemed to give Rachel strength. It was amazing.'

Alessandro mulled over her words for a moment, then said in a voice that was strangely lacking in emotion, 'So you are marrying me because you think I will make a good father?'

'Well, you will,' she countered, confused by the strong hint of affront in his manner.

'Thank you,' he said, not looking overjoyed by the compliment.

He seemed to be waiting, so she added, 'And a child needs

two parents.' *And I need you.* 'But of course there must be some ground rules.'

Alessandro raised his brows, but didn't interrupt as she continued.

'I'll try not to interfere with your life any more than absolutely necessary…'

His hand fell away from her face. 'That is very good of you,' he said, walking towards the carved Adam fireplace.

'I'm a realist. I just want you to be discreet.'

Alessandro, who had been standing looking at the room reflected in the over-mantel mirror, spun back. 'Can it be that you are giving me permission to take lovers? Does that mean *you* intend to take lovers, to satisfy your newly awakened appetite for sex?'

The colour flew to her face. 'What a question!'

'You introduced the subject,' he pointed out. 'Do you not believe in equality of the sexes?'

'Of course. But I'm surprised if you do.'

'If I am at liberty to seek entertainment outside the marriage bed, would it not be right for you to do the same?'

The thought of any man other than Alessandro touching her filled her with repugnance. 'I'm pregnant,' she reminded him.

'This is not something I am in any danger of forgetting.'

The dry insertion made her eyes slide from his. She didn't need reminding that this marriage wouldn't be happening if it wasn't for the baby.

'When you have my ring on your finger I think you will find that I can satisfy you, and if our relationship continues as it has begun, moral issues aside— Oh, yes,' he said, seeing her expression, 'I *am* acquainted with morals.'

Sam belatedly realised that he was furious. 'I didn't mean that—'

'Moral issues aside,' he gritted, ignoring her, 'I will not have the energy to seek excitement outside the marriage bed.'

'So long as I amuse you.'

Alessandro's accent was significantly stronger as he ground out, 'You do not *amuse* me. You infuriate and provoke me.'

'The feeling's mutual,' she flared.

Alessandro, his jaw clenched, said something under his breath.

Sam's eyes narrowed. 'I'm going to learn Italian, and then you won't be able to do that,' she warned him.

'You want to know what I said? No problem. I said I'm not going to fight with you.'

'Why not?'

'Because we will end up in bed.'

Sam didn't know which upset her more—the assumption that they'd end up in bed, or the implication that it was somewhere he wanted to avoid!

'And, as much as I would like to…you need to rest.'

'I suppose I *should* go home,' she admitted, slightly mollified by his qualification and the frustrated gleam in his eyes.

'No need. You can stay here, where I can keep an eye on you.'

It turned out he meant it quite literally. When Sam woke it was around three in the morning, in a strange bed. It took her a little while to recollect why she was in a strange bed wearing her underwear, and a few seconds longer to notice the figure in the armchair.

Alessandro was sitting with his hands resting on his thighs, his body hunched forward.

'What are you doing?' she asked, struggling into a sitting position.

'Watching you. I like watching you.'

The throaty confidence sent a sharp thrill of sexual excitement through her body. No longer feeling at all sleepy, she threw back the covers and patted the bed. 'You can watch me just as well from here.'

Even though he was sitting several feet away, she could hear the raw sound of his harsh inhalation.

'I like to watch you too,' she said as he rose to his feet, a dark, shadowy figure. 'Even if you just want to sleep,' she added, in case he thought she was being pushy.

Sam heard the sound of a zip being unfastened and swallowed.

'You will find, *cara*, that I actually need very little sleep.' But one thing Alessandro had discovered he could not do without was a redhead with eyes like the sea...

CHAPTER FOURTEEN

THE wedding took place a week later, in a tiny chapel on Alessandro's Tuscan estate which was just as spectacularly lovely as Emma had suggested.

There were few people in attendance. Besides her parents, Sam had invited Emma and Paul. Other than his sister and Dorothy Smith, Alessandro had invited half a dozen close friends, but the only one Sam was conscious of was the dark-haired beauty who appeared to be in tears when she embraced Alessandro after the ceremony. Marisa Sinclair.

Sam sealed her feelings behind a frozen smile, while inside her hurt and fury silently grew. Neither emotion found any release until after the wedding meal, which had been served in a room where the ceiling was covered in the most incredible frescoes. They and their guests, carrying drinks, had drifted out through the wide doors into the *palazzo* gardens.

Sam was talking to the best man, whom she would have considered the best-looking male she had even seen if she hadn't seen Alessandro first, when Emma hurried over. She thrust a slim mobile phone at Sam and announced, 'You'll want to hear this personally.'

As Sam stood there, emotional tears of relief streaming down her cheeks, Emma explained to the best man, 'Our friend's little boy has been very ill in hospital, and the doctors have just given him the all-clear.'

When Sam had finished talking to Rachel, Emma took back the phone.

'Kind of makes the day perfect, don't you think?' she said happily. 'Will you tell Alessandro the good news or shall I…?'

'You do it,' said Sam.

'Any idea where…?' began Emma, looking around.

Look for the gorgeous brunette and you should find him, thought Sam, but said, 'I think he was on the terrace.'

Sam had just finished receiving a lecture on the antiquity and history of the *palazzo* from Dorothy Smith when Alessandro materialised at her side.

'Do you mind if I borrow my bride for one minute, Smithie?'

'Well, considering you have her for the rest of your life I consider that selfish. But who am I to stand in the way of true love?'

Sam was so embarrassed by the comment that she couldn't even look at Alessandro as he drew her indoors.

'A lot of books,' she said, looking around the room—anywhere rather than at him as he closed the door. In her head she was seeing the beautiful lawyer with her arms wound around his neck. She pressed her fingers to her drumming temples. Suddenly crimes of passion made a lot more sense.

'That is not uncommon for a library.'

Sam made herself look at him. He looked, of course, totally incredible. Every long, lean inch of him so rampantly male that her stomach muscles quivered. 'What do you want, Alessandro?' she asked, wiping her damp palms along the silk skirt of her wedding gown.

'I want a wife who can behave with some degree of circumspection,' he announced frigidly.

Sam did not have to pretend total incomprehension as she stared at him. 'What…?' For the first time she registered the anger in his body language.

'You will *not* make assignations with Jonny Trelevan.'

Sam's wide eyes attached themselves to the nerve leaping in his lean cheek.

'In fact,' he decreed autocratically, 'as you obviously have no self-control or sense of what is fitting where he is concerned, in the future you will not be alone with that man.'

The throbbing silence stretched, until Sam drew a long, shaky breath and, planting her hands on her slim hips, walked towards him. 'For starters,' she said, her voice shaking as she fought to control her anger, 'I haven't the faintest idea what you are talking about...*assignations...*?'

Alessandro's lip curled contemptuously as he dragged a hand through his dark hair. 'Before we dined you vanished, and so did Trelevan.' One dark brow elevated. 'A coincidence?' he suggested. 'I don't think so.'

'You think I—?' She broke off, shaking her head incredulously as she drew in air through her flared nostrils. 'I'm really touched by your faith in me,' she choked bitterly, 'and I'm sorry I can't live down to your expectations of me. But if you had taken the trouble you might also have noticed that my mother was not in the room either. I spilled some wine on my dress.' She touched her shaking hand to the spot on the pearl-encrusted bodice of her gown where the liquid had spilled. 'Mum was sponging it off. You could always ask her to confirm my story—though of course,' she added sarcastically, 'she might be covering for me...'

The muscles in Alessandro's brown throat worked as his eyes locked with hers. 'Your *mother*...?'

Sam nodded, and watched the dark colour rise up his neck.

His jaw tightened another notch, and a hint of defensiveness entered his voice as he said, 'Trelevan was not in the room.'

'You really do have a nerve, Alessandro.'

'I might,' he conceded stiffly, 'have made a mistake.'

'I *know* I've made a mistake. I walked up the aisle,' she retorted, too angry to notice that her comment had made the colour leave his face. 'You're acting like a little boy who doesn't want to share his toys with another kid.' As she saw the incredulous anger flare in his eyes she realised the analogy might have been better.

'*Madre di Dio,* I am a *man* who doesn't want to share his *wife* with another *man*. And if you flout me on this, Samantha, you will find I do more than throw a tantrum.'

'I don't think under the circumstances anyone would blame me for slipping off into the shrubbery for a snog.' Ignoring his hissing inhalation, Sam continued in the same hard, angry voice. 'My h…husband invites his mistress to the wedding!' she yelled. 'And then has the cheek to fling around ultimatums!'

'I have no idea what you're talking about.' Alessandro, conscious of the dull roar of blood thundering in his ears, could see very little but the image her angry words had implanted in his skull. His wife in another man's arms.

Sam released an incredulous laugh. 'I'm talking,' she told him, 'about Marisa Sinclair—your mistress—who you expect me to smile at and say *Delighted to meet you.* Well, I'm *not!*' she cried, catching her trembling lower lip between her teeth and dashing the tears from her eyes with the back of her hand. 'I'm not at all happy!'

A shuttered look came over his face. 'Marisa is an old and valued friend.'

'Oh, is that what they call it now?' she sneered. 'You know, she is much prettier in the flesh than she looked in the newspapers—but then you already know that, don't you?'

Alessandro studied her face for a moment, before saying quietly, 'You have nothing to fear from Marisa.'

'You mean you're not sleeping with her any longer? Gosh,' she intoned sarcastically, 'I feel better already—because you always tell me the truth.'

'I do not wish to discuss my relationship with Marisa with you. It is not relevant to us.' Alessandro, whose breathing had steadied, added softly, 'You've never seemed jealous that Jonny has Katerina, but the idea of me with Marisa…'

'I'm not in—' Sam stopped abruptly, her eyes sliding from his as the colour rushed to her pale cheeks. 'I'm not married to him. Now,' she went on backing towards the door, 'I need to get out of this—' she fingered the strapless neckline of her wedding gown '—if we're to get back to London tonight.'

'Did I say? You look very beautiful today, Samantha.'

His accented voice sent shivers up her spine.

'No, you didn't say,' she admitted huskily as, her hand on the door handle, she spun back. She glanced down at the slim silk dress that revealed the creamy upper slopes of her breasts and clung to her still-slender waist before flaring out from the hip to swish sexily around her legs. 'My mum helped me choose it.'

'The dress?' He dismissed the designer creation with a graceful wave of his hand. 'I was not talking about the dress. I am sorry we have to get back tonight, but I promise we *will* have a honeymoon.'

She was within a hair's breadth of responding to the earthy invitation in his eyes when she recalled that he had offered no concrete explanation or even an apology for Marisa Sinclair's presence. Lips set in a hard line, she enquired bitterly, 'Is Marisa coming too?'

As she fled, before he could respond to her sarcastic retort, it hit her: *I'm married.* No matter how many times she said it, it still didn't feel real.

The next day, back in London, her sense of unreality persisted. They had arrived so late the night before that she had fallen asleep fully dressed on the big four-poster. When she'd woken later that night she'd been wearing her underclothes. In the darkness she had made out Alessandro's profile. She'd lain there listening to the even sound of his breathing, experiencing a longing as strong as the one which caused her to breathe—a longing to feel his skin against her own, to taste him, to merge with him.

It had been only the memory of their unresolved argument and the painfully awkward journey back to London that had held her back.

It was light when she next woke, and Alessandro was already up and dressed. She barely had time to register his silent presence at her bedside and recall that he was now her husband, even if she didn't feel married, when she had to dash to the bathroom.

Her morning sickness was particularly vile, and she was soon on her knees in the bathroom—a great image of his wife for him to carry through the day when he had to leave!

When a guilty-sounding Emma rang before lunch, Sam was glad of the interruption.

'I know this is the cheekiest thing to ask you when you're on your honeymoon—'

'A honeymoon requires two people,' Sam inserted drily. 'Ask away. The truth is, I'd be glad of the distraction.'

'You know I've got that interview this afternoon—which is why we flew back this morning?'

'Problem with the interview?'

'Not the interview—my sitter. Paul was going to watch Laurie, but his boss has just rung and there's some enormous crisis. So…?'

'Bring her on over,' said Sam.

'You look…' Emma's glance dropped down Sam's slim body. 'Actually, you look terrible,' she observed with a frown.

As if she needed any reminder that she look drained and terrible. 'Sorry I can't live up to *your* high standards, superwoman.'

'I was just saying…and I'm *not* superwoman,' Emma protested.

Sam rolled her eyes. 'What would you call someone who goes into labour on a building site and drives herself to the hospital *after* sorting out a building regulations wrangle? You,' Sam contended, only half joking, 'are one of those women who make the rest of us feel inadequate.' Or me, at least. With her constant tiredness and mood swings, not to mention the nausea, Sam was quite aware that she did not resemble the glowing image of motherhood so often portrayed on the covers of magazines.

'I had morning sickness,' Emma protested.

'No, you had heartburn. Once. After eating a hot curry.' Sam, who was unclipping the harness that secured Laurie in her buggy, stopped what she was doing and angled a questioning look at her best friend. 'Why are you whispering?'

Emma raised her brows and looked around the painting-lined walls of the formal drawing room. 'I feel like I'm being watched,' she admitted. 'Not exactly cosy, is it? Oh, my, that's a real Monet, isn't it? And is that a—?'

'They're all real,' Sam admitted guiltily as she bent down to extract her goddaughter from her buggy.

Emma began to study the carpet she was standing on. 'I'm assuming this is priceless or something?' she said rubbing her toe cautiously into the soft pile of the Aubusson rug. 'You know, on second thoughts, I think it might be better to leave Laurie in the buggy—safer...'

'Don't you dare!' Sam retorted. 'A few grubby fingerprints will make the place more homely.'

An hour later, with toys strewn all over the floor and the remnants of the sandwich lunch they had chosen to eat cross-legged on the floor, it was even homier.

'I hope that's non-toxic,' Sam said to herself as she removed a crayon from Laurie's mouth.

Laurie released a childish cry of anger.

'I prefer the orange myself,' Sam said, and remembered the DVD that Emma had said soothed the baby. Putting down the fractious tot, she inserted it in the machine. Muttering under her breath, she tried to turn it on, but when she pressed the appropriate buttons all she got was a montage of television channels. She tried again, and got the channels again—but this time minus the sound.

She glared at the offending remote. 'Damn! Where is—?' She lifted her head from the remote to look at the screen and stopped dead, the colour fading dramatically from her face as the remote slipped from her fingers and onto the floor. The baby in her arms, she sank down until she was sitting cross-legged on the floor, staring at the screen.

The subtitles beneath the picture for the benefit of the hard of hearing—or people unable to locate the volume on the remote—pronounced that amongst the famous people present for a charity luncheon was Mr Alessandro Di Livio, a generous benefactor.

Alessandro's lean, photogenic face filled the screen—until the woman sitting beside him leaned across, blocking him from the camera's view. Sam went cold inside as the woman tilted her head and laughed up at her handsome companion.

It was Marisa Sinclair.

You could see why so many people had predicted that the clever lawyer would end up marrying Alessandro. She did look the part. Elegant and beautifully groomed, she was wearing a slim-fitting cream silk jacket, cut low to display her cleavage and lots of smooth, tanned flesh.

'Not a freckle in sight!' To cut off her hysterical-sounding laugh Sam pressed a hand to her mouth and turned away from the screen.

No wonder Alessandro hadn't laughed at her crack about the other woman coming along on the honeymoon! Some 'negotiations' he'd had to rush back for.

It was one thing to have a mistress. It was another entirely to flaunt the fact. Actually, no, she thought, brushing a tear angrily from her cheek. The having was just as unacceptable as the flaunting.

They had married in order to give their child a stable environment. And even if *she* hadn't see this televisual proof personally there were plenty of people who knew them both who would have. Clearly he didn't care if the rest of the world knew their marriage was a sham, and clearly he cared even less about humiliating *her*!

Or maybe he hadn't thought? Maybe he couldn't help himself around Marisa Sinclair? A victim to blind lust or love… Either option made Sam equally furious.

Breathing hard, her paper-white face set in hard, angry lines, she forced herself to look at the screen. The camera remained on Marisa Sinclair. Her lovely lips were moving. Sam had no doubt that her words were as sincere as the expression on her lovely face. The strength of the hatred she felt for the other woman was shocking.

If she had stopped long enough to think about the consequences she might not have done it… But what had Alessandro said? *Any woman worth her salt would fight for the man she loved.* Well, she was going to fight. Of course it might have been easier minus the fretful child in her arms…

Entry to the charity event proved a lot easier than she had expected. The name Di Livio certainly opened doors—either that, or people were scared of saying no to a dangerous-looking madwoman carrying a screaming baby.

Muttering about the shallowness of people who were willing to overlook anything if you were rich enough or famous enough, her head held high, she stalked down the carpeted hallway.

As she stepped through the open double doors that led to the flower bedecked ballroom the adrenaline high that had got her this far took a sudden dip. *Bad timing*, she thought, looking around a room filled with smartly dressed and in many cases famous people. A plus point was that so far nobody had noticed her—they were all too busy enthusiastically clapping the minor royal who was at that moment stepping down from the dais set up at one end of the room.

Sam took a moment to stiffen her resolve. As she scanned the room her narrowed gaze skipped over the well-known faces she saw. There was only one face she was interested in, and when she saw it the breath caught in her throat.

Closing her eyes momentarily, she sucked in a big breath and straightened her shoulders. *Any woman worth anything would fight for the man she loved.* As she wove her way through the tightly packed tables she gathered more and more attention. But Sam was past caring.

It wasn't Alessandro but Marisa who noticed her.

Sam watched as, in response to the scarlet fingers tugging at his sleeve, Alessandro bent his head towards his companion. At her urgent murmur he lifted his head. Sam was close enough to see the shock in his eyes when he saw her.

You can run, buster, but you can't hide, she thought viciously.

Actually, Alessandro showed no inclination to run or hide. He rose in an almost languid manner to his feet and waited, one eyebrow raised, for her to reach his table. By the time Sam reached her goal her breath was coming in short, breathy gasps, and she had the attention of just about every eye in the room.

'Who is that child?' Alessandro asked, as though the baby in her arms was the most unusual aspect of his wife appearing unannounced at this glittering public event, wearing jeans and a T-shirt with orange crayon down the front, while he was playing footsie with his girlfriend.

'It's Laurie. I'm babysitting for Emma,' she snarled.

His dark eyes moved over the baby. 'She has grown.'

'That's what babies do…at least the females do. Emotionally, most males never make it past puberty.' Sam shot her husband a look of pure loathing. 'Sorry to crash your cosy assignation, Marisa…' she gritted, all the time glaring at Alessandro.

'I would not choose to hold an assignation, cosy or otherwise, in the full view of television cameras. Why are you here, Sam?'

'I came—' Sam stopped. What was she supposed to say? *I came here to tell your girlfriend to back off, to tell her that you're mine…*

As a wave of desolation washed over her, her shoulders slumped, and she turned her head momentarily into the soft sweet-smelling curls of the baby in her arms. Even the baby smell could offer her no comfort.

'It doesn't matter.'

'Well, now you are here, you will sit down and have a drink with us.'

Sam stared at him. 'I will what?'

'And smile—people are looking.'

'Is that all you care about? What people will think?' The inner rage she felt suddenly exploded inside her head like crystal shattering. 'Well, let's see what they think of this, shall we?'

Sam managed to pick up a glass and throw its contents in Alessandro's face in one smooth motion.

She knew that the image of his incredulous rage as he stood there with wine dripping down his face would be etched permanently in her brain. And she knew with equal certainty that Alessandro would never forgive her for humiliating him in public this way.

'It could have been worse. It could have been red.'

She managed not to start crying until she was safely back in the taxi.

CHAPTER FIFTEEN

MARISA SINCLAIR, whose dark, glossy head had been tilted back whilst she admired the chandeliers overhead, turned as she heard the echo of Sam's shoes on the marble floor of the hall.

'I've always loved this place.'

And you'd look so at home here, Sam thought, imagining the brunette gracefully ascending the sweeping staircase, diamonds glittering at her lovely throat. The image increased the tight feeling in her chest.

'I prefer something a little cosier.' *Me, I'd spoil my big entrance by falling flat on my face.* 'If you came expecting me to apologise, forget it. I'm not sorry. Alessandro isn't here—but I expect you already know that.'

Encountering the frigid touch of Sam's eyes, the older woman winced. 'You really don't like me, do you? And I don't actually blame you,' she admitted.

'That's *terribly* good of you.'

The butler, who had notified Sam of her visitor's arrival, responded to Sam's nod and retreated, leaving the two women alone.

'He's protective…' Marisa observed, as the austere-looking thickset Italian vanished from view. 'I virtually had to refuse to budge before he agreed to tell you I was here.'

Sam's brows lifted as she flashed the other woman a cold smile. 'And why *are* you here?'

'I came because I think there are some things you should know.'

Presumably that my husband loves you? She looked at the woman with a frozen expression. 'And you decided that someone should be you?'

'Well, I know Alessandro isn't going to tell you.'

'Decided to spare my feelings has he? Well, I think it's a bit late for that, don't you?'

Marisa's feathery brows twitched into a frown. 'Alessandro *couldn't* tell you. He's the sort of man who doesn't break promises.'

This admiring comment drew an ironic laugh from Sam's pale lips.

The concern in the older woman's dark eyes deepened as she scanned Sam's pale features. 'You look terrible.'

Of course I look terrible. My husband skipped his honeymoon so he could spend the day with you. Does she think I've not got the message? The idea that this woman had come to drive the message home sent a shaft of revitalising anger through Sam.

'Did Alessandro send you?' she demanded.

'Good God, no. He doesn't know I'm here!' Marisa exclaimed. The guilty little glance over her shoulder that she could not repress seemed to suggest that she was telling the truth. 'When he finds out,' she admitted cheerfully, 'he'll probably kill me.'

'Your secret is safe with me.'

The older woman responded to Sam's promise with an unexpected high-pitched laugh that made Sam realise for the first time that for once the other woman was neither serene or calm. 'Secrets,' she said, heaving a sigh. 'Secrets are the problem.'

Mystified by this cryptic utterance, Sam shrugged. 'If you say so. Myself, I thought it was more to do with cheating husbands.'

Marisa shook her head hard enough to dislodge a few

strands of glossy dark hair from the chignon she wore. 'Alessandro has not been unfaithful to you…at least not with me. The only thing Alessandro has been to me and Timothy is a good friend, and I'm afraid,' she admitted with a shame-faced grimace, 'we have abused that friendship.'

'Sleeping with his oldest friend's wife hardly makes Alessandro the innocent party.'

'But—'

Cutting across the other woman's protest, Sam said wearily, 'You'd better come in,' and opened the door that led to the morning room.

Sam stood with her shoulders braced against the wall, breathing in the heady scent of the winter jasmine she had cut the previous day. She knew the fragrance would forever be associated in her mind with this day, when Alessandro's mistress had come to stake her claim. The day she realised that she had lost her husband before she had even won him.

'Good thriller,' Marisa observed, picking up the paperback Sam had been reading from the table.

Sam's brows lifted. 'Books…husbands… Who knows what else we have in common?'

Marisa didn't respond to Sam's acid jibe, but continued to pace around the sun-filled room.

'I hate to hurry you, but I have other things to do.' Such as what? she asked herself. Find a good divorce lawyer? The reality of what was happening suddenly hit her with the force of a tidal wave. Her anger and aggression evaporated…and it turned out they were the only things keeping her standing.

'I—' Turning, Marisa saw Sam sway, and with a cry of alarm ran to her side. 'That's it—sit down there,' she said, dragging Sam a couple of steps towards the nearest chair. As Sam sank into it she gave a heavy sigh of relief. 'Can I get you something? Water…?' She looked around the room as if seeking inspiration. 'I'm totally hopeless when people are ill,' she confessed in a tone of self-disgust. 'Shall I ring for some tea?'

Conscious that if she tried to speak the sobs that were aching for release in her throat would escape, Sam shook her head mutely.

'Well, you just sit there…' Marisa recommended.

Sam, who couldn't have done anything else even had she felt the urge to do so, almost smiled.

'Yes, you sit—and I'll talk…' she said. 'Tim and I knew each other when we were growing up, and I always thought I would marry him… I suppose that seems pretty strange to you?'

Sam touched her tongue to the salty beads of moisture that dotted her upper lip. The faintness had passed, but she still felt nauseous. 'As a matter of fact, no, it doesn't.' Though the fact that she had ever mistaken her feelings for Jonny for love now seemed almost laughable.

'Have you ever wanted something so much that you'd do anything to get it, but when you do it's not at all what you expected? Well, that was what being married to Tim was like for me…anticlimax I suppose would be the best word. It wasn't a bad marriage, we were friends, but there were no…fireworks. If you take my meaning.'

'So you looked elsewhere for fireworks?' *And found them!*

Marisa shook her head. 'No, not me. Tim. He came to me and told me he'd met someone. He said he'd fallen in love with his secretary.'

'Not very original.'

Marisa gave a mirthless laugh. 'You think…? Tim's secretary was not only tall, blond, beautiful and a *cordon bleu* cook, but I think the fact he shared Tim's passion for Man United was actually the all-important factor that swung it. How,' she asked with an ironic shrug, 'could I compete with that?'

'*He…?*'

Marisa laughed at her expression and sank down gracefully in a chair opposite. 'Yeah—he. It seems Tim had been in denial about his sexuality for years. When I said I wanted a divorce he panicked. He said if people found out that he was gay his political career would be over.'

'There are gay politicians,' Sam protested weakly. *Could this be true?*

'True, but none that get voted in on the clean-living, family values ticket. And even if that wasn't the case Tim didn't want to come out. That was where Alessandro came in. He walked into the middle of a big row we were having one day. Considering how *not* shocked he was when Tim told him he was gay,' she recalled thoughtfully, 'I think he'd already suspected. But then I expect you've noticed it's really hard to pull the wool over Alessandro's eyes.'

Sam's gave a gasp, her eyes widening. 'My God—you asked him to pretend to be your lover!' *Or was it pretend…?*

'No, that was his idea.' She angled a shrewd look at Sam's face. 'I wouldn't have minded things getting real,' she admitted. 'But he wasn't interested.'

The relief that had flooded through Sam when she realised that Alessandro wasn't in love with this woman suddenly turned to horror. 'Oh, no!' she gasped. 'What have I done?'

The older woman gave a grimace of sympathy and patted her shoulder.

After Marisa had left, Sam wandered out to the walled rear garden. It began to rain, which suited her mood. She tried to sort out her thoughts, but realised almost immediately that there wasn't much to sort. It was all pretty straightforward.

She had in a matter of minutes effectively killed stone-dead any chance she'd had of any sort of relationship with Alessandro.

She ran her finger over the wet face of a stone heron and sighed. 'He's just never going to forgive me for this,' she said, seeing his face again as the wine had hit him.

'Who is not going to forgive you?'

The colour drained from her face as she spun around to see her husband, standing there watching her.

'What are you doing here?' Her eyes were drawn to the stains down the front of his once white shirt.

'I would have been here sooner had another hysterical woman not waylaid me. Though this one did not throw wine in my face.'

'Hysterical woman…?'

'Katerina. I was just about to get in my car when she arrived. It took me the best part of an hour to get her to calm down enough to tell me what was wrong. When she did, I drove her home.'

'What was wrong?'

'She's pregnant.'

'*Pregnant!*'

'And it would seem that she's afraid to tell her husband.'

'What?' ejaculated Sam. 'Jonny hasn't told her! He's such an *idiot*!'

As this heartfelt comment was music to Alessandro's ears, he felt he could be generous. 'Having displayed no small degree of idiocy myself recently, I do not feel in a position to throw stones. However, you will be pleased to hear that he has now told her of his money problems—and of your role in helping him out of them.'

Sam struggled to take on board this glut of information. 'What's going to happen?'

'My sister has announced her intention of taking over the running of the stores. Jonny is apparently happy to diversify and use his contacts. Katerina has told him he will leave the finances to her, and utilise his talents crafting individually designed surfboards. Excuse my ignorance, the technicalities passed over my head, but apparently people are prepared to pay a great deal of money for such things…'

'Then they're all right…?'

'I think you could say that my first and only foray into marriage guidance has been a success,' he agreed. 'Would that gaining access to my own home had gone as smoothly…'

'Did you forget your key?' Sam studied his face, which was wet and getting wetter with each passing second. He *had* to be totally furious—but oddly it wasn't fury that was coming across in his facial expression or his body language. But that fury was as far as she got when it came to interpreting the rigidity in his manner.

'No, but when I opened the door Carlo looked as though he would have liked very much to close it in my face…'

Sam gave a confused blink. '*Carlo?* Why would he want to do that?' she asked, genuinely mystified.

One side of Alessandro's mobile mouth lifted. 'It would appear he feels protective towards you, *cara*…'

'*Me?*'

'And not just him. The members of staff who I have encountered so far have all looked at me as though I am some unpleasant sub-species. Still,' he mused, reaching across and taking her chin in his hand, 'I suppose I must get used to being treated like the villain in a Victorian melodrama.'

Sam, whose barely functioning brain had gone into shock when his thumb had slid down the curve of her cheek, was only capable of echoing faintly. 'Victorian melodrama…?' *Why isn't he shouting? Why isn't he yelling? Why isn't he telling me that marrying me is the worst thing he has ever done?*

'Yes. I think it was the crying baby clutched to your breast that captured the imagination of the nation.' He looked around. 'No baby?'

'Paul picked her up.'

Sam looked at him blankly as he cupped the back of her head in his hand and said, 'You're getting very wet,' as he sank his long fingers into her wet hair.

'I don't understand,' she said, grabbing a handful of his shirt to steady herself as her knees started to fold. She was shaking from head to toe.

'There were television cameras there…' he reminded her gently.

'Oh, my God…' As she half closed her eyes she wondered why this should come as such a shock—after all, it had been the television coverage that had prompted her mad *get your hands off my man* crusade.

Unable to contemplate the sheer awfulness of having the most humiliating moment of her life being recorded for posterity, Sam let her head fall forward against his chest. She could feel the warmth of his skin through the dampness of his shirt. She just wanted to close her eyes and lean into his warmth, have his arms close around her and stay that way for ever.

It was several seconds before she could force herself to step back. She swallowed and whispered hoarsely, 'They won't actually show it?'

'From the way my loyal staff have been looking at me, I'd say they already have.'

She gave a groan, amber flecks swirling in her green-blue eyes as they flew, wide and stricken, to his face. 'Couldn't you sue them or something…?'

The total lack of concern he was showing at having his reputation torn to shreds on national television was extremely disconcerting.

His lips curved into a sardonic smile. 'For telling the truth…?'

'The people who write stuff about you wouldn't know the truth if they fell over it!' she exclaimed, unable to hide her indignation at what he had suffered at the hands of the press.

In the act of dragging a hand through his hair, Alessandro stopped. Eye contact was hard to maintain, but he levelled his interrogative stare directly at her wary face. After a moment his hand fell away and comprehension filtered into his dark gaze. 'So Marisa has been talking…?'

Her lips tightened. 'Well, you weren't going to, were you?'

'That was not possible.'

'Oh, I know you'd given your word and all that stuff. And I'm sure it's great having honour and so forth. But forgive me for not patting you on the back. I was the one left thinking…' She caught the strange way he was looking at her and stopped, began to study her hands.

'What were you thinking?'

Her head jerked up. 'Well, what would *you* think if you turned on the TV and saw me next to some gorgeous bloke I had a well-documented history with? Then saw him gaze at me as though looking at me made him hear heavenly music? I know this requires some imagination…'

This bitter addition caused Alessandro, whose expression had been growing increasingly austere as she described this imaginary scenario, to smile. 'Leaving aside the fact that before you entered the room Margaret Danes was the most beautiful woman in the room—'

Sam's eyes widened in protest as she recognised the name of a revered actress who had recently been made a dame. 'Margaret Danes is seventy!' she protested.

'She was a beautiful woman at twenty and she is today. True beauty is not dimmed by the ravages of time. It has to do with an inner glow.'

Midway through his dissertation on beauty, Sam stopped listening. 'Until *I* walked into the room…?' She thought of the way she had marched in, screaming baby under one arm, maniacal gleam in her eyes, and started shaking her head. She didn't stop until he took hold of her chin between his finger and thumb and tilted her face up to him.

'You are a beautiful woman.'

She opened her mouth, but before she could deny this claim she connected with his deep, fabulously dark eyes and lost the power of speech totally. She thought about the incredibly glamorous females who had been present at the glitzy event and looked down at her own jeans. She released a choked laugh. *He had to be joking!*

'And you are my wife,' he finished simply.

The breath snagged in Sam's throat as she lifted her head. Her head started to spin as she registered the incredible tenderness in his face.

'But, leaving aside those factors, you have no history with any man but me. And since you wear my ring on your finger…' Sam trembled a little, but didn't resist as he took her small hand in his. As he stroked his finger against first the plain gold band and then the square-cut emerald in its antique setting she held her breath and tensed expectantly.

The silence stretched, tearing her shredded nerves to breaking point and beyond. The tension was almost unendurable as she waited for him to continue. When he did she jumped and gave a tiny startled cry.

'You never will have history with any other man but me.'

His eyes lifted and melded to hers, and the possessive glow in them sent a corresponding surge of heat through her own body. He released her hand and ran a finger along the soft curve of her cheek until it rested on the small indentation in her chin.

'Don't worry—your future is taken care of, *cara*. I can tolerate a man hearing heavenly music when he looks at you, but if he showed any inclination to do more than gaze at you I would…' His slight smile widened into a wolfish grin. 'Discourage him,' he finished silkily.

'You would?'

He nodded.

Sam, who had started to dare to think that maybe this situation could be saved, took a deep breath and slanted a wary look at him through her lashes. 'I don't blame you for being as mad as hell with me.' *Except he wasn't.* 'If you'd told me this morning that you were going to that darned thing…'

'I was about to tell you this morning, when you announced that you didn't feel married,' he recalled bitterly.

'Did I *say* that?' she gasped.

He nodded. 'It is not what a man enjoys to hear when he

is leaving his wife for the day. Then you had to throw up...that tends to cut short a conversation.'

'I can see that,' she admitted with a rueful grimace. 'I suppose you expect me to explain why I...?'

'Made a national laughing-stock of me?' he inserted. 'No, I don't expect that.'

Her eyes flew to his. They were a deep green. 'You don't?'

He shook his head. 'I already know why you did it.'

She stared up at him.

'You came to fight for your man.' He took her face between both his hands. 'You love me.'

Sam's heart stopped. She opened her mouth and tried to laugh, but nothing but a strangled squeak emerged. The rampant hunger in his eyes made her head spin. 'Marisa is actually very nice,' she heard herself say stupidly. 'We should invite her to dinner some time.'

'Why are we talking about Marisa?' he growled.

'Well, she would have made you a perfect wife.'

'Marisa is beautiful and talented. She probably is perfect,' he admitted. 'But for one thing...'

'What thing?'

A slow smile that made Sam's heart thud spread across his face. 'She isn't you, *tesoro mio*,' he said simply. 'She isn't you, and I have discovered,' he explained against her trembling lips, 'that nothing else will do for me. Say it!'

'Say what?'

'Tell me I'm right—tell me you stormed the ceremony because you were willing to fight for me.' His voice dropped a husky octave as he went on in the same driven tone, 'Tell me that you love me and can't bear the idea of living without me. Tell me that your life without me is empty.'

'All those things,' she gulped.

She felt the deep sigh that shuddered through his lean body. And then, as he angled her face up to his, she recognised the gleam of male triumph in his spectacular eyes. Her eyes closed as he gathered her to him and kissed her—tenderly at first, and then with a growing hunger and lack of control. When he dragged his mouth from hers with a groan he was breathing hard.

'You want me, Alessandro?' she said, wary still of the happiness that was flooding her body.

'I think I loved you from the first moment I saw you.'

'First moment!' she exclaimed, recalling the way he had looked at her on every occasion they had met. 'I don't think so.'

'It's true. I couldn't take my eyes off you. The way you moved, your face, your laugh…' His eyes left hers for a second as he swallowed. 'And then…' His eyes darkened as they met hers. 'Then, Samantha, I saw you look at Trelevan. And I knew that you loved him. I told myself that it was my duty to watch you, to make sure you did not do anything to hurt Katerina.' His lips sketched a derisive smile. 'I carried on telling myself that when I rearranged my schedule time and time again, in order to accept every invitation that came my way if I knew there was a chance you would be there. I couldn't admit that I just wanted to see your face. And the more often I saw it,' he admitted, framing her face in his hands, 'the more I needed to.

'It wasn't until I got you into my bed that I recognised my self-deception for what it was. And then to realise that you had not given yourself to another man… It made me feel—' His voice thickened as he broke off and kissed her parted lips hungrily. 'For the first time in my life I contemplated a meaningful relationship that was more than fleeting gratification. Imagine, then, my feelings when you declared that you only wanted me as a sex toy.'

'I didn't say that!' she protested, absolutely stunned by his revelations.

'As good as,' he insisted.

'I was trying to be what you wanted. I sort of half convinced myself that was what I wanted too—but then it got so hard. I had to throw your number away to stop myself ringing you.'

The confession made him laugh. Then, as the laughter died from his face, their eyes connected and his love was there for her to see. She shed the doubts and fears of the past weeks as though they had never been.

'The only time it ever mattered to me what a woman thought of my scars was with you, and you're the only woman who has kissed them, *cara*.'

Her lips quivered. 'I hate the idea of you hurting and me not being there.'

'You have healed me. I used to have flashbacks of the accident, but since the first time we made love there has been nothing.'

'Flashbacks!' She looked horrified. 'Did you go to therapy?'

'I didn't need therapy,' he scorned. 'I needed you.'

He bent his head to kiss her, and as much as Sam wanted to let him she knew there was something left to clear up. 'There's something I have to say, Alessandro. About Jonny. What I felt for him—it wasn't…real.' Lifting her eyes to his, she pressed a hand to her heart. 'What I feel for you—it's in here. It's real. I didn't know what love was until you taught me. You are my perfect lover, Alessandro, but I think you could be a perfect husband too, and a better than perfect father.'

He covered her hand with his. 'That is quite a title,' he said, his voice suspiciously husky. 'But,' he promised, 'I will try to live up to it every day of my life.'

Tears of joy stood out in her eyes as Sam's throat closed over with emotion. 'I thought you married me because of the baby,' she admitted.

'I was knocked sideways to hear about the baby,' he admitted quietly. 'And I am looking forward to being a father. But when I arrived at your flat that day I had this ring in my pocket.' He lifted her hand and touched the emerald that shone on her finger.

Sam's eyes widened. 'You were going to propose?' she whispered.

He nodded. 'And if I had got in my proposal before I learnt about the baby I think perhaps we would both have been saved some heartache… But that,' he said, 'is the past. We have the future to look forward to. Don't look now, but here comes Carlo with an umbrella, looking most disapproving. When we are alone he will scold me for letting you get wet. We should go indoors.'

Sam, her eyes shining with love, looked up at her tall, handsome husband and smiled. 'I'd go anywhere with you,' she told him, meaning it literally.

'When you look at me like that all I want to do is make love to you.'

'What's stopping you…?'

'Good point,' he said, scooping her up into his arms and carrying her, laughing, past a very startled-looking butler.

The Italian's
Forced Bride

KATE WALKER

Kate Walker was born in Nottinghamshire, but as she grew up in Yorkshire she has always felt that her roots are there. She met her husband at university and originally worked as a children's librarian, but after the birth of her son she returned to her old childhood love of writing. When she's not working, she divides her time between her family, their three cats and her interests of embroidery, antiques, film and theatre, and, of course, reading. You can visit Kate at www.kate-walker.com

CHAPTER ONE

ALICE HOWARD knew just who was at the door from the very first second she heard the bell ring.

She knew who it was; knew who was there. And she also knew that he was the last person on earth that she wanted to face. Even though, at the same time, he was the person she most wanted to see in all the world.

Just the thought of opening the door to him turned her legs to water so that she couldn't stand up or go to the window to look out and see if she was right about the identity of her unexpected visitor. But then she didn't need to. She was sure in her mind of that—and more so in her heart, where it mattered most.

The timing was right—just three days after she had sent the letter to tell him she had something important they had to talk about… Her hand slid down and curved protectively over the spot where she had only recently learned that her baby—and this man's child—was beginning to grow. *Something very, very important,* she had said—and it was certainly that.

The atmosphere was right too. The arrival totally out of the blue. No warning. Not even the sound of a car coming up the small country lane and pulling up outside her gate had alerted her to the fact that he was there.

And even the sound was just right. The hard, loud, unceasing ring of the bell, echoing through the quiet of the afternoon and the silence in the small house, was like an imperious, autocratic summons. As cold and proud and unyielding as Domenico himself.

Domenico.

There, now she'd let his name into her thoughts. She'd finally admitted who she was expecting her unwanted visitor to be.

The man whose arrival on her doorstep she was dreading most.

Or did she mean longing for most…?

She couldn't answer that and shook her dark head slowly, sending her long hair flying around her pale, oval-shaped face. Sharp white teeth worried at the fullness of her bottom lip and her blue eyes were clouded by the deep shadows left by long nights, lack of sleep and that extra little secret as well.

'Domenico.'

His name slipped from Alice's lips as she sat back on the small single bed in the tiny, shabbily decorated bedroom, hands clenched tightly in her lap as she fought against the craven impulse to rush to her feet, dash across the pale green carpet and peer out of the window.

Safely hidden behind the faded velvet curtains, of course.

But she didn't need to look. She already knew exactly what she would see. His image was imprinted on her mind, the strong features and powerful physique, black hair and dark gold eyes etched into her thoughts by the power of the love she had once felt for him. All the tears she had shed since their parting—and before—hadn't been enough to wipe away the memories of the man who had once meant more to her than her own life.

The man who had once held her heart in his hands, to do with as he wished. But he had been totally careless of the gift she had given him. He had treated it callously and cruelly, without a thought for the way she had made herself so vulnerable to him. And so, in the end, unable to take any more, she had had to leave.

She had thought that she had gone far enough away. That by heading back to England, to her home, to the village so many hundreds of miles away from the sophisticated Italian city of Florence where he lived, she had escaped his malign influence. That here, in the quiet of the countryside, she would have a chance to lick her wounds in private and somehow find the strength to face the world again, start over.

'Alice!'

If she had had the slightest belief that she was wrong and that the person at the door was not who she feared, then that belief was shattered instantly at the sound of her name.

'Alice!'

Only Domenico used her name in that way. Only he could take the simple syllables and, with the help of his musical Italian accent lengthening the *i* in the middle to a long, soft *ee*, turn them into something so lyrical that it sounded like a poem instead of just a name.

'Alice!'

But there was nothing musical or poetic about the way he used her name right now.

His tone was the opposite of soft, the cold, slashing sound of his voice like a shower of sleet falling on the soft spring air, the barely controlled anger giving it a brutal edge.

'Open this door, damn you! I know you're there!'

He couldn't *know* that, Alice told herself, struggling to still the racing thud of her heart. He was simply challenging her, being deliberately provocative—being Domenico.

Domenico, who had never, to her knowledge, ever admitted to being wrong or even unsure about anything. Domenico who knew everything, understood everything, handled everything that life ever threw at him. He must have been born with that supreme self-confidence. Lying in his cot, he must have looked out on the world with the arrogance of a tiny Roman emperor, knowing he had only to make the slightest sound and his doting attendants would rush to his side.

So now he was just frustrated at the way she hadn't jumped to answer his command, the way that everyone else in his life did. He was challenging her, wanting to push her into revealing herself.

'Go away!' She mouthed the comment in the direction of the window, secure in the fact that he couldn't see her, had no proof that she was even in the house.

She had simply to stay where she was, well back from the window, hidden by the cottage's thick stone walls, and eventually his frustration would turn to boredom, boredom to anger, and he would slam himself into his car in disgust, drive away with a screech of tyres on the pebbled drive.

And she would be free of him.

For a while at least.

Oh, she knew she couldn't hope that he would get so annoyed he would leave for good—never coming back. That was too much to dream of. Domenico Parrisi didn't give up that easily. Not after just one attempt.

In fact, Domenico Parrisi didn't give up *at all*. He was renowned for it; his reputation for determination and refusal to surrender second to none.

He would be back, sooner rather than later. To have the talk she'd said she wanted. But at least she would have had a little more breathing space. A little more time to think, and to work out just how she was going to handle things. What she was going to say to him.

It had gone suspiciously quiet outside. The awful noise of the bell ringing on and on and on had stopped, and so had the sound of Domenico's voice. She hadn't heard the car leave—but then she hadn't heard it arrive either!

Had he gone? Had she actually been lucky this time and got away with avoiding the confrontation he'd evidently planned? She couldn't quite believe it.

Edging closer to the window, she tried to peer out but the faded green velvet curtain blocked her view. Twitching it aside by just an inch or two, she leaned forward, looked out…

And looked straight into a darkly handsome face, her startled blue eyes clashing with the burning bronze gaze of the man below.

He had moved back from the cottage door and was leaning against the bonnet of the car—something sleekly low-slung and metallic grey—his long legs crossed at the ankles, strong arms folded firmly across his broad chest. The weak spring sunlight made his jet-black hair gleam and a soft breeze lifted and ruffled the shining strands. His head was thrown back, the fierce profile in stark relief against the pale blue sky.

He was waiting and watching, like some big, powerful black cat sitting patiently by the hole in the skirting board, knowing exactly where the small, nervous mouse had disappeared. And knowing just where it ultimately would have to come out of hiding and into the open again. So he was quite content to wait and watch—and pounce if his victim so much as showed a whisker.

And he was looking straight at her. Eyes hooded, mouth—a mouth that was normally a sultry, sexual temptation—drawn into a thin, controlled line, lips compressed. The coldness in his eyes seemed to slice into her like an icy laser, cutting straight through to her heart.

And then he lifted his arm, waved a hand in an imperious gesture, pointed.

The message behind that particular signal couldn't have

been clearer if he'd written it in large red letters along the length of his expensive car.

Get yourself down here, it said. And be quick about it.

Immediately her mood changed.

'All right,' she muttered to him from the security of behind the pane of glass. 'All right, I'll come down. But, I warn you, you might just regret it when I do.'

So she *was* at home, Domenico reflected grimly, watching Alice's face disappear from the window. And a damn good thing that she was. Otherwise he would have made this journey for nothing. And he didn't have the time or inclination to waste precious hours on 'nothing'.

When the detective he had hired to find Alice for him had come back with this address, he'd thought long and hard about whether it was worth making the journey all this way to seek her out.

Wouldn't it have been better to dismiss her from his thoughts just as easily as Alice had been able to dismiss the months they had spent together from hers? But the problem was that once he'd let a single thought into his head, it had been followed by others, dozens of them. Thoughts he'd told himself he'd forgotten. Memories he didn't want to recall.

Memories he damn well wasn't going to recall now!

He and Alice Howard had had a relationship. Well, he'd thought it was a relationship; she, evidently, had thought otherwise. She had just been 'having fun', she'd told him in that last cold-blooded confrontation, but now it wasn't fun any more and she was leaving.

And that was that. She had packed her bags and walked.

Walked out of his home, out of his life, out of his world. She hadn't spared a backward glance; hadn't given him any sort of explanation—just gone, making it plain that she no longer had any time for him or interest in him.

Certainly the woman who had peered down at him from the first-floor window of this tiny, shabby cottage didn't appear at all enthusiastic at seeing him. In fact, everything about her gave the opposite impression. She was staring at him as if he was some particularly nasty form of life that had just crawled out of the overgrown pond in the middle of the unkempt lawn, and she appeared to have frozen into immobility, rather than making any move to let him in.

But she had walked out on him—and that was something he wasn't used to. Truth to tell, he was always—*always*—the one who did the walking. And that was the way he liked it. It meant that when it was over, it was over. There were no hanging, frayed loose ends.

Loose ends got in the way. They could trip you up, stop you from moving on. Domenico preferred things clear-cut. Things with Alice had been far from clear-cut.

And so he had snatched at time he didn't actually have to make the journey here. He was not going to be pleased if she stayed hidden away and didn't let him in, and the whole journey was a waste of time. He certainly didn't plan on coming back again if she changed her mind a second time and decided she *did* want to see him after all.

In fact, he wasn't at all sure just why he was here now. He...

His thoughts stopped dead at the sound of the door handle moving. The white-painted wood swung open and Alice stood in the space of the doorway.

'Dannazione!'

Domenico swore under his breath as he felt the effect that her appearance alone had on him. The kick of response low down in his body told him the unwelcome truth about why he had been so reluctant—and yet so determined—to come here today.

He still wanted this woman.

He'd wanted her from the moment he'd first set eyes on her, and he still did, damn it! And he sure as hell didn't want to feel that way.

She was far more casually dressed than he had seen her for a long time. The loose lilac T-shirt was long, almost like a tunic over the top of black jeans, and she had pulled on a black cotton cardigan over the top, leaving it hanging open. The worn denim shaped the long, slender lines of her legs and the way the soft cotton of the T-shirt clung to the rounded curves of her hips made his mouth dry in the heat of sudden desire. Her feet were bare and looking down at the way that the small pink toes curled and flexed on the cool stone of the doorstep brought a sudden, blazing memory of how it had felt to have one of those narrow, soft feet slide erotically up and down the exposed skin of his own calf, over his knee…along his thigh…

'Well?' Alice said sharply.

The cold, brittle tone of the single word shattered the heated illusion that had gripped him. This was the woman who had walked out on him, he reminded himself. The woman who had done what no other woman had ever done.

'Buon giorno, Signorina Howard.'

Domenico forced himself to speak, fighting against the husky sound that the dryness in his throat had created.

Perhaps it was the sombre colour against her skin, or the way that her dark hair tumbled rather wildly about her shoulders, but she looked paler than usual, the deep blue eyes like clouded pools above the slanting cheekbones. And there was a coldness in those stunning eyes that might have frozen a lesser man, leaving him incapable of speech.

But *frozen* was not how Domenico felt. Quite the opposite. She could never look anything but stunning, and somehow the two months' absence had increased rather than lessened the impact of her deeply sensual femininity.

He had told himself that in his memories he had exaggerated the potent appeal of her beauty, the lush curves of her body, but the instant electric sting of desire that tormented him just at seeing her revealed that unfounded confidence as the lie it was.

There was no way he was over this woman. And seeing her here, like this, had driven that point home with a force that made his head spin. Everything that was male in him responded to her femaleness on the most primitive, basic level, heating his blood and demanding satisfaction right here, right now. The impulse to march across the few metres of pebbled drive between them, snatch her up into his arms and carry her inside to the nearest bed—the nearest floor—was such a struggle to resist that the tension tightened his muscles, tied painful knots in his nerves as he fought to control it.

'I understand that you wanted to talk to me,' he continued.

It seemed that the strain had reached his vocal cords too, making his voice sound harsh and raw, almost brutally aggressive. But then that only matched the cold welcome she had given him.

And she showed no sign of being pleased, or even relieved to see him. Instead, those deep blue eyes were as cold and distant as the ocean—the *English* sea, he amended, recalling the way that the water on the coast here had been so very different from the warm blue of the Mediterranean that surrounded his own country.

'So talk,' he growled in irritation.

Talk!

The word—the command, for that was what it was—reverberated inside Alice's head.

Talk, he said, standing there, lean hips propped against the low bonnet of his car, powerful arms folded across his chest like a determined barrier, beautiful eyes gleaming bronze in the weak April sunlight.

Talk.

But what could she say? What was it safe to talk about? She couldn't just plunge straight in and announce starkly that she was pregnant.

'I think we'd do better to discuss this inside.'

'If you prefer.'

His voice was hard and unyielding, totally uncompromising, just like his expression.

This far and no further, was what the look he shot her said. *You can bring me to your door, but you can't make me do anything I don't want to do.* And Alice felt the force of that look almost as if it had been a deliberate slap in the face.

How could she talk to a man who was so obviously armoured against her? A man who, it seemed, had dropped even the pretence of caring that he had displayed when they had been together.

But, of course, the truth was that now she knew it had only been a pretence. Then, she had been totally convinced of his honesty, and had gullibly swallowed the stories he'd spun her.

She certainly couldn't tell him just like that—totally cold. Not with her secret gnawing at her deep inside, the dread of seeing his expression when she spoke. Not knowing at all just how he would take the news of her pregnancy, this man who had openly declared that he 'didn't do marriage'. If nothing else, she needed a few moments to gather herself.

'Well, I need a drink.'

She tried to make it sound as if she didn't give a damn what *he* wanted. In fact, she was actually turning her back on him as she spoke.

'You can come in or wait out here as you please.'

She left the door open behind her as she walked back into the house, not daring even to glance back over her shoulder to see if he followed her. She didn't care if he did or not, she told herself, trying to make herself believe it. But all the while she knew that she was only kidding herself.

Just seeing him here like this had rocked her world. Already her heart was beating hard and fast inside her chest, making her breathing painfully shallow and rapid so that her head swam uncomfortably. She was shivering faintly as if she was in a state of shock, and her stomach clenched on an uncomfortable wave of nausea.

She had had to fight so hard to get away from him. And the worst battle had been with herself. But now it seemed that she had been flung back right into the maelstrom of feelings that simply being with Domenico could create; and she didn't know how to handle them.

Why was he here? Why had he finally decided, after eight long weeks, to come after her?

'One drink, then.'

She hadn't heard him come in after her, so that now his voice, sounding so suddenly behind her back, made her jump like a frightened cat, the glass she had picked up to fill with water clattering sharply against the tap.

'My, you are jumpy, aren't you?' Domenico drawled cynically. 'What's the problem? A guilty conscience?'

'Not at all.'

Alice fought for control over her voice and her hands before she put the glass under the tap to fill. But even then she had to concentrate fiercely on holding it straight and not letting the betraying tremble in her fingers give her away too much.

Somehow she managed to complete the action, turning

with what she hoped was the right amount of nonchalance and taking a careful sip of her drink as she faced him again.

'It's just that I thought you were determined to stay outside. But now that you are here, what can I get you? Tea? Coffee?'

'You know that I never drink tea,' Domenico returned with a faint shudder. He had never understood her very English addiction to the drink and always tried to avoid so much as a sip of it when she made a pot for herself. 'Surely you can't have forgotten that already?'

'Out of sight, out of mind.'

Oh, he hadn't liked that! The burning glare he turned on her made her throat constrict so that she thought she would choke on her second sip of water.

But angering him was a bad mistake. She was going to need him in a mood to listen and if she drove him into one of his black rages then there was little chance of that ever happening. So she carefully toned down the sharpness of her response.

'For all I know, you might have had a complete change of heart about a lot of things in the time since we were together,' Alice went on with careful coolness. 'And I'm not at all sure that I really knew you that well anyway.'

'We spent over six months together.'

'Six months in which you were at work or in some other country for more time than you were ever in Italy,' she reminded him.

'I warned you what it would be like,' Domenico stated flatly. 'I never left you with any illusion that it could be otherwise.'

'No,' Alice admitted. 'You were perfectly straight about that.'

He had been totally upfront about the fact that his work was his life. He hadn't made it to where he was—from nowhere to head of the multi-million-pound Parrisi computer empire— by sitting back and contemplating. Domenico was a force to be reckoned with.

No one knew very much about him. He kept his back-ground—where he came from, who he was—intensely private. It was rumoured that he never slept, rarely ate. That the only leisure activity he had time for were the nights he spent with beautiful women.

The beautiful, glamorous women who were seen on his arm at all the right places.

But, as she had cause to know only too well, it was not the women who were seen on his arm that mattered.

'So that wasn't why you walked out?'

The question took her by surprise. As did the fact that he suddenly seemed so very much closer. Dangerously so.

When had he moved? He must have been as silent on his feet as a panther stalking its prey, prowling up behind her when she wasn't looking and making the small kitchen seem suddenly even smaller until no matter which way she turned the place was full of Domenico. His height and strength dominated the space between them, the sheer impact of his tautly muscled body overwhelming. He had tugged his tie loose at the neck and unfastened the top two buttons and she could see the faint shadowing of dark body hair in the opening of the light blue cotton. The clean, masculine scent of his skin, overlaid with the subtle tang of some expensive cologne, filled her nostrils and the soft sound of his breathing was in her ears.

Her heart had started to thud again, but this time it was with a very different sort of pulse, one that unwillingly she had to acknowledge that she recognised only too well. This was the heavy, heated beat of awareness that had always assailed her in the past. The way that she had felt from the first moment she had seen him and had never really recovered from since.

It was the sheer concentrated physical impact that he had on her. And the pulse that throbbed through her veins was one of deep, sensual arousal. It was as if everything that was male in him was calling to her own essential femininity on the deepest, most primitive level, in a way that made her head spin.

'I told you why I left.'

'Yeah, you stopped having fun.'

There was something in his voice that caught and held her. Some soft undertone that seemed to reach out and enclose her, like the delicate but constricting lines of a spider's web. She felt it coil round her, lightly seductive but dangerously transfixing.

'Why was that, *cara*, hmm?'

'I…'

Her voice had failed her, no matter how hard she tried to make it work. Her mouth opened and closed but no sound came out. She felt she must look like some stupid, gaping fish, but something about her expression made Domenico smile.

'When did the fun go out of things? Because it never did for me.'

'Never?'

Was that stupid, squeaky little voice really hers?

'Never.' Domenico's echoing of the word was much lower, deeper, rich with a sensuality that tugged at something deep inside her.

'Coffee.' She tried for common sense, for practicality.

Domenico shook his dark head slowly, that smile growing wickedly.

'I think not,' he murmured.

No? Once again Alice tried to form the word but failed, her throat closing. Nervously she slicked her tongue over painfully dry lips, determined to try again, only to have the determination evaporate like mist before the sun as she saw the way his bronze gaze dropped to follow the betraying movement, the intensity with which it fixed on her mouth.

'What?' she managed to croak, rough and uneven.

'There is something I would like so much more.'

And before she could snatch in another breath his mouth came down on hers, taking it in a slow, seductive kiss.

CHAPTER TWO

HE HADN'T been able to resist it, Domenico admitted to himself. He had come into the house determined to hold back, to keep himself to himself, to watch and wait, and only decide what his next move should be when he had found out just which way the land was lying.

But from the moment he'd set eyes on Alice once again, he had been caught up in the familiar burn of desire that always took his body by storm whenever she was around.

He had been determined to stay outside at first. At least that way he could keep some distance between himself and the beguiling enticement offered by her sexy body. An enticement that twisted in his guts, coiled around his senses, stopped him from thinking straight.

He wasn't going to jump in with both feet this time, he'd told himself. Not the way he had done last time. Then he had wanted her in his life just five minutes after meeting her, had had her in his bed within a day. He had been so obsessed, so physically enslaved by her that he hadn't been able to *think*, except with one very basic part of his anatomy.

And look where that had got him! After six short months she had walked out on him, declaring she'd had enough and she wasn't coming back.

So this time he had vowed that he was going to take things steady.

That he was going to think before he acted, pause before he moved. And was very definitely going to put his brain in charge instead of his libido.

But from the moment she had appeared in the doorway he had known that thinking was not what he wanted to be doing. He had fought down the carnal urges that stung at him, not even allowing himself to look too closely at her—until she had turned to walk away.

The sway of her hips had been his downfall. The sight of the neat, curved behind in the tight black jeans had set his pulse rate soaring, scrambling his thought processes.

He had been without this woman in his bed for two months and that was long enough.

More than long enough.

And he was going to do something about it.

'Something I want a hell of a lot more,' he murmured now against her mouth, 'than any damn coffee.'

Her first response was to stiffen under his caress. To freeze into immobility, her slender body held taut, inches away from his.

But she hadn't pulled away. She wasn't fighting him.

So he kissed her again. Harder this time. Firmer.

He slid his hands up into the dark silkiness of her hair, cupping the fine bones of her skull in his palms as he angled her head so that it was positioned just right.

And she went with him all the way. Let him do just as he pleased. Her eyes were closed and there was a new and very different tension in her muscles now. Her mouth softened under his, her lips parting on a sigh of response, of surrender, but she hadn't yet let herself go, hadn't leaned into him.

'Alice, *carina…*'

He pressed home his advantage, sliding one hand down the long length of her spine, curving it around her waist and sliding it under the loose-fitting T-shirt, bringing it up to cup the warm, soft side of one breast.

She jumped slightly, tensed a little, then stilled. But her clinging mouth never left his; her tongue danced with his in an echo of the intimacy she was inviting.

But that tiny hesitation warned him not to rush things. To slow down, take a step back. If he pushed too hard now he might drive her away and that was not what he wanted at all.

And so he eased his mouth away from hers, brought his hand back down to her waist, smoothing the lilac cotton straight as he did so.

'No…' he said slowly, softly, the effort it cost him to keep it that way, the stinging protest from his heavily aroused body, putting a convincing unevenness into his tone. 'No.'

And watched her eyes fly open in disconcerted amazement.

'No?' she asked sharply, obviously bewildered.

Just what was happening? Alice asked herself, struggling to get a grip on her feelings—and on Domenico's constantly changing moods.

He had arrived here in a state of cold anger, obviously totally armoured against her, so much so that she had been convinced he wouldn't even set foot in the house. He had insisted that she talk and made her afraid that he knew her secret. Then suddenly he had changed again, become Domenico the seductive—a Domenico she knew only too well.

Perhaps it was because she knew that Domenico so well that she had responded to him so easily, let her defences down without thinking. One touch of his lips on hers and she had been lost. Lost in the so-familiar taste, the familiar scent, the heat of his skin, the strength of his hands on her head.

Lost in the sensual spell that he wove so effortlessly.

'Not a wise move,' Domenico said now. 'At least, not yet.'

The audacious assumption of that 'not yet' took her breath away. She had to clamp her mouth tight shut, teeth digging into her tongue, so as not to fling a furious retort at him, her fingers itching to swipe the self-assured smile from his stunning face.

She knew she had only herself to blame for that arrogant confidence. After all, he had only to touch her and she became putty in his hands. It was as if they had never been apart. He knew just the way to hold her, to kiss her, to caress her, and she went up in flames. Her body was still shaking from the erotic assault of his kiss. That brief, fleeting touch of his hard fingers against her breast, so newly sensitised by the changes in her body, had set her senses singing.

The need for more was a deep ache low down in her body, a heated pulse between her legs. But the emotional need was worse; the knowledge of what she had wanted so much from this man and how he had broken her heart when she had realised that he would never provide it.

'Coffee,' she said again, hoping she sounded more determined than she felt.

'Coffee,' Domenico echoed, but he didn't move away. He didn't smile, either, but watched her, his burning gaze disturbingly intent. She felt like a small, uncertain creature being watched by a large, predatory jungle cat, one that was trying to make up his mind whether it was worth the trouble of pouncing.

So had that kiss meant nothing to him at all?

Had he just wanted to see how she would react? Or had he not been able to stop himself?

Or worse, had he simply kissed her because he could—as an act of power?

The thought sent a shiver down her spine, making her hand unsteady as she reached for the coffee jar and the cafetière.

Now was completely the wrong time to remember that one of the side effects of her pregnancy was the fact that she had suddenly developed a hatred for the scent of coffee grounds. The smell caught in her throat, twisted round her stomach, making her feel horribly nauseous and unwell.

Briefly she closed her eyes, fighting the sensation.

'Is something wrong?' Domenico had noticed her reaction and pounced swiftly.

'No!'

Alice forced her eyes open sharply, fighting to hold her breath, not to inhale the nauseating smell as she spooned coffee into the glass jug.

'I'm fine.'

'You don't look it.'

'I—I wasn't expecting you to just turn up like that.'

If she was honest, she hadn't expected him to come here at all. The most she had hoped for was a phone call in response to her note saying that they needed to talk. The way he had appeared on her doorstep had rocked her right off balance.

'I couldn't stay away.'

'And you expect me to believe that?'

Broad shoulders lifted in a shrug that said he didn't really give a damn whether she did or not.

'You're not an easy woman to find.'

'Maybe I didn't want to be found.'

But then the realisation of just what he had said hit her hard, bringing her head up sharply.

'You were looking for me?'

Her voice squeaked ridiculously as her eyes flew to his face. It was difficult to read anything into that dark, shuttered expression, the way his eyes met hers head on, unyielding and unrevealing.

'Of course.'

'I find that hard to believe.'

She hoped she sounded calmer than she felt, but the tremor in her hands scattered the coffee over the edge of the jug and onto the worktop.

'Damn!'

Painfully aware of Domenico's dark bronze eyes on her pink face, she snatched up a piece of paper towel and swiped at the spilled coffee grounds, only succeeding in sending them flying further.

'Let me.'

She jumped sharply as Domenico's hand came down over her own, stilling the nervous movement. In a moment, the mess had been cleared up, swiftly and efficiently and using only one hand. And what made her tremble inside was the way that the other hand still lingered on hers, its hold so light but somehow impossible to break away from.

'I'm all fingers and thumbs!' she managed, her voice shaking with nervous response. Her heart was racing, thudding against the wall of her chest, making her breathless and unsteady.

That burning gaze dropped to their joined hands.

'But beautiful,' he said, so softly, and his accent was so thick on the two words that for a second she blinked uncertainly, wondering if she had heard right.

'What?'

'You have beautiful hands…'

Domenico's thumb moved as he spoke, stroking down the length of her middle finger, over the knuckle and smoothing the skin of her hand. His touch was warm and delicate and made her bare toes curl on the terracotta tiles of the kitchen floor, a sensual shiver snaking its way down her spine.

'*Bella.*'

'Dom...' Alice tried, the word drying on her lips. And it was only as the silence closed in around them that she realised that, unable to finish, she had croaked the shortened form of his name that she had used when they were together.

The shortened, *affectionate* form of his name.

The one that it had taken her so long to work round to using.

The one that, she had once thought, he had allowed only her to use. She had been so proud of that small fact, thinking that it meant she was somehow special to him.

'Why would I not want to find you when you are so beautiful? I said, you have beautiful hands...'

Once more that caressing thumb moved over Alice's skin, making her shudder in response.

'And a beautiful face.'

That burning gaze lifted to lock with hers, holding her transfixed and unable to look away. The touch that held her fingers still kept them captive while his other hand rose, touched her forehead, her temple, traced a heated path down the side of her cheek, coming to rest underneath her jaw line, lightly cupping her chin. The way he held her lifted her face towards his, forcing her to look into the heated depths of his eyes.

And what she saw there was something she recognised only too well.

Desire.

Stark, burning, undisguised desire.

A physical need that turned his gaze molten, that made his pupils expand, turn jet black, deep and impenetrable.

A desire that she knew was burning in her own veins, woken by the touch of his hands on her skin, the scent of his body all around her.

'Dom...' She tried again but he wasn't listening.

'You have beautiful eyes,' he murmured, leaning forward

to drop a warm kiss on one eyelid, pressing it closed. 'And beautiful hair.'

Behind the enclosing darkness of her lids, she felt his mouth on her hair, felt another kiss whisper across the silky strands, and knew the sudden clutch of a harsh, primitive hunger low down in her body, pulsing cruelly.

Too cruelly, too heavily to let her think straight.

'And a very, very beautiful mouth.'

Even though her eyes were still closed she knew that he was very near. She could feel the warmth of his breath on her lips, almost taste it in her mouth.

He was going to kiss her again, she knew. And if he did then she would be lost. Helpless. Unable to resist him.

She had barely escaped with her sanity a moment ago when he had taken her into his arms. She had almost surrendered totally to him then, giving in to feelings she couldn't control.

No!

From behind the protective cover of her eyelids, she mentally shook herself fiercely.

She was not going to let this happen to her. Not going to give in to those feelings. They were not stronger than her, not uncontrollable. They were habit; nothing more!

She had been with Domenico for six months. They had been lovers from the start; she hadn't been able to resist him. And in that time she had grown so strongly accustomed to his kisses, his caresses. He knew just where to touch—how to kiss. And her body, so well attuned to his, responded instinctively, like the finest of musical instruments to the touch of a master.

It was only habit, she told herself. It sounded right—so why didn't it help?

'Alice…' Domenico breathed and she forced her eyes

open, finding that he was even closer than she had thought. His face was only inches from her own, with his eyes burning into hers, the impossibly long, rich black lashes almost brushing her skin when he blinked.

And she couldn't look away, even when he moved just that last tiny bit closer and let his mouth brush hers. Just a touch. The briefest, lightest touch before he lifted his head away again. But just a touch was all it took to set her body clamouring again.

'Dom, please,' she sighed. 'Don't…stop…'

She felt that sinfully beautiful mouth smile against her own, and knew with a terrible sinking of her heart just what was coming.

'"Don't. Stop"?' Domenico questioned silkily. 'Or…"Don't stop"?'

There was no way she could answer him. She couldn't even answer herself to explain what she had meant. Even as she'd formed the words, her mind had been warring with itself, torn between the two meanings, wanting to say them both— neither—but never, ever able to decide between the two.

Domenico wasn't waiting for an answer. Bending close again, he took her mouth with his, tilting his head just so to get the perfect angle, the exact pressure he wanted, to let his tongue slide along the barely closed line of her lips.

And Alice knew she was lost. She had been so close to insanity that first time. This time she had no hope of holding back.

This wasn't habit, or anything like it, she told herself as the hot waves of sensuality broke over her, drowning her thoughts. This was passion, carnal hunger, need—desire.

Lust.

Love?

Oh, dear God, no! Not love.

Please let love not be part of this. Not any more!

Lust she could cope with. Desire she understood. Passion—Domenico had always brought out a burning, searing passion in her. One she couldn't control; couldn't escape. It had been her downfall from the start—and it looked as if it was going to pull her right down that heated path again.

But she didn't want to be in love with him. That had hurt too much. So much that she had barely escaped with her sanity.

'Don't tell me to stop,' Domenico muttered against her mouth, and it was impossible to tell if it was an order or if he was pleading with her, begging her not to say it, not to hold him back.

'I—'

'I can't stop!' It was harsher, thicker, roughened by the same hunger that was firing through her veins.

Between each word he snatched another kiss, each one harder, stronger, deeper than before.

And each kiss broke down another part of Alice's resistance, chipping away at it until it crumbled under the onslaught and had her clinging to him, arms tight around his neck, soft body pressed up against his hardness, her mouth opening under his, inviting more, inviting him in.

'I can't stop! I won't!'

'Don't,' Alice choked and this time she knew exactly what she meant to say; what she wanted.

What she wanted was to know this powerful passion just once more. To feel his strength around her, his touch on her skin, his kiss on her mouth.

She might be deceiving herself but deep inside her heart there was a tiny speck of hope. A small glow that time was fanning into a flame. A flame that no common sense would ever extinguish, no matter how hard she tried.

I couldn't stay away.

The words swung round and round in her head, drowning out all other thoughts.

You're not an easy woman to find.

He had been looking for her. He hadn't just arrived here because of the letter she had sent him. He had been looking for her. And now he was here, and she was in his arms, and he was kissing her.

And the powerful throb of her need for him would drive her mad if she didn't give in to it.

'Don't stop…'she sighed against his mouth and sensed rather than saw the hard, quick smile of deep satisfaction that curved those sinfully seductive lips.

'I won't,' he promised deeply. 'I swear to you I won't stop until we're both too exhausted to think—too sated to breathe.'

And, gathering her up into his arms, he turned towards the door.

'Upstairs?' he muttered, his voice dark and husky, his accent more pronounced than ever before.

'Upstairs,'Alice murmured in acceptance, knowing that this was what she wanted, no matter what happened afterwards.

CHAPTER THREE

IF THE kitchen had seemed small with Domenico in it, then
her bedroom appeared to have shrunk to doll's-house proportions. His dark strength and size dwarfed everything, standing out starkly amongst the white and green flowered decor,
the elderly pine furniture.

At one side of the room the roof sloped downwards so that
he had to stoop, bending low, as he carried her towards the
bed. And even as he laid her on the old-fashioned quilted
bedspread and came to sit beside her, he still had to keep his
head bent so as not to bang it against the ceiling.

But then he had also to keep his head low to capture her
mouth in another of those long, powerful, drugging kisses that
shattered her thought processes, drove her senses wild and had
her clasping her hands behind his neck, fingers threading
through the jet-black softness of his hair, and pulling his face
down towards hers, while she strained upwards to meet him.

'I've missed this... Missed it so damn much.'

It was just a rough mutter, almost incomprehensible in the
thickness of Domenico's accent, blending with the harshness
that desire put onto his tongue.

But Alice didn't need to hear the words clearly to understand. She could feel the strength of his need for her in the

forceful touch of his hands, the impatient, urgent way he tugged the cardigan down her arms and off, pushing the loose T-shirt aside at her waist. Hard fingers burned their way across her skin, shaping the curve of her body, smoothing upwards over the lines of her ribcage.

Her breath caught in her throat as each big hand curved around the soft underside of her breasts, cupping the warm skin.

'No bra?' he questioned softly, the gleam deep in the darkness of his eyes telling her how much that small discovery pleased him.

'No—I…'

She caught in her breath at the realisation of just how close she had come to giving away her secret.

She had avoided wearing a bra whenever possible over the past few weeks because of the way it made her feel. With her breasts newly sensitive and tender, she avoided the constriction of the underwear as much as she could, finding even the faint pressure of satin and lace almost unbearable at times.

Already she could tell that her body had altered. That her figure was developing, ripening, becoming more rounded. She was so sensitive to the changes herself but would Domenico too see the difference in the body he had once, not so long ago, known so intimately? Would he feel…?

But then those knowing hands closed over her breasts and she found that the new and heightened sensitivity to his touch made her mind swim, her head falling back against the pillows, his name escaping her on a long moan of delight.

'You like that?'

Domenico's smile had nothing in it but the deep, predatory satisfaction of a sexual male at the realisation that his touch could send a woman spinning out of control. He seemed to have taken her sudden gasp of response, her indrawn breath as nothing more than the natural reaction of uncontrolled delight he expected.

'Oh yes, you like that,' he declared with arrogant conviction. 'I *know* you like that—and that you like this.'

Slowly, deliberately, he rubbed the pads of his thumbs over her taut and yearning nipples, smiling his dark pleasure, watching her writhe as the stinging electric current of pleasure ran through her.

'You see, *I* have not forgotten! For me it is not "out of sight, out of mind"! You have never been out of my mind since that day when I came home to find you had gone.'

'Never?' Alice croaked, her mouth dry with the need that was burning her up.

'Never,' Domenico assured her. 'How could I ever think to forget this…?'

His lips took hers, the hard pressure, the intimate dance of his tongue, heightening the heated pleasure she already felt, raising it to boiling point until she felt that her brain had melted with the blaze of it.

'Or this…?'

The feel of that wicked mouth closing over her breast loosened the last remnants of any control Alice had over her tongue. The increased sensitivity that her pregnancy had brought turned his gentle suckling into a pleasure-pain that was like a wild explosion along the path of every single nerve she possessed.

'Domenico!'

His name was a moan of delight, a long, yearning sigh of need. She moved instinctively to help him ease the T-shirt from her body, lay tense with anticipation as he unfastened the black jeans and slid them down the length of her legs, tormenting every inch of her skin with hot, ruthlessly arousing kisses as he went.

'Oh, please!' Alice cried out sharply. 'Domenico—please!'

It was impossible to hold back, impossible to stem the tide of hunger that had her in its grip. She didn't know how Domenico kept his control, what ruthless grip he had on his passion so that he wasn't tearing off his own clothes, flinging himself upon her, easing the hunger of his body in the welcoming warmth of her own.

Because he *was* hungry for her. How could he not be when the forceful evidence of his body's need strained against the constriction of his trousers, crushed into the cradle of her pelvis by the weight and strength of him? The heat of it reached her through the fine material, seeming to scorch her skin and making her move restlessly under his imprisoning bulk.

The friction of her skin against his aroused body made Domenico groan aloud, flinging his proud head back, dark eyes glittering as he looked down into her upturned, rose-flushed face.

'Oh, please…' he echoed mockingly, in a mercilessly accurate mimicry of her tone.

One long-fingered hand swept down the length of her body, from the burning cheek, down over the smooth skin of her rounded shoulder, pausing for a tormenting second on the swell of her breast where the hardened nipple pushed wantonly at his palm, seeming to demand more of the electrifying pleasure he had given it only seconds before. But this time Domenico spared her only a second of the sensual delight before sliding his palm down further, lower, easing under the elastic at the top of her knickers, closing over the hot, damp curls at the juncture of her thighs.

'So what is this, hmm, Alicia, *mi bella*? Could it be that you too are remembering just what it was like? That perhaps you have not forgotten…?'

Forgotten! The word was like a roar of horror in her thoughts, one she had to deny.

Forgotten? How could she have forgotten anything? She had tried to forget—tried to wipe every last memory of her time with Domenico from her mind—but had failed. The endless, restless nights she had spent alone, trying to sleep, were evidence of that. The hours when she had thought of nothing but Domenico, the long, sensual hours she had spent with him in the privacy of the big, deep bed in his Milan apartment or in the villa outside Florence, the wild abandon of their lovemaking, the sensual satisfaction that had left her exhausted but contented, right to the depths of her soul.

How could she ever have forgotten that?

Even when she fell asleep her dreams were full of burning, erotic images, memories that stirred her blood and heated her body so that she tossed and turned, often moaning aloud in the night. So many times she had woken in a tangle of bedclothes, with her heart racing, her breath coming wildly, her skin sheened with the sweat that simply imagining him here with her had brought to the surface.

So now, with her dreams made reality, with Domenico's strength surrounding her, his hands caressing her body, the clean, male scent of his skin in her nostrils, she knew only too well what she had been missing; what had kept her from any real sense of rest every night they had been apart. The emptiness that only he could fill.

And she knew there was no way at all she could turn back now.

She didn't care if it was only for today, if this one last time with Domenico was all she would have, if they had any future—the future of which his appearance at the cottage seemed to hold out a promise to her. The only thing she had was here and now, and she had to grab at it with both hands because she felt that she would die if she did not.

And so she stirred once more under his imprisoning

weight, deliberately arching her back slightly to press herself against the heated swell of his erection, bringing her hands up to tug at the buttons on his shirt, working them from their fastenings.

'I've not forgotten,' she admitted roughly, hiding her face against his cheek so that she didn't have to look into his eyes as she spoke, pressing her lips so close to the olive-toned skin that she felt the faint beginnings of the dark stubble against their softness. 'Never forgotten. How could I?'

Domenico's response was a laugh of triumph, low in his throat, and his hands came up to help her with the buttons, swiftly and efficiently dealing with them in contrast to the fumbling hash she had been making of it. A couple of seconds and his shirt was free. Sitting up slightly, he pushed it back, shedding both it and the superbly tailored jacket in one go, tossing them to one side without a care for the way that the beautiful garments tumbled into a crumpled heap on the floor.

But she had forgotten this, Alice admitted to herself. Well, not forgotten how beautiful his skin was, how smooth and sleek, like hot olive silk, sliding tautly over the powerful muscles, the straight, square shoulders. But in her mind she had been unable to hold on to just how sensual a delight Domenico's stunning body was, both to look at and to touch. Across his chest it was hazed with jet-black hair that she had always loved to feel underneath her fingertips, tracing the lines of it along the powerful bones of his ribcage and down, down to where the most intensely masculine part of him throbbed below the narrow waist.

When she had thought that she would never be able to do so again, having the freedom to touch him in this way was such an erotic charge that it went straight to her head like a gulp of the strongest brandy, making her giddy with pleasure and excitement in the space of a heartbeat. She couldn't hold back, had to stroke, to caress, to *feel*. She even found the nerve to press her lips against the heated flesh, remembering the unique taste of his skin, the scent of it, the sensation of feeling the strong, heavy beat of his heart beneath her mouth, the sound of it like thunder in her ears.

'Alice!' Domenico groaned in raw response, his loss of control showing in the way that the sound of her name again became not the soft English pronunciation, but the much more exotic *Aleeece*, a version that only he had ever used.

Hard hands pushed under the fall of her hair, clenching round the shining dark length and wrenching her head back as he clamped his lips down savagely on her mouth again. Still holding her prisoner with one hand, he fumbled impatiently with his belt, the fastening of his trousers, cursing in violent Italian when the clasp would not open quickly enough.

'Let me…' Alice managed, scarcely any more in control or any less clumsy as she dealt with the fastening, slid down the zip so that his erection spilled, hot and hard, into her seeking hands.

And with that one, soft touch, any remaining control that Domenico possessed evaporated right away. With her name hissing through his teeth on a sound that was somehow both violent and tender, he pushed her back down against the pillows, one hand still holding her head at just the right angle so that he could kiss her hard and strong and deeply intimately. The other hand, more roughly, pulled at the scrap of satin and lace that was all the covering she still had on. So roughly that she heard the delicate material tear, felt the elastic band at the waist split completely.

Not that she cared a damn. All she cared about was the feel of Domenico's mouth on hers, the hot thrust and flavour of his tongue invading her, tasting the essence of her. And below her waist those knowing fingers were now wreaking havoc on her most intimate senses, touching, stroking, teasing, tantalising, *exciting*, until she felt that she would explode with the force of the sensual stimulation.

But just as she felt she must abandon herself totally to the stunning sensations, the wicked provocation stopped and Domenico pushed one long, hair-roughened knee between her thighs, moving her legs apart and opening her up to him.

'This is what I remember,' he muttered, his accent so thick and pronounced that the words were all but incomprehensible. 'This is what I had with you—what I wanted from you— what I always wanted…'

Wrenching his mouth from hers, he took a couple of seconds to administer a sensual onslaught to her breasts, taking first one and then the other nipple into his mouth and suckling hard, building up a pleasure so savage it was almost a torture to endure. And before she had come down from the brainstorm of delight that he'd created, he lifted his powerful body, positioning himself exactly at the spot where she craved him most, the hot power pushing at her throbbing core.

'And I've certainly never forgotten *this*…' he muttered, thick and raw, pushing himself into her in one long, powerful thrust.

Alice was already so close to total fulfilment that just the feel of him almost took her over the edge. In less than the space of a heartbeat she was clinging to him, arching her hungry body closer and closer, opening herself to him, welcoming the force of his possession.

He thrust in as deep as he could go, withdrew, but only to push forward again, hard and strong and utterly devastating. One more pulse was all it took to splinter Alice's control into tiny pieces and have her spinning wildly and totally into a whirling vortex of delight, abandoning herself so completely that she lost all track of time and place, lost consciousness, oblivious to anything but the explosive sensations that suffused her body, and the powerful, forceful, dominant male who had made her so entirely his.

And somewhere, in the seconds before the unconsciousness of ecstasy took her over completely, she heard Domenico's hoarse, wild cry of fulfilment and knew that he too had lost himself in the blazing consummation of their lovemaking.

She had no idea how long it took her to come back down to earth. She only knew that as she floated hazily, lazily, back to reality, her body still humming with the aftershocks of the wild delight that had taken hold of her, all she could hear in her mind, in her memory were the echoes of the words Domenico had said, the things he had revealed in the heat of their passion—and before.

I couldn't stay away.

You're not an easy woman to find.

And then that final, triumphant, totally abandoned declaration: *And I've certainly never forgotten this,* as he'd taken possession of her, made her his.

She wasn't too sure just what would happen now; didn't know quite what Domenico's next move might be or how he would want to deal with things, but right now she had to admit that she didn't really care.

All that mattered was that he was here, with her, in this bed. He had been looking for her and as soon as she had written to him he had come at once, not even hesitating, not phoning or writing but appearing here, in person, declaring that he couldn't stay away. And he had just made love to her in a way that surely revealed a depth of feeling she had never suspected before.

There might be some awkwardness; they certainly had a lot of things to sort out. She needed to know the truth about Pippa Marinelli, and she had yet to tell Domenico that he was about to become a father. But all that could wait until the right moment. They had time, she was sure of that. Time to talk, to *really* talk, to put things right—and then, hopefully, move forward into a future.

But for now, Domenico was back. He was in her bed, and he had just made wonderful, stunning, mind-blowing love to her. For now that would do. All the rest would follow in its own good time.

Sated, exhausted, wonderfully content, she drifted asleep.

Consciousness returned slowly. Swimming back to the surface from the deep, deep sleep into which she had fallen, it was the silence that struck her first.

Had Domenico fallen asleep too? Was he still asleep? Still in the relaxed, totally satisfied mood into which he had collapsed with a cry of fulfilment just after her own?

Now was the time that she could tell him, she thought. Now, while he was at ease and languid with pleasure. She could tell him the reason she had asked him to come here and hope to have a fair hearing. Maybe she could even have some hope of a future for herself and her child that included the baby's father.

But as she came more awake herself, she realised that this was an unexpected, uncomfortable, strained, *watchful* sort of silence. One that tugged at her nerves, twisting some uncertain, wary, uneasy sensation deep in the pit of her stomach. She had no idea what gave her that feeling. Domenico was still lying beside her; she could feel the heat of his long body, the dip in the mattress underneath his weight. He was probably, like her, just coming back to wakefulness.

And if she knew Domenico, he would be stirring in other ways too. He had always had extraordinary powers of recovery, and a demanding sexual appetite. Glorious, explosive, orgasmic as it had been, that one passionate coming together would not be enough to satisfy him. He would already be anticipating a repeat performance, perhaps was already aroused...

But some instinct warned her that that was not the case. There was something in the atmosphere that was not the indolent, sensual, indulgent feeling she had anticipated. Some unexpected tension in the powerful masculine frame next to her, some unusual rhythm to his breathing alerted her that his mood had changed—and not in the way that she had anticipated.

It sent a cold whisper of unease sliding down her spine, chilled the passion-warmed skin, stilled her stretching limbs.

Slowly, uncertainly, she opened her eyes and looked straight up into the cold bronze stare of the man beside her.

He had woken before her, in fact. Woken first and, levering himself up into a half-upright position, had rested his elbow on the pillow, supporting his dark head on one hand, and had been watching her silently and intently as she lay asleep. Perhaps it had been some unconscious awareness of that silent scrutiny, some touch on her skin as if that stare had an actual physical force, that had penetrated the depths of exhaustion into which she had fallen and brought her slowly back to consciousness. But she had no idea why.

And that stunning, harshly carved, beautifully masculine face above her was giving nothing away. His features might have been set in stone for all the response he gave to the tentative, uncertain smile she gave, the wary attempt at a greeting. The glowing eyes were hooded, all emotion hidden from her, and the sensual, sexy mouth was set in a firm, unyielding line, no trace of an answering smile curving it up at the corners.

'Hi...' she managed softly, trying for another smile, only to have it fade away weakly in the face of his unresponsive expression. 'H-how long have you been awake?'

Domenico ignored the question, not even sparing it a second or two of consideration. Instead he looked her up and down, his eyes pure ice as they took in her relaxed body, still sprawled in the indolent aftermath of the sexual explosion that had shaken her. A slow, emotionless assessment swept over her in the long moment before the gaze returned once more to her uncertain and watchful face.

'No fun any more, huh?' he drawled, obvious disbelief in every word. 'Well, I'm sorry, Alicia, *cara*—but I really don't believe you. I think that what happened just now proved you a liar. And not a very good one, at that.'

'I—I…'

Alice struggled for words, trying to find some answer, any answer for him, but failing miserably. She knew that the hot colour she could feel rushing into her face was flooding her body too, the rosy colour betraying the way his words had caught her on the raw, leaving her unable to find anything to say.

'I think that that very definitely comes under the heading *fun*,' Domenico went on, totally ignoring her consternation, her awkward attempt to respond. 'And it was the sort of *fun* I would very much like to enjoy again—and again—until I've had my fill. Which is why I came after you, *bella mia*. You see, you may have claimed that you were growing jaded, that you were no longer getting what you wanted from our relationship, but I was most definitely *not* getting tired. I still want you—more than ever, in fact. And as long as I want you, then this relationship continues. No woman walks out on me—none ever has and none ever will.'

Leaning forward, he dropped a kiss on her startled mouth, but it was a cold, emotionless kiss, a kiss of pure control and not of feeling. There was not even any hint of passion or desire in it. All emotion had been wiped from it, leaving it cold and indifferent, chilling her right through to her soul.

'This relationship isn't over, Alice, not until I say so. As long as I want you, you stay—and you only leave when I give you permission to go.'

CHAPTER FOUR

ALICE felt as if that kiss had been a slap in the face.

A hard, cruel, cold-blooded slap that had knocked all the sense from her thoughts, leaving her gasping for breath like a stranded fish, her mind reeling in pain.

'I... You...'

If he had woken her by dumping a bucket full of icy water right over her head, she couldn't have been more shocked, more horrified. With a terrible sense of devastation she felt all her hopes and dreams, those lovely warm, anticipatory dreams, those promising, positive dreams, evaporate out of her heart, leaving her shivering in shock as reality hit home.

As long as I want you, you stay.

That was why Domenico had come after her. Not because he still cared about her—if in fact he had ever really cared—but because he felt he owned her. He regarded her more as a possession, as something that was his and stayed his as long as he wanted it to.

The thought slashed at her, stabbing straight to her weak and foolish heart and wounding it so badly she thought she might faint from the pain. In an instinctive reaction of self-protection she grabbed at the sheets, yanking them up to cover her exposed body, needing desperately to hide at least some part of her from those coldly assessing, coldly possessive eyes.

But somehow the gesture had exactly the opposite effect. Eyes like bronze chips of ice watched her frantic reaction with an almost analytical interest. Domenico was saying nothing, his beautifully carved features expressing nothing, but there was something in his stare, in the set of that once sensual, now deeply controlled mouth that said without words that he regarded her response as foolish and totally unnecessary. After all, he'd seen everything there was to see, touched everything, kissed everything, so what was the point in trying to hide now?

Because those kisses had been Judas kisses! Alice wanted to fling at him. Because they had been lying, deceiving gestures, seeming to speak of caring—she had even been foolish enough to allow the word *love* into her mind. And all the time he had been thinking only of power, of a ruthless need to impose his dominance over her, and to get her exactly where he wanted her—in his bed and at his mercy.

'I don't….' She tried again but her voice still wasn't ready to express how she felt. Shock seemed to have paralysed her vocal cords and as soon as she tried to speak she just managed a couple of words before the sound faded into an embarrassing and revealing squeak.

'You don't…?' Domenico questioned and his faintly mocking tone caught her on the raw, new strength flaring through her, her courage bolstered by a wave of anger.

'Don't I get any say in this matter?'

'Any say?'

Domenico appeared to consider the question, though she was quite sure that his mind was already made up. That he knew exactly what he was going to say—and that no, her opinion didn't matter at all.

'I think you've already made your feelings only too plain,' he declared, leaning back against the pillows with his arms crossed behind him, his head resting on them. The movement made the sheet, all that covered him, slide lower at his narrow waist, almost exposing his hips, but unlike her he appeared totally unconcerned by his near-nakedness. Instead he looked totally at home—totally in control.

'I have?'

Domenico nodded his dark head.

'Would you be here if you hadn't? I don't remember forcing you to come to bed with me. In fact, I seem to recall that you were only too willing.'

'I...'

Alice tried to growl a protest then found she couldn't think of any way of continuing and she stared down at the sheet that covered her, her fingers moving restlessly to pleat the white cotton over and over on her knees. The glare she directed at the nervous gesture was the one she wanted to turn on Domenico, directing it right into his arrogant, smug face, but the knowledge of how she had been wrong-footed held her back.

Her own voice rang in her ears, the cries of delight she had been unable to restrain, the moans of encouragement she had given him coming back to haunt her, now sounding like the worst reproaches, all the more embarrassing because she couldn't deny them even in the privacy of her own thoughts.

'Are you saying now that you didn't want to make love—?'

'No!' Alice flung out, cutting in before he could complete the sentence.

It was precisely because she had thought—foolishly, weakly, *stupidly*—that he might have been doing something close to making *love* that she had wanted it so much. But now that it was obvious she had been blindly deluded, there was no way on earth that she was going to admit to the truth.

What could she say?

I thought you were here because you really cared for me. Because you realised that you didn't want that other woman. I thought you had come because you realised you missed me and that you wanted me back.

Well, yes, he'd felt that all right but not in the way she'd been weak enough to allow herself to believe.

'I'm not saying that I didn't *want* you. Only that…'

Suddenly unable to stay where she was a moment longer, unable to bear lying here, like this, stark naked, beside an equally nude male, Alice pushed herself out of the bed, dragging the sheet with her, and reached for the white cotton robe that was hanging on the back of the door.

Ramming her arms into the sleeves, she pulled the soft material round her and belted the garment tight around her waist. It was a futile gesture, she knew, and far, far too late, but at least she felt better for being clothed, as if the robe provided some much-needed armour against Domenico's barbed remarks.

'Only that…?' came the pointed prompt from behind her, sparking wild anger, making her whirl round to him in a fury.

'Only that my wanting you sexually doesn't mean you own me!'

'I don't want to *own* you,' Domenico tossed back. 'And I don't recall ever saying that I did! But I am saying that I'm not yet tired of this relationship, that I still want you—and I'm damn sure you want me.'

'But I ended the relationship!'

'And I just restarted it.'

'You can't restart it—not without my agreement.'

With the haze of anger slowly fading from her eyes, Alice suddenly deeply regretted the fact that she had turned round. She hadn't thought that when she'd got up and taken the sheet with her, she'd also snatched away the only covering Domenico had. Not that he appeared to care—damn him. Instead he lay there, totally at his ease, as if only too aware of the glorious picture he made lying there, the golden skin seeming to glow in contrast to the white of the sheets, his long body fully relaxed and shockingly beautiful, almost spotlit by the shaft of sunlight that came through the bedroom window.

There wasn't an ounce of spare flesh on his muscular frame and he was everything a man should be. Strong, lean, shockingly handsome with those dark bronze eyes and black, black hair. His long limbs were arranged with a supreme elegance that showed them to their best advantage and Alice felt her throat dry at the memory of how it had felt to be held close to such male beauty, the feelings that had stormed through her at the touch of his hands, the kiss of that gorgeous mouth.

And she had only just let herself remember how much that feeling meant to her. She had given in to the longing she had felt and like an addict had returned to the source of her obsession. Only to regret it instantly and to wish she had never given in to the craving.

Because now she had to wean herself off it all over again. She had to endure once more the longing and the despair that being without what she most wanted could bring. She had been through it all once and had barely survived. Now she had to do it again—and this time it would be so much worse because she knew how hard it would be.

'Shouldn't you put some clothes on?'

Domenico's response was a nonchalant shrug that infuriatingly made Alice reflect on just how broad and strong his shoulders were, the impressiveness of muscle sliding under the tanned skin.

'I'd rather have a shower,' he returned. 'In fact I had hoped that we could have one together.'

'Hope away,' Alice retorted. 'That's something that's never going to happen.'

A faint smile greeted her angry outburst, one that only served to fan the flames of her irritation.

'You used to enjoy it. It was something we always did after—'

'Exactly! I *used* to enjoy it!'

She couldn't bear it if he said those lying words 'after we made love' once again.

'Past tense. It *was* something we *did*…'

'And something I would like to do again.'

Domenico was uncoiling his long body as he spoke, stretching lazily and getting to his feet. Having wanted him to move from his place on the bed, Alice now found herself wishing that he hadn't done any such thing. On his feet, he was too tall, too imposing, too *male* for the confined and very feminine space of her bedroom. The width of his shoulders blocked the sun from the window, casting a shadow over her face, and he was once again having to stoop slightly to avoid hitting his head on the sloping roof.

'But it's something I would *not* want to do again!'

'Why not?'

To her relief, Domenico had at least reached for his undershorts and trousers, pulling them on but leaving the waist and zip unfastened. Disturbingly, it didn't seem to make any difference to the heat of the blood in her veins, the heavy, sensual thud of her heart. Her fingers itched to reach out again and touch that smooth, golden skin and she had to cram them fiercely into the pockets of the white robe to keep them under control.

Oh, why had he had to mention those showers they'd shared? Showers that had been so much a part of every lovemaking session that they had been almost a continuation of the passion, rather than a cooling-off after it. In fact, more times than not they merged straight into another erotic encounter. The memory of the times they had made love up against cool, smooth tiles, with the warm water sluicing down on them, the scent of the shower gel in her nostrils, the bubbles foaming over her body, made her tremble in instant and devastating reaction.

'Is that something else you've decided is no longer any "fun"? Well, you'll have to forgive me if I don't believe you.'

Those deep-set eyes drifted to the bed, scanning the crumpled sheets, the disarray created by their passionate coupling such a short time before.

'Seems to me we had a lot of *fun*…'

Just what was going through this woman's head? Domenico asked himself. It seemed that she was changing her mood and her mind so often that it made his head spin. She had been so many different people since he had arrived at this cottage and not one of them had been the Alice he knew—or thought he knew.

No… Once more his eyes went back to the mess they had made of the bed.

There was one time, one place when she had been the Alice he knew—the Alice he wanted. In that bed, in his arms, she had been the woman with whom he had spent six glorious months. The woman who could make him want her just by breathing. Whose smile had an effect like setting a match to the fuse that led straight to his libido, triggering off an explosion in seconds.

The woman without whom his life and his bed had seemed so empty and cold ever since she had walked out on him.

And the woman who had so obviously been lying when she'd declared that their relationship was no longer any fun.

But she was equally obviously determined not to admit to

any such thing, damn her. For some hidden personal reason she was hell-bent on denying the truth, and for the life of him he couldn't see why.

Well, he was damned if he was going to let her get away with it. She was lying and one way or another he was going to make her admit that she was.

'Well, I hope it was enough *fun* to keep you satisfied for the rest of your life,' she snarled. 'Because, believe me, it's never going to happen again.'

'No?'

He almost laughed out loud at the furious indignation of her tone, the way that she drew herself up to her full height, the blue-eyed glare she flung right into his face. Couldn't she see that the very drama of the way she was behaving, the over-the-top reaction to everything he said, was making it impossible to believe her? It was a total contradiction to the way she had been in his arms, the wild, passionate creature she had been just a short time ago.

'You don't mean that.'

'Oh, don't I?'

That tone was enough to crush the urge to laugh, make him swallow his amusement down before it escaped. Laughter was not a good move at the moment. It would just make her angrier than ever, and that would just make sure that she wouldn't admit to whatever was bugging her.

Because something was bugging her. Something she wasn't yet prepared to admit to. But he would get it out of her. He was getting damn tired of her playing games, blowing hot and cold; a passionate sex queen one minute, an ice maiden the next.

'I meant it when I said I was leaving, didn't I? You didn't believe me then, if I remember rightly!'

That particular dig hit home, Domenico admitted. He hadn't believed her when she'd said she was going. He'd thought it was just a temporary storm, one they could easily weather. Then he'd come home to an empty house, an empty bed. Not even a note on the table.

'I don't know what the hell you do mean!' he exploded. 'You haven't even given me any sort of an explanation for why you walked out in the first place. One moment everything was fine, the next—'

'The next I found out about your other woman!'

'You what?'

It was so unexpected it hit him in the face like a slap. His head actually went back with the shock of it, his eyes narrowing sharply. She'd certainly meant that. It was there in her tone, in the way she held herself so stiffly upright. The stony-eyed look she'd turned on him.

'Explain that!' he rapped out. 'I want to know just what the hell you mean.'

Alice's chin lifted a shade higher, the muscles in her jaw tight and stiff. But her gaze didn't flinch from meeting his head on, the blue eyes colder now than they had been in the first moments after his arrival.

'What does the phrase usually mean? Don't tell me your English isn't good enough to understand.'

'Oh, I understand what it means all right, damn it!'

Domenico took a swift, angry step towards her, then thought better of it as he saw the way she was fighting with herself not to shrink back in the face of his advance.

'What I don't get is just what *you* mean.'

That determined, stubborn chin went even higher. And her eyes flashed with a mixture of anger and rejection that told him that this time was real. That this time was something she was not about to change her mind over.

'I mean just two words,' she declared fiercely. 'And I'm sure even you will understand what they mean.'

Domenico leaned back against the window frame, crossing his arms across his chest.

'And those two words are?'

Alice took a deep breath, hesitated briefly then brought it out in a rush.

'Pippa Marinelli.'

Pippa Marinelli!

His thoughts spun, his brain seeming to short-circuit in a shower of sparks. He had tried to be so careful; he didn't want anyone finding out about his meetings with Pippa and jumping to conclusions.

He'd thought she would never know.

'How the hell did you find out about her?'

CHAPTER FIVE

How had she found out?

A demand, Alice noted miserably; not a defence. Domenico hadn't attempted to deny the existence of Pippa Marinelli in his life. He hadn't tried to pretend he didn't know what she had meant by her accusation, or to say he didn't recognise the name.

Instead he had gone straight on to the attack with his biting query.

'Does it matter?' she managed, her voice giving way and breaking painfully in the middle of the question. 'Isn't it enough that I know?'

'Of course it matters.'

Domenico's eyes were blazing in cold rejection. The skin on his face seemed to have been draw tight over the stunning bone structure and his mouth had clamped tight into a cold, unyielding line. But then what had she expected? Guilt? Embarrassment?

He didn't look as if he had a guilty bone in his body.

'Then you should be more careful about leaving your mobile phone lying around.'

'You answered it? Read my messages?'

He didn't need to launch into a savage roar to show how

furious he was at just the thought. His anger was there in the white marks etched around his eyes and his mouth, the deadly venom in the dangerously quiet voice.

'Of course not! What do you think I am? But I—I did pick it up. It must have fallen from your pocket or something—I found it under the bed. And the name—her name—was still on the screen.'

There had been other signs too. A letter, hastily pushed aside when she'd come to him in his office. Under other circumstances she might not have noticed but, with the missed phone call still in her mind, the swift glance that had caught the name 'Pippa' had alerted her suspicions.

She had tried not to connect the unknown woman's name with Domenico's frequent unexplained absences, and perhaps if things had been easier between them she might have succeeded. But for weeks he had been difficult and unapproachable, rarely coming home until late, going out again early in the morning. The most damning evidence had been the reduction in the times that they made love. Some nights—many of them—she had been asleep before he came home. Or he had made some excuse that he had to work on something important, leaving her alone in the bed that then seemed so much bigger than even its king-size label merited.

And at the same time there had been so many swiftly broken-off conversations. Times when the phone had been put down as she came through the door, or when Domenico had said he couldn't talk right now but he'd ring back later.

'So you didn't talk to her?'

'No, I didn't—but would it have mattered if I did? I presume you'd have had some story ready—some cover plan! But you obviously weren't quite as discreet as you thought. People must have seen you—they were starting to talk.'

The faint pause was meant to give him a moment to say

something—anything—and she fully expected him to use it to jump to his own defence. But Domenico didn't say a word. Instead he stayed exactly where he was, withdrawn, unmoving, his expression as still and cold as if it had been carved from marble. Even the brilliant golden-brown eyes were hooded and unrevealing as he watched her face, obviously waiting for her to say more.

'Do—do you know what it's like?' she flung at him in the end, unable to bear the silence any longer. 'Do you know how it feels to be in a restaurant—in the ladies' loo in an elegant hotel of all places!—and to hear three women gossiping about you? To hear them call you a poor, deluded, naive fool—a woman who doesn't even know that her partner's playing away—that he's been seen in there and in two other places with his latest squeeze—his new mistress, Pippa Marinelli?'

'You left me because of gossip?' The contempt in Domenico's voice threatened to flay the skin from her bones.

'Not just—'

'She isn't my mistress!'

It came low and hard and deadly. No hesitation. He didn't even attempt to raise his voice above a dark mutter, but he meant to be heard. There was no doubt about that.

Just as there was no room for doubt about the conviction in his tone, a conviction that cut straight through what she had been about to say and had her freezing into silence, her mouth still partly open, eyes wide, staring straight at him.

'What did you say?'

You heard! The dark scowl he turned on her needed no words to express his meaning, but all the same he still took the trouble to repeat what he had said, making it clear that he had no intention of being misunderstood.

'Pippa Marinelli is not my mistress. I don't give a damn what the gossips say. I don't care what amazing scenarios that wild imagination of yours has created—none of them are true. I'll say this only once more and then never again. Pippa Marinelli is not my mistress.'

There was no mistaking the conviction in his voice; in his face. Alice could have no doubt that he was telling her the truth. He couldn't be lying and meet her accusing glare with that steady, direct gaze. There was no deceit in those clear bronze eyes, nothing hidden or fake.

'Do you believe me?'

What else could she say? 'If you say so, then yes—I believe you.' Though it tore at her heart to see the way his tight muscles relaxed, the faint smile that softened his mouth.

Two months before, yesterday perhaps, even an hour or so ago, she would have given the world to see that. She would have dreamed of being told that her suspicion about Pippa Marinelli was just fantasy, the creation of a combination of cruel gossip and awkward coincidences. Would have prayed to see Domenico here, with that smile on his face, knowing he could explain away her fears, put her mind at rest.

But it wasn't possible now.

Those dreams had been before Domenico had appeared on her doorstep with seductive words on his lips and a ruthless determination in his heart. Before he had enticed her into bed with the practised ease of a man who was used to getting what he wanted, whenever he wanted, and taken her blind foolish heart and used it for his own selfish purposes.

Before he had declared that she could only leave him when he gave her permission to go.

'I believe you,' she repeated, but it was a low, despondent sigh rather than a confident statement of fact.

'Good.'

Domenico had pushed himself away from the wall, standing upright. He was about to come towards her, about to take her in his arms. She could see his intent in his face.

She had to stop him. If he touched her, she would be lost. And although it hurt like hell to do so, she forced herself to put up a hand to stop him.

'But if she's not your mistress then who is she?'

That stopped him all right. He stilled instantly, that smile fading in the blink of an eyelid, his expression hardening again, closing off from her.

'It's not important,' he said stiffly.

'It is to me.'

'It's none of your business. She's nothing to you.'

He caught the look she turned on him, the dark scowl growing blacker.

'I told you I'm not sleeping with her. What more do you want?'

Everything.

Nothing.

Alice didn't know which response to give.

It was the fact that he didn't see that was what mattered.

'You don't trust me,' he said.

'Trust was never the problem.'

And that was the truth; she saw that now. Pippa Marinelli had just been the last straw.

She had known for weeks—for months—that Domenico didn't really care for her. She had fallen head over heels in love with him and as a result had tumbled into his hands, his life—his bed—without hesitation and without thinking. And even when she had surfaced from the huge, heated pool of sensuality for just a brief moment, getting her head above water just enough to snatch in a much-needed cooling breath, a reality check, she had still not taken the time or the trouble to *think*.

She had just gone along with the delight of being in his

company, being able to make love with him, sharing his life. Domenico had been all the world to her. It was only much later that she began to realise, slowly and painfully, just how small a part of his world she actually was.

'So what was the problem? No—don't tell me...' Cynicism dripped from every word. 'You weren't having *fun* any more.'

'That's right!'

Alice tried to make the words sound casual, even flippant. She'd picked on that line as as good an excuse as she was going to get for leaving when the truth was that leaving was the last thing she had ever wanted to do. It fitted with the person she had been trying to be—the person she'd thought that Domenico wanted her to be.

They'd met by accident when Domenico had come into the restaurant where she had taken a temporary job as a waitress. Back home, in England, she'd been a management trainee in a big clothing store but she'd hated it. Throwing the job up, she'd decided on a working holiday in Italy while she took the time to think about her life, about where she wanted to go, what she wanted to do. She'd got as far as Florence, and gone no further. She'd met Domenico and immediately had the feeling that she'd come home. That she'd found the whole point to her life.

Domenico, however, hadn't felt that way at all.

Oh, he'd been attracted to her from the start. He couldn't have made that any plainer. He wanted her in his life, in his bed—but he didn't want anything more. As far as he was concerned, she was there for relaxation: someone to be seen on his arm when they went out; someone with whom he enjoyed the blazingly passionate desire that had flared between them from the first moment their eyes had met.

But he didn't want anything more. Words like commitment, a future, *love*, didn't come into his vocabulary. Within a very few weeks, Alice had known that she wanted—needed more. But Domenico was quite content with what they had.

She'd tried, she'd really tried to go along with it, and for a while it had worked. But the more she had tried to squash down her emotional needs, the more they grew. She had tried to put on a brave face, to act as if she was having the 'fun' she'd told Domenico was all she was looking for, but inside she felt as if her soul was dying. The love that was supposed to fill her life had instead made her feel lost and empty and alone.

So when she'd heard the gossip about Pippa Marinelli, she'd seen it as a lifeline—or a kick in the pants. Something to bring her up short and make her realise just what she was doing to herself. Was she going to stay around, living this half-life, just waiting until Pippa Marinelli—or some other new flame in Domenico's life—superseded her?

Better to jump before she was pushed. At least that way she still had some pride left—and the wound of separation would be cold and quick and clean. So hopefully that way it would heal much more quickly.

The problem was that she hadn't reckoned on being pregnant. *Pregnant!*

Oh, dear heaven, she'd actually forgotten why she had asked Domenico to come here in the first place! Events had caught her up, taken her so much by storm that she hadn't even had a moment to think about the truth.

But now she was forced to think of it, she had no idea what she was going to do. She had to tell Domenico about the baby; it was his child, after all, and as the father he had rights—if he wanted them. But would the Domenico to whom commitment was a dirty word want anything to do with fatherhood and all the ties that brought?

Always supposing she gathered up the courage to tell him. She had to tell him but she didn't know how. It would have been hard enough at the start, when he'd arrived in that stiffly distant mood. But this cold-voiced, cold-eyed monster who stood before her was something else again. That black fury that blazed in his eyes scared her so much that she didn't think she could even remember her own name if he'd asked her what it was.

'Our relationship had stopped being right a while before I left,' she managed, her tongue stumbling awkwardly over the words, perhaps because they were closer to the truth than anything she had said before. 'It wasn't what I wanted any more.'

'So how much *fun* did you want to have?' Domenico enquired now, each word as cold as steel, scorn sharpening them to a brutal knife edge.

She'd been restless that last couple of weeks, he reflected, looking back on the time after Alice had moved in with him. But he'd thought that it was just a temporary thing. It would pass. His time with Pippa had been so important; he'd assumed that Alice would still be there when everything was done. He'd been wrong.

'Where did we go wrong? Not enough parties?'

Her eyes actually widened in outrage as she turned them on him, that neat chin lifting again as she glared at him.

'It wasn't like that at all!'

'So what was it like, *bella*? What else should I have given you? More clothes? More travel?'

'I said—'

'Oh, I know what you said!' Domenico's hand came up between them in a wild, slashing movement as if cutting off any hope of a connection to her. 'Not what you wanted. But what *did* you want?'

What the hell was she holding out for? Surely she knew she only had to ask and he would give it to her?

'More money? Should I have given you a bigger allowance?'

'*No!*'

She actually looked appalled, her skin whitening over her cheekbones, her big blue eyes like dark pools.

Not money, then. It should have made him feel better to know that she didn't just see him as a bottomless wallet, a limitless credit card, but somehow it didn't. Just what the hell…?

Then suddenly he thought he had it. There was only one other thing this could all be about.

'Oh, I get it. Are you angling for marriage? Is that it, Alicia, *cara*? You want a gold band on your finger?'

It looked as if he'd hit the target, right in the centre of the gold. For once she didn't have a word to say, and that was so unlike the Alice he knew that her silence might as well have been a clear, definite statement of fact. He'd caught her on the raw there, left her gasping for breath, unable to deny the fact that he'd hit home. It made his throat tighten, brought a sour taste to his mouth, to realise that she was, after all, going for the big one.

It was marriage or nothing, it seemed. That was why she had walked out on him. He was being held to ransom, and the price was a ring on her finger and his name on a marriage certificate.

'I told you—I don't do marriage, not ever. I thought I made that clear from the start.'

'You did.'

It was a strangled little voice, the words barely comprehensible, but Domenico was past caring. If she could deliver ultimatums, then he could too.

'There's only one thing that would ever make that a possibility and that's never going to happen…'

Something had changed in her face. A new expression had come into her eyes, a haunted, hunted look that gave him a grim sense of satisfaction to see it. His lovely Alice was finally beginning to realise that her dreams of becoming

Signora Domenico Parrisi were just that—dreams. And they had no more hope of coming true than he had of claiming an English title and setting up home in a castle.

She had gambled all she had in her hand on the fact that if she walked out he would come after her and offer her anything she wanted just to get her back. Gambled and lost. OK, so he was here—he had come after her—but marriage wasn't on the table. And the fact was that he doubted if she'd really want it if she knew the whole truth.

So she'd played her trump card by making it plain that if he didn't offer marriage she wasn't staying around. But there was one important thing she hadn't reckoned on, one thing that could wreck her plan completely.

His eyes went back to the disordered bed, the covers still tangled and dishevelled in the evidence of the passion they had shared. A passion she had been every bit as unable to resist as he had. Cool, calculating Alice—an Alice he had to admit he hadn't even guessed existed—had made one fatal miscalculation when working out the odds.

Banking on the fact that he would be unable to stay away, she hadn't taken into account the possibility that she might not be able to control her own feelings quite as well as she had hoped. She had had him at her beck and call, but one touch, one kiss and suddenly all bets were off. She might not like it—she clearly didn't want to admit it—but she could no more resist him than he could control his passions where she was concerned. His cool, controlled Englishwoman wanted him so much that when they kissed every last trace of sanity flew out the window.

'What…?'

Alice seemed to be having trouble forming any words at all. Probably because she had just realised that she had no more cards to play. Her blue eyes looked faintly dazed with the shock of being outmanoeuvred, and she slicked a soft pink tongue over suddenly parched lips.

'What would that be?' she croaked, reaching out a hand to grab hold of a nearby chair as if she suddenly needed its support.

'Nothing either of us would want to even consider right now. I don't think we need to concern ourselves with anything more than the fact that I'm not looking for marriage, and if you're wise neither will you.'

'If I'm *wise*?'

She made it into a sound of disgust at the same time that it had a questioning note at the end.

'And just why would I need to be wise?'

'If you want this relationship to continue.'

Alice's breath actually hissed in between her teeth and her eyes sparked in irritation.

'I seem to recall that you were the one insisting that we stay together. If you remember, *you* were the one laying down the law and declaring that things weren't over until you said they were. I'd have been much happier if you'd stayed well away!'

'That's not what you were saying a short time ago.'

Once more Domenico's eyes swept over the disordered bed then up to Alice's white, tense face, noting the sudden burn of colour high along each cheekbone, the way that her teeth dug into the softness of her lower lip.

'With your body, if not actually in words.'

'What my body was saying…'

The tremor in her voice made the words break up, but the stiffness of the words, the tightness of that kissable mouth made it plain that it was a cold anger rather than any upset that made her tongue stumble. In fact he doubted if he had ever heard such a note of ice in her tone in all the time he had known her. He had definitely caught her on the raw with his comments about marriage.

'What my *body* was saying was that you're a sexy guy. I thought so when I first met you—and nothing has happened to change that opinion of you! You're an extremely attractive man and you must know that. There's no need for false modesty.'

It was almost a compliment, but that freezing tone, the flash of antagonism that turned the blue eyes almost silver warned him that it was meant as anything but. That look, combined with the way in which she had spoken, turned the phrase 'extremely attractive man' into something that was light-years away from the surface meaning, and made that 'sexy guy' sting like a dark insult.

'But I don't have to want a relationship with someone—or even to like them—to want to go to bed with them. I'm a woman, I have as much red blood in my veins as any man, and I have needs as much as the next person.'

'And my arrival just happened to coincide with a particularly—needy moment?'

Domenico didn't even recognise his own intonation. But at least it accurately echoed the mixture of thoughts in his head—scepticism, scorn and sheer anger at the thought that he had been used uppermost in all of them.

'That's right.'

She even smiled as she said it but it was a cool, distant, brittle little smile, one that had no warmth or genuine amusement in it.

'And I think you felt the same way. I mean—have you found a replacement for me yet?'

'Have I...?'

The directness of the question actually stopped his thoughts dead just for a second. The next moment, shock was replaced by a rush of outrage that she should consider him so shallow, and so irresponsible.

'No, I damn well haven't! What the hell do you think I am?'

He wouldn't have thought it was possible but her second smile was even tighter and more distant than the first.

'Frustrated? Two whole months of abstinence—how wonderfully restrained of you! Then you'll know how I was feeling. It must have been mutual.'

'Just what—?'

'What am I saying? Do I have to put it bluntly? OK—I'll do that. It was a moment of madness, nothing more! But now that madness is over and I really should thank you.'

'Thank me?'

If Alice had turned into a furious cobra, spitting venom right into his face, he couldn't have been more appalled. He didn't recognise the ice-eyed, cold-voiced woman who stood before him. The total transformation took his breath away, scrambling his brains. Domenico reached for his shirt as a distraction and pulled it on. He started to fasten the first couple of buttons then abandoned the enterprise, leaving the rest undone.

'Yes, thank you! If I'd had any stupid ideas of thinking about taking you back, then you've made me realise just how foolish a decision that would be. To put it very bluntly, Domenico, you were an itch I had to scratch. But that was all. And now I'd be really grateful if you'd leave.'

'I don't think so,' Domenico declared, not moving an inch.

'And I don't *think*; I know,' Alice corrected pointedly. 'I know I want you out of here.'

Dark head high, long, slender back straight and stiff, she marched to the door and pulled it open.

'Now,' she added meaningfully when he didn't move.

But Domenico's attention had been distracted. Either the

waft of air from the way she had stalked across the room, or one created by her pulling the door open so violently had caused a draught that had set a small pile of papers flying from their place on top of the chest of drawers. Floating in the air for a moment, they had blown partway across the carpet and come down to land on the floor almost at his feet.

And a heading on the topmost sheet had caught his eye.

Caught and held it in shocked disbelief.

'Domenico?' Alice suddenly became aware of his distraction—and the reason for it. 'I said I wanted you to— No!'

Abandoning her position by the door, she dashed forward, one hand outstretched to stop him just as Domenico bent to pick up the letter, his eyes fixed on the printed words.

'No!' she said but in a very different and much less assertive tone of voice.

'Yes…'

Domenico's own hand went out but towards her, with the aim of keeping her securely at a distance while he read and reread the words on the page before him. For a moment Alice struggled, fought to get free, to grab at the letter, but he clamped one big hand around both her wrists and held her still, his eyes on what he was reading.

It took some absorbing.

In fact, he had read it twice and still couldn't believe that he had actually seen what was in front of him.

Not that the letter was long. In fact, quite the opposite. It was short and to the point.

Very much to the point.

Dear Miss Howard…appointment…antenatal clinic…

Antenatal clinic.

No matter how many times he read those words, they still said the same thing.

Antenatal clinic.

'Are you…?'

He turned to glare at Alice, took one look at her face and knew that the question didn't have to be asked.

'You're pregnant!'

Alice had expected a roar of anger or some sort of hostile re-action. This cold, calm—far too calm—declaration of fact was unnerving. Its very coolness, its total composure rocked her sense of reality, knocking her mentally off balance and leaving her floundering for words.

'This is a date and time for an antenatal appointment,' Domenico went on, as clinical as the letter itself. 'You are pregnant.'

'I— Yes,' Alice managed, because there was nothing else to say.

Abruptly Domenico released her hands, letting them drop so suddenly that it jarred her shoulders, adding physical dis-comfort to the mental distress she was feeling.

'Is it mine?'

His hands were busy, surprisingly so. He was buttoning up the rest of his shirt, fastening it across his chest, the action making it look as if he was closing it against her, creating a defensive shield against her.

'Of course. Who else's could it be?'

'How?'

For the tiniest moment, her shaken mind toyed with the idea of a flippant response. Something on the lines of 'Well, you know what we were just doing in that bed…?'

But even as she thought of it her throat closed up in panic at the anticipation of the way he would react, and she decided that it was much safer to take the question the way she knew he meant it.

'That time when I had the stomach upset. I took the Pill,

but being ill must have—have affected how it worked. I'm not quite ten weeks…'

Just for a second, his dark eyes searched her face, probing deeply so that she had to struggle to meet that searing gaze. But then, just as she thought she couldn't bear it any longer, he gave a single hard, decisive nod.

'Mine,' he said with unexpected firmness, but somehow his easy acceptance of her assertion did nothing to set her mind at rest. He believed the baby was his, but instead of reassuring, his statement set every nerve tingling, lifting the tiny hairs all over her skin in a way that made her shiver in fearful reaction.

'Yes…' she began but her voice clashed with Domenico's.

'Mine,' he repeated on a very different note. 'I see.'

He wasn't looking at her. In fact, he was looking down and it took her a minute to realise that he was searching for his shoes. A moment later he had found them, stamped his feet into them without even troubling to find his socks, at the same time snatching up his jacket from the nearby chair.

'Domenico…' Alice tried but when he turned to her at the sound of her voice and she saw the wild blaze of fury in his eyes, her voice failed her completely and she froze into stillness and silence.

'You're carrying my baby—my child—and you never told me.'

'N-no—but…'

'And you would have let me walk out of here, without saying a word!'

But that's why you're here, she wanted to say. *That's why I asked you to come here. What I said we have to talk about.*

But to her shock and horror she was confronting the empty air. Without another word, Domenico had turned on his heel and marched across the room, disappearing out of the door before she had time to take in what was happening.

Still unable to move, she heard his heavy, rapid footsteps descending the stairs, the sound of the front door being wrenched open and then slamming shut again behind him.

It was when she heard the roar of the car's engine outside, the spurt of the gravel under the wheels as he put the power-ful vehicle into gear and sped away, that she realised what had happened.

After all her failed attempts earlier to get him to go, it seemed that the revelation of her pregnancy had achieved just what she had wanted. But at precisely the point at which she hadn't wanted him to leave at all.

CHAPTER SIX

WELL, if she faced facts squarely, Alice told herself as the afternoon faded into dusk, dusk into rainy, miserable night, she was no worse off than she had been at the start of the day.

When this morning had dawned, she had been living in this cottage, on her aunt's generosity, no job, no money, alone and pregnant.

She still was.

Nothing had changed. Domenico had blown in and out of her day like a fierce, icy hurricane. He had turned things upside down and inside out for a few brief moments, and then he was gone again, heading out of the door and driving off down the lanes as if all the devils in hell were after him. She was still in exactly the same position as she had been when she'd woken that morning. So why did it feel so much worse?

Because this morning, she had had hope. Oh, she knew it had been a wild, foolish, totally unfounded sort of hope. But she had had a tiny thread of hope.

Hope!

Alice flung herself away from the window out of which she had been staring sightlessly as darkness fell over the little garden.

Hope? Who was she trying to kid?

She might have dreamed that Domenico would listen when she told him she was unexpectedly pregnant. That he would offer to stand by her, to help, to be there for the baby. But from the moment he had appeared things had started to go crazy. She had felt as if she was on a wild, whirling carousel, unable to get off. Every time she had thought to tell him the truth something had interfered or it hadn't seemed like the right time.

Now it seemed that there had been no such thing as the *right* time.

Domenico didn't do marriage, and his reaction just now showed that he most definitely didn't do fatherhood.

Slowly she smoothed her hand down over the front of the jeans and lilac T-shirt that she had dressed herself in again shortly after Domenico had stormed out. She had made herself do it, telling herself that if, just supposing, he changed his mind and came back again, she didn't want him thinking that she had been sitting here all that time, too miserable even to get dressed. It might have been close to the truth but she was determined that she wouldn't let him see that.

If he came back.

She'd still been fool enough to hang on to that tiny thread of hope. But not now.

Hope had gone right out of the window. She was on her own with this one.

Her hand slowed, stopped, curving protectively over her lower body. Over the spot where her baby lay, still only a tiny form, not even creating a bump to show its existence.

'It's just you and me now, sweetheart,' she whispered. 'Just you and me.'

But she'd take care of this child, she vowed to herself. It might not have been conceived in the best of circumstances, and her heart might ache desperately for the father who didn't want it—the man she loved—but she would love and care for his child as best she could.

And she'd start by having an early night. She'd take a cup of tea up to bed…

The sound of a car pulling up outside was so much something she had dreamed of in the loneliness of the afternoon that for a couple of seconds she refused to believe it was actually real. It couldn't be. It had to be something that her imagination had conjured up out of a longing that went so deep that she didn't dare even acknowledge it in her heart.

It wasn't happening…

But the slam of a metal door, the hurried stride of footsteps over the gravel could not be denied.

Halfway between the living room and the kitchen Alice froze, her heart thudding painfully high up in her throat so that she could hardly breathe. The handle of the front door turned, it was pushed open roughly, and Domenico strode into the narrow hallway, coming to an abrupt halt at the sight of her standing there.

He didn't say a word, and Alice found that she couldn't speak either. Her throat had dried, her tongue felt like a block of wood in her mouth, and all she could do was stare, unable to believe her eyes.

The wild weather outside had whipped his jet-black hair into disarray, spattering it with tiny diamond studs of raindrops. Similar drops of moisture spattered his face, looking unnervingly like the glisten of tears and spiking the thick, lush darkness of his lashes around those incredible eyes.

Tears? Domenico? Don't be stupid, Alice berated herself. Tears were another thing that Domenico didn't do.

The jacket he was wearing was unfastened and the wind had blown it wide open so that the rain had soaked into his shirt, plastering it against the hard, tight lines of his chest. She could see the golden tone of his skin, the black haze of chest hair through the saturated material in a way that made her wonder if he had been exposed to much more of the storm than just the brief walk from his car to her door. Certainly the heavy damp patches on his shoulders and sleeves seemed to indicate that he had been out of his car before this, and for quite some time. The black trousers clung soddenly to his muscular thighs too, and his shoes were spattered with mud.

He still had no socks on, she realised with a jolt to her heart. The glimpse of his ankles, which she could see between the hem of his trousers and those muddy shoes, were as bare as when he had marched out of her house several hours before. For some reason that realisation caught on something raw and sensitive deep inside her, making her gasp in sudden shock and pushing her into uncertain speech.

'D-Domenico…' she managed, cursing the inanity of it, the way that her voice shook in reaction to his sudden appearance. 'You came back.'

His beautiful mouth twisted in cynical response to the obviousness of her comment.

'I came back,' he echoed her words with a dark, mocking irony. 'As you see.'

'But—why? What are you doing here?'

'Isn't it obvious?'

The brusque, aggressive lift of his head dislodged a raindrop from the raven's-wing fall of his hair over the broad forehead and sent it splashing down onto his cheek. Domenico scrubbed at it with the back of his hand in an impatient, angry gesture, flicking the moisture off his fingers so that it fell against the cream-painted wall of the hallway.

'I've come back for my child.'

If he had shaken himself like a big black aggressive dog, until all the raindrops on his hair, his face, his clothes had sprayed over her in a cold shower, it couldn't have brought a rush of ice to her soul as quickly as his words. Alice felt as if some freezing hand had enclosed her heart in a cruel grip and was squeezing, hard and tight, taking all the life out of her.

He'd come back because of the baby she was carrying—but not because he cared at all about her.

'But—you can't have the baby without me...'

Domenico dismissed her protest with an arrogant, impatient wave of his hand. That was a small matter, the gesture said, and one that was easily dealt with.

'I know,' he said, hooded eyes clashing with her stunned, bewildered gaze. 'Of course I know that—that's why I've decided that we are going to marry.'

He'd known it was the only answer from the minute that he'd seen that damn letter. In fact, if his brain had been working properly he'd have proposed right there and then.

No, not proposed. Proposing meant asking, giving the other person an option, presenting them with a choice and a chance to say no. He didn't intend that Alice should have any such choice.

Just as he had no other option in this matter.

There was no choice. They had made a child between them, and so everything else had to take second place. No child of his was going to grow up not knowing who its father was, as he had done. The baby had to have his name and so they had to marry. After that, they could take a breath; take a look at the situation.

He should have said that straight away. But just the fact of taking in what that letter said, and what it meant, had blown all his thoughts right off course. He had felt hunted, cornered, *trapped*. Only a few moments before he had been declaring that marriage was not for him; that, no matter how much Alice angled for it, manipulated things, she was never going to get a ring on his finger.

And then he had seen that letter and known that the only course open to him was the one he had been so angrily refusing.

He had felt as if his head was going to explode. He had had to get out of there. It was either that or tell her just what he thought; just how he felt. And if he'd done that, there would have been no room at all for negotiation.

No matter how much it stuck in his throat, he had to open negotiations with this woman because she was the mother of his child. But the one thing that was non-negotiable was marriage.

Those were the thoughts that had come to him, the decisions he'd wrestled with in the hours since he'd walked out. He'd never actually gone very far away from the cottage—a few miles down the road, in fact. He'd parked the car and got out and walked and walked. He'd walked himself to a standstill. Until his thoughts were resigned and his heart had stopped racing.

He'd walked until he was as calm as he could be. And then he had come back here to tell Alice what he had decided.

'We are going to get married—and as soon as possible,' he said again, as much to make sure there was no going back as to convince her.

Because Alice wasn't looking at him the way he had expected. She wasn't looking anything like the way he had thought she would. Considering how much she had been angling for marriage earlier, this stunned, blank expression was the last thing he had anticipated. He'd been convinced that she would bite his hand off in her eagerness to take the wedding ring he offered. Instead she looked almost shocked. Almost as if she might actually say no.

'But you don't do marriage,' Alice said at last, and her voice sounded as rough as he felt, raw and off balance, totally uneven.

'I do when it's a matter of getting a legal claim to my baby. That *is* my baby you're carrying?'

'Of course it is! I told you that! I've never slept with any other man since I met you—I don't do that! And if you don't believe me—'

'I believe you.'

If he had had any lingering doubts at all, then the vehemence of her declaration drove them right out of his mind. Whatever else Alice might be—and right now he was beginning to wonder just how much he had ever known her at all—she was not the type to sleep around. He'd had one hell of a job to persuade her into bed with *him* so quickly, even though it had been blatantly obvious that she'd wanted to be there every bit as much as he'd wanted her. And once she was there, she had never looked at another man. That was why her sudden declaration that she was no longer having any fun and she was moving on had hit him like a ton of bricks.

Besides, there was something in her eyes, in her expression, in the sheer fury with which she had responded that convinced him that she was telling the truth. That and the dates told him that this baby was his.

'That's why we're getting married.'

'I don't have a choice?' Alice questioned sharply.

'No more than I have.'

'And what if I won't agree to marry you?'

Don't be stupid, the scornful glance he turned on her said only too clearly. *Of course you'll agree to it!* It was, after all, what she'd been angling for just a short time earlier. But perhaps she was determined to make him pay for the rejection he had flung at her back then.

Well, if she needed a little persuasion, he'd persuade. He supposed she was getting back at him for saying that there was no way he would marry her.

'I'll make it worth your while. I'll give you everything you want—anything you want.'

'Anything?' It had clearly made her think. 'Why?'

'No child of mine is going to be born illegitimate.'

He didn't realise how aggressive he had sounded until he saw the way her head came up, the uneasy step backwards she took. It twisted something sharply in his conscience, made him regret the shift in the balance of their relationship, but there was no going back now. He had set out on this path and he had too much to lose if he turned back.

But Alice was not giving in.

'I'll put your name on the birth certificate.'

'Not good enough,' Domenico stated ruthlessly, giving his dark head a fierce shake. 'It's marriage or—'

'Oh, you've changed your tune!' Alice mocked in a tone so brittle he almost wondered if speaking would snap it in two. 'A couple of hours ago it was no marriage, not ever! Now you can't seem to wait to get a ring on my finger! So tell me, marriage—or what?'

'Or I'll fight you.'

He waited just a nicely calculated moment as he saw the statement hit home. Saw the way her face lost what little colour it had, the sudden wary apprehension in the beautiful eyes. He had her, if not exactly on the run, then certainly slowly starting to retreat.

'Can you risk a major legal battle? A drawn-out custody case? I'll bring in the best lawyers money can buy.'

'And you can afford the *very* best!' Alice flung into that shuttered, unyielding face.

'Of course.'

If he caught the sting of her sarcasm he didn't even acknowledge it by so much as a glance; not even the tiniest change in his expression revealed that her bitterness had hit home.

Suddenly Alice couldn't bear to be still any longer. She felt dizzy and faint, as if she had been standing in the glare of the sun for too long. Which, in a way, she supposed that she had. Facing up to Domenico was like being at the eye of a storm, struggling with something fiercely elemental. And she had been battling with him all day; a cruel, emotional battle that had taken its toll on her.

She couldn't face that harsh, predatory stare any longer. Her legs felt insecure beneath her, shaky and weak.

'I—I have to sit down.'

Turning away hastily, she headed into the living room, stumbling slightly at the move from wooden flooring to the shabby carpet.

Behind her she heard Domenico mutter something, thick and raw in shock—and was that a note of concern that had sharpened his voice? She couldn't tell and she really couldn't even begin to think as her unwary movement made her head spin nauseously.

'Alice?'

He was close behind her, his hands fastening over her arms, taking her weight, supporting her as he half walked, half carried her towards the settee.

'Are you OK? Sit down… Can I get you something?'

Stunningly gentle for a big man, he guided her down onto the cushions, putting one hand behind her back, another at her head as she lay back. The room was spinning and she closed her eyes against the sensation.

'Here.'

She had barely noticed that he had gone but suddenly he was back again, sitting beside her and holding out a glass of cool water. Alice took it and sipped gratefully, feeling the dizziness recede slightly.

'When did you last eat?'

Cool and sharp, Domenico's question went straight to the heart of the problem, making Alice feel very small and very stupid.

'I—I tried to have something at breakfast…'

Even as she said it, she expected—and got—his wordless sound of disapproval.

'*Idiota!* You must eat! You are pregnant.'

Of course. His concern would be for the baby.

'I felt sick and then…'

Then he had arrived and it seemed as if the world had gone crazy. She felt as if she had been picked up and whirled away from everything she knew, everything that kept her sane. And now she didn't know if she was on her head or her heels. One moment he was saying that he wanted her but would never marry her—the next he was insisting that they marry for the baby's sake.

Ah, yes—*for the baby's sake.* The thought of how little she actually mattered in all this slashed at her like a cruel knife and made a small, weak gasp escape her painfully dry lips.

'Relax!' Domenico had misunderstood the reason for her reaction. 'I'll get you something, then you'll feel better. What do you think you could manage?'

'Some toast.'

'And soup,' Domenico insisted. 'You need to eat something substantial if you've been fasting all day.'

'And soup,' Alice conceded, knowing it would do her no good to argue.

She really didn't think she could manage anything. Her stomach was so upset and the way that her nerves seemed to be tying themselves into tight, painful knots only added to the problem. She might be able to snatch a few quiet moments while Domenico disappeared into the kitchen but it would only be a brief respite. And somehow she had to think, had to try and find some way of coming to a decision about his proposal—his *demand* that she marry him.

But her thoughts wouldn't come together into any coherent form. Even though Domenico had left her side, she was still so sharply aware of him, just through the doorway in the tiny kitchen. She could hear him clattering about, opening doors, slamming them shut again.

Clearly he wasn't finding what he wanted as he muttered curses in explosive, frustrated Italian, and the sound of his fury at several inanimate objects brought a wry smile to her lips.

'The bread is in the wooden bin by the fridge,' she said into a rare moment of silence. 'And the butter in the—'

'Bread?' Clearly Domenico had found the remains of the small sliced loaf that was all the bread bin contained. 'You call this bread?'

The wooden lid banged down in a sound of disgust and another cupboard was opened—then another.

'And *where* will I find the toaster?'

Alice's smile grew. Something of the faintness was receding; enough to give her the strength to enjoy his discomfiture.

'There isn't one. You have to light the grill and use that.'

More expressive Italian issued from the kitchen.

'How the devil can you manage in such a place?'

'It's all I can afford. We're not all multimillionaires. Do you need me to come and help you with that?'

The outraged silence that greeted her question spoke more expressively of his indignation than anything he might actually say.

'I will manage, Alice. I do know how to cook.'

'You do?'

That was a surprise to her. She had lived for six months with this man but she had never learned that simple fact. In his city apartment, and at his villa outside Florence, he had always had a troop of servants to attend to his every need.

Her astonishment had shown in her tone and Domenico appeared in the doorway in response to her comment.

'I was not always a multimillionaire.'

'I know that. But—but you never actually wanted for anything.'

He had never talked of his past in any depth. Never let her in to any intimate secrets about his childhood or his youth, so it stunned her to find that he seemed prepared to do so now.

The black brows twitched together in a dark frown and the muscles in Domenico's jaw tightened, compressing his mouth as if he was determined to hold something back. But then, to her astonishment, he shrugged off the momentary hesitation.

'In my childhood I would have thought that this place was a palace,' he declared, making her jaw drop in genuine amazement. 'That is why I cannot believe that you would insist on bringing up our child in a dump like this when you know what I have to offer now.'

He might as well have thrown the knife he was holding straight into her heart. It wouldn't have hurt any more. Probably a lot less because the physical hurt was light in comparison to the emotional anguish that seared through her.

She'd been stupid enough to let her guard down, to forget just why he was here. But he had had no hesitation in reminding her of just what was uppermost in his mind—and it wasn't a concern for her welfare.

'So you think you can buy me?' she flung at him, pain making her voice colder than she had ever intended.

But it seemed that the accusation just bounced off Domenico's tough hide as if it was armour-plated.

'Not *buy, cara*,' he reproved with stinging gentleness. 'I merely suggested an arrangement that would suit us both.'

'But why does it have to be marriage?'

'I told you—no child of mine is going to be born illegitimate.'

'But that doesn't matter at all these days.'

'It matters to me.'

And there was no point in her arguing with that; no point at all. It was stamped into every hard line of his face, etched along each bone, each muscle in his body. Even the way he held himself told her that he was braced for a fight—for as long and as hard a fight as it took him to get what he wanted—and he had no intention of losing.

But how could she marry him; give up everything she was—her freedom—and go and live with a man who didn't love her? A man who only wanted her because of the precious baby she was carrying?

'Don't fight me on this, Alice,' Domenico said harshly, making her head spin in shock at the way it seemed that he had listened in to her thoughts and was now almost quoting them back at her. 'Because you won't win—you can't win. I want my child, and I'll fight you till the end of time to get it.'

Not waiting for her to answer, or even to attempt it, he turned on his heel and went back into the kitchen. A few moments later the savoury smell of soup crept into the living room, making Alice's ravenous stomach growl its emptiness.

Perhaps she could eat something after all. And perhaps, with something warm inside her, she might be able to think more clearly. Find some argument that would convince him she wasn't going to tie herself to a man she....

But that was where her thoughts floundered and came to a stumbling halt.

A man she...

It was no good. Try as she might, she couldn't force herself to say it even in the privacy of her own thoughts. Couldn't make herself say 'a man she didn't love'. Because the truth was the exact opposite.

She still loved Domenico.

She always had and she always would. She hadn't left him because she had fallen out of love with him, because she no longer cared, but because she adored him and she knew that he did not love her. She had never had any illusions that their relationship was for ever—and she had certainly never dreamed of marriage. She had fled because she'd feared that one day, and probably one day soon, Domenico would tire of her and she would find herself replaced by a newer model. And hearing stories of him with Pippa Marinelli had just been the last straw.

But then fate had conspired against her and she had found that she was pregnant. Or had that really been a gift from heaven? Because now Domenico had offered her marriage so that he could have his child.

What was she fighting for? She had always known that Domenico didn't love her; that hadn't changed. But so much else had. As his wife she would be part of his life, able to be with him every day. And perhaps that way, some time in the future, he might actually come to care for her.

And if he didn't, there would always be their baby. The child they had made between them. She had no doubt at all that Domenico would love the son or daughter he so clearly longed for, and she would love them both. It would be enough. It had to be enough—for now. She wouldn't hope for more—but nothing could stop her from dreaming.

'I make no promises about the soup.'

Domenico had come back into the room with a tray on which he'd placed a bowl and a plateful of toast.

'On the tin, they had the audacity to call it minestrone—but this looks nothing like any *minestrone* I've ever tasted.'

Setting the tray down on a small coffee-table, he moved it so that it was within reach of Alice, then flung himself down in the chair opposite, watching intently as she sat forward and picked up her spoon to eat.

'But I want to see you eat all of it.'

She would have a hard job swallowing anything with him sitting there, head back on the cushions, long legs stretched out in front of him, sockless ankles crossed. He gave an impression of being relaxed and at ease, but the long fingers of the hands that rested on the arms of the chair were moving restlessly, tapping out an impatient rhythm on the flowered fabric.

She didn't expect that he would wait very long before he went on to the attack again and she was proved right. She had barely got halfway down the bowl when he returned to the subject that was clearly uppermost in his mind.

'OK, how much is this going to cost me?'

'Cost?'

It wasn't the approach she'd been expecting. What she'd been dreading was another threat of legal action, of a court case that she couldn't hope to afford. So his talk of costs threw her off balance.

'What sort of a settlement would make the idea of marriage appeal?'

'I don't want a settlement.'

Porca miseria, but she was stubborn! Domenico cursed to himself. Stubborn and totally unpredictable. He could have sworn that she had been angling for a ring on her finger with this damn running-away business, the whole 'not having fun any more' blatantly a cover-up for something else. But now that he had *offered* marriage, she'd tossed it back in his face as if it was the last thing she wanted.

'Alicia, a marriage between us could work in other ways than just the fact that we are going to become parents. I'm not proposing just some marriage of convenience.'

He had her attention now. The spoon had paused, halfway to her mouth, and she was staring at him, watching him like some wary animal suddenly caught in the headlights.

'We would have a real marriage. You would be my wife—in my home, in my life…in my bed.'

That spoon was moving again, but not towards her mouth. Instead it was slowly put down again, into the bowl, the handle resting against the side.

She was definitely listening now so he pressed home his advantage.

'And surely what happened between us here today tells you that we could be good together—great together.'

'In bed?' It was a strangely rough-edged question but at least it was not the determined, cold-eyed refusal he'd met with before.

'In bed or out of bed. I told you, *mia bella*, you may have tired of our relationship, but I have never grown tired of you. I still want you, as much as, if not more than, when we were together.'

Alice opened her mouth as if to speak, but no sound came out. He watched her fight with the moment of weakness, saw the elegant lines of her throat move as she swallowed hard.

'You do?'

Domenico's laughter was low and sceptical. Did she doubt it? How could she doubt it?

Sitting forward, he leaned towards her, his arms resting on his knees, his fingers spread in an open gesture. His eyes locked with her uncertain blue ones, seeing the dark pupils, the wide-eyed stare, the long, curving lashes.

'Did you listen to a word I said earlier? Didn't what happened in your bed tell you anything? I want you—and I want our baby—and I'll do whatever it takes to make sure that our child is born into a legitimate marriage.'

'Why is that so important to you? I'd give you access…'

She broke off abruptly, blinking hard in shock, as he shook his head in adamant rejection of her tentative suggestion.

'No?'

'No. Access isn't good enough, Alice. I want marriage.'

'But why? Tell me why it has to be this way. You can't expect me to marry you if you don't.'

She didn't know what she was asking. No one had ever
delved so deeply into his life, or come so close to things he
had kept hidden. He had never let any woman open up that
part of him.

But if it meant getting his child—being a father to his son
or daughter—and getting Alice into the bargain, having this
woman in his bed every night...

'Dom?'

Dom.

It was the name she had once said with such warmth—with
such affection. She'd used it in passion too, in a husky whisper in his ear at the most intimate of moments as he'd taken
her as his own, sheathing his hungry body in her welcoming
warmth. And she'd cried out in ecstasy as she came, keening
his name on a long, drawn-out sigh.

Dom.

He had given no one else the right to use that name. And
hearing it now seemed to crack something open inside him,
bringing him hard up against the fact that it was let her in—
or lose her. Lose his rights to her and the child, except for what
she would allow him.

Unable to keep still, he pushed himself out of his chair,
turning towards the window and staring out at the dark night
where the rain was still falling, lashing against the glass, whirling in the wind. He didn't know where to start or how to say
it. He had kept it to himself for the thirty-four years of his life.

But then she said it again.

'Dom?'

And that brought him whirling round, seeing her upturned

face, those blue, blue eyes watching him. Watching and waiting for an answer.

Abruptly he held out a hand to her. And she took it, letting him pull her upright, draw her close to him.

Still holding her, looking deep into her eyes, he let his free hand rest on her body, low down, where his child was beginning to grow.

'My parents are both dead.'

She knew that much already. He had told her at the very beginning of their relationship that he had no mother or father.

'I have no other relatives.'

Alice's tiny gasp escaped her involuntarily.

'None?'

'No one.'

'Not a cousin or…?'

'No one.'

His hand moved, fingers splayed across her belly.

'This child—our baby—is the only other living person in the whole world who has my blood in its veins. I want that child—my child—to have my name.'

It was only part of the truth, but he prayed it was enough to satisfy her. The rest he had never told anyone, and would willingly go to his grave without ever speaking of it.

'So tell me what it will cost me and I'll pay any price.'

Her silence seemed to drag on for an eternity. But then, at last she slicked a moistening tongue over her dry lips and drew in a long, slow breath.

'Just marriage,' she said, so softly that he barely caught it and thought he hadn't heard right.

'What?'

He ducked his head until her mouth was close to his ear. In this position he had nowhere to look but at the swell of her breasts, rising and falling with the unsteady, rapid rate of her breathing. The scent of her skin was both a delight and a torment to senses that were already over-stimulated, nerves that seemed tight with too much tension.

'What did you say?'

'Just marriage,' Alice repeated, still in a whisper, but more firmly this time. 'All I want is marriage.'

'You'll marry me?'

And ask for nothing more? It seemed impossible.

But she was nodding silently, her head down, her eyes closed. Nodding agreement.

'Yes, I'll marry you,' she said, making sure there could be no mistake.

Suddenly she flung up her head and looked him straight in the eye.

'But Pippa Marinelli…'

'Pippa Marinelli is no threat to you,' he hastened to reassure her. 'You will never have to hear about her again. I swear to you.'

Slowly Alice nodded her head again, this time more confidently.

'In that case, I'll marry you and we'll raise this child together.'

Domenico was thankful that her upturned head offered him her mouth, suggesting without words that they seal their bargain with a kiss. A handshake didn't seem quite appropriate, for all that it was a business agreement they had finalised, for a marriage that was all formality and nothing of feeling, except that they both cared for the child that was to be born to them.

It was as he angled his head to take the kiss that the kick of reality hit, landing hard in the pit of his stomach.

Just marriage. Of course.

Just marriage was quite enough for any woman. *Just marriage* gave her the rights to half of everything he owned. She didn't have to name her price for agreeing to his terms—it was right there in her statement.

Just marriage.

But then their lips met and in the sensual explosion the sensation sparked off he managed just one thought before his mind went into total meltdown.

He didn't care. He didn't give a damn at all.

It was worth handing over half of everything he owned to have this woman back in his bed, and to know that she was bringing his child into his life.

CHAPTER SEVEN

PRECISELY two weeks ago, at exactly this time of night, she had been standing at a window, staring out at the dark garden. Now she was doing just that again. But the view that met her eyes and the circumstances in which she found herself couldn't be more different.

Then the garden had been tiny, windswept and rain-soaked, and she had been under cooler skies at her English cottage. Now she was looking down at the extensive grounds of Domenico's elegant Italian villa, after a day of warm sunshine and blue, blue skies.

And tomorrow was her wedding day.

Out there, beyond the window, still visible because of the lights that lined the long, sweeping drive, workers were still making sure that the gardens were immaculate and the huge ornate fountain in perfect working order, ready for the big day. Downstairs, in the villa's huge ballroom, the floral decorations were being set up and the tables prepared for the reception after the ceremony in the morning. They were to be married in the village church and then come back to the Villa d'Acqua in a horse-drawn coach that had been freshly scrubbed and painted, ready to transport her and her new husband to their marital home.

'My husband…'

Alice whispered the words under her breath because she still couldn't quite believe this was actually happening.

This time tomorrow she would be Signora Domenico Parrisi. She would have Domenico's ring on her finger and they would be man and wife.

And her baby would grow up knowing its father. Knowing it was loved.

'Loved.'

Alice winced away from the stab of pain that just saying that word brought to her. It was impossible to think of her coming wedding without wishing that it could be perfect in every way. But perfect would mean that she had Domenico's love. And that was the one thing that tomorrow's wedding would be lacking.

She couldn't fault her husband-to-be in anything else. In the two weeks since she had said she would be his wife, he had taken care of everything—dealt with every need she might possibly have and a few that hadn't even crossed her mind.

He had taken charge immediately, organised everything, taken every last responsibility from her, and all she had had to do was to pack a small case with the things she needed to settle herself into the villa—and plan the dress she was to wear for the wedding.

Even there, Domenico had made things easy for her. A designer had been contacted, summoned to the villa. She was to choose anything she wanted—exactly what she wanted—and it would be provided for her. Now the most beautiful dress, the dress of her dreams, hung in the dressing room, carefully shrouded in protective plastic, waiting for her to put it on tomorrow morning. And tomorrow her father would walk her down the aisle.

Domenico had arranged that as well, contacting her parents in New Zealand where they now lived, arranging first-class flights for them—and for all her friends—so that they could be here, with her on the big day. He had never put a single foot wrong.

And perhaps that was the reason for her uneasiness and edgy feeling tonight, Alice told herself as she moved away from the window, wandering restlessly about the large, elegant room. Domenico had been polite, considerate, generosity itself, but he had always remained—well, the only word she could come up with was…

Distant.

From the moment that he had had her answer to his proposal—his demand that she marry him, from the time that she had said yes, she would be his wife, he had totally withdrawn from her so that at times he no longer seemed like the same man. His courtesy was impeccable; he had done everything he could to make sure she was comfortable and had everything she needed. But it was as if someone had put up a glass wall between the two of them, with each on different sides, so that they could see and hear each other, but not reach out. Not touch.

Except where the baby was concerned.

Oh, yes, where the baby was concerned Domenico was all interest, all attention. The first thing he had done when she had agreed to marry him—even before he had started any arrangements for tomorrow's marriage ceremony—was to arrange for the best medical care that money could buy. She had been examined, assessed, had every blood test known to medical science. And only then had Domenico agreed to let her travel to his home outside Pavia to join in the wedding preparations.

A light tap at the door brought her head round quickly, a movement she regretted as it made her head spin. This had happened several times in the last few days, something she put down to her non-stop tiredness and the persistent nausea that dogged her days.

'Come in,' she said but Domenico had already opened the door and was halfway into the room.

'I told you to rest,' he said reprovingly as soon as he saw that she was not, as he had instructed, lying down with her feet up.

'I was too nervous to sleep,' she admitted. 'There's so much to remember—so much to do before tomorrow.'

'And none of it that you need to trouble your head with. Everything's under control. But you have been looking tired—you're too pale. And you barely ate a thing at lunch.'

Did he notice everything she did—or didn't do? He must have eyes like a hawk, because she had been convinced that she had made a fair pretence of eating the light meal served to her. And she had thought that Domenico had been intent on talking to her father so that her non-existent appetite would go unobserved.

'It's this sickness.' She grimaced wryly. 'They might call it morning sickness but it doesn't just appear in the morning! If it did, I might be able to cope. As far as I can see, it's all-day sickness really.'

'And you've been overdoing things.'

His hand came up to touch her face, smoothing a long finger across the top of her cheek, and her heart seemed to stand still suddenly at the unexpectedness of his touch.

He had barely come near her in the two weeks since he had proposed this marriage, and in spite of his protestations that he wanted her more than ever before he had made no move to take her to bed or even to show any sign of warmth towards her. In fact she had become so used to him keeping a strict distance between them that it had rocked her sense of balance when, arriving back from the airport, where he had collected her parents from their flight, he had greeted her with an apparently affectionate kiss on the cheek.

It had taken a moment for her to realise that it was precisely because of her mother's smiling presence just behind him that he had even made the gesture. They were to act as if this marriage was a real one, he had told her. No one was even to suspect that they were marrying for any reasons other than the fact that it was a perfect love match. And so of course he had put on an act, setting out to impress his potential in-laws from the start.

'You have shadows under your eyes,' he said now, the sharpness of the words crushing down the weak rush of hope that his touch had been a caress and not the criticism it had turned out to be. 'And you're losing weight.'

His hands came round her waist, measuring it against the span of his fingers, and his frown said that he was not at all pleased with what he saw. Alice didn't need any tape measure or scales to tell her how the weight was dropping off her. She felt so sick all the time that it was a constant struggle to eat, and when she did manage to swallow something, it didn't always stay down. She'd hoped that as she got further into her pregnancy the nausea would wear off, but, if anything, the past two weeks had been worse.

'Well, it's just as well I'm not putting on too much or I'd never get into that outrageously expensive dress I'm planning to wear tomorrow.'

Alice tried for lightness, but knew that her attempt to soften his mood even a little had failed when she saw his black brows twitch together in a dark frown, his features freezing into such a hard expression that she felt her attempt at a smile might actually bounce back off its rigidity and hit her in the face like a reproach.

'It doesn't suit you,' he snapped coldly. 'And it won't be good for the baby. You really should take better care of yourself.'

'Better care of your son or daughter, don't you mean?' Alice flung back, the stinging pain of rejection so sharp that she couldn't even try to hold back her reproach. 'I'm surprised that you even notice I exist, except as the incubator in which your precious heir is growing!'

'Oh, I notice all right,' Domenico snarled irritably. 'I can't help but notice—and I don't like what I see. You don't look strong enough to stand on your own two feet, let alone nurture a child. How would you feel if something happened—?'

'How would *you* feel if something happened, you mean!'

Alice pulled herself away from his restraining grasp, unable to bear his critical gaze, the dark reproof in his frowning eyes. 'After all, that would mean that you'd wasted your time and money—and married me for nothing!'

Domenico's reaction was not what she expected. That dark frown was replaced by a cool, assessing narrowing of his bronze gaze. And his response was low and fast as a striking snake as he demanded, 'Is that what you want? To call the wedding off? Are you going back on your word?'

It was only what he had been expecting, after all, Domenico reflected. He had pushed her into this marriage for his own reasons, offering her nothing but financial security in return. Perhaps she was now regretting her decision, wishing she had chosen that 'fun' she'd said she wanted. Certainly that seemed possible from the way that she was hesitating over her answer now.

'Is that it?'

'No.' Her response was low, but firm. 'No, that's not what I want. I said I'd marry you and I will. After all, who would turn down a chance to become mistress of all this?'

The wave of her hand took in the luxurious room furnished in cream and gold, the adjoining dressing room and *en suite* bathroom, and beyond the windows the expanse of the beautiful grounds sweeping right down to the banks of the river that had given the villa its name.

'You needn't worry that I'll jilt you at the altar. I'll be there tomorrow, never fear. That is, if you still want me.'

If he still wanted her! *Dio*, was the woman blind? Didn't she know what it did to him just to be near her, the way that his body responded instantly to her presence, the raging desire that scrambled his thoughts in seconds? The need that he had had to clamp down on since that day in her cottage? That he had had to bury in concern for her well-being?

She had looked so pale, so ill from the first moment that he had brought her here. At first he had thought that it was the after-effects of the journey, but she hadn't seemed to pull round very quickly. If anything, she had looked worse, more fragile, with every day that passed.

Her hand moved, lightly covering the spot where his child lay.

'If you still want us,' she amended softly.

'Of course I want you. What man wouldn't want a beautiful woman as his wife and the prospect of his first-born child arriving just a few months from now?'

'First-born?'

He wouldn't have thought that it was possible for Alice to look any paler; her skin was almost translucent as it was. But as she echoed his words it seemed that even the faintest wash of rose fled from her cheeks and her eyes were smoky with shock as they stared into his face.

'*First*-born?' she repeated. 'I don't recall agreeing to any more children.'

'And I thought you understood that this was to be a real marriage—not just a business arrangement.'

'Real—for how long?'

Did she really believe that all he wanted was her name on

a marriage certificate and then she was free—free to have fun, he presumed?

'For as long as it takes,' he stated bluntly. 'I want my child to grow up in a real family, with two parents—brothers and sisters if possible.'

'Are—are you saying…?'

'I'm saying that when I make those vows tomorrow I mean to keep them. This isn't going to be just a show marriage, Alicia, *cara*. I will be a father to my child—and a husband to you.'

'You're surely not saying—t-till death do us part?' she managed in a whisper.

'I'm certainly not looking at any temporary arrangement.'

'But—we don't love each other.'

'Love!'

Domenico couldn't hold back the cynical laughter that escaped him at the word. Was it love that had brought him into the world? It had been more of another, very different, four-letter word. He had been created by lust, pure and simple—not that there had been anything *pure* about a quick, sordid and rough event.

'And do you believe in "love"?' he questioned sharply. 'Is there really such an emotion? And what makes you think that any marriage based on *amore* has any better chance of lasting than one grounded in sound, practical reasons for its existence?'

'Practical?'

Somehow she managed to make the word sound like the greatest insult possible.

'Surely you're not deluding yourself with some dream of a happy-ever-after with the one love of your life? You must know that that is only an illusion of songwriters and fantasy novelists. Arranged marriages have worked very well for centuries—and often with less between the participants than we have.'

'And we have…?'

'Oh, *mia bella*—don't pretend that you have to ask! You know what we have. We have this…'

He caught her wrist, drawing her gently towards him. Sliding one hand under her chin, he lifted her face to his and bent his head to take her lips softly. He had to fight to hold back on the hot passion that flashed its way through his body as his mouth touched hers, crushing down the need to snatch her up in his arms and carry her over to the bed, flinging her down on the gold-coloured coverlet…

And she didn't help matters because after a tiny heartbeat of hesitation, the briefest snatching in of a breath, she just melted into him, her mouth clinging, opening softly under his, her sigh tormenting him with its sound of surrender, just when he knew he must not act on it.

Her hands came up around his neck, sliding into the dark hair at the back of his skull, smoothing, stroking. The softness of her breasts was crushed against his chest, and the slender curve of her hips was cradled by his pelvis, heating and hardening his body in an instant so that it was impossible she couldn't feel the power of his hunger for her, the rigid force of his need.

In spite of himself, his arms came tight round her, crushing her to him, but as soon as they did so, he felt the thinness of her, the delicacy of her frame, the fragility of her bones. And she was all bone. So finely spun that he feared that if he used even one small part of his strength to hold her, she might actually crack into a thousand tiny pieces.

'Dear God, *cara*,' he muttered against her lips. 'Don't do this to me—don't—*stop*!'

He regretted the word as soon as it had escaped him; regretted the force of the command, the instant effect that it had on her.

She froze in his arms, her dark head bent, resting against his chest, eyes hidden from him. But there was a new tension in the slender form, one that held her totally distant from him even though she was still standing so very close.

'I thought…you wanted…'

Her voice was muffled against his shirt but he thought he could hear the thickness of tears in her stumbling words. And when he gently brought her head up so that he could see her face, those deep blue eyes were sheened with moisture that she tried vainly to hide, struggling to pull her chin away from his firm, restraining grip.

'I *want* you,' he assured her deeply. 'Never doubt that. I've never wanted any woman more.'

She tried for a response, that soft pink mouth opened, worked, but no sound came out. And so Domenico bent his head, risking a brief, delicate kiss, shuddering faintly as he endured the stinging pulse of primitive need that tormented his yearning body all over again.

'But don't you have a tradition that the groom must sleep apart from his bride on the eve of their wedding night?'

'It's supposed to be bad luck if they don't,' Alice agreed, her tiredness showing in her tone, which was flat and lifeless. No emotion in it at all.

'Then we don't want to risk that. Besides, you look worn out. The preparations for the wedding have taken it out of you. You need to rest—take care of the baby.'

'The baby,' Alice echoed, but she nodded slowly. 'I could do with an early night.'

'You have one.'

Domenico dropped a kiss on her forehead, easing himself away with a care that was as much to appease the screaming protest from his own aroused body as to make Alice feel that he was not keen to leave. If he didn't get out of here fast, then he would never leave.

He'd fought the need to hold her, to kiss her, to *have* her for as long as he could. He wanted to give her time and space and consideration, but he was only human. If he stayed a second longer with her in his arms, with the soft scent of her skin mixed with some subtle rose-based perfume tormenting his nostrils, weaving through his thoughts like warm, intoxicating smoke, then he would not be able to hold out any longer.

The temptation that the big, soft, inviting bed offered was almost more than he could stand. He was going *now*—*pronto*—before he did something damn stupid. Something he would always regret.

'It will be a long day tomorrow,' he said, ruthlessly erasing every note of regret from his voice. 'But when we're man and wife there will be a lifetime of nights we can share. Goodnight, *cara*. I'll see you in church.'

A lifetime of nights, Alice repeated in her thoughts as she watched him walk away from her and out of the room. Never once did he hesitate or look back, and he closed the door so firmly behind him that he might have been going away for good; never coming back.

A lifetime of nights we can share.

But tonight was the night that she needed him. The one night that would have meant so much. The night when, if he had stayed, if he had held her in his arms, kissed her, taken her to bed, she might have been able to feel that he wanted her, really wanted her, for herself.

Not just as the prospective mother of his child—of his 'first-born'—and the potential breeder of the brothers and sisters he wanted this baby to have, but as Alice. As the woman he said he wanted but who, once he'd had her agreement to marry him and his ring on her finger, he hadn't even touched since she had come into this house.

Until tonight.

Tonight he had at least held her. He'd kissed her. But when she'd made it plain that she would love to take things further he had removed himself, disentangling himself from her clutching hands and putting her carefully aside. Oh, he had been gentle, considerate, courteous even. But he had not wanted to make love to her.

Because she had to take care of the baby.

Alice sighed, deep and low, blinking back tears as she rubbed at her back, where tired muscles ached miserably. Domenico was right, of course. She was worn out, and she hadn't been feeling well for days.

But the fact that he was right didn't make things feel any better. If anything, they made them worse. He was right—and he had thought of her as the mother of his child, taking care of her needs, concerned for her health, her strength—and for the baby!

'And I wanted him to care for *me*!'

She wished he had felt so overwhelmed by his feeling for her—even if it was only physical—that he had not been able to tear himself away and had taken her to bed, to lie with her through the long hours of the night, and wake at her side on the special morning that tomorrow was going to be.

She didn't give a damn about bad luck! It was only superstition, and she didn't believe in superstition.

The truth was that for Domenico tomorrow wasn't going to be such a special day at all. He might talk about a *real marriage,* about spending a lifetime together, about having more children after this precious baby who had brought him to the altar when it was the last thing he had planned and the last thing he had wanted.

But he had shown no feeling about it. In fact he had said

straight out that he didn't believe in love, stating openly that he wanted a practical, arranged marriage and had only chosen her because she was pregnant with his baby.

But how could she fault a man who cared about his unborn child as deeply as Domenico so obviously did? She had felt the heated hardness of his body when she'd cuddled close. She recognised, though he would hate it if he knew, the struggle that he had had to pull away from her, the fight he had had not to give in to the passion that flared between them. How could she not recognise it when it was the same primitive need that had racked her too? She didn't possess Domenico's ruthless self-control, his unyielding determination, and would have given in to it if he had not decided for her.

And the truth was that she was tired, bone weary, with that hateful nausea making her stomach roil, her head spin.

But oh, how she wished he had stayed.

When he was here it all seemed easier. She could even ignore the sickness to a degree, drawing strength from his big, strong, comforting presence; feeling his arms around her for support.

Now that he was gone she felt doubly bereft, lonely, lost—and ill. And she didn't know how she was going to get to sleep.

She'd run a bath. A deep, deep, warm bath. And she'd soak in it for as long as she could, lying there in the soothing water, feeling it ease away the aches in her back, the uncomfortable twinges that seemed to be coming and going all over her body. She'd linger until she felt relaxed enough to sleep—until she was too tired to do anything else—and then she'd crawl into bed and hope that oblivion would claim her and keep her from thinking, or from dreaming, until the morning of her wedding day dawned.

The bath worked. Or perhaps it was just the sheer exhaustion that overwhelmed her, dropping her suddenly into total blankness almost as soon as she lay down and closed her eyes. She knew nothing, felt nothing for hours, lying dead to the world as the night slipped away and the morning came closer.

Until something invaded her sleep and brought her rushing awake with a jolting shock.

She didn't know what had happened; what nightmare had invaded her sleep and forced her to open her eyes. But it had to have been something dreadful because she found herself sitting half-upright, staring straight ahead, heart racing, her shaking body slicked with sweat as if she had been running from some appalling horror.

'Oh, help…' she groaned, rubbing a trembling hand across her face to drive away the sleep demons that had pursued her into her dreams.

And as she did so it happened again.

And it wasn't a nightmare, or a fantasy demon. It wasn't anything imaginary at all.

The monster that had grabbed at her, pulling her out of sleep and into the dreadfully cold light of the dawn, was a cruel, physical, painful reality.

It came as a savage wave of dizziness, a shuddering nausea and an agonising, brutal cramping sensation that had her hand flying to her abdomen in shock.

'Ooof!'

The sound was pushed from her as she held her stomach, gasping in pain, her mouth wide open, breath catching in her throat.

'Ouch!'

For a couple of seconds that was all she could manage— simply handling the pain took all the strength she had. It was as the cramping pain subsided, leaving her panting and weak, that some ability to think returned and with it the devastation of realising just what was happening.

'No! Oh, *no!*'

The baby…

She couldn't…

Oh, no, please, *no*! Not the baby.

The receding pain gave her the momentary strength to fling herself out of bed, stand upright, though her head whirled sickeningly and her eyes blurred into sightlessness.

Domenico.

His name was the one clear, focused thought inside her panic-stricken mind.

Domenico—she had to get to Domenico. He would know what to do. He would be able to get help, he would—

'Ohh… Oh!' she gasped as another wave of pain attacked from out of nowhere.

By the time it had subsided again she was sweating hard and breathing rawly. Her legs were trembling badly, barely supporting her, but she forced herself to move, stumbling across the carpet and out into the long, dark corridor.

Domenico's room was just a few doors down, directly opposite the huge suite that would be theirs when they were married.

If they were married. Because surely this…

Another clutch of pain destroyed her thought processes, taking with them any hope of following through on what she had been wondering. Instead she wilted against the wall, grateful for its hard support at her back as she panted her way through the agonising contraction, her concentration too fierce to allow her to think of anything but that.

And that was something for which she was thankful when her brain started working again. Because thinking hurt too—bringing with it the anguish of knowing that there was only one possible reason for this terrible pain.

'Domenico…'

It was muttered through teeth gritted against the fear and

the horror, her jaw tight with determination to get to his room, to get to him.

'Domenico…'

Her feet dragged, every step was an effort, but eventually she made it to the door, her fingers reaching for the handle.

She didn't have time—didn't have the strength—to knock and wait, and she could only summon up the energy to swipe a perfunctory slap of her hand on the wooden panels as she turned the handle, tried to push it open.

For the space of a couple of agonised heartbeats, she thought that it was not going to move, that it was locked against her, but then, just as a despairing moan rose to her lips, she felt it give, fly inwards, taking her with it.

'What the—? Alice?'

It was Domenico's voice, harsh with shock, but, her eyes blurred with panic, Alice couldn't see where it was coming from until, blinking frantically, she managed to focus her vision better.

Her first thought was a sense of shock that the room wasn't in the semi-darkness of the dawn as she had expected, but filled with the bright light of the several lamps that were burning.

The next was that Domenico was not in his bed. Instead he was up—and fully dressed, dark and devastating in a black T-shirt and jeans.

Had he too been unable to sleep? she wondered, briefly diverted, her whirling mind latching on to any distraction from the blackness of reality.

'I'm sorry—' she tried, only to have the words snatched away from her by another vicious crush of pain. 'Dom!' His name was a high, desperate cry of panic.

'Alicia, carissima—tesora—cosa c'e che non va?'

Domenico was coming towards her, his hands out to her, his face white, all his English deserting him in his shock.

'Oh, *Dom!* The baby—I think—I'm losing the baby!'

It was the last thing she could manage, the last coherent thought she had. The next second she had lost herself in a world of fear and dread and total misery and all she knew was that Domenico had reached her. That he was by her side.

Her mind was closing up. She was losing touch with the world, with consciousness and all that mattered was that he was there, big and strong and dependable.

She'd reached home, she knew. She could leave everything up to Domenico now.

And giving up the battle to stay on her feet and fight for consciousness, she collapsed thankfully into the welcoming safety of his arms.

CHAPTER EIGHT

DOMENICO shifted slightly stiffly in his chair, and stretched limbs cramped with being still for too long. He'd been sitting beside the hospital bed for hours, waiting for Alice to wake up.

And he had no idea what he was going to say to her when she did.

At the moment she lay quiet and peaceful, her eyes closed, long black lashes lying in a luxuriant arc on her colourless skin, her breathing slow and relaxed.

It was all so very different from the moments of horror when she had collapsed in his arms in the bedroom in the early hours of the morning. Then she had been out of her mind in panic, whiter than the hospital sheets, her eyes just unfocused black pools, and her breathing had been so raw and ragged that it had been painful to hear.

He could only be thankful that restless thoughts, and an even more restless body, had stopped him from sleeping, got him out of bed just as dawn was breaking. He had spent too long lying awake, tossing and turning in a mess of heated bed-clothes, not knowing which was worse: closing his eyes and seeing images of Alice's seductive naked body playing out against the screen of his lids—or opening them again and fighting hard against the knowledge that his lover, soon to be his bride, lay in a bed just a short distance away down the corridor and only some feeble English superstition was keeping him from being there with her.

No. Some feeble English superstition and his own sense of unease about this coming wedding.

Because the truth was that from the moment he'd had her agreement to become his wife in the knowledge that her only reasons for giving it had been purely financial, he'd found he just couldn't look at Alice in the same way.

Only marriage, she'd said. But it wasn't *only* marriage she had wanted, was it?

He didn't recognise the woman Alice had become. She wasn't the Alice he had first met, the bright, vivacious, delightful girl who had charmed him with her wide smile, her easy confidence. Nor was she the sensual temptress she had become in those first months of living together, her delight in her seductive power over him growing as she gained more confidence in the bedroom.

She wasn't even the Alice who had left him, walked out on their relationship and out of his life because she wasn't having fun any more.

No, in the moment that he had discovered the truth about her pregnancy, she had become something else entirely. Something he had never known before in his life.

Alice and the baby growing inside her were now the family he had never had.

The family he had never had. The family he had told himself he never wanted. The family that was a totally unknown quantity in his life.

'My parents are both dead,' he'd said. 'I have no other relatives.'

And that was the truth—or, rather, the truth as far as he knew it.

The real truth was that he had no idea where his parents were, or even who they had been. Brought up an orphan, in a children's home run by nuns, he had no idea of what having a family might mean, no experience of any such thing.

It had thrown him completely. He had been so knocked off balance that he didn't know what to think, how to react. He didn't know who Alice was, and he didn't know who the hell *he* was.

And so he'd taken several careful steps back, keeping his distance as he tried to assess just how things stood.

'Dom…'

A sigh, the sound of faint movement from the bed brought his eyes back to Alice in a rush.

'Alice? Are you awake?'

She had come round once from the anaesthetic for the operation she had needed this afternoon, but then she had been only half-conscious and not really aware of where she was or what was happening. She had fallen into an exhausted sleep within minutes, and he had been waiting for her to come properly awake ever since.

But no, she had simply stirred in her sleep, coming close to surfacing for a moment and then drifting back into unconsciousness with another sigh.

That sigh twisted something deep inside him as he reached out a hand to smooth the tangled, tumbled hair away from her forehead, his fingers stroking it down onto the pillow.

'Hush, *cara*,' he soothed, keeping his voice low and soft. 'Sleep now—rest while you can…'

It was better for her that way, Domenico told himself. Better that she should get as much rest as she could, to help her recovery on the way.

There would be sorrow and pain enough for her to face when she did wake.

She didn't know it but there had been times in the past

when he had sat and watched her sleeping just as he was doing now, or lain beside her, just staring down into her sleeping face, watching her muscles relax in sleep, seeing the soft
curves of her breasts rise and fall with each breath she took.
On those occasions he had often had a fierce, determined
struggle with himself, the need to lie still and not disturb her
warring with the deeper, more primitive need to wake her gently and set himself to seducing her, rousing her body to passionate life beneath his hands and his mouth.

And the more basic need had usually won. He had never been
capable of restraint where her luscious body was concerned.

But there were no such thoughts in his head today—tonight, he corrected himself, checking his watch and seeing
that the trauma of events had swallowed up most of what
should have been his wedding day, so that it was now late evening and the point at which he and his new wife should have
been about to depart on their honeymoon.

But there would be no honeymoon, just as there had been no
wedding—and, most devastating of all, there would be no baby.

*'This child—our baby—is the only other living person in
the whole world who has my blood in its veins.'*

His own words came back to haunt him, twisting a knife
in his soul.

The baby would have been his only blood relative, his only
family, but now there was no baby.

With a rough, jerky movement, Domenico brushed fiercely
at his eyes with the back of his hand, dashing away the stinging tears that had blurred his vision. He had never thought
about having children—a family—until he'd learned that
Alice was pregnant, but over the past two weeks that fact had
started to change his world. But now that change would never
happen. And the truth was that he had never known how much
he had wanted that child until it was too late.

And what about Alice? How would she react when she realised that the only reason for her agreeing to marry him no longer existed? Would she stay with him or would she see this as the perfect excuse to leave, to find someone new, someone who could give her the sort of life that she had been looking for when she had left him that first time?

'Dom…?'

Another sound from the bed snatched his attention back to where Alice lay, to see that this time she was really waking. Her heavy eyelids fluttered, her head stirred on the pillow and she sighed again.

'Dom?'

'Here,' he said softly, watching as her eyes flew open and went straight to his.

She didn't have to speak a word. Didn't have to ask the question that was so obviously uppermost in her thoughts. It was there, in the darkness of her gaze, in the clouded blue depths of her eyes.

She still had a tiny hope; and he had to be the one who took it away from her. Reaching for her hand, he closed his fingers around it, knowing that even the small gesture was telling her all she needed to know.

'I'm sorry,' he said huskily.

Alice hadn't needed any words to confirm her worst fears. Deep inside, she had known the truth from the moment that consciousness had started to return to her mind.

The last thing she had really registered was arriving in Domenico's room and seeing him there, tall and strong and dependable, when she most needed him. After that, things had just been one terrible whirl of confusion, horror and pain, and through it all she had held on to Domenico's strength as if it was her only lifeline to reality.

She had heard his voice roaring for help, known that she

had been snatched up into his arms and carried out of the room, taking her down into the villa's main hall. The car had been summoned, the chauffeur at the wheel, and Domenico had cradled her close all through the long, fearful journey to the hospital.

At that point she had lost all track of time and place and events. There had been many faces, all unknown, all asking complicated questions in complicated Italian that she couldn't understand.

But once again Domenico had taken charge, answering questions and firing off demands in swift, brusque tones. Weak, in pain and distressed, Alice had simply left everything to him and sunk back inside herself in a desperate attempt to cope. From then on, events had become a terrifying blur in which nothing made sense, until at last the oblivion of unconsciousness had saved her from the worst reality.

She had come round to the silence and the whiteness of the single private room. To soft pillows, crisp, clean sheets and the awareness of the lean, dark, silent figure of Domenico sitting in a chair beside her bed. He had been there every time she had surfaced, opening her eyes just a little, and she had drifted in and out of sleep with a sense of safety and security, knowing he was still there with her, for her.

But there was no hope of staying asleep all the time. She had to wake up and face the truth of what had happened. And if she had had any doubts at all about just what *had* happened then the look in Domenico's eyes, the dark burning gold dulled and clouded, the bruised shadows underneath them, took away any last remaining hope she had.

'I'm sorry,' he said again, his voice gruff and harsh as if coming from a painfully tight throat, and she knew that her baby was gone.

'Oh, no…'

She didn't have the mental strength to lift her head; could only lie there and look into his drawn, shadowed face, seeing her own loss etched there in the lines around his nose and mouth, the tightness of control in the muscles of his jaw.

'Oh, Dom—no.'

The big hand that enclosed hers tightened, squeezing hard as if he wanted to transfer his strength to her.

'Your mother's here—she's just outside. Do you want me to fetch her?'

'No…'

That single word, 'mother', was just too much. It breached all her defences, broke down the barriers she had built up around herself and let the real pain in.

'No,' she managed again. 'I just want you.'

Hot tears flooded her eyes, spilled out down her cheeks and soaked into the white cotton of the pillow case. She didn't have the strength to hold them back, or even to sob in the way her aching heart needed to express itself, but just let them flow.

'*Porca miseria!*'

As if from a great distance, she heard Domenico mutter fierce imprecations in his native Italian. The next moment he had got up and out of his chair and he was coming down onto the bed beside her, easing her across the mattress gently to make room for his large frame.

'Come here, *cara*.'

His arms came round her, gathered her close, pulled her until she was lying with her head resting against his chest, the soft cotton of his T-shirt beneath her cheek, the heavy thud of his heart in her ear. In the space of only a couple of seconds his shirt was soaked with her tears.

'I'm sorry…' she began, rubbing at her eyes, trying to pull away, but he held her close.

'No,' he said, low, husky and intense. 'No, you need to cry—we both need to mourn. Don't hold back.'

And he held her while the tears poured out of her and she wept and wept until she had cried herself to a standstill.

'The doctor says you can go home today.'

It was Alice's mother who spoke, her tone that determinedly bright one that she had adopted from the very first moment she had visited her daughter in hospital after her miscarriage.

'That will make you feel so much better, won't it?'

Alice managed a murmur in reply that might have been agreement. She didn't know what to say—and she wasn't at all sure that her mother's description of the Villa d'Acqua as 'home' was at all appropriate.

Domenico hadn't suggested that she go anywhere else. Like her mother, he seemed to have assumed that she was going back to the villa, at least at first, once she left the hospital and needed to recuperate.

But under what circumstances would she be able to live in Domenico's home—and for how long?

She had arrived here less than three weeks before as Domenico's fiancée; the mother of his unborn child. Another day—just a few short hours more—and she would have been his legal wife, with everything signed and sealed, and then the villa would have been her home too. Her home—and that of her child.

Now she had nothing. No baby. No marriage. No home…

And no Domenico?

She didn't know the answer to that question, she admitted as she packed her few belongings into the case her mother had brought with her. Domenico had proposed marriage to her only because she was pregnant. He had changed his mind, moved from his adamant position that he didn't 'do marriage' only because she was pregnant and he was determined that his child should bear his name.

And she had believed that loving both Domenico and his child would be enough to make it worth her while. Now she had no idea if Dom would want her without the baby that had been so important to him. And even if he did, was loving him enough to help her bear a loveless marriage?

A large, wet tear dropped from her cheek onto the night-dress she was laying in the case, leaving a darker, damp patch on the fine silk, and she heard her mother's concerned sigh.

'Oh, darling—don't! It will all come right in the end, you'll see. Give it a few weeks and you'll feel so much better—and then you and Domenico can try again.'

'I don't know if I want to try again, Mum,' Alice admitted. 'I don't want another baby—I wanted this one.'

'Oh, I know—but I don't mean that you should replace the baby you lost. There will always be a place in your heart that is for that baby. But another child to love…'

Another child that would force Domenico into a marriage he didn't want. That would tie him to a marriage with her just to give his baby his name?

'Last time was an accident, Mum,' she said, concentrating fiercely on fastening the case. 'I never meant it to happen. I don't think I want to be a mother after all.'

Something about her mother's silence, a strained quality in the air, made her look up, glancing in the direction of Patricia Howard's face, and then following the direction of the older woman's gaze.

Domenico stood in the doorway. He had appeared, soft-footed and silent, at some point during her conversation with her mother—but she had no idea at just what stage he had actually arrived.

So how much had he heard? It was obvious that he had caught at least part of her last declaration. Alice opened her mouth to take it back, or at least explain, but then, on a hasty second thought, closed it just as quickly again.

It was better this way. Safer. Easier.

If he thought that she never wanted his child in the future, then he wouldn't feel obliged to keep to his offer to marry her. He could be in no doubt that he could have his freedom back. And the man who didn't do marriage would know that she wasn't looking to be his wife in the future.

But if he had heard, he was giving nothing away. His face was closed up, his eyes as unresponsive as the blank stares of marble statues as he came further into the room, reaching out a hand for the case she had just finished packing.

'The car's outside,' he said, his words perfectly even, flat and expressionless. 'Are you ready?'

'Ready as I'll ever be.'

She made it sound as if she really meant it, but the truth was that she was terrified of leaving. The small blue-painted room with its pristine white sheets and narrow single bed had become like a haven to her over the past few days. A tiny sanctuary where she could hide away from the world, give herself up to her grief at her loss and not have to think about the harsh realities of the outside world.

Now she was going to have to leave the security of her little hideaway and go back into living—and she had no idea at all what the future held for her.

'Come on, then.'

Domenico held out his arm to her and, knowing she had no choice but to do so, she took it and let him lead her out of the door.

CHAPTER NINE

THE journey back to the villa was as silent, calm and sedate as the desperate journey to the hospital had been frantic, fearful and filled with pain. But for Alice this trip was the time of real desolation. Those words, 'going home', kept repeating inside her head, each time with the dragging sense of dread at the thought that the Villa d'Acqua wasn't home to her at all, and probably never would be now.

She was going back to *Domenico's* home, feeling empty, lost and, in spite of her mother's presence in the car and the fact that her father was waiting for her at the villa, totally alone.

The feeling of loss was almost unbearable.

Alice folded her arms across her body, as if trying to hold herself together, to will her baby to still be there, to make this terrible thing not have happened. But it had, and the misery was compounded by the fact that by losing the baby she had probably lost Domenico too. He had only wanted her as the mother of his child. Now she was no longer that, he couldn't possibly feel the same way.

And that was a thought that was reinforced by the sights that greeted her as they arrived at the villa.

At first she couldn't quite take in what she was seeing. Still numb with shock, it took her bruised mind several lingering seconds to absorb the fact that something was different from the last time she'd been here and process that into a realisation of what had happened—what Domenico had done.

Because only Domenico could have given the order to have all the decorative lights that should have lined the driveway taken down and put away. Only Domenico could have told the gardeners to remove the floral decorations that had been around the huge fountain, flowing over the great stone steps, hanging from the low walls of the terraces.

Only Domenico could have ordered that every trace of their wedding should be removed, erased from existence as if they had never been. Just like the wedding that had never been.

And the wedding that would now never take place?

'We're here,' Domenico announced unnecessarily, bringing the car to a halt at the foot of the steps to the huge main door.

Was the look he turned on her as blank as she read it, or was it just her own battered sensitivity that made it seem so? Was there some hint of question in those brilliant eyes, or was she just imagining everything?

'Are you OK?'

Her hesitation had made him frown.

'I— You had the flowers taken down.'

'I thought it best.'

Now was the time that she had to be strong. She had to hold on to her dignity and face him with a strength she hadn't known she possessed until now. It was time to go back to the pretence she had put on when she had found out about Pippa Marinelli. Time to hide her real feelings behind that mask again.

'Yes,' she said carefully, almost lightly. She even managed a quick, nervous, on-and-off smile. 'I think you're right. It probably is for the best.'

'I'm glad you agree.' Domenico's voice was unexpectedly

gruff. 'Now, can you manage to get up the steps or shall I carry you?'

'I'm all right.'

She'd manage if it killed her. She didn't want to show a moment's weakness, or even response. Domenico's cool indifference on that 'I thought it best' had taken her breath away, and with it all her earlier fears had rushed back with a vengeance.

It was the same once they were inside the house.

All the flowers there had disappeared too. The polished tables, the fine damask cloths, the glittering crystalware might never have been out on display a few short days before. It was as if they had dematerialised, leaving no trace behind.

And she didn't dare to raise a protest, make a comment.

I thought it best.

That was what Domenico would say. Cool and flat and adamant. Totally unyielding. It was not something he was prepared to be moved on—or even argue about—and so she might as well not waste her time or deplete the precious little emotional energy that was left to her.

But she couldn't sit and play the loving fiancée to this man, the polite, unconcerned host to her mother and father. She just couldn't do it. She wanted to run and hide, to bury her face in her pillows and pull soft blankets up over her head as she had done in the hospital, and wish the world would go away.

So when Domenico turned to her with that carefully controlled expression on his face, with that social smile that meant nothing at all, and said in a quiet and perfectly pitched tone, 'Would you like something to eat—or a drink?' she simply shook her head, reacting instinctively, defensively.

'I don't need anything—except I'm a little tired. I'd like to lie down.'

'Of course.'

For a moment she was terrified that he would actually suggest coming with her. That he might take her arm to help her up the stairs or, worse, would once again offer to carry her in his arms up to her room. And she just wouldn't be able to bear it.

If he touched her she would break, splintering into a million tiny pieces, and it would be impossible to put her back together again. If Domenico's hand touched hers, or she felt the strength of his arms, the warmth of his body, then she would be lost, remembering what she had once had and what now, it seemed, might have been taken away from her forever.

But something of her thoughts must have shown in her face. Domenico looked into her eyes and read her feelings intuitively and accurately. If he had been about to offer help, then he swallowed the words. He stepped back and away from her, giving her space and leaving the way to the stairs—and to escape—open to her.

'You know where everything is. If you want anything…'

'No! Nothing!'

It was too sharp, too defiant, and it revealed too much. Hastily Alice swallowed down the tension that was twisting her nerves into tight, painful knots. Made herself smile an acknowledgement.

'I'll be fine, thanks,' she managed. 'I just need to rest.'

And before he could say or do anything more, anything that might shatter what little was left of her precarious self-control, she flung herself into climbing up the wide staircase, rushing up the steps as if all the devils in hell were after her and she had to get away from their grasping claws.

She hadn't expected how hard it would be to go into her room. As she put her hand on the door the memories crowded round her, beating at her head and making her hesitate, trembling on the threshold.

The last time she had been here had been on that dreadful night when she had woken in pain and distress and she had fled down the corridor, seeking Domenico and safety. She didn't know if she could make herself go in.

As she stood there she heard quiet footsteps on the polished wooden floor behind her, the sound bringing her head round sharply. Domenico had come up behind her, her small bag in his hand.

'I brought this in case you needed it,' he said, but those narrowed eyes went to her face, took in her hand on the door, her hesitation that told its own story.

'Let me,' he said and, reaching out, he put his fingers over hers, warm and strong, and turned the handle.

He gave the door a little push with his foot so that it moved, swinging open to give her a clear view of…

But it wasn't her room!

Oh, it was the same *room*—there was the big window giving the wonderful view of the sweeping drive, the big fountain, the glorious gardens, the door to the *en suite* bathroom to her right, the big dressing room to her left…but it was not the room she had left. The place had been totally transformed. The cream and gold decor had vanished, to be replaced with a soft green and white colour scheme, not unlike her bedroom back in the cottage in England. Everything was fresh and crisp and obviously new.

'I had it redecorated,' Domenico said quietly from behind her and, stunned into silence, Alice could only nod blankly, still staring at the scene before her. Taking in the changes that wiped away the links to the terrible memories of that night.

He'd done this for her. He'd known how hard it would be to go into the room, and he'd had it changed so that it was still her bedroom, but it was not the room she had woken up in in the darkest hour of the dawn and known that she was miscarrying.

'Thank you,' she said at last. 'Thank you so much.'

There was no response. Nothing. And suddenly a quality

about the silence at her back made her turn sharply, a startled gasp escaping her lips as she realised that there was no one there.

As quietly as he had come, Domenico had disappeared again, moving silently off down the corridor and back down the stairs. Only the case still standing on the floor at her side showed that he had ever been there.

Had he heard her words of thanks? Did he know how much his thoughtfulness in changing the room had meant to her? Alice wasn't sure and for a moment or two she considered going after him to give him her thanks in person, but then, re-thinking, she hesitated.

If Domenico had wanted her thanks, he would have stayed around to hear it. Instead he had deposited her case on the floor and gone. He would be back downstairs with her parents again now and he probably wouldn't want her to come rushing down and interrupting things. Besides, the tiredness that she had claimed as an excuse to go to her room had now become a reality. She was still recovering from the physical trauma she'd experienced, and the emotional turmoil that had assailed her since she had left the hospital had reduced her to a limp weariness that meant she only had the energy to head into the room and nowhere else.

Meaning only to dump the case before getting into bed, she headed for the dressing room, freezing in appalled shock as she opened that door and looked inside.

I thought it best.

Domenico's voice, controlled, distant, unemotional, came back to her as clearly as if he were standing beside her and speaking the words right in her ear.

I thought it best.

Her wedding dress was gone.

Not only her wedding dress but also her shoes, the veil, the delicate headdress. Everything that had been laid out so carefully in the dressing room, ready for her to come and dress herself in them, waiting for the dawn of her wedding day.

The day that had never come.

The day that had never happened and, it seemed, the day of which Domenico was determined to erase every trace from his life—and hers.

She had coped with the disappearance of the flowers and the lights, the changes downstairs that had removed every sign of the festivities that had been planned but had been so abruptly cancelled. But this...

This careful, deliberate removal of the most personal, most intimate items that had meant her wedding day to her was more than she could bear. It seemed to her that Domenico had set out to obliterate any reminder that there would ever have been a wedding now that in his mind there was no reason for him to marry her after all.

I thought it best.

And she had been forced to agree with him. What other choice did she have?

Domenico might not have told her to her face that their marriage was no longer on the cards, but he had found a way to get his message across loud and clear.

In the sunlit garden room downstairs, Domenico finally gave up on his attempt to follow the conversation that Alice's mother and father were having and let his thoughts turn inwards, brooding on the situation in which he found himself.

At some point he knew he was going to have to ask Alice what her thoughts on her future—their future—were. But not now. Not yet.

He had to give her time to heal, to recover from this traumatic loss, before they could look at where they went from here.

Everything had changed so fast. A couple of weeks ago, life had been simple and uncomplicated. Twenty-four hours had changed all that. By the end of one single day he had been anticipating the two major life changes he had thought would never happen to him.

He was going to be a father, and he was getting married.

'I think that would be best. Don't you agree, Domenico?' Patricia asked, turning towards him suddenly.

'*Si...*' he responded absently, not at all sure what he was agreeing to.

All that he could focus on was just how much like her daughter Patricia Howard was. They had the same deep blue eyes, the same dark, fine hair. Though Patricia's hair was cut into a smooth, elegant style, much shorter than Alice's tumbling mass of waves.

But in another twenty-five years or so, Alice would look much as her mother did now. Smiling, elegant, composed...

Happy?

Dio mio, but he hoped so.

'Alice should feel better after she's rested,' Alice's father, David, was saying now. 'Just take things one day at a time. In fact, I think it's probably best if we went home—left you two alone.'

'I agree...'

The rest of Patricia's words faded into an inaudible blur inside Domenico's head. It wasn't the words he was concerned with—it was the smile that she had turned on her husband that caught him and held him transfixed.

It was a smile of agreement and yet it was so much more. It was a smile of trust, of total confidence—the sort of knowledge of a person that could only come from long years of knowing them. Of being together.

And suddenly he had a mental image of Alice, somewhere down the line, twenty, or twenty-five years from now, turning that smile...

On someone else.

No!

The rejection of the thought, of the image sounded so violently inside his head that for a moment he was stunned that Patricia and David hadn't heard it. But they continued with their discussion as if nothing had happened—which, to them, it hadn't. And Domenico could only be thankful that they were absorbed in their conversation and didn't seem to notice how he had withdrawn, getting up and pacing to the open French doors and onto the terrace, staring out at the gathering dusk as it crept across the garden.

But he wasn't seeing the expanse of lawn that swept down to the river's edge. He didn't see anything of the vast property he owned and had earned for himself from nothing. From a start with no home, no family, not even a name.

All he could see inside his thoughts was that smile. A smile that told him what it meant to be part of a family. To share a life. To be married.

Two weeks ago his life had changed. Suddenly he was going to be married. And he was going to be a father.

Two weeks ago he'd put those in a different order. He'd been going to be a father, and so he was getting married.

And now suddenly both of them had been taken away from him. He was no longer going to be a father and...

And marriage?

His thoughts went back to the moment they'd arrived back at the house earlier. The moment that Alice had looked around and noticed the things he'd had done while she was in the hospital. When she'd commented, he'd given her an honest response. 'I thought it best.'

He had thought it was for the best. The reason for their getting married in the first place was gone. Alice had only agreed to marry him because of the baby. Before that—before she'd discovered she was pregnant—she had left him, saying she'd had enough of their relationship.

So with no baby to hold them together, would she stay or would she be glad of the excuse to leave once again and never come back?

He'd thought it best to remove all the signs of the wedding that neither of them had wanted, and Alice had agreed with him.

'I think you're right,' she'd said, as calmly as could be. 'It probably is for the best.'

He'd made the right decision. He was doing what had felt right—and his instincts had been spot on where Alice was concerned. She'd been grateful to see all the evidence of the wedding removed. She'd even managed a smile as a result— the first and only smile since she'd come to him in the grey-ness of the dawn with a face as white as a sheet and panic darkening her eyes.

She'd smiled. And that smile had told him that she was grateful that he'd anticipated what she wanted and done it without being asked.

Definitely the right thing.

So why the hell did he feel as if he'd just made the worst possible mistake of his life?

CHAPTER TEN

'YOUR mother and father should be landing about now.'

Domenico made it sound as if his statement was just a casual remark, everyday conversation, but there was still enough of an edge on the words that they made Alice sit up straighter in her chair.

'That's right,' she said carefully, aiming to keep her tone as strictly neutral as his. 'They said it would be at about eight in the evening, our time.'

Now she had to nerve herself for the 'and' or the 'but' that she knew instinctively was coming. She didn't have to wait long.

'Pat said that she asked you to go back with them.'

He didn't lift his eyes from the letter he was reading, keeping them focused on the page, but an unnatural stillness about his posture, a unnecessary ferocity in his concentration revealed the fact that there was a lot more behind the easy comment than he was letting on.

'Yes—she suggested it might be therapeutic to have a holiday.'

'But you decided not to go?'

'No. Do you think I should have done?'

Oh, this was ridiculous! The two of them were like a pair of hostile cats, nervously circling each other, neither of them daring to look the other straight in the eye for fear that it would spark them into launching a direct attack. So they were both using sidelong glances, oblique approaches, in the hope of suggesting a problem rather than bringing it right out into the open.

And that was 'the problem' right there in that sentence.

Ever since she had come back from the hospital, relations with Domenico had been like this—strained, cautious, careful in the extreme. Nothing was said about the events of the past week, the loss of the baby, and the way it would affect them from now on. Domenico had never, ever raised the topic of what it meant for the future of their relationship—or even if they *had* a relationship that might have a future to follow.

Certainly if she read his behaviour right since she'd come out of hospital, then Domenico had already written off the relationship they'd had and was simply waiting for her to realise it.

'Do you think I should have gone to New Zealand with Mum and Dad?' Alice repeated now, more emphatically. At least if he had to answer that then she might get some clue as to how his mind was working, where his thoughts were heading, so that she might have an idea of how to proceed.

And at least her pointed tone made Domenico pause, lift his head, meet her questioning stare head on.

'Do you?'

Domenico shrugged off the question with a nonchalant lift of one shoulder.

'That depends on what you would like to do. Did you want to go?'

Alice clenched her hand tightly round her water glass until the knuckles showed white.

No! she wanted to scream. No, I do *not* want to go to New Zealand—I don't want to go anywhere! What I want to do is to stay here with you and…

But there her mind blew a fuse. What she wanted was for time to go back, for things to be as they had been before she had lost her baby. But she knew that that was impossible. It could never be.

The problem was that she had no idea what would happen if she stayed. She only knew that since she had come out of hospital living with Domenico had been like walking on eggshells—and eggshells filled with broken glass, at that!

'I don't think so,' she said cautiously, watching his face intently from between her lashes, waiting to see if some change of expression, some reaction, however small, would give her a clue as to what he was thinking or feeling.

But there was none. Just as there had been no reaction, no show of any emotion, to anything all week. He had been politeness and courtesy itself. If there was anything she wanted, needed or even just had a passing whim for, then it was hers. But what she wanted was some sign of Domenico himself. The real man behind the unrevealing mask which was all he was showing her.

And that she was not allowed to see.

'Then you're better staying here,' Domenico returned calmly, dropping his gaze back to the letter in his hand.

'You don't mind?'

'Why should I mind? There's plenty of room and if you don't feel up to travelling…'

'It isn't the travelling that bothers me!'

His indifference stung. If he had made up his mind about their future, then he was not saying. If he had any thoughts at all about where they went from here then he clearly had no plans to share them with her.

'I just think Mum and Dad need time to themselves without me around. After all, they're almost newly-weds in a way.'

That got his attention. He actually put the letter aside as

his eyes went to her face, a faint frown of confusion drawing his brows together.

'How can they be newly-weds? They must have been together—what, twenty-six years?'

'Because I'm twenty-five? Well, yes, they were together twenty-six years ago, but they haven't always been together in between.'

'They split up?'

'About eight years ago. They were rowing all the time and they decided on a separation. They'd even put the divorce in motion. That was when Mum moved to New Zealand—she has a sister out there. But one day Dad's company sent him out to Auckland to complete a deal. On an impulse, he decided to look up Mum. They had a meal together—and another… In the end they realised they didn't want to divorce at all. So they cancelled the whole thing.'

'And your father moved out to New Zealand too?'

Alice nodded, a faint smile curving her mouth.

'They felt they needed a new start—and that New Zealand had been lucky for them, so they wanted to stay there. That's why I said they're only like newly-weds really. They've just bought a new house and are enjoying rediscovering each other. I'm so happy for them and I wouldn't want to…'

Her voice caught in her throat as her gaze tangled with his and she caught the expression in the darkness of his eyes, snagging on something raw and unshielded that was hidden there.

'How does it feel?' he said suddenly and for a moment she couldn't understand what he was asking, or even why he had come out with the question.

'How…?'

'How does it feel to be able to talk like that? To know about your parents; who they are, where they live—what they did in the past?'

'It…'

Alice found she couldn't answer him. To her, it just felt normal. Perfectly ordinary. She couldn't begin to think what it would feel like *not* to know.

'Did you never know your parents?'

'Never.'

'Oh, Dom! I can't imagine what that feels like. For me, Mum and Dad have always been there. Even when they split up they were there for me. They're part of my life and always have been. They're what helps me define myself. And of course my past—my memories—are full of them.'

'I have no memories.'

'None at all?'

Everything in her was pushing her to get out of her chair, go over to him, take his hand…but one look at his dark, controlled face warned that her actions would not be welcome.

'You—you must have been very young when they died.'

'I was *neonato*—newborn.'

It was the sheer matter-of-factness of the statement that caught on Alice's heart and twisted. He showed no emotion, no sense of horror, while even to imagine anything happening to either of her parents, never mind both, brought the hot sting of tears to her eyes.

But then, of course, Domenico had been too young to register his parents, too young to remember anything about them.

'What—?' she began, but Domenico either wasn't listening or was determined to cut her off before she probed any deeper.

'That's why I'm not exactly used to having someone's parents around the house.'

Was he saying that was also why he had been so distant and impenetrable for the past few days? That it was because of her parents and not because their relationship was over as far as he was concerned? Or was it that he hadn't felt right at the thought of finishing things with her while her parents were here?

'Is that why you kept your distance while Mum and Dad were here?'

She meant it to sound joking but it somehow got mangled up between her thoughts and her tongue and came out as provocative instead.

'You needn't have worried—they're no prudes. They would expect us—as an engaged couple—to share a bed.'

The sensation of having put her foot squarely in her mouth hit home with a sickening sense of horror uncoiling in the pit of her stomach.

Engaged.

Were they engaged?

He had proposed marriage because she was pregnant with his child, and only because she was pregnant. So did he still consider his offer binding now that she had lost the baby?

She opened her mouth to ask but lost her nerve and found herself saying instead, 'Did you really think that they'd play the heavy parents because—?'

'That is a very stupid question,' Domenico inserted with a razor-sharp edge to the words. 'Do you really think that I'm crass enough to force myself on you when you've just been through such a trauma?'

And did she really think that he had forgotten it already? That he could just switch off from the memories of just over a week ago? Hell, if he closed his eyes now, he could still see her the way she'd been when she'd burst into his room, with her eyes wide and staring in shock, her face whiter than the nightdress she was wearing, the spots of blood on the silky material that had told their own story of horror and loss.

'I do have some sense of control, even if you might find it hard to believe.'

He wished he'd moderated his tone better when he saw her flinch, but she'd caught him on the raw. For the past few days she'd drifted through his life like a pale, withdrawn wraith. She would neither talk about the miscarriage nor let him get anywhere near her. She had seemed as hard to get close to, get hold of, as a rainbow or a drift of snow in the wind.

And now *she* was accusing *him* of keeping his distance!

'So it's just "control", is it?' Alice challenged, suddenly more animated than she'd been in days. Her head had come up, tossing back the cloud of dark hair that tumbled round her face, and her big eyes had a flash of life in them that had been missing ever since she'd woken up in the hospital. Nothing else?'

'And what does that mean?'

'Exactly what I said. That it's only a "sense of control" that's keeping you in your room and not in mine?'

'That's what I said.'

'Yes, I know that's what you said, but is that the truth? Are you sure that there's nothing else that might be causing the problem?'

'What else would there be?'

Tossing the letter down onto the table, Domenico raked both hands through his hair as he tried to follow her abrupt changes of mood, struggling to see any logic behind them. He believed he had behaved like a gentleman, but it seemed that in her mind she was accusing him of something else entirely.

'Alice—this is—'

'Stupid! Yes, I know!' she interrupted, her voice so brittle that he expected the words to splinter into tiny pieces on the carpet in front of him. 'I know—it's stupid—'

Flinging herself to her feet, she paced restlessly about the room, hands shoved into the side-pockets of her deep pink dress, the flowing skirt swirling about her legs with each brusque, jagged movement.

'I'm stupid!'

'Damn it, Alice!'

Disbelief, annoyance and a great wave of exasperation swept through him, pushing him out of his chair and across the room towards her. Grabbing hold of her arms, he pulled her to a halt, the force of the action swinging her round to face him. She was paler than ever, but this time it was the pallor of suppressed emotion, her eyes clashing violently with his, her expression radiating defiance and rejection.

'Just when did I say you were stupid? I never said any such thing and you know I didn't! Just what is going through that muddled head of yours that makes you think such crazy thoughts?'

'First stupid—now crazy, huh?'

Alice's face was sending him completely contradictory messages to her voice. Her words were cold and sharp, impossibly harsh, while her facial expression was a blend of defiance and distress, her chin tilted challengingly, her blue eyes sheened with tears. But were they tears of anger or unhappiness? He couldn't judge, and, given the volatile mood she was in, she would probably go up in flames if he even asked.

Clearly he was supposed to know just what was going on in her mind, without being given so much as a clue.

'I'm surprised that you want to waste your time with a mad woman like me—that you'll even give me houseroom.'

'Give you—' Domenico began, but Alice's tongue was running away with her and she cut straight across him without even listening to what he was saying.

'But then, of course, it wouldn't do to show me the door when my parents were here, now, would it? I mean that would be really "crass" and of course you don't do crass just as you don't do—' Abruptly she swallowed down whatever she had been about to say. 'As you don't do loss of control!'

'So now my restraint is being held against me, is that it?'

Domenico could feel his grip on the reins of his temper sliding away from him. He was beyond knowing which way she was going to jump next. And his attempts at guessing what she wanted from him were exploding right in his face. It seemed that he was expected to know without any clues and then get shot down anyway, no matter what happened.

'I'm trying to be considerate here, Alice, but you're not making it easy!'

'Considerate!'

Alice wrenched herself away from his grip, whirling round and flouncing off across the room. When the barrier of the wall blocked her way, she swung back again to face him, hands on hips, eyes flashing, mouth set.

'So you're trying to be *considerate,* are you, Dom? *Considerate!* So tell me—what's considerate about the way you behaved when you brought me back here? When I'd just got out of hospital?'

'You're going to have to explain that accusation.' Domenico's fight to keep his temper damped down turned his voice into a cold snarl, made his words snap out like the toughest commands. 'Because it seems to me that I'm being tried and condemned before I even know what I'm charged with! It's obvious that you think I'm guilty, but of what?'

'You don't know?'

The look she flung in his direction was openly sceptical, taking any remaining warmth from her face and turning it into the face of an ice maiden, bloodless, frozen and totally remote. She was completely armoured against him, shields up to repel any advances, and she had no intention of letting anyone get past any of her defences.

'Obviously I don't know or I wouldn't be asking! Alice…at least sit down and let's discuss this rationally.'

'I don't want to sit down!'

Her hands came up before her face in a wild, defensive motion that also had the effect of cutting off all communication between them, breaking even the delicate strands of eye contact.

'And I don't want to do as you tell me—and I most definitely do not feel rational about this! But I'll just bet that you felt totally rational—and so much in control when you—'

'When I what?'

Domenico's control cracked and he couldn't hold back the roar of frustration; couldn't disguise the exasperation that was chafing at him, fraying his ability to keep his irritation in check.

He had thought he'd been prepared for anything that might result as an after-effect of the miscarriage. Depression, withdrawal—he'd expected those. Tetchiness and a volatile mixture of emotions...those too. But this was something else. This cold-eyed, cold-voiced woman with the colourless face and the ice-blue eyes was an Alice he had never encountered before. A chilly, hissing harridan who clearly loathed him.

'If you're going to start treating me as the devil incarnate, or as some sort of beast from the primeval swamps, then at least do me the courtesy of explaining *why*. Even a serial killer gets a chance to defend himself! To answer the crimes he's accused of!'

'Crimes!'

It came on a cynical laugh, one that he doubted he'd ever heard from Alice before. And it didn't sound at all right coming from her soft mouth while scepticism shadowed her beautiful eyes. If he'd thought earlier that her appearance was at odds with her voice, then it was happening again. But this time it was impossible to believe that such bitterness, such black sarcasm could come from someone as delicately beautiful as the woman before him.

It might be fury that sparked in her eyes, but it gave them

a glow like the most beautiful, most polished sapphires he had ever seen. And even though cynicism and accusation were what came from her mouth, they were still the most sensual, most kissable lips he had ever seen. And if she tossed her proud head once more, flinging back the shining dark mane of hair and stamping her foot like the proudest, most glorious, thoroughbred Arab mare, then he was going to lose all control.

He just wanted to stride forward and grab her. To slide his hands into that fall of hair and twist it around his fingers, holding her tight. He wanted to turn that proud head towards his and take the softness of her mouth under his, kissing her until she was lost in sensation, until those angry blue eyes shut and she softened under his caress, forgetting all the wild accusations in the moment of yielding up to him, moving instantly from the fierce arousal of fury to the softer but no less potent excitement of pleasure.

But as he took a single step forward, she edged away again, nervous as a wary cat, the look in her eyes warning that if he tried that again then she would run.

And so he forced himself to stay where he was. Forced his mouth to speak softly, to control the urge to lash out, match her accusations with some of his own, parry the slashing attacks of her tongue with a ferocity that matched and outstripped her rage.

'Yes—if you're going to start throwing accusations around then at least tell me the crimes I've committed.'

'Do I have to spell it out? Oh, but I see that I do, because you don't even care what you've done—you don't even *see* it.'

'*Porca miseria!* I don't know what the devil I'm supposed to see!'

'Well, what about the sight that greeted me when I came ho—when I got back here from the hospital? What about the way that all the flowers had vanished—all the lights? All the decorations and the candles?'

'I thought—'

But Alice rushed on.

'What about the way that every trace of our wedding had disappeared—the cake, the marquee—even…'?

Her voice broke on a sob that stopped her speech for a moment. Once again Domenico tried to take a step forward but a furious hand came up to wave him away.

'Even my wedding dress? Do you know how I felt when I looked in that room and my dress had gone? And you call that considerate?'

'Yes, I do, damn you! I do!'

'Then what the blazes are you like when you're being inconsiderate? Because if this is your *consideration,* then I'd sure as hell hate to be around when you're being *mean!*'

'Oh, I can be mean if you want me to, Alice.' Domenico's tone had smoothed to a silken purr, a purr that was soft as a tiger's paw—with lethal, cruel claws concealed just out of sight. 'But I swear you wouldn't like it. And I wasn't being cruel when I—'

'No, of course not!' Alice spat at him, blue eyes flashing fire. 'Of course not! You just—'

She broke off in shock as Domenico flung up his arms in exasperation.

'I thought you wouldn't want reminding of the wedding that your pregnancy had forced you into! I thought that you already had enough on your plate without worrying about a promise that you'd made under duress. I thought—'

'You thought it best!'

'Yes!'

'You thought it *best*—and you thought of everything! Well, no, not everything…'

Her left hand came up, fingers spread. With her right one she was tugging at something on the third finger.

The ring. The engagement ring that he had insisted on buying when she had agreed to marry him. The ring he had chosen with such care, because she had given him something he had never thought he would have—the chance of a family of his own.

'That—' he began but had to leave the sentence hanging when she flung the ring at him with such force that he had to turn his face aside swiftly to avoid being hit on the cheek.

'There was no need—' he tried again.

'There was every need!' she cut across him, tossing her hair back as she faced him with challenge and defiance stamped into every inch of her. 'Because now you have everything! Every damn thing that would ever remind me of that unwanted wedding! You have everything—and I'm free!'

Well, that told him, Domenico reflected cynically. Now he knew exactly where he stood; exactly what she thought of his proposal, of the thought of ever being married to him.

And he could only be thankful that he'd never opened his stupid mouth and let her in on his thoughts—the momentary dream—of the night that he had brought her home from the hospital. Now, as then, silence was clearly the best policy.

'Yes,' he said stiffly, 'you're free to do whatever you want.'

'Well, in that case, I'm sure you won't mind if I pack! I can be out of here in an hour and then you'll never have to see me again!'

He meant to let her go. He really did. It was so obvious that all she wanted was to get out of here—and fast—that he knew he would just be wasting his time even attempting to dissuade her.

He even stood back to allow her space to get past him, a free path to the door.

And he clamped his mouth shut, pushed his hands deep into his pockets, to armour himself against any weak and foolish attempt to hold her back.

He was fine while she was still; while she was standing there, glaring at him, her slender body stiff and taut with rejection, her eyes blue chips of ice. But something happened as she came past him.

Perhaps it was the brush of the skirt of her dress against his body. Perhaps it was the waft of her perfume on the air, the scent of her skin that seemed to reach out with delicate, sensitive fingers and coil around him, chaining him to her with strands so fine and yet so strong that he knew he would never be free.

Or maybe it was the flash of something in her eyes as, just for a second, she turned her head and looked straight into his face. Something that clashed with his own gaze, then snagged and caught—and held it...

'No!' he said, the word breaking from him, impossible to hold back. 'No!'

And, wrenching his hands from his pockets, he reached out and grabbed at her arm, hauling her to a halt and holding her there.

CHAPTER ELEVEN

'No?'

Alice couldn't believe what she had heard.

It wasn't possible.

And yet it was such a simple word, one that barely sounded like anything else. So what else could it be? What else could it mean?

And there was that hand on her arm, strong fingers curled around it, just above her elbow. What else could it mean, when combined with that single syllable but...?

'No?' she repeated, searching his face for clues and finding none.

'Don't go.' Domenico spoke with husky ferocity. 'I don't want you to go.'

Her heart jerked violently in her chest. Was this real? Had he actually said...?

'Wh-what did you say?'

'I said don't go.'

'Why?' she croaked, forcing the word past lips that were painfully dry and tight even though she had slicked them with a moist pink tongue just seconds before.

'Why?' Domenico echoed on a questioning note and there was a small smile that curled his lips as if he couldn't believe that she had even had to ask. 'Does this give you a clue?'

And he slid his free hand under her chin, holding her face up to his as he bent his head and closed his lips over hers.

Alice had never known a kiss like it. It was long and slow and drugging in its sensuality, but at the same time it had a fierce intensity that made her head spin. It was searching, demanding, infinitely hungry and yet it also enticed and cajoled, seeming to draw her heart out of her body and have her soul follow it.

His tongue slid across her mouth, marking the line where her lips had parted, not intruding, not invading, but gently inviting her to open up to him. And Alice could do nothing but respond, her lips parting on a gasp of delight and surrender, her mouth opening, her own tongue enticing him in.

Domenico made a low, raw sound deep in his throat and gathered her close to him, one arm coming round her, to pull her up against his body, the other sliding into her hair, tangling in the dark strands, hard fingers splaying against the curving bone of her skull. Gently but irresistibly, he turned her to him, angling her head just so that he could kiss her again, harder this time, taking her mouth on a long, slow, sensual journey that burned his brand on her lips, turned her blood molten in her veins and set her senses zinging with electricity all over her body.

'Get the idea?' he muttered against her mouth. And Alice could only sigh a wordless sound of agreement and acquiescence as her lips sought his again, needing the hot pressure even after that tiny space of snatched speech that had stopped him kissing her.

Her own hands had gone up and around his neck, pulling his head down to hers, as she stood on tiptoe to press herself closer, giving back every bit as much as he had given her, and adding something more. The heat from his body against which she was pressed seemed to sear her from top to toe, burning through the fine material of her dress and scorching the wakened flesh beneath.

But it wasn't enough. It could never be enough. Not when what she truly wanted was his hands on her, the burn of his palms on her skin, the hardness and strength of his fingers caressing the most delicate points on her body. The heavy pulse of need low down in her body set every nerve throbbing in aching hunger.

She had thought that she was being dismissed, that he wanted no more of her, and this sudden about-turn made her head swim. She felt as if she had been starving and now she was finally being offered something. It wasn't enough to appease her aching hunger, and it probably wouldn't sustain her for more than a very short space of time, but she was so, so hungry that she knew she was going to grab at it with both hands before it evaporated totally.

'So you do still want me—want me here?'

'Want you?' Domenico's laughter was raw-edged, catching in his throat as he vented it. 'Oh, *cara*, do you have to ask?'

Did she need to ask? Well, no, not really. The heavy pounding of his blood that built a pulse at the base of his throat, the heat that radiated from his skin, the ragged, uneven breathing all told their own story. She had known and loved this man so long that she was attuned to every tiny sign that revealed how aroused he was, and she couldn't doubt them now.

She knew that he *wanted* her, and that was enough for him. But was it enough for her?

Was she really so desperate that she would take whatever crumbs he would toss her and accept them gratefully, as being just enough to stop her from starving without ever actually nourishing any part of her?

But then Domenico's mouth touched her ear, his lips warm and his tongue moistly tracing the contours of the skin, his teeth faintly grazing the curving outer edge, and everything inside her melted in the rush of heat along every nerve path. The tips of her breasts stung where they were crushed against the hard wall of his chest, her lower body moved sinuously against his, bringing a low groan to his mouth as she slid against the swelling force of his arousal, feeling its heat even through their clothes.

His dark head came down to kiss her again, his mouth crushing hers, his tongue invading, stroking intimately over the soft inner tissues so that she shivered in excitement.

The hand that had held her had loosened and was stroking slowly, softly down the bare skin of her arm. Tantalising caresses circled over her hand, moving down each finger in turn before he caught her palm in his and lifted it to the warm pressure of his mouth. This time it was his lips that kissed their way down each finger, lingering over the spot where her engagement ring had been and enclosing the now empty space in a warmth that seemed to ease the sense of loss. And all the time he was muttering soft words in her ear, husky, caressing, cajoling words in liquid Italian that made her heart melt as she caught at their meaning. She spoke enough of the language to recognise the ardent praise of her beauty, the declarations of adoration, the need, the hunger that was driving him wild, making him crazy.

And her own mouth moved almost silently, echoing and repeating the phrases to him, pressing the words against his skin in slow, tender kisses on the lean planes of his cheek. The rough growth of beard abraded her lips and she let the tip of her tongue slide out to touch the warmth of his skin. The clean, faintly salty taste of his flesh and the heady, male scent rushed to her head like a potent wine, intoxicating and stimulating.

She felt drunk in seconds—drunk on pleasure—and the small, provocative taste was just not enough.

'Dom!'

With a small, whimpering moan, she sought his mouth again, becoming braver now, more demanding, pressing her lips to his, letting her own tongue mimic his explorations earlier, and smiled inwardly as she felt his instant response. The stroke of his hands over her body became harder, hungrier, more urgent. His caresses found the swell of her breasts, cupping and enclosing each one in a searing heat so that she writhed in uncontrolled response, pressing her needy body closer into his hands, hungry nipples peaking against the warmth of his palms.

'Alicia—*carissima…*'

With a gasp he wrenched his mouth away to snatch in a much-needed breath, his broad chest heaving. Looking down into her face, his molten bronze eyes met the yearning blue of hers and he reached up a noticeably unsteady hand to push it through her hair once more, holding her head just so—tilted up to him. Their gazes locked, unable to look away.

'Come with me, *mi fidanzata,*' he muttered in a voice that was thickened with passion. 'Come upstairs with me and let me show you that I want you—let me show you how much I want you here, with me…'

Mi fidanzata.

My fiancée.

Alice's already whirling brain could only fasten on that one word and the important meaning it had—the way that Domenico had used it when he could have said so many others.

Mi fidanzata.

Just two small words but they were enough.

'Come with me now,' Domenico said again, and she looked

up into those burning eyes, seeing the way that the pupils had expanded, huge and dark with just a circle of glowing gold around the rim. She couldn't speak, though her mouth opened to try, but she didn't need to because something in her face had given her away.

And Domenico had caught it. She saw his eyes narrow, saw him register the silent answer she had given him with a quick, decisive nod. The next moment he had crushed another hard, fierce kiss on her parted lips before catching her up in his arms, lifting her and carrying her towards the sweeping stairs.

Instinctively Alice's arms went around his neck, though she knew she was held safely, with his strength supporting her. Her eyes were still locked with his so she barely saw their progress up the polished wood, or even registered just where they were on their journey to the wide expanse of the landing. She only knew the feel of the wall against her back as, every couple of steps or so, he paused to kiss her again, turning their progress into a form of foreplay that inflamed her senses and heated her blood.

By the time they reached the landing, she was gasping with need and had already tugged loose the top four buttons on his shirt that were all she could reach. But it was enough to reveal the powerful straight lines of his shoulders, the pulse that beat at the base of his neck, against which she pressed her hungry mouth, licking, sucking and nibbling the exposed skin, feeling his pulse kick up a beat under her caresses, his raw groan of response a husky sound low in his throat.

As he lowered her to her feet he let her body slide down the length of his, chest to chest, thigh to thigh, the slenderness of her hips cradled in the strong bones of his pelvis. By the time she was standing on her own feet, her legs were trembling almost too much to support her as a result of the onslaught on her senses and her knees threatened to buckle beneath her.

But Domenico didn't intend that she should stay there long. As soon as he had a hand free he found the long zip that fastened her dress at the back and slid it swiftly down. A heartbeat or two later the whole dress slithered down her body, falling to the floor to pool in a swirl of pink linen on the deep blue carpet.

Deep blue.

It was only then that Alice registered just where she was. That Domenico had brought her up and into *his* room, not hers. That fact seemed significant, but for the life of her she couldn't quite put her finger on why. And her whirling brain's scrabble to find an explanation spun off into oblivion as Domenico kissed her again and slid her unfastened bra from her aching breasts, dropping it to the floor to lie, pale pink against dark, on top of her crumpled dress.

'Alicia, cara...'

Her name was a crooning litany against her skin as he swept her up again, carried her to the bed and came down beside her.

'Carina, adorata, tesora...'

With gentle hands he shaped her body, lingering at the curves of breasts and hips, his eyes hooding and a smile curving his mouth as he watched her writhe underneath his touch, her yearning body arching upwards, pressing herself against him.

'Dom...'

The affectionate form of his name escaped her on a cry of need as his touch tormented the aching tips of her breasts, tugging lightly on the tightened nipples.

'Dom...please...'

Experience of loving her in the past told him just what she wanted and he bent his proud head to take one of the rosy pink tips in his mouth, swirling his tongue around and over it, bringing it to burning, stinging life before closing his lips over it and suckling hard.

And as it had always been in the past, that was the point at which her fraying hold on her control broke. Her head flung back against the pillows, her body arcing into his, as her impatient fingers completed the task of unfastening and removing his shirt that she had begun on the journey upstairs.

Domenico helped her, shrugging his broad shoulders out of the garment and tossing it to the floor. His trousers followed, and then the black trunks that Alice had been pushing at impatiently, desperate to have the whole man as naked as she was, the whole muscular length of his hot, satin flesh covering hers.

For as long as it took to draw in a breath or two that satisfied them, but no longer. As soon as Alice's wandering hands found their way down the long, straight line of his back and smoothed the tight curve of his buttocks, Domenico moved convulsively, jerking in response to her caress. And that abrupt movement brought the heated power of his erection into burning contact with the nest of dark curls at the juncture of her thighs.

Immediately her fingers slid between their bodies, touching softly, smoothing over the heated velvet that sheathed the masculine force of him, making him buck in uncontrolled reaction, his own hands tightening in the dark cloud of hair spread out around her head.

'Careful,' he muttered, thick and raw. 'Don't…Alice— don't!—Momento…'

In a frantic movement he pulled away, twisting on the bed and reaching for the small cabinet that stood beside it. Wrenching open a drawer, he pulled out a small foil packet and ripped it open.

Alice had barely time to register what was happening before he had sheathed himself and was once more lying with her, the hair-hazed strength of one leg coming between hers, nudging her thighs aside, sliding between them.

Cupping her head in both his hands, he looked down deep into her face, his glittering eyes searching her passion-scorched features. His black hair had fallen forward over his broad forehead and high on the carved cheekbones a raw slash of colour burned his skin.

Bending to touch her lips, he took them once in a long, drugging kiss before lifting his head just inches so that his nose was against hers and the breath from his mouth was warm on her cheek.

'Now,' he muttered roughly as the tip of his masculinity probed the moist core of her. 'Now I will show you how much I want you. And why I want you here…with me…'

With each phrase he thrust himself into her, a little further and a little harder every time, making her hungry body clench around him, a moan of response escaping her lips.

Domenico moved again. In…and almost out…and in again.

As his thrusts picked up strength and speed, Alice moaned, her head tossing on the pillow, long dark hair flying over her face, catching on her lips. Domenico kissed it aside, took her mouth for his own.

With his hands on her body too, she was lost in a world of sensation, swimming in it, drowning in it, going down under swirling waves of pleasure. Giving her whole self up to it, she closed her eyes tight, concentrating fiercely on the glorious pressure building up and up, deep inside her. But even as she felt it grow, knew where it was heading, Domenico moved again, shifting his lips to take one pouting nipple hard into his mouth and suckling on it hard.

Immediately Alice's control shattered, taking any form of rational or coherent thought with it. Losing herself completely, she arced her body upwards, giving herself totally to this man, taking him totally into herself. A wild, keening cry of stunned delight broke from her as the pleasure flooded through her, taking all defences, all restraint along with it. Somewhere in the back of what tiny fragment of her mind was still functioning, she was instinctively aware of the fact that Domenico too had reached the same peak at the same time, as a hoarse cry of fulfilment was torn from him, his long body tensing, his dark head thrown back as her heated inner-most core convulsed around him. But that was the last thing she knew as the next moment the stormy waves of orgasm broke inside her body, swarmed through every nerve, crashed over her head, and took her whirling and spinning and sobbing out loud into the blind oblivion of ecstasy.

CHAPTER TWELVE

THE MUTED buzzing of his mobile phone, somewhere in the room, was the last thing on earth that Domenico wanted to hear.

He didn't want to know about the outside world, didn't want to *think* about anything else but what he had here, in this space, in the heat and comfort of this bed, with this woman at his side, her glorious female body limp and exhausted, satiated as he was by the fiery passion that had consumed them both.

Satiated? Well, temporarily.

His heart was still slowing from the frantic, urgent racing of fulfilment. His breathing had eased, returning to normal from the raw rasp of sexual ecstasy, and the sheen of sweat had evaporated from his body. Already his recovery was close to complete.

In his mind he was already there, already anticipating the point when, with the afterglow of gratification ebbing away at last, and the nagging tug of need driving away the lazy contentment of this moment, he would reach for Alice once more. He would kiss the softness of her yielding, giving lips, savour the intimate, uniquely personal taste of her mouth, bury his tongue in its moist, welcoming warmth. His hands would explore the silken contours of her body, tracing paths they'd been before, finding pleasure spots he knew from a lover's experience always drove her wild. Maybe he'd find some that even he had yet to discover, the hidden secrets of her beauty that would take him a lifetime to fully enjoy, to truly appreciate. His touch would arouse his own hunger with each kiss and each caress, awakening a matching desire in her, nurturing the still-glowing embers of their passion until they flared once more into the wild and unstoppable fire of need that would consume them both in its demanding force.

It was a prospect that he anticipated with the deepest pleasure. Even now, just thinking about it, he felt his body already growing hard and hot, his senses starting to rediscover the anticipation and primitive excitement that he knew would soon build to a brutal demand for fulfilment if he denied them too long.

But the persistent electronic buzzing of his phone forced itself into his consciousness, driving through the clinging cobwebs of his lethargy and demanding his attention *now*, before it woke Alice too, and turned her mind to more practical and mundane matters than the sensual feast he had been anticipating. Already she was beginning to stir and mutter faintly, a small frown creasing the smooth space between her fine, dark brows.

'Porca miseria!' Domenico swore under his breath as, flinging back the bedclothes, he forced his unwilling body out of the bed, swinging his legs to the floor and standing up reluctantly.

Where the devil was the damn thing? Why hadn't he left it in his jacket pocket as he usually did? Then it would still be downstairs and the unwelcome caller wouldn't have intruded on the sensual idyll that he had been enjoying.

The idyll he had every intention of prolonging right through the night. He had every intention of making love to Alice again and again, over and over, in every way he could imagine and some he had yet to dream up—but ones he was sure that the combination of her luscious sensuality and his erotic imagination could invent for their drawn-out delight.

'Go away!'

Mentally he cursed the caller's persistence, wishing on them a battery failure, a power cut, the loss of credit—anything just so that they would go away and leave him alone to….

But then he realised what time it was; recalled just who he had asked to ring him at this hour, why he had told her to use the mobile and not the main house phone, and what her call might mean. Immediately the slow reluctance of lethargy dropped from him and he moved quickly to where the tangled bundle of his clothes lay abandoned on the carpet. Snatching up the crumpled trousers, he tugged the slim, silver-coloured phone from their pocket and thumbed it on.

'*Si?*'

The voice that answered him in Italian was the female one he had been expecting; the one that made it awkward and impossible to take the phone call where he was. He couldn't talk freely and, besides, in the bed Alice was stirring again, her tousled head turning on the pillow, her long, smooth limbs stretching and relaxing as she drifted closer to wakefulness.

'I'll ring you back,' he said softly, hastily switching off the phone again and gathering up the rest of his clothes in one hand as he moved swiftly to Alice's side of the bed and knelt down on the rich blue carpet at her side, gently stroking the tangled dark hair away from her face with the hand that still held the phone.

'*Cara…*'

It was low-voiced, soothing, stilling her restless movement, making her smile in recognition of his voice.

Smiling too, in unseen response, and unable to resist it, he bent his head and took her mouth in a lingering kiss, then cursed inwardly as the intimate caress created a savage kick of primal need low down in his body. A need that he knew he

was going to have to deny himself the pleasure of indulging—
for a little while at least.

'Dom…'

His name was a sleepy sound of pleasure on Alice's
tongue, twisting his physical and mental discomfort several
notches higher as she stirred languorously and reached out
sleepy arms to fold around his neck. The dreamy smile on
her soft pink lips was almost irresistible, but Domenico knew
that if he gave in to temptation then the next phone call that
interrupted them would be impossible to conceal. Alice
would want to know who it was from and he could not lie
to her.

And there would be another phone call—and soon, he
knew. Pippa Marinelli was not a patient woman, and she
wouldn't take kindly to being kept waiting.

'I have to take this, *cara*,' he said, kissing her closed eyelids instead.

He wanted her to keep them closed; was not at all sure that
if she woke up properly, opened her eyes, she might not read
something in his face that would make her want to enquire
further into the reason for his leaving her right now. She might
even guess at the identity of the caller, and they had too much
to talk about as it was.

'I'll answer it downstairs. I know…' he murmured ruefully,
anticipating her frown of displeasure, the small pout of her
lips. 'I know, and I don't want to, either. But I won't be long.
And now that you're staying we have all the time in the world.'

His smile grew, became a wide, reminiscent grin, even
though he knew that she couldn't see it.

'I knew I could make you stay. Knew you'd see we're not
ready to be apart—not now…'

Not ever? his unguarded mind added in the privacy of his
own thoughts. But that was another subject he could only raise

when they had enough time—more time than was available to him now.

'Sleep now.'

'But…'

Once again her mouth formed that sexy little moue of protest, threatening both his composure and his resolve. But each movement of his left hand brought the sleek lines of his cellphone back into the range of his vision, reminding him that he didn't have the time to indulge the yearning demands of his senses,

'You need to rest, *cara*,' he insisted. 'And I'll be back by the time you wake. Wait here for me and we'll take up where we left off. I'll tell you when you can get up.'

And that was as much delay as he dared risk, so he gently but firmly eased himself from her entwining arms, tucking them down at her sides and pulling the bedclothes up around her, hiding the provocative temptation of her naked body from his hungry gaze. He couldn't resist one last snatched moment to press a lingering kiss on the rounded curve of her shoulder, almost groaning aloud as she murmured softly, the faint, warm sound of sensual contentment twisting nerves already tight with the struggle to resist.

'Come back soon,' she murmured, nestling down deeper into the pillows and sighing reluctantly.

'Oh, I will,' he promised, huskily fervent. 'As soon as I can.'

And then, because it was either leave *now*—and fast—or abandon all attempts to go and give in to the need that was driving him half-insane, he forced himself to his feet, and out of the door.

He was more than halfway down the landing, almost at the top of the stairs, before he felt ready enough to stop, draw in a deep, ragged breath and bring himself under the control needed to pull on his clothes and restore himself to some degree of normality.

The phone he still left switched off, however. Out of sight of Alice's feminine temptations, he was at last beginning to think rationally again. He was not prepared to take any risks, he told himself as he ran down the stairs and headed for his office. There was still the possibility that Alice might awaken and come after him. He wanted to have this conversation in complete privacy before he decided whether he was prepared to share the contents of it with anyone or not.

In the privacy of his study he shut the door carefully. Then pulled the phone out of his pocket again and thumbed it on.

'Pippa? What have you got to tell me?'

At first, Alice was quite content to lie where she was and wait for Domenico to come back. She was warm and comfortable and very relaxed, and so indolently satisfied that for a while she was not even remotely inclined to move. It was just so easy to lie there, and doze, and think of the passionate lovemaking she'd just shared with Domenico, the memories bringing a smile to her face at the same time as her toes curled as she anticipated his return and a repeat performance. It was only slowly, as the time ticked past, that she began to wonder what had happened, and where her ardent lover had got to. And that was when a sneaking feeling of unease crept its way into her soul.

What was taking him so long? What was it about the phone call that had been so important that he had to answer it now—and away from her?

Alice's eyes flew open, all remnants of sleep deserting her in a second as her thoughts went back over the things Domenico had said before he'd left the room.

'Now that you're staying we have all the time in the world.'
Now that you're staying.

She hadn't said anything about staying. Hadn't agreed to anything. Knocked off balance by the passion of Domenico's kiss, swamped by the hungry feelings it had awoken in her, she had been thrilled to hear him say that he didn't want her to go. But she hadn't actually agreed to anything. His confident assumption that all was now well and that she was going to fit in with what he wanted suddenly jarred uncomfortably, making her pull herself up on the pillows, thinking back over everything else he'd said.

I knew I could make you stay. Alice flinched inside at the memory of the arrogant declaration. Was that the triumphant exclamation of an ardent lover or a man who had just carried out a cold-blooded, deliberate manipulation of the woman in his bed?

I knew I could make you stay...

Suddenly desperately afraid to face her uncomfortable thoughts, Alice shifted uneasily against the pillows, trying to find another way of looking at things. But no matter which way she tried to send her thoughts to come up with another explanation, they always came back to the same thing.

I knew I could make you stay.

What did that remind her of? It was something that made her mind restless, setting her nerves on edge.

I'll tell you when you can get up.

I'll tell you...

'Oh, heaven help me!'

The words escaped in a panicked rush and she realised just what the nasty, nagging suspicion at the back of her mind was trying to tell her. She remembered now and it made her feel dreadful—taken for granted—manipulated...

Used.

How could she have forgotten the very first day that Domenico had come back into her life after she'd tried to walk away from him? The day that he'd arrived at her cottage and openly declared just why he was there.

'This relationship isn't over, Alice, not until I say so. As long as I want you, you stay—and you only leave when I give you permission to go.'

She'd been such a fool! She'd allowed herself to think—allowed herself to feel—allowed herself to be seduced into believing that Domenico's declaration that he wanted her to stay was because he cared for her. Because he couldn't bear to let her go. But she'd forgotten one important thing.

She'd forgotten how he always had to be in control.

Once before, she'd tried to walk out on Domenico Parrisi when he had not been ready to let her go. He'd come after her and brought her back into line, using exactly the same tactics as he'd just employed on her tonight. He'd cold-bloodedly seduced her back into his bed and into his life. And she had been enough of a blind, besotted fool to let it happen.

'Oh, you idiot! *Idiot!*' she reproved herself, clenching her hand into a fist and slamming it down onto the bed in a rush of impotent rage. 'You let him do it! You let him walk all over you!'

She had been just too weak, too stupid. Totally at the mercy of her feelings for this man, she had let him use and manipulate her into doing exactly as he wanted.

Or had she? There had been that look in his eyes, a note in his voice. There had been *something* there—hadn't there?

Or had she simply been fooling herself? Letting herself believe because it was what she wanted most in all the world? Because her days had been filled with hopes, her nights with dreams, that one day, some day, Domenico might come to feel a little for her.

But that had been when she had thought she was going to become his wife. When she had still been carrying his baby, and Domenico had wanted the child so much that he had been prepared to take her along with it. And now that there was to be no baby, there would be no marriage, no future for her and Domenico in any way.

But of course there had been more to it than that. More that Domenico had wanted out of the arrangement, anyway.

He had made it plain that he still lusted after her—that he still wanted her so much, physically at least. Hadn't he declared that to her face so openly?

I still want you—more than ever, in fact. And as long as I want you, then this relationship continues. No woman walks out on me—none ever has and none ever will.

Too upset, too restless to stay still, Alice flung back the bedclothes and flung herself out of the bed. The idea of staying there, just waiting patiently and obediently for her man to return to her, waiting for his attentions, was abhorrent to her. She had to get a grip on herself and make up her mind just what she was going to do.

Going to do?

'Oh, dear heaven!' Alice crammed her knuckles against her mouth in an effort to crush back the cry of pain that was almost like the howl of a wounded animal.

What *could* she do? There was only one course of action left open to her.

She'd told herself that if she was no longer considered as Domenico's bride-to-be then she was going to take her dismissal with dignity. All those weeks before, when she had accepted that the man she loved would never love her back, she had packed her bags and gone. If she had to, she would do that again.

And it looked as if she had to.

She might have been weak this once, might have let him win her over this once. She might have succumbed weakly to soft words and even softer kisses, but if she kept doing that, if she kept on letting him use her in this way, then it would destroy her.

She had accepted that he was never going to marry her now, but to be nothing but a mistress like this, doing his bidding, jumping when he said jump, obeying every command, was more than she could bear. She had to get out of here.

Oh, but it would be so much harder this time. Because the first time she had never known how hard it would be to endure the long, lonely days, the dark, even lonelier nights without a sight of Domenico in her life, without ever hearing his voice.

She had been through all that once, and barely survived. She had had to survive because in the middle of the misery she had discovered that she was pregnant. And because of the baby she had had to keep going. Now she was completely on her own, and she didn't know how she was going to survive.

She had to get out of here. She had to get dressed and ready before Domenico came back. She couldn't face him like this. She had to be clothed—armoured—feeling strong and ready before he came back into the room and she had to confront him with her decision.

If he came back now… If he touched her…

'No!'

Whirling round, she grabbed at her clothes where they lay scattered about the room, fallen on the carpet. She wouldn't let herself think about how they had come to be there, about the wildly passionate moments when Domenico had stripped her—and she had stripped him—and they had left their clothes anywhere they had landed. She had been so hopeful then, so joyful, so optimistic…

So blindly, stupidly, crazily deceived.

She had let him do whatever he had wanted with her and she hadn't even questioned why.

Domenico must have thought that he had her totally in his power; that she was his to do with as he pleased.

And why not? Hadn't she given him every reason to think so?

'Oh, damn it!'

The exclamation escaped her as she grabbed up an abandoned shoe, at the same time spinning round to see if she could find its partner. Her grip on the leather was not secure and the sandal went flying from her hand, landing with a thud on top of a dresser near by.

On top of the dresser was Domenico's laptop, still open, with the screen up and the keyboard exposed.

A keyboard that one edge of her shoe had obviously caught on, briefly pressing a key before it bounced off again and fell back to the floor.

The slim computer had obviously not been switched off but had been left there, abandoned in standby mode, and Domenico had planned to get back to it well before now. It hummed for a second, buzzed, flickered and then came back to life. The screen lit up and Alice found herself staring at the rows of lettering.

Rows of names and message titles. Domenico had obviously been checking his email messages when he had left the machine switched on.

Alice was just about to turn away and find her shoe again when one of the names caught her eye. A very recent message, it must just have come in in the last hour or so because it lay at the very top of the list, the first thing on the screen. And of course the message subject was in Italian. But it wasn't that that Alice was looking at. Instead, her eyes had focused on the list of names at the left-hand side of the screen, and fixed on one name in particular.

A name that she hadn't heard of for a month or more.

A name that she had thought she would never have to hear of again.

A name that Domenico had *sworn* she would never have to hear of again.

Pippa Marinelli.

The woman Domenico had refused to tell her about. The woman he had declared had never been his mistress, but the woman with whom Alice had heard gossip link him so closely in the weeks before she had left him that first time.

As she stood and stared at the screen, and that name, it was as if she was once more back in the ladies' room at one of the most elegant hotels in Milan, where she and Domenico had been attending a reception. Shut in one of the cubicles, Alice had been invisible to the group of women who had come in after she had shut the door. The group of women who had then set themselves to primping and preening in front of the mirror while chattering and gossiping non-stop.

It was when she had caught her own name, and then Domenico's, in the middle of the high-speed rush of Italian that Alice had frozen into total stillness, listening hard.

'And did you see that poor stupid English girl—that Alice Howard—draping herself all over Domenico Parrisi out on the dance floor? She was gazing up into his eyes like a lovesick rabbit—and she doesn't even know she's being taken for a ride. Luisa and I were at a restaurant the other night and we saw him there with someone else—another woman. They were dining together—dining on each other, more like! They had eyes only for each other…Luisa said her name is Pippa Marinelli…'

Pippa Marinelli.

Alice closed her eyes sharply against the white-hot stab of pain that seemed to sear right through to her soul.

Domenico had said that Pippa Marinelli was not a danger to their marriage—and she had believed him.

But of course that had been when they were going to get married. Now the engagement was off, the wedding had been cancelled; even her dress had been taken away…

And it seemed that Pippa Marinelli was back in town and back in Domenico's life.

She knew she shouldn't do it, but she really couldn't help herself. She wouldn't have been human if she'd been able to resist the temptation.

Reaching out a hand that shook terribly, Alice clicked on the message and watched it open up onto the screen.

'Dom…'

That was the first pain and one that stabbed straight to her heart.

Dom.

The shortened, warm, affectionate form of his name. The name he let so few people use—the name, in fact, that she had believed he let only her use. And it had taken her months of being with him, living with him, loving him, before he had let her use it easily.

And Pippa Marinelli began her email, *'Dom…'*

Alice had to fight a brutal little struggle with herself to clear the tears from her eyes so that she could focus on the screen again and read the rest of the message. She blinked hard, swallowed harder and forced herself to stare at the brief lines before her.

Dom—of course I understand why you want me to be more careful. If Alice has miscarried then, naturally, she will be upset and sensitive to everything at the moment, and you don't want her suspecting anything, or trying to probe into areas you don't want her to know about. But don't worry—she won't find out anything from me. I do know how to be discreet.

Pippa.

'I do know how to be discreet!'

Shock and pain made Alice's head spin so hard that she had to grab hold of the dresser for support.

He had promised! He had *sworn!*

She felt as if everything she had ever believed, every hope, every dream had been snatched away from her and then thrown aside like so much garbage. She wanted to run—she wanted to cry—she wanted to fold her arms around herself. To keep the pain out and to hold herself together.

But then, just as a moan of savage agony escaped her, she knew another feeling. A sudden rush of a new and very different sort of emotion—a wild, fierce pulse of pure, blinding, exhilarating, liberating rage.

She was *furious!*

How could Domenico treat her like this? How dare he?

But of course he had never thought, never suspected that she would ever find out. He had thought that he was home and dry, safe with his *discreet* other woman—while he kept his poor, blind, *stupid* current mistress dangling on a string.

Well, not any more! Her time of being taken for a fool was well and truly over. She was going to confront Domenico over this—and she was going to make sure he knew exactly how she felt.

Dropping the bundle of clothes to the floor, abandoning the dress as too complicated and fussy to get into in the state of mind she was in, she kicked it out of the way and snatched at the nearest thing to hand—the black towelling robe that lay across a chair near by.

Domenico's robe. And it still bore the scent of his body, bringing her up short with a desperate shudder of miserable memory.

But her anger was still boiling high enough to overcome her momentary cowardice. She needed protective clothing and she needed it fast—and this was the best she was going to get. If she hesitated now, she might have second thoughts and lose this glorious rush of heady fury that would give her the strength to confront him as she needed to.

Steeling herself against the intimate scent that twisted in her nerves, threatening to destroy her, she pushed her arms roughly into the sleeves, pulled the towelling closely round her and yanked hard on the belt to fasten it tightly.

Then, before she could have a chance to think, determined not to let herself think in case she weakened in a panic, she pulled open the bedroom door and set off down the long landing, running down the stairs, silent in her bare feet, looking for Domenico, ready to give him more than a piece of the bitterness and rage that was in her mind.

CHAPTER THIRTEEN

DOMENICO was getting impatient.

This phone call had been going on for far too long, and it was going nowhere. Or perhaps the truth was that it seemed to be going nowhere because his mind just wasn't on anything that was being said. His thoughts weren't even here in this room but upstairs, where the most beautiful woman in the world was lying in his bed, waiting for him.

'So you see…'

The female voice at the other end of the line launched into yet another explanation but her words didn't seem to make any sense. Instead, they all appeared to blur into one another so that he couldn't make out a single separate syllable, let alone a complete word. All he could think of was the image of Alice.

Beautiful, sensual, sexy Alice as he had left her lying naked in his bed. Warm and content, her eyes sleepy, her mouth softened and smiling, her gorgeous body still flushed a faint pink in the aftermath of the passion that had brought them together.

A stunning, devastating, unique passion that he had known with no one else—and that he desperately wanted to experience all over again. Already, just remembering, he felt his body go hard and hot and hungry and he fought the impulse to tell Pippa to go to hell, to fling the phone down and…

'Do you understand that?' Pippa Marinelli asked suddenly.

Understand what? What had she said?

'Yes—of course,' he replied firmly, knowing that he had no idea at all what he was agreeing to.

Somewhere in the house a faint sound caught his ears and he tilted his head slightly, listening hard. Was Alice moving?

But he could hear nothing else and so he relaxed back against the desk against which he was leaning and prepared to bring the conversation to a halt.

'Well, it's a disappointment, but it can't be helped; I do understand that. And I'm grateful to you for what you've done. But I think we'll leave it there— What?'

He broke off, listening, as Pippa spoke again. Then shook his head even though he knew she couldn't see him.

'No, I'm sorry, but I can't do that. I really can't see you this week. In fact—'

He broke off abruptly as another faint sound, a change in the air behind him, brought him spinning round to see the woman who had just pulled the door open and come into the room.

Alice.

A tangle-haired, bare-footed Alice, who was dressed— swamped would be a better description—in his black towelling robe, the soft material wrapped almost twice around her slender frame and the belt pulled tight at her narrow waist.

His first thought was the wild, crazy feeling that the room had suddenly brightened; that it was as if someone had just switched on a brilliant light—no, more that the sun had suddenly come out from behind a cloud and flooded the whole space with warmth and glory. Which was totally ridiculous when he remembered that it was well after nine at night and the sun had already set hours before.

That was when he realised that the brilliance, the warmth, was not a real one, but an outward reflection of the effect that seeing Alice had had on him. And just for a moment he allowed himself to hold on to that feeling, to clasp it to him, to let it into his heart. And to recognise exactly what it meant for him and for his future.

But then she took a step forward into the room and the way she looked, the way she moved created another very different thought—the dangerously sensual one that underneath that wrapped and belted towelling she was naked. He could barely see a glimpse of flesh at the neck or almost all of the way down her legs, but he sensed that she had just got out of bed, grabbed the robe and headed downstairs to find him. And suddenly he knew precisely why, in days long gone, when women had dressed in long dresses, with gloves and hats, with almost every part of them covered up, a flash of ankle would send men into a frenzy of desire. The sight of those long, narrow pink feet planted firmly on the polished wooden floor was having such an erotic effect on him that his mind was heading for meltdown and the temptation to toss the phone aside and reach for her was one he was having to fight hard to overcome.

So instead he looked into her face, into those glorious blue eyes that were no longer sleepy but wide awake and glittering with something distinctly worrying, and his wanton thoughts jolted to an uncomfortable stop. The soft, sexy mouth was no longer smiling sleepily—in fact, it was not smiling at all but was clamped into a set, hard line, and every muscle in her throat and jaw was clenched taut as if to hold back some powerful emotion.

This was not the Alice he had left upstairs, he realised uneasily. Something had happened and it had changed her mood completely.

But first he had to get away from this phone call.

'Pippa…' he said, breaking in on the woman's monologue. 'Pippa!'

It was Alice who spoke, the single word coming swift and low but with such an intonation of deadly fury that it brought Domenico up short, silencing him like a slap in the face.

'Pippa Marinelli!'

And before he could blink, before he could even focus his thoughts, she had marched into the room and snatched the phone from his hand, sending a furious glare right into his face as she did so. Her eyes were even brighter now—but it was the brilliance of anger and rejection he saw, her face white with the control she was fighting to impose on her temper.

'Alice…' he began but she ignored him completely, turning her attention to the phone she held instead.

'Pippa Marinelli?'

He had never heard that tone on Alice's tongue before, even when she'd been furious with him. Never heard the way that each syllable sounded as if it were formed in ice, so that he almost expected to see the frozen letters tumble from her mouth and onto the floor, to lie in slowly melting pools of water.

'This is Alice Howard, Signorina Marinelli. I just wanted to make sure that you heard Domenico right—he *really* can't see you this week. In fact, he really can't see you ever again! If you have any sense of decency at all—which I very much doubt— you'll stay right away from my fiancé in future. Goodbye.'

As Domenico was still stunned into silence by her action, her icy-voiced outburst, she switched off the phone, gave a small, determined nod of satisfaction.

'There, that's dealt with your little floozy. Now it's time to deal with *you*!'

And, directing that look of ice into his face, she lifted her arm and flung the cellphone straight at him.

Alice couldn't believe that she'd actually gone quite that far. It was only as the phone left her hand that she realised just what she'd done—and the potential results of her unthinking actions. Thrown with all the force of the fury in her soul, the small silver-coloured phone would have done some real damage if it had landed squarely where it was aimed, right in Domenico's smiling face. But luckily some defensive instinct, some sixth sense alerted him, and with reflexes as swift as a cat's, his hand came up, caught it squarely and then dropped it onto the desk beside him with a small clatter.

And all the time his eyes never left her face. And all the time he kept on smiling. In fact, he looked like a man whose dreams had just come true.

'Why the hell are you smiling like that?' she demanded, thoroughly thrown off balance.

He shouldn't be *smiling*. He should be looking—well, at least he should be looking disconcerted, uneasy—*worried*. After all, she'd just walked in on him on the phone to his other woman—and she'd told that other woman to get out of his life in no uncertain terms.

At the very least he was going to have to do some very careful explaining and soothing. At the worst—and oh, how she hoped for the worst!—he had lost Pippa Marinelli for good. And he was *smiling*.

'Why?' she asked again, even more forcefully, using the violence of her tone to try to push some sense into the stupid, crazy brain of hers that was trying to force her away from the justified fury she was feeling and into a weak-minded appreciation of just how stunning Domenico looked. Standing there with his black hair falling forward over his face, his bronze eyes burning brilliantly, his wickedly sensual mouth curved into that wide, shocking smile, he was having a lethal effect on her senses. His long body was devastatingly attractive even in the simplest of clothes, the white shirt and jeans that she had taken off him only a short time ago...

No!

She must not think of what had happened such a short time before. Mustn't remember the final betrayal of that coldly calculated lovemaking. The deliberate seduction that had brought her back under his control, made her do exactly as he wanted and ensured that he would have everything the way he wanted in the future.

Or so he thought.

But if that smile was one of triumph, then she was very definitely going to enjoy disillusioning him on that score.

'Tell me!' she snapped when he just continued to look at her with that damn light in his eye, the wicked smile on his lips. 'Why—why—*why* are you smiling?'

'Isn't it obvious?' Domenico said at last and the lightness of his tone was positively the very last straw.

'No, it isn't!'

'It should be,' he countered. 'After all, what man wouldn't smile when he heard his woman claim him as her own with quite that degree of determination and emphasis?'

'Claim—*his woman?*'

Alice found the words were getting tangled up in the tightness of her throat. She could hardly get them past the choking knot that seemed to have formed there.

'I am *not* your woman! And I did *not* claim you as mine!'

Domenico dismissed her furious indignation with a wave of his hand, his casual nonchalance heaping fuel on the fire of her rage.

'Oh, yes, you did, *carissima,*' he assured her.

And then, when she frowned her disbelief, he went on, using a voice that she could only assume was mimicking her own.

'"If you have any sense of decency at all—which I very much doubt—you'll stay right away from *my fiancé* in future."'

Had she really sounded as cold and determined as that? Alice almost winced at hearing her words reproduced in this way. But then she realised just what words Domenico had emphasised—and just what the deliberate emphasis had meant. And the powerful effect of the fury that had buoyed her up so much until now suddenly evaporated in a rush, leaving her as limp and deflated as a suddenly pricked balloon.

My fiancé.

And if she really had claimed Domenico as hers in quite that deeply possessive way, then it was no wonder he was smiling; no wonder his eyes were alight with satisfaction.

He really must think he had her right where he wanted her.

'I wasn't *claiming* you—I was putting her off!'

'Same thing,' Domenico returned easily.

'No, it's *not* the same thing at all. If you must know I only used that phrase to get rid of her—and the truth is that I came down here to do the same to you.'

If she had actually hit him in the face with the phone, or at least slapped him hard, then the tormenting smile couldn't have vanished any quicker. It faded abruptly and without it his handsome face looked totally different.

'Alice—no!'

'Alice—yes!'

She had to harden her heart to say it, fighting hard not to be deceived by the loss of all warmth from his features, the way the bronze eyes looked bleak and clouded.

'I came here to say goodbye to you—I just got distracted by Signorina "I can be discreet" Marinelli.'

'You saw the email.'

'I saw the email.'

The fact that he recognised the quote immediately gave another twist to the knife in her already desolated heart. He didn't even try to deny anything. Didn't try to pretend that he didn't know what she was talking about.

'And don't expect me to apologise for prying into your private correspondence—'

'I'm not.'

Domenico took a couple of steps towards her, then stopped as her head came up and she eyed him warily, ready to back away if he came any closer.

'I'm glad you found it. Glad it's all out in the open.'

That was the last thing she had expected and her thoughts reeled a little at the shock of it.

'You're glad?'

Was that high-pitched, brittle-enough-to-break voice really hers? She sounded right on the edge of despair—which might be how she was feeling but was most definitely not how she wanted Domenico to see her.

'You swore that that woman was not your mistress!'

'She's not.'

'That you weren't sleeping with her.'

'Alicia, *adorata*—I'm not.'

'You said that Pi—that she was no threat…that I would never have to hear about her again…'

'I meant it. And if you hadn't seen that email then you never would have heard about her! I was just paying her off.'

'What?'

Momentarily distracted by that *'adorata'*—that lying, scheming, calculated *'adorata'*—Alice couldn't believe what she was hearing.

'You were paying—and that is supposed to make me feel better?'

Domenico's hands came up in a gesture of exasperation combined with determination to be heard.

'I was doing what you wanted—I was getting her out of my life, our life, so that—'

Seeing him like this, knowing he believed he was making things better—that he was winning her round—Alice felt her control break completely.

'Paying her off! Getting her out of...! Dom—she called you *Dom*!'

She could barely get the last word out, huge, racking sobs choking her. And in spite of all her determination, her resolve that this was not going to happen, she found that she couldn't hold back the tears that were now streaming down her cheeks.

'Oh, sweetheart!'

Domenico moved forward so swiftly, his arms coming round her before she had any chance of anticipating it. She tried to fight against his hold, but her struggles were impotent against his strength.

'Alice, *cara*, if that's what's troubling you, I never said she could. In fact, I've asked her time and again to stop using that name—your name—but she is a very stubborn woman and she just wasn't listening.'

'Maybe you didn't insist hard enough.'

Through the whirling confusion in her thoughts, it was all that she could manage.

'Or perhaps you didn't want to drive her away.'

'That's certainly part of it,' Domenico agreed, so soberly that it shocked Alice rigid. 'I certainly didn't want her to give up on me and the project we had together.'

CHAPTER FOURTEEN

'PROJECT?'

Alice found she was actually shaking her head in disbelief, her eyes clouded in confusion as she looked up into Domenico's face.

'What project?'

But Domenico didn't answer her immediately. Instead he unfastened his arms from around her body and, with her hand in his, led her to the big, black, leather-covered settee that stood on the far side of the room. Pressing her down onto the soft cushions, he went back to the desk and took something from a drawer, then came and sat beside her, holding a tooled leather wallet out to her.

'What's this?' Alice's tone, like her body, was rigid with suspicion and rejection.

Domenico looked straight into her eyes, his bronze gaze firm and unflinching, disturbingly reassuring when she didn't believe she could be reassured—wasn't even sure if she *wanted* to be reassured.

'Open it.'

Then, when she didn't move, he opened the wallet himself and placed it upright in her lap. But all Alice could do was still to stare into his face, unable to look away, unable to trust the

wickedly weak feelings of longing and hope that were creeping into her mind, in spite of her efforts to push them back.

'*Look,*' Domenico said, so insistently that she obeyed him
automatically, dropping her gaze to what she held.

And she saw at once just what he wanted her to find.

The small white piece of card was tucked into a side-panel
in the wallet. And the name on it caught her eye immediately.

Pippa Marinelli—who else? But it was the next line that
snagged her attention and held it.

'Pippa Marinelli—private investigator? Dom—what was
she investigating?'

His smile was more of a wry grimace, strangely boyish and
disarming, and in his eyes there lurked something she couldn't
interpret. In any other man she would have said it was a sort
of defensive apprehension—but in Domenico?

'Me,' he said.

'You? But what…?'

Her hand moved, her fingers closing around the card,
meaning to pick it up, study it more closely, but Domenico's
touch stopped her, held her frozen.

'Wait,' was all he said, and, riveted by the raw note in his
voice, she could only sit there in silence and do as he asked.

This time, Domenico reached into a larger section of the
wallet and took out a small white envelope. Handling it with
care, he opened it and took out the piece of paper it contained,
then held it out to Alice.

Her confusion growing with every second, she took it with
a care that matched his and stared in bewilderment at the image she held. Printed on cheap paper and in rather garish colours, now rather faded, it was a shabby, worn holy picture of
the type that many Catholic Italians put into their prayer
books. A picture of a tonsured monk in white robes with a
black over-garment that fell almost to the floor, exposing only
his bare feet in rough leather sandals.

'Who?'

'St Dominic,' Domenico told her. 'My patron saint.'

'Your…?'

She was reduced to nothing but single syllables, unable to think in any other way.

'Let me explain.'

Domenico didn't touch her, or make any move to try. He didn't need to. There was something so raw and open in his voice, in the bronze burn of those amazing eyes, that she couldn't have looked away if she'd wanted to. He held her effortlessly and mesmerically just by the sheer force of his tone, his absolute stillness.

'I told you that both my parents are dead. It's not the truth—well…'

He caught himself up, sighed deeply then raked both hands through the jet-black sleekness of his hair, ruffling it desperately.

'The truth is, I don't know. I don't know if my parents are alive or dead. I don't even know who my parents are, or were—and neither does anyone else. Even my name is not my own.'

'What?' That brought the startled question from her lips as she struggled to take in just what he was saying.

'I was abandoned as a baby—left on the steps of the church. The church of Santo Domenico in a little town called Parrisi.'

He sat back and watched as Alice absorbed these facts, slowly thinking them through, trying to make them make sense.

'Domenico—Parrisi…'

'That was the name the nuns in the orphanage gave me. Because of where I was found and because of this…'

One long finger touched the shabby little picture that still lay in Alice's open palm, and his eyes were darkly shadowed as he looked down at it.

'This was left with me—it was in the blanket that was wrapped around me. My mother must have put it there because she at least wanted me to be given the name she'd cho-

sen for me. It's the only thing I have of her. The nuns gave it
to me when I was five and...'

The way he hesitated, the deliberate pause before he went
on and the intent burn of his eyes on her face left Alice in no
doubt at all that what he was about to say was the most important thing of all.

'No one—*no one* else has ever seen that or touched it until today.'

'No one...' Alice echoed, beginning to understand the
meaning of what he was saying, but unable to believe the sig-
nificance of what it seemed to mean for her.

'I hired Pippa because someone I knew said that she had
had some success in tracking down the parents of adopted children,' Domenico was saying, his voice seeming to come from
a long distance away. 'I thought she might be able to help me
find my parents, or at least my mother, but I needed someone
who could be discreet. For all I knew, I could be the result of
a rape, or my mother might just have been little more than a
child herself—so I made her swear to keep things quiet.'

'To be discreet,' Alice managed hollowly, going over that
revealing email in her mind and now seeing it in a very different light.

There were new tears on her cheeks, tears she had barely
been aware of having shed. But this time they were tears *for*
Domenico, not tears of pain at something he had done.

'So you see, Pippa was never any threat to you—except in
one way.'

The sudden deepening of his tone brought Alice's head up,
looking at him through tear-filmed eyes.

'What way?' she managed hoarsely.

'I was afraid that she might turn up something so terrible
from my past that I would never be able to ask you to marry
me. But then—'

'No, wait a minute!'

Unthinking, Alice lifted her hand and laid it across his mouth, gently stopping his words.

'You—are you saying that you hired Pippa before I left you?'

He had to have done, because already then his name was being linked with the other woman. The lunches he had had with her had been spotted—gossip had started.

'And that was because—because…'

She couldn't continue. Didn't dare to go any further in case it didn't mean what she was beginning to suspect—to hope—that it meant. But Domenico answered her without the slightest hesitation.

'Because I was hoping to ask you to marry me but I didn't think it was right to do so when I knew nothing about my-self—about my background, my parents. What did I have to offer you—?'

'You had the only thing that really mattered—you had yourself.'

Her voice shook as she spoke, the full impact of what he was saying finally hitting home.

The man who had claimed that he didn't do marriage had been planning this all the time. He had brought in a private investigator, let her into secrets he had been carrying with him for all his adult life—and all because he had wanted a chance to propose marriage. And she—Alice—had walked out on him, declaring that she wanted more fun!

The memory made her so restless and uneasy that she couldn't sit there and stay still a moment longer. Releasing the precious picture back into Domenico's hands and getting to her feet, she prowled around the room for a moment, try-ing to find the strength to speak, and knowing that Domenico was watching her all the time.

'That fun thing…' she muttered at last, turning back to him and looking down into his deep, dark eyes. 'I never meant it. It was what I heard about Pippa and—and—the fact that I didn't think you loved me.'

'I didn't make it easy for you.' Domenico got slowly to his feet, his eyes locked with hers all the time. 'But I didn't want to say anything in case…'

'I know.'

Once more Alice laid a finger across his mouth to silence him. She wanted to kiss him into quietness but she didn't yet dare.

'I understand.'

When he held out his hands to her she took them, feeling their warmth and strength close around her, holding her tight.

'But I couldn't let you go,' Domenico continued. 'So when I came to find you—'

'To find me?' Alice broke in. 'But I sent you a message saying…'

'Saying you needed to talk to me, I know. But I was already coming after you. And then you had my ring on your finger so nothing else mattered.'

'Your ring…'

Once more Alice was blinking away tears, but this time they were not tears of sympathy but ones of real distress.

'I wore your ring, but only because—'

'No!'

It was Domenico's turn to silence her, and this time he did it with a kiss. A kiss that was so strong and tender and so— so *loving* that it took Alice's breath away, destroying all her words with it.

'No, *cara, no*! Never. It wasn't just because of the baby— though I tried to tell myself that was the only reason at the time. I wanted you in my life, I couldn't live without you, and when I thought that you were going to have my child—a family of my own at last—I felt as if I'd been given the world.'

'The world—a family—but I lost…I failed…'

Now the tears would not be held back. They tumbled down her cheeks, thick and fast, but Domenico gently wiped them away and kissed the places where they had been.

'Oh, no, beloved, never think that. I would have wanted

that child, would have loved him or her so much, but you are my family—you are my world. If I have you in my life then it will be enough.'

His kiss was long and slow and it spoke of promises, of futures—of happiness. But there was still one thing nagging at Alice's thoughts.

'But—the wedding. When I came back from the hospital, you'd got rid of everything—even my dress. I thought that was because you didn't want to think about marriage any more—that you...'

'That I wouldn't want to marry you because you were no longer pregnant with my child?' Domenico put in when she hesitated, his voice as deep and burningly sincere as the passion in his eyes. 'You couldn't be more wrong, my love. I had everything cleared away because I didn't want to pressure you. Because I wanted you to know that you were free—free to make whatever decision you wanted, without being tied to a promise you had made under duress. I wanted to give you time and space to recover from the miscarriage and then I was going to ask you to marry me all over again—and this time I was going to do it properly. I wanted to marry you even more than before because I'd had a taste of what it could be like to have a wife, a child—to be a...a family.'

If Alice had had any doubts before then there were none in her mind now. To see a man as strong and sure as Domenico always appeared suddenly stumbling over his words, to catch the glint of sheening tears behind the fringe of thick dark lashes shielding his bronze eyes, was something that struck straight to her heart with its message of love and need and the loneliness of loss.

And now at last she dared to move forward, sliding her arms around him and pressing close, lifting her face, taking his mouth in the kiss she had been yearning to give for so long—for a lifetime, it seemed.

And Domenico responded ardently, taking all that she was

offering, and giving it back a hundredfold. Giving her his love, his devotion, all his heart in that one kiss.

Alice could have stayed like that forever. Either that, or she would have wanted to take Domenico back upstairs to bed, to give herself to him in the truth of love and the knowledge that he felt the same. But Domenico was strangely resistant to her gentle urging, her attempts to edge him towards the door.

'*Momento, cara,*' he said softly. 'Wait—there is something I must do…'

And as Alice stared in astonishment he suddenly dropped down onto one knee and caught hold of her hand, pressing a lingering, loving kiss on the back of it.

'Alice—my love—I want to do this properly this time. I want you to know, to be in no doubt that I adore you, that without you my world is empty…'

Disbelievingly she saw him pull something from his pocket and recognised it as the engagement ring that she had flung at him in a fury earlier that evening. He must have gone back to the living room and hunted for it, keeping it with just this moment in mind.

'Beloved Alice—my life, my heart are yours. Will you marry me and be my wife, my family, for the rest of my life?'

Reacting purely instinctively, Alice knelt too, coming down on the carpet beside him, deep blue eyes locking with the longing, loving gaze of this man she loved so deeply.

'I'd be honoured to do so,' she told him with deep-voiced fervour, every last trace of uncertainty or tremor gone from her voice. 'Oh, yes, yes, my darling. Yes, I'll marry you.'

In the same hospital where just fifteen months before he had kept a long, lonely vigil at Alice's bedside, Domenico once again sat beside her sleeping form, but this time in a totally different frame of mind.

This time he couldn't wait for her to wake, couldn't wait

to see her smile and know that her happiness was mirrored in his own face.

Even as he thought it Alice stirred, murmured sleepily, opened her eyes and looked around.

'Dom?' she asked softly. 'Was it real? Or did I dream?'

'No dream, my love,' he hastened to assure her. 'It's perfectly, wonderfully real. Our son was born last night and he's as perfect, as healthy and strong as any baby should be.'

'Our son,' Alice echoed happily, her joy glowing in the deep blue eyes. 'Can I hold him?'

'Of course.'

Crossing to the bassinet that stood on the other side of the bed, Domenico gently lifted his tiny, twelve-hour-old son from the mattress and handed him carefully to his mother, watching as she cuddled him close, dropping a soft kiss on the little upturned nose.

'How can I ever thank you for this gift?' he said, coming to sit beside Alice on the bed, putting one arm round her and with the other helping her support their child.

Alice looked up into the intent, loving gaze of the man who was her husband, the father of her child, and her heart clenched in love and understanding.

When Domenico had been no older than her newborn son, his mother had wrapped him in a scruffy blanket, put the picture of St Dominic in the bundle with him, and abandoned him on the stone steps leading up to a village church. She could only be thankful that a much happier fate awaited her already beloved baby son.

'You don't need to thank me,' she told Domenico softly. 'Just promise to love me—and this little treasure—for the rest of your life.'

'I promise,' Domenico told her, and as his mouth took hers in a long, deeply passionate kiss she knew that it was a promise he had every intention of keeping.

The Mancini Marriage Bargain

TRISH MOREY

Trish Morey is an Australian who's also spent time living and working in New Zealand and England. Now she's settled with her husband and four young daughters in a special part of South Australia, surrounded by orchards and bushland, and visited by the occasional koala and kangaroo. With a life-long love of reading, she penned her first book at age eleven, after which life, career and a growing family kept her busy, until once again she could indulge her desire to create characters and stories – this time in romance. Having her work published is a dream come true. Visit Trish at her website, www. trishmorey.com

Look for Trish Morey's latest exciting novel, *His Prisoner in Paradise*, available in August 2010 from Mills & Boon® Modern™ romance.

CHAPTER ONE

THE noise woke her—the insistent dull pounding that crashed its way into her receding dreams and brought Helene Grainger to wakefulness in a foggy panic. One blurred glance at the red electronic display and her head momentarily flopped back onto her pillow with relief. She'd been asleep less than an hour—she wasn't late for her early morning taxi after all.

The thumping cranked up a notch and she staggered out of bed, shrugging into her silk robe and slippers, her mind clicking into gear. So if it wasn't a burly taxi driver anxious not to lose his hefty fare to Charles de Gaulle airport, who the hell would be beating their fist against her door at this time of night? *Unless Agathe from the apartment next door had had another seizure.*

Her slippered feet padded faster along the passageway. Maybe she'd fallen? Eugene wouldn't be able to lift her on his own. *'Je viens!'* she called. *I'm coming.*

Throwing security measures aside in her rush to help, she pulled open the door only to instantly recoil, her insides performing a slow roll, her mind turning cartwheels while she absorbed the frozen snapshot before her.

His fist was curled and raised ready for another blow, his eyes were wild and tormented and his dark hair mussed and troubled, as if his hand had been

5

giving it grief until he'd taken to pounding her door with it instead. His other hand gripped white-knuckled onto some kind of leather folio.

'Paolo.' She whispered his name on a breath, aching under the weight of years of pointless longing and wasted nights. But it was cold dread that flavoured her thoughts right now. She'd always known that one day he'd come—but she'd never imagined it would be like this, that Paolo would look so strained, so intense. 'What is it?'

He sucked in a lungful of air, holding it in his broad chest as he let his fist slowly melt back into a hand and drop down to his side. A muscle in his whiskered unshaven jaw twitched, pulling up one side of his mouth into a half-smile, half-grimace as he suddenly let go the breath he'd been holding. A hint of coffee laced with whiskey, overlaid with the unmistakable essence of Paolo himself—the very taste of him curled into her senses as his agonised eyes continued to hold hers.

Then slowly, almost imperceptibly, he shook his head. 'It's over.'

The sound of locks being pulled back, of a security chain being hooked into place and a doorknob turning, all of these things leapt to centre stage in her consciousness even as Paolo's words struck a chilling void in her heart.

It's over. But why should that come as such a shock? She'd been expecting this moment for nearly half her life yet all those years of waiting, all those years of knowing, in no way diminished the pain.

Because she'd never wanted it to be over.

The door to the adjacent apartment opened on a creak, jerking to a stop against the short chain.

'Helene! Dois-j'appeler la police?' Eugene's voice croaked from behind the door, frail and betraying its owner's octogenarian status. Late-night visitors to her apartment were unheard of; no wonder he had thoughts of calling the police.

Stepping past Paolo and into the dim glow of the night-time hall lighting, she could just make out Eugene's gnarled features peering inquisitively around the door. *'Mais non, Eugene,'* she said, setting her voice to soothe. *'C'est juste un vieil ami.'*

Through the crack in the door Eugene's scowl deepened. She could almost see the cogs in his ancient mind turning—an old friend who made such a racket?

'Je suis désolée du bruit,' she said, apologising for the noise.

'Bon,' he said gruffly, as if he didn't mean it, with a last nervous sideways twitch of his eyes before retreating inside his apartment, his door closing behind him and the bolts sliding home once more.

She turned back to Paolo and their eyes collided. His dark scrutiny held such raw pain she could feel its jagged edges reaching out to scrape uncomfortably against her own feelings. Yet he was a man who would soon be free. What had happened to cause him such anguish?

'I guess you'd better come in,' she said at last, reverting to her native English, her heart thumping louder under the weight of his leaden gaze. Even Eugene's interruption couldn't stall the mounting trepidation in her body, the dread as she battled to come to terms with Paolo's spoken words.

Because this was no social call.

'I should come back tomorrow,' he said, backing away as if suddenly struck by the late hour. 'I'm disturbing your neighbours.'

'You've disturbed all of us already,' she stated plainly. 'But I'm leaving in the morning. Let's get this over with.'

Instinctively she reached for his forearm as she stepped back into the doorway, looking to draw him inside, but one touch of his arm, one hint of the tight flesh, the corded muscles hidden beneath his leather coat, and her hand jerked away.

He wasn't hers to touch.

He never had been.

A pity that hadn't stopped the thrill.

He watched her turn and lead the way into her apartment as he sucked in a breath. She seemed as strung out as he felt, though that was hardly surprising. She'd probably done her best to forget about him—to forget all about the circumstances that had brought them together in the first place.

Dio—he'd done his best to as well! And for the most part it had worked—until just lately, when their shared past had come crashing back in glorious widescreen detail.

His eyes followed her progress into the apartment. He could still walk away. Come back at a better time. Maybe even just send a fax and make the whole deal more official. He was a lawyer, for God's sake; he dealt with much bigger stuff than this unemotionally all the time.

And he almost did. But there was something about her—the crazy waves her ash-blonde hair had formed when pressed against her pillow, the shadowed eyes that hinted of secrets, the full lips plumped and pink with the scraping action of her upper teeth…

She was so much like the girl he'd known years ago, her genteel British accent unchanged, her attitude the same mixture of defiance and vulnerability, and yet he could see there was more.

He closed his eyes and called upon a mightier strength. Because the seductive sway of her hips underneath the silky robe made him forget the pain of why he was here, and made him ache for much more than anything to which he was entitled.

With a sigh he followed her into the apartment, unable to pull his eyes from her retreating form even if he'd wanted to.

Had Helene been so beguiling twelve years ago? Had their problems back then been so paramount that he'd simply never noticed, or was it just that time had transformed a pretty young student into a stunning woman?

With a struggle his mind clicked back into logic mode. It was academic really—it was a bit late to start noticing how good-looking a woman was a mere ten minutes before you divorced her.

She turned and waited for him in her tastefully decorated reception room, switching on a low leadlight table lamp in deference to the late hour, the coloured glass segments of the shade casting a soft, comfortable glow over the room. The truth was stark enough without illuminating it in the glare of one hundred watts.

'Can I get you a drink?'

He definitely looked as if he needed one, but that wasn't the only reason she'd asked. Right now she needed space to breathe. Because no matter that she'd anticipated this moment for twelve long years it was still too sudden, too unwanted, too damned painful.

It was time to get rid of her.

She concentrated on keeping her breathing calm, on keeping her hands from tangling with each other as she awaited his response. He seemed to fill the space in the modest-sized room, making the furniture look too small. He warmed the air around her until her face felt bright and flushed. He made her wish she had a whole lot more on under this robe than one tiny pair of pink cotton panties.

He seemed to think about her question for a while and then, 'Coffee?'

With relief she darted for the kitchen. If the silence between them had stretched out any longer, something would have snapped—probably her. She flicked on the kettle, piled the grounds into the plunger, tinkering with cups, but her mind refused to focus on simply making coffee.

Twelve years had seen the lean, good-looking student turn into a man who looked as if he could have been carved from stone. Even sporting a late-o'clock shadow, troubled eyes and mussed hair Paolo looked good. Better than good, and in fact better even than the pictures of him she'd pored over from time to time when she'd stumbled upon them in her hairdresser's magazines. Somehow in those he'd always seemed to be glaring at the photographer, as if resentful of being captured on film.

The woman on his arm had been less camera-shy, smiling radiantly as they had been captured on film. But who could blame her for looking so happy? She had it all. A successful designer for the Milan-based fashion house of Bacelli, she was simply stunning, and she had Paolo.

Sapphire Clemenger.

There was no way Helene could forget her name. The woman-in-waiting, the imminent Mrs Paolo Mancini, according to the social pages. Well, if Paolo's sudden visit was any indication, it looked as if she was about to get her opportunity. Paolo obviously couldn't wait to be free so they could tie the knot.

'You don't seem very happy to see me.'

Her spine stiffened and she took the time to draw in a fortifying breath, depressing the plunger before she turned. He was standing in the doorway, one arm resting up against the jamb. He'd taken off his coat and the white shirt fitted without clinging, showing off the width of his chest and the long, lean line of his body. Her mouth went dry.

'It's late,' she said on a swallow. 'I thought something had happened to Agathe next door; she's got a bad heart. I was worried about her and Eugene. They know to call me if anything happens...'

Her rambling words trailed off, evaporated, in the heat from his gaze.

'You must know why I'm here.'

She nodded, fighting her shoulders' determination to sag. She couldn't show him how much she was affected by this. 'Khaled's married, then.'

'Yes.'

The word sliced through her heart.

Knowledge wasn't power.

Knowledge was pain.

Yet it was crazy. She should be happy to escape from the shadows of Khaled Al-Ateeq, the man she'd been promised to when barely seventeen, brokered as part of a deal with Khaled's father to further her own father's oil interests in the Middle East, and the man she'd enraged by running off with Paolo and marrying him first.

Their short, civil ceremony had sounded the death knell for the arranged marriage and for the deal. And still she'd been so terrified that Khaled might persist in his attempts to come after her that Paolo had vowed to stay married to her until Khaled had taken another wife.

It had been such a simple plan—foolproof—and neither of them had thought Khaled would take longer than a year or two to find a new wife.

Instead, for more than a decade the threat of retribution had loomed long and large over their lives, a permanent and poisoned cloud that had threatened to snuff out any and all relationships she'd had with men and any chance that Paolo had had to start a real family of his own.

Until now.

Now that Khaled was married they were both free.

Except that, for her, freedom meant severing the very tie she had with the only man she'd ever wanted.

'He certainly took his time about it.'

A muscled worked in his jaw. Something fleeting skidded across his eyes and she realised her attempt to lighten the mood had fallen flat.

'You don't have to be worried about him any more. You're safe. He'll never trouble you again.'

Emotion hitched in his words, forcing her to really look at him, and guilt speared her deep inside. For twelve years he'd stuck by his promise to her. He could have been married already with a houseful of children. He should have been! Instead he'd been lumbered with a wife he'd never wanted and a promise he'd had no idea would be so binding.

No wonder he wanted out.

'So you've brought me some papers to sign?' she asked, pushing past with the tray, trying not to breathe in as she moved past him, trying not to breathe in the scent she'd so quickly have to forget all over again.

He nodded in the direction of the sitting room. 'They're in the folio.'

'Then let's get started,' she said brightly, trying to infuse her words with something more closely resembling enthusiasm.

He pulled out the documents while she poured the coffee, all the while wondering why she hadn't had the sense to make herself a cup of herbal tea instead. It was late and she needed to get some sleep before her early morning flight. The last thing she wanted after tonight's visitor was a caffeine-induced think-fest.

Then she took one look at Paolo and realised she was kidding herself. Whatever she drank tonight there was no hope of getting any sleep. Not now. Not knowing it had all come to an end at last.

He sat down alongside her on the settee, brushing the long length of his upper leg against hers and inadvertently snaring one side of the fabric of her robe.

Too late she realised what was happening. By the time she'd shifted herself away, one side of the slippery fabric was well and truly wedged under his thigh, totally exposing her left leg from her knee all the way past her too-brief panties.

She grasped the other side of the robe and pulled it over before the gap could expose more of her midriff than it already did, instantly regretting her decision not to have taken the opportunity while she'd had it to put more layers of clothing between her and Paolo. But given that she normally slept naked, it was lucky she had anything on at all underneath her robe.

Luck was hardly what she was feeling right now, though, as a combination of exposure to the cool air and a major dose of embarrassment turned her skin to goose-bumps.

He seemed to take an inordinately long time to register her distress, although it could very well have taken the space of one hitched breath as her whole world ground to a halt. His eyes shifted from the papers he was holding to her knee and then all too slowly drifted up, way up. He blinked, dangerously slowly, when his eyes reached where the skin disappeared under her robe. Then his eyes moved to where her hands gripped white-knuckled at her waist-tie, and finally to her face, although she was sure there was just a moment there where they'd hesitated, without a doubt registering the points of her nipples, straining firm and insistent against the perilously thin fabric.

His jaw tightened and something flared in his eyes, something hot and dangerous and powerfully magnetic. Blood pulsed in secret places as his heated gaze turned her embarrassment into something much, much more primal. Then, almost as quickly, his eyes cooled to apology mode. A second later he was out of his seat and across the room from her, feigning sudden interest in the items on her mantelpiece.

'I'm sorry,' he said, his voice sounding unusually thick.

She covered herself, tucking the newly freed fabric securely around her while her skin burned with mortification.

Oh, she'd seen that look before; she'd heard those very words from his mouth. Surely he hadn't thought she'd been trying to seduce him again? She was no naïve seventeen-year-old on her wedding night. She wasn't stupid enough to try that again.

Her memory vividly played back his words, still startlingly fresh despite the weight of the intervening years. *'I'm sorry,'* he'd told her back then, unwinding her arms from where she'd wrapped them around his neck, *'But this marriage isn't about sex.'*

He couldn't possibly think she'd want to bring that humiliation upon herself again? He hadn't wanted her on their wedding night and he'd just made it doubly plain that he didn't want her now. Why the hell would he when finally he had his chance to be rid of her for ever? Did he really think she still cared enough to try, even after twelve years of nothing more than an occasional Christmas card from his law office?

He'd be crazy to think it.

Totally crazy.

Except that she did.

Time and pain hadn't erased the attraction at all. If anything they'd honed it, sharpened it to such a fine point that when she'd opened the door tonight it had felt like a needle exploding in her heart, its fragments burying themselves deep into her flesh like tiny splinters.

Damn, but how could a man you'd promised yourself years ago that you'd forget still manage to turn you to pulp? It was hardly fair. Especially when all he wanted was to be free to marry someone else.

Then again, if he deserved anything after being faithful to his promise for so long, it was a rapid release from the ties that bound them together. At the very least she owed him that.

'No apology required,' she said quietly into the low-lit room as he continued to study the objects and the few photographs on her mantelpiece. 'I'm sure you're in a hurry to get going.' *To get married.* 'Give me the papers to sign while you have your coffee.'

He could sure do with coffee. Or something stronger. But at least now he could turn around safely without her thinking he'd come here tonight to get a whole lot more than just her signature.

It had been a long time since he'd had a woman. Months. But he hadn't realised how long until his need had threatened to spin out of control just then.

And the last twelve years had shaped Helene into a very desirable woman indeed. Her greenish eyes flickered with gold in the lamplight and spoke of both intelligence and warmth; her chin might be firmly angled like her father's, yet her lips were full and inviting. And as he dipped lower to place the papers in front of her even the faint remnants of her chosen fragrance melded with her own natural scent, making something new, something utterly feminine and alluring.

She was one attractive woman all right. But it had been the sight of all that creamy skin on a leg that seemed to go forever coupled with the knowledge that she couldn't be wearing a whole lot more than a tiny pair of pink pants under that robe that had made him suddenly wish he could tumble her straight back into the bed his late-night visit had pulled her from.

Or maybe she hadn't been alone.

All of a sudden he wanted to know more about her. What had she been doing for the last twelve years? Who had she been with?

And was someone waiting in bed for her even now?

A glance at her photographs revealed nothing. There was no evidence of anyone else in the apartment, no trace of masculine input into the soft decor, but still he burned to know.

'The places where you need to sign are flagged,' he offered. 'Are you sure I'm not disturbing anyone else by being here this late? A flatmate? A boyfriend?'

Her eyes snapped from the papers straight up to his. 'Perfectly sure,' she replied coolly.

He cursed inwardly. It wasn't the answer he wanted. It told him nothing more than he already knew.

'So you don't have a boyfriend, or he doesn't live here?'

She put the pen down and looked up at him again through narrowed eyes. 'I didn't realise that's what you were asking. For what it's worth there's no boyfriend, live-in or live-out. There's also no flatmate. Obviously I don't have a husband, except you of course. The sooner you let me sign these papers, though, the sooner I'll have that sorted.'

'I would have thought they'd be queuing at the door,' he said through barely separated lips, resuming his investigation of her room, leaving her to study the papers. Was she that desperate to sign?

His eyes fell on an old photograph of a couple he recognised instantly. Her parents. *His parents-in-law.* Caroline Grainger was smiling into the camera, looking every bit the society wife, smiling benignly in her neat-trimmed jacket and pearls, her hair immaculate, while Richard Grainger's cold blue eyes gazed smugly at the camera as if he owned the world. Given his business interests all over the globe, he just about did.

'How are your parents?' he asked, over his shoulder.

'I don't know,' she said.

He put the picture down and turned to face her. He sensed a note in there that suggested things weren't at all right. 'You don't know?'

She dropped the pen on the table and took a deep breath, running her hands back through her hair. Fascinated, he watched the way it straightened out long under her fingers only to bounce back into its shoulder-length waves. He liked the way her hand could bury itself in its thick depths. It was the kind of hair you could lose yourself in.

'The last time I heard from my father,' she said, pulling his focus back onto her words, 'was four weeks after our wedding. You'd returned to Milan by then and I'd just found my first flat in Paris. That's where his solicitor's letter finally caught up with me. In it he told me he considered he'd never had a daughter and that I'd never speak to either of them again.'

'He disowned you?'

'That's about the size of it.'

'I never knew.'

She shrugged. 'I expected him to be angry. We'd blown his deal sky-high. He'd not only lost face, he'd lost millions—potentially billions if the venture had been the success they expected. He wasn't about to let me get off easily after that. He wanted me to pay.'

'But to cut you off like that—and from your mother.'

'It's okay really,' she said, much too quickly for him to believe it was. 'I got what I wanted after all. I have a good career with the International Bureau for Women and I've made a good life here in Paris.' She smiled weakly up at him. 'To think I owe it all to you.'

'No,' he said. 'You've made your life a success all by yourself.'

'But I would never have had the opportunity without you. Nobody else cared enough to stop what was going on and, even if they had, the prospect of acting in defiance of my father would have turned them to jelly. You were the only person who cared enough to stand up for me, who wouldn't let me be traded off as just another piece of merchandise in my father's bizarre business deal.'

He wasn't sure his actions had been all that noble. He'd been enraged that a fellow student, a good friend, could be placed in such a position by her family, and with the impetuosity of youth and the certainty that they were wrong he'd been determined that their plan to sell off their daughter would be foiled. And he and Helene had simply found a way to do it.

He took a deep breath. Looking back, knowing what he knew now, knowing what he had set in train, maybe he should never have got involved. Maybe he should have turned his back on her and let her marry Khaled.

'Don't you understand,' she continued, 'that you gave me my freedom at the cost of your own? I know I can never repay you for the years you wasted being tied to me, but you have to know that I will always, always be grateful for what you have done.'

She smiled again, belying the moisture filming her eyes, and something pulled tight inside him. How could he have abandoned her? How could he have even considered that he might have? It was all he could do to stand in one spot and not rush over to collect her into her arms and kiss her pain away.

But he dared not do it. Once already he'd come close to losing control. If he kissed her, there'd be no way he'd want to stop, because he knew without a doubt that it would help erase his own pain.

Instead he forced a smile to his own lips and tried not to think about the devastating consequences of something they had both done so long ago, tried not to think about another woman, now tied to the very same man he'd saved Helene from.

So what that he'd saved Helene? He'd done nothing to save Sapphy from the same fate. He'd as good as delivered her to Khaled on a platter. He had little to feel proud of.

He needed to close this conversation down. It was getting too dangerous, too close to the bone. 'It was the least I could do,' he said, his voice a dry rasp as he turned back to her small collection of photographs before she detected anything was wrong. A few seconds later the sounds of pages turning told him she'd directed her attentions back onto the documents.

He let go a breath he hadn't realised he'd been holding. Coming tonight had been a mad idea. He should have sent the papers. Coming here was like ripping off a bandage on a wound that had never healed and that now lay exposed, raw and weeping and edged with decay.

'There's something I don't understand,' she said after a little while, interrupting his thoughts. 'These are papers for what looks like a regular divorce. Only I thought—'

He looked around and waited, watching the colour in her cheeks rising. Then, when it was clear she wasn't going to go on, asked, 'You thought what?'

'Well, I just had it in mind that we would be seeking an annulment. You know, given…'

Again she trailed off and he took a step closer, watching the turmoil of emotions flashing through her eyes.

'Given that we never actually consummated the marriage?'

She nodded, her exposed skin colouring brighter by the second. Her chin kicked up on a swallow and he followed the movement in her throat, watching it disappear into the spot where her skin dipped into the hollow just above her collar-bone.

Such smooth skin, fair and creamy all the way to where it disappeared behind the V of her robe. All the way down and all the way up, if what he'd seen before was any indication. He swallowed, amazed that they'd never taken that one extra step to consummate their marriage.

She'd wanted to, he remembered. After the tension of carrying out their plan, after he'd successfully whisked her away from her mother while on a London shopping trip and kept her hidden until he'd slipped a ring on her finger, they'd both been on a high. They'd outsmarted both her domineering family and the heir to an independent Arab state, they'd foiled Richard Grainger's attempt to sell off his daughter to the highest bidder, and they'd managed to get away with it.

After dispatching copies of the photographic evidence and the marriage certificate to her family, they'd celebrated in true student style in a friend's shabby bedsit with a bottle of cheap fizz, congratulating themselves on how clever they were and laughing and dancing into the night.

And then she'd kissed him and suggested they go to bed together and suddenly everything had become a whole lot more complicated...

He could easily have made love to her that night. Very easily. But he hadn't wanted to take advantage of her while she'd been high on their success and cheap wine. And he hadn't wanted her to think he was expecting her to pay him back in sex. He remembered he'd tried to explain and made a mess of it, but she'd made no further attempts to get physical, so no doubt she must have been relieved he hadn't taken her up on the offer. He had been at the time too, although now he wasn't so sure.

It was clear to Helene he hadn't forgotten either. She could just about see the frame-by-frame action replaying on the screen of his dark chocolate eyes. What an idiot she'd been back then, and how incredibly stupid of her to bring it up again now. It was bad enough thinking back on the humiliating experience herself without reminding Paolo of her embarrassment.

He suddenly shook his head, as if trying to rid himself of the images. 'In legal terms, it's not actually relevant. It's a common misconception, but lack of consummation isn't usually sufficient grounds for annulment.'

Not relevant? Her mind reeled as her perspective on the past shifted. She'd imagined he'd turned her down that night because making love might have hurt their chances of escaping the marriage. It might have damaged their right to an annulment. But, from what Paolo was saying, that had never been an option. Which meant he'd turned her down because he hadn't wanted to make love to her at all.

What a total fool she'd been all these years!

'Our cause,' he said, his voice breaking into her thoughts, 'is separation for at least two years with mutual consent.'

She clenched the pen, her fingers tight and stiff. Just sign the papers, she told herself, doing her best to suppress the stinging sensation behind her eyes. Sign the papers and let him go.

Because he was never yours to begin with.

Without bothering to read the small print, she turned up the first page flagged for her signature and scrawled off her name.

'Aren't you going to read it first?'

'I've read enough,' she said, her throat oppressively tight. 'Besides, you're a lawyer, I assume you know what you're doing.'

Something in her voice alerted him and he took a step closer to the coffee-table.

'Helene?'

She looked up briefly and he saw the moisture pooling in her eyes. She was crying?

'What?'

'I thought you'd be happy about this—about Khaled getting married at last.'

'Of course, I'm happy,' she said, reeling off another crazy looped signature, another nail in the lid of the coffin of their marriage. She swiped at her eyes with her pen hand when she was done. 'It's wonderful news. You must be relieved yourself.'

Ignoring his own advice to himself, he sat down nearby and placed one hand under her chin, gently directing her to face him. 'Then why are you crying?'

'Happy tears,' she said, twisting her lips into a wonky smile as she pulled her chin away. 'It's great news really. So who's the poor bride? Anyone we know?'

His swift intake of air pulled her straight back out of the documents.

'What's wrong?'

His eyes swirled with pain, the flesh of his face

pinched and tightened, and instantly she knew that this was no accidental marriage. 'Who is she?'

His eyes stared back at her, but she could tell they saw nothing. They were blank, empty shells, his thoughts obviously centred on somewhere else— *someone* else—and her blood ran cold with fear.

'Khaled promised he would take his revenge upon me. He warned me that one day he would steal some-one close to me, steal them away from me, as I had done to him.' His eyes changed and she knew he'd brought her back into focus. 'Just as your father wanted you to pay, Khaled could not let me go.'

'Oh, no!' she said, one hand pressed against her mouth.

'And he did. He took someone I care deeply for. Just as he'd promised. Just as he'd sworn.'

His words snagged and he stopped, hauling in a breath. She waited in dread for him to go on, wit-nessing the turmoil in his eyes, sensing the devasta-tion of his pain.

'And he married her?' she asked with disbelief.

He smiled, but it wasn't with joy or elation. It was a smile empty of any emotions, a hollow smile that spoke of his loss.

'Oh, yes. He married her.'

'Who is she?' Her voice was no more than a whis-per, her dread a living thing, threatening to strangle her words.

'I don't know if you ever heard of her. She is—or rather was—a fashion designer for the House of Bacelli in Milan. Her name is Sapphy—Sapphire Cle-menger.'

CHAPTER TWO

'OH, MY God! No, Paolo… Not Sapphire! I heard— I thought—-oh, my God!'

Helene burst out of the settee, arms wrapped tightly around herself, shaking her head, trying to come to grips with the disaster that she'd caused, the anguish that she alone was responsible for. Unable to stand still, she paced the carpet, unable to stop, unable to rest with the knowledge of what she'd done.

Paolo's late-night visit, his stressed-out state, the pounding on the door—suddenly it all made sense. This was a man in mourning. A man bereft. And she was to blame.

'This is all my fault!'

'Helene. Don't think that.'

'But it is. All of it is down to me. Down to what I wanted. Don't you see?' She turned to face him, throwing her hands out wide. 'If you hadn't married me back then, none of this would have happened.'

'And what was the alternative?' He was up now, his voice raised, his eyes blazing. 'Marry Khaled? That was never an alternative and you know it.'

'But look what's happened because of it. It's been like a dark threat hanging over our lives for twelve long years. And now just look at what it's done to your life and to Sapphire's! It's too high a price to pay. I never should have asked it of you. I had no right.'

The weight of all the things she'd cost him bore heavily down upon her—twelve years of his life ripped away, twelve years of being unable to commit to a relationship, twelve years of being denied the chance to start a family. And as if that weren't enough, now she'd cost him the woman he'd wanted for his wife.

It was too much!

She sucked in a shuddering breath as she covered her mouth with her hands. 'I'm sorry, Paolo. I'm so very, very sorry.'

Then she couldn't speak any more as the sobs overtook her, great heaving sobs that racked her chest, doubling her over with the pain of knowing what his promise to her had cost him.

She was barely aware that he'd touched her, but then he was straightening her up and pulling her in close to him. Gratefully she collapsed against his chest, tangling her fists in his shirt as his arms wound around her, while the tears continued to fall, the sobs unrelenting.

'Let it go,' he said softly. 'Let it all out.'

She had no choice. She had no energy to fight it. It was all coming out anyway, a torrent of emotion that had been walled up all this time, buried away, deep inside.

Once again she felt her shock at the callousness of her father when he'd coldly informed her of his decision to trade her off. She felt the despair when her mother had ignored her pleas for help and she relived the fear and desperation that had driven her to find any solution, anything that would save her from her fate.

She cried with the relief she'd felt when Paolo had come up with his crazy plan, the answer to her prayers. He'd done more than offer her a lifeline. He'd literally saved her life when it had seemed that the only way out of her predicament was to throw hers away.

And her tears mourned for Paolo and for the life he should have had, the life now denied to him for ever.

Her breathing was still nowhere near normal when she noticed the rocking. Paolo's arms were locked around her, his chin resting against her head, and he was swaying, gently moving from side to side, an age-old soothing motion. It felt good. Paolo felt good.

His shirt was wet through under her face, but it was far from uncomfortable. Instead the steady pounding of his heartbeat, the warm, musky scent of skin made her want to bury her face deeper into him. She could taste him in her breath. She could feel his strength feeding into hers, calming her ragged sighs.

And yet she didn't belong here, in Paolo's arms. She needed to sign the papers and let him get out of here and get on with his life. Reluctantly she lifted her head from his chest. Her eyes fixed on his shirt, she drew the back of one hand across her cheeks, but she knew there was little point trying to look presentable. She looked up and saw it then, the moisture filming his own eyes. And then he blinked and it was almost gone, except for the dampness clinging to his long lashes, making them shine glossy and thick.

'Oh, Paolo,' she uttered on a breath, her heart breaking even more, knowing that she was the one responsible for his tears. 'I'm so sorry—for every-thing.'

He loosened one arm and for a moment she thought he was going to let her go completely, but one hand splayed in the centre of her back, keeping her close, as his other found her chin, tilting it up towards him.

'Enough with the apologies.'

'But, Paolo—'

'Enough.' He touched his finger to her lips to shush her, his eyes narrowing as he looked down, while the heat inside them cranked up.

It was contagious. Like a pilot light suddenly given a flow of fuel, something flared into life inside her, coursing through her and warming everywhere it touched.

And everywhere she touched him.

Heat gathered and pooled in low places as every point of their contact became more significant. Her breasts felt swollen and full, her nipples hard even as they butted into his chest, her thighs wedged tight against his.

Something had changed. No longer was he merely someone holding her, soothing her. He was a man, all man, and a man whose body was showing unmis-takable signs of arousal.

Her heart stopped. Or was it just her breath? Whatever, it seemed the whole world was waiting for something to happen.

And then his mouth was on hers and she didn't need to breathe, didn't even need to think. She had everything she needed and more in his sweet kiss. Softly, tenderly, his lips brushed against hers, the supple warmth of his mouth like a salve to her hurt, the rasp of his chin like a gentle file scraping away her pain.

Her hands untangled themselves from the knots they'd formed in his shirt as her body relaxed into his, and her fingers flexed against the fine fabric, exploring, learning, drinking in the feel of the firm, muscled flesh beneath.

His kiss deepened in response, demanding more of her and taking more. Much more. The taste of him filled her, fuelled her, obliterating every last trace of logic from her mind.

Why was he here after all this time? Why had he come? She didn't really care. Because warm breath was skidding across her cheek, heavily laced with the taste of their kiss and the scent of desire, and that was all that mattered.

Heat followed the course of his hands, transmitting through the thin silk of her robe as if it wasn't there. And then his mouth was at her throat, setting off new fires under her skin and making her hungry—hungry for him.

His hand pulled back the side of her robe and his mouth followed the movement, tracing the line of her collar-bone to her shoulder. She shuddered against him, her spine melting, every part of her skin looking to be the next place in line under his hot mouth.

He returned to her lips before trailing kisses down the other side, pulling away that side of her robe in his quest. She clung to his back, relying on him to keep her upright, knowing that her knees couldn't support her while she concentrated on the magic from his mouth.

Then his lips were at her breast, on her breast, his

tongue rolling around the hard bud, and sensation speared through her, setting off a desperate need deep inside. Tissues tingled, moisture welled as her body prepared to open itself to him.

He lifted his mouth away, his eyes fixed on the fabric, now moulded to the firm nub of her nipple. A low rumble, like a growl melded with passion, emanated from his throat and his eyes flicked up to hers.

Hunger filled their dark depths. Hunger and need. She was afraid to let her eyes slide away in case she missed something, but even so she was afraid to hold them, in case he might read too much in hers.

Whatever he saw, it gave him what he was looking for. He tugged one end of the looped tie at her waist. She sucked in a breath as the tie fell undone and the sides of her robe slid slowly apart.

Breath hissed through his teeth, his eyes glowing in frank appreciation as he drank in her near nakedness. Her breasts seemed to swell even harder in response, the points of her nipples achingly taut as anticipation built to fever pitch inside her.

'*Perfezione,*' he said, resorting to his native tongue on a breath that sounded almost like worship.

And then things sped up. His arms swept around her, dislodging the robe hanging from her shoulders. The fabric pooled behind her, but there was no time to mourn its loss, not with Paolo's mouth on hers, his hands exploring every dip and curve of her skin, his arousal a pressing imperative between them.

She pushed herself against him, need driving her to force her hips ever closer. His hands skimmed her back, tucking under the band on her panties and capturing her naked flesh, wedging her neatly between his pressing hands and the grinding force of his own desire.

His mouth dipped to her throat and she gasped for air, but the oxygen was consumed more rapidly than she could suck it in, burning white hot in the heat of their passion. Each breath, each second burned the flames higher, the need greater.

The need to touch his skin.

The need to feel his skin against hers.

The need to have him inside her.

It was all-consuming. And she wanted to be consumed. She wanted him, deep inside her. Only that could quell this desperate, mounting ache.

Frantically she scrabbled for the buttons of his shirt, not caring whether they came undone or flew off in her quest to get at his body, while his kisses continued their way down towards her breasts. She pulled the shirt open and her hands revelled in the satiny touch of his skin, the well-defined muscles below, in the contrast of the springy hairs that swirled between his pebble-hard nipples.

Her hands followed the line of his muscled chest down, over an abdomen that tightened deliciously under her touch as he caught his breath. She reached the band on his trousers, slipping the pads of her fingers beneath. Steel bands trapped her wrists and his mouth nuzzled her ear.

'Have mercy,' he said, his voice rough and edgy. 'It's been a while.'

He had to be kidding. It had been for ever. Or that was how it seemed. Two boyfriends in twelve years. Two unsatisfactory love affairs that had left her thinking she had some kind of problem. Maybe she did.

Certainly neither man had made her feel a fraction of what she was feeling right now. Neither had ever come close to setting her alight. Right now she couldn't even remember their names.

And he wanted mercy?

She curved one hand out of his grasp, turning it palm down against the straining fabric, her fingers instinctively tightening around the rigid proof of his desire.

'Not a chance,' she whispered.

His mouth and body stilled and for a cold, hard moment she thought she'd blown it and gone too far, and her spirits plummeted. She'd never tried a move so bold and outrageous before because she'd never before felt so driven, so motivated by need. But maybe she just wasn't cut out for coming the temptress.

And then he groaned, a low guttural sound, a warning of things to come, and expectation resumed its heady build-up through her veins.

He drew her back into his arms and carried her through to her bedroom, placing her with almost reverential awe on her bed. In almost the same next movement he'd shrugged off his shirt and shoes. She didn't have a chance to feel overdressed because in a moment his pants were similarly dispensed with, her pink panties meeting the same fate.

His eyes drank her in.

'So beautiful, *bella donna*,' he said, lying alongside her. Then his lips found her again.

His liquid voice and his generous words fed into her senses. The passion in his eyes set her extremities alight.

And his mouth…

Oh, his hot mouth made magic on her skin, casting spells with his lips, weaving charms with his tongue. It was witchcraft, seduction by sorcery, pure enchantment, and she was completely and utterly bewitched.

It was all she could do to cling to him as his hands made complementary havoc elsewhere. Everywhere they touched produced sparks and fireworks, but none so much as when his fingers lingered over the spring of her curls.

Breath caught in her chest as his fingers dipped lower, slipping amidst her most intimate place with an apparent knowingness that felt so right.

Hot kisses returned to her mouth and she let herself open to his fiery onslaught. Then she heard his breath catch on a groan and he shifted over her. She felt his weight pressing between her legs and the insistent column of his erection between them.

'I want you,' he said, his eyes burning with need, and she almost believed him. But then amidst the desire she also saw the clouds scudding across their surface, as if he were doing battle with demons.

It hit her like a blow to the chest. *Sapphire! He's seeing Sapphire. He's thinking she should be the one he is with.*

And there was nothing left for her but to try and help him forget. Maybe just for a little while she could help dull the pain of his loss.

She closed her eyes as she felt him pressing up against her. So hard and yet so warm. So smooth and yet so powerful. Muscles spasmed in reaction to his touch, as if by their invitation they could draw him in. He leaned further over, drinking in her mouth with his, plundering with his tongue and then meeting her need with one long thrust that made her arch her back and threw her reeling from the kiss.

Slowly he withdrew, only to fill her again, lunging himself to the hilt.

She matched his movements, tilting her hips to receive him, tightening around him to prolong the pleasure, working in with the rhythm he established. She wanted to give him pleasure, to make him forget, to pay him back something of the loss she had caused him, but it was building, her own feelings escalating into something potent, something dangerously close to boiling over.

And there was nothing at all she could do about it. Then his mouth moved to her breast, his teeth tugging on the tight peak, his tongue curling and cajoling, and it happened.

She felt herself come in high-definition colours, colours that shattered and fragmented into a million tiny shards that hovered in the air like sparkling fireflies. His own release prolonged her own, so that wave after wave of shuddering sensations followed, throwing up more clouds of the shimmering lights, glistening and sparkling and eventually fading like spent fireworks as her body slowly came back to earth.

They collapsed together amongst the pillows, breathing deep, the scent of their lovemaking a blanket to warm them. She must have dozed off, when a sound, his voice, brought her to.

'Did you say something?' she murmured.

'I said I'm sorry.'

Her warm feelings turned decidedly chilly. 'You don't need to be sorry. I believe I was a willing partner.'

He shook his head where it rested against her shoulder. 'I didn't use protection. That's never happened before.'

His words were a harsh dose of reality. What the hell had they been thinking? Except obviously they hadn't been thinking, not beyond the frantic desperation of their coupling.

'Is there reason for me to be worried?' she ventured. 'I can guarantee you're at no risk from me.'

'It's not just that,' he said. 'The last thing we both need is a baby, especially since we're about to become divorced.'

'Oh, of course.' The divorce. Her teeth dragged across her bottom lip, now plump and tender from his passionate ministrations. Of course the divorce would be uppermost in his mind. Naturally after twelve years he was looking to destroy the links that tied them together. Not forge new ones.

That's what had brought him here after all. Tonight's lovemaking was simply something that had happened between two consenting adults. It wasn't as if she meant anything to him.

'Do you take some form of contraception?'

She started to say yes, but then she remembered. She *had* been on the pill, had been on it for years to battle irregular and crampy periods. Until last month when her doctor had recommended she take a break. But she couldn't get pregnant. People tried for months after going off the pill to have a baby, didn't they? Besides, it was much too late in her cycle. She was due any day.

'I'm safe,' she said, as certain as she could be.

He pulled her to him and kissed her gently. 'Not to mention beautiful.'

The constant hum of jet engines was neither soothing enough to let her sleep, nor loud enough to drown out the memories. And she wanted to sleep. She was tired and aching and desperately, desperately running on empty. Instead she was reliving last night's lovemaking, over and over, replaying the scenes in her head, feeling the shadow of the sensations he'd awakened in her.

How many times had they made love last night? She'd lost count together with her sleep.

Thankfully he hadn't stirred when she'd left, because she had no idea what she would have said to him this morning anyway. It had been easier to write a note—although even that had taken her half a dozen attempts before she'd been satisfied. What did you say to someone you'd just made the most amazing love to all night and whom you were never likely to see again—happy divorce?

And without a doubt he'd be relieved he didn't have to worry about any awkward morning-after scenes too. She'd made sure she'd signed the papers before she'd left so he'd have nothing to complain about. He'd got what he'd come for and then some.

As for her?

She sighed, finding it impossible to get comfortable

in spite of the wide business-class seat. She'd had the night of her life. She had memories—bittersweet memories that would live in her heart for ever. Memories of a night when for just a few hours she'd been able to pretend that there was more to her relationship with Paolo than a cold, contractual arrangement—a contractual arrangement now as good as dead.

And put to death by her own hand. She'd checked and double-checked to ensure she hadn't missed a signature. She didn't want to cause him any more grief than she already had.

Because Paolo was right. It was over.

She was gone. Her side of the bed was cold, no hint of her body warmth anywhere when finally he stirred, the apartment strangely quiet. The door to the *en suite* was open, the light off. There were no sounds or smells from the kitchen, no radio or television to cover the muted traffic noise from outside.

He picked up his watch and looked disbelievingly at the hands. It was almost afternoon. He must have slept for hours when they'd finally fallen asleep. He couldn't remember sleeping this solidly in months.

But where was she? His mind searched for a clue, trying to play back their conversation from last night. But actions spoke louder than words and visions of Helene, naked and coming apart in his arms, interfered with his thought processes. She'd been so responsive, so soft and giving of herself.

After they'd made love he'd carried her into the shower and they'd washed each other and it had been another voyage of discovery. The water cascading over them both, streaming over her skin, forming rivulets down her breasts, tiny waterfalls spinning down off her nipples, his mouth lapping the tiny stream away.

And her mouth, setting his skin alight once more, building fires and need until their bodies had merged once again in their liquid world.

'*Dio!*' he swore as the pictures stirred his masculine response into life once more. He didn't need this right now!

The scene in the hallway gradually drifted uppermost in his mind. Hadn't she said something about leaving today? But where?

She couldn't be gone. Surely she would have said goodbye?

He called her name, waiting for a response in her soft tones, but there was none. Nothing but the womanly scent of her still lingering in the sheets, the fragrant trace of her hair on her pillow.

There was something else too. He raised himself up onto one elbow and reached over. The papers, he realised, as something small fluttered off the top and over the side of the bed. He ignored it for a moment as he leafed through the pages. She'd signed everywhere indicated and then left the papers where he had no chance to miss them.

Something inside him snapped.

Last night he'd got the impression she was almost saddened at the prospect of their phony marriage coming to a conclusion. She'd made love like a goddess, letting him worship her and giving her sweet body to him in return. And yet by her actions this morning she'd shown herself to be another person from the woman he'd met last night. To leave this way after what they'd shared—he hadn't given her credit for being so coldly calculating.

The papers could have waited. There was no real rush now, not from his perspective. It wouldn't have mattered if the papers hadn't been signed until her return from wherever it was she was going. She could have had more time to go through them, ensuring the arrangement was as they'd agreed all those years ago.

But she'd taken no time. She'd asked for none. She'd completed the papers and left them where her intention was unmistakable.

She couldn't wait to be free of him.

He threw himself out of the bed, noticing again the scrap of note paper, now on the floor, and he reached down to snatch it up, his spirits rising. So she had left him a note after all? Maybe a phone number where she could be contacted wherever she'd gone. There was no reason why they shouldn't remain friends.

Her tight, looping script stared back at him as he took in the message, his anger building more with what wasn't said than what was.

> Paolo,
> Help yourself to whatever you need. Let yourself out—the cleaner is coming at one.
> Helene

That was it? Breath rushed out of him as if he'd been sucker punched. She didn't want him to know where she was. She obviously didn't want him to contact her. And she didn't want her cleaner to find him still here.

He screwed up the note, tossing it into the corner of the room. *Let the cleaner find that!*

He was out of here.

CHAPTER THREE

THE physician had such compassionate eyes, making it much easier to feel comfortable with him than Helene had expected. He was older than her own doctor back in Paris, maybe sixty or so, his skin ruddy in places, his jowls just starting to slip from his cheekbones, and yet his eyes were the kindest, most reassuring blue.

He'd waited outside while she'd dressed and he smiled now as he sat back down again behind his desk, making her wonder why on earth it had taken her so long to make an appointment to see someone. Sure, her three-month secondment to the New York office was nearly over and she'd be back in Paris again in two more weeks, but she'd put up with this situation for too long already and it was starting to affect her job.

The sooner she got another prescription for the pill, the sooner she'd be back to normal. Already she'd missed work on a couple of occasions, and had been tempted to take more sick leave because of the cramping and general malaise. For someone who'd only ever taken time out for rare dental appointments it was too much. She'd had enough of the discomfort and the irregular periods.

The doctor picked up a pair of glasses from the desk and without unfolding them, lifted the lenses briefly to his eyes to look down at his notes. 'Miss

Grainger,' he said, turning his attention back to her. 'How long before you're due to return to France?'

'Two weeks.' Disappointment welled as she anticipated where his line of questioning was going. Maybe she'd wasted her time coming after all. 'Surely you're not saying I should wait until I get home to get a new prescription?'

He shook his head, 'No. Merely that we've got a bit of time in that case, so I think it might pay for you to have a couple of tests before you leave for home.'

'Why? Whatever for?'

He held up one hand to quell her reaction, his eyes crinkling with compassion again. 'Nothing serious, but I think for your own peace of mind you might want to have them done as soon as possible.'

'I don't understand.'

He smiled across at her, pinching the bridge of his nose with his fingers. 'Miss Grainger,' he continued, 'I'm not aware of your personal circumstances so I don't know if this might potentially be good news or bad news, but have you considered the possibility that you might be pregnant?'

Somehow she'd managed the short journey back to her apartment. It must have been on autopilot as there'd been no conscious thought processes involved. Her mind was way too concerned with matters far more momentous.

She was pregnant.

It couldn't have been possible and she'd wanted to argue with the doctor. But with the very first test, a specimen she'd given the nurse, the results had confirmed what the physician had surmised during his examination.

And now she was having a baby, a *child*. She placed one hand over her abdomen in wonderment. Below her hand somewhere there was a tiny baby growing. And in only another six months or so that baby would be hers to hold.

There was too much to come to terms with. It was all too sudden—all too hard to believe. After all, she'd been having periods—admittedly irregular and not at all like normal, but that was half what she'd expected. Her own doctor had warned it could take a while for her cycle to settle down after taking her off the pill. She groaned at her own recklessness. It should have clicked that he'd been referring to ovulation as well.

And she'd told Paolo she was safe!

With a cry of despair, she dropped her head into her hands.

Things couldn't get any worse.

She wasn't just pregnant.

She was having Paolo's child!

And he would be furious. His words came back to her with chilling clarity. 'The last thing we both need is a baby, especially since we're about to become divorced.'

But the last thing they'd needed had happened. The last thing they'd wanted had happened.

For on the very same night they'd severed the only bond they'd had, they'd created another that would tie them together for ever.

She tried to laugh out loud with the irony of it all, but the only sound she could make came out brittle and false and couldn't be sustained anyway—not when all she really wanted to do was to descend into tears.

It was a mess, a horrible mess and there was no way out. And if it weren't bad enough that she had to come to terms with her newly found discovery herself, the knowledge she'd have to tell Paolo certainly was.

And he had to be told. Despite the reaction she knew she'd get, he had to know he was going to be a father and that she, Helene, the woman he'd just divorced, was going to have his child.

She'd contact his law firm, get them to put her in touch, find a way to tell him.

Assuming everything was all right.

She fished the appointment card for tomorrow's obstetric ultrasound from her purse, mulling over the doctor's words. Discarding the 'routine' and 'to confirm dates', she instead focused on what he'd really only hinted at—that the scan would show if her blood loss was caused by any underlying problems that could endanger, or might already have endangered, the life of her baby.

It was only another day. There was no point getting in touch with Paolo before then. Not if there was any chance…

With a sudden burst of guilt she threw herself out of her chair. She needed to get busy—keep busy. She wouldn't think about the possibilities. It didn't matter that she'd only just found out that she was pregnant. It didn't matter that she'd have to tell Paolo and that it would be the most difficult thing she had ever done. She would find a way to do that somehow.

What was paramount now was that her baby was healthy. She wouldn't think about the other options. She wouldn't wish this baby away. She couldn't do that to her child. Maybe she was new at this pregnancy business, but even she realised that this baby needed her to protect it and keep it safe. Even she knew that her baby needed her love. She wouldn't abandon it, as her parents had done to her, coldly cutting her off as if she'd never been their own. This baby would be wanted. It would be loved.

Work had granted her request to take the next day off, for which she was grateful. The scan was going to be hard enough to deal with without having to front her colleagues afterwards and pretend it was business as usual. She still had to get used to the idea she was pregnant herself.

From her windows overlooking Central Park, she could see it was a fine day, the gentle movement through the treetops signalling just a slight late-spring breeze. She slipped on a lightweight jacket over her linen dress and, doing her best to ignore the discomfort of holding onto the best part of a litre of water inside her, pulled open the door.

'Paolo!'

'We have to stop meeting like this,' he said, one side of his mouth angled up, although his cold eyes beamed imperiously down at her.

'What are you doing here? How did you find me?'

His eyebrows jagged upwards. 'And how lovely to see you too. Aren't you going to invite me in?'

'How did you get past Security?'

'Why aren't you at work?' he countered, ignoring

her questions and not waiting for an invitation as he pushed past her into the apartment. 'They told me you were taking sick leave.' His eyes narrowed as they raked over her, frankly assessing, taking in her coat and bag. 'But you don't look sick. And you're going out somewhere. So why would you be skipping work on such a beautiful day? Unless you're on your way to meet someone. Is that where you're going? You have a man waiting for you?'

She stayed where she was at the door, the shock at his sudden appearance turning into a slow-simmering resentment. 'I don't remember inviting you in.'

His gaze moved from her to scan the apartment and its contents. She got the distinct impression he was taking inventory. Then his eyes zapped back onto hers.

'Is there a man? Is that why you're going out?'

'Paolo, just stop it. This is crazy. What are you doing here? Did I miss a signature somewhere?'

His eyes blazed cold heat down upon her. 'Oh, no, you signed every last place. You didn't miss one.'

Confusion jangled with her thoughts. If she hadn't blown his chances for a speedy divorce, then why was he turning up now looking so upset? If he'd got what he wanted, why did his words sound so damning?

'So why are you here?'

'Why didn't you tell me you were coming to New York?'

Anger surged through her veins, escalating with every pump of her heart.

'You didn't ask.'

'You left, without a word—'

'I left a note!'

'That said nothing!'

'What did you expect me to say? *Happy divorce?*' She took a deep breath and put a hand to her forehead, though the discomfort she was experiencing was coming from a much lower region of her body. If she didn't calm down it wouldn't only be her blood pressure that burst. 'What's going on, Paolo?'

He took a step closer, his eyes hooded and dark, his expression grim.

'I came to see you as it happens. I found out where you were working and decided to look you up—*for old times' sake.*' He just about spat the words out. 'I didn't realise you'd be otherwise engaged.'

She glanced at her watch, anxious to be away.

'Late for your assignation?' he accused.

'Late for my appointment. I have to go.'

'And you expect me to let you.'

'As it happens, no. I have a much better idea.' She caught the look of surprise on his face and knew it was almost worth the change in plans to pull the rug out from underneath his arrogant feet. 'I think it's far better that you accompany me.'

Immediately his brow furrowed, calculating. 'Why? Where are you going?'

'You mean you don't know? And yet you seemed so certain a minute ago. Not that it's any business of yours, but I do expect to meet a man, actually. I think you should come along and meet him too. Just don't get upset if he makes me take my clothes off.'

He covered the distance between then them in an instant, gripping onto her shoulders, so tight that she knew instinctively that if her legs gave way she still wouldn't drop an inch.

'What are you talking about? Tell me.'

The power came off him in waves, the pure animal aggression that no doubt cut swathes through board-room bureaucracy and decimated his courtroom op-position. His eyes glowered darkly down on her, his nostrils flaring, his signature male scent tugging at her senses.

It could tug all it liked. She'd been intoxicated by the man that night in Paris, but she wasn't about to make the same mistake now. Not now when she was so damned angry.

She looked squarely into his eyes and met them head-on. 'I'm having a scan. An obstetric ultrasound.'

'What for? What's going on?'

But even as he fired at her the questions it was clear that the cogs of his mind were spinning fiercely, searching for answers, clicking into place. She watched his face change, move through the stages of confusion, uncertainty, disbelief.

'But that would mean…'

And the swirling unknowns cleared from his dark eyes as she witnessed the moment, the very instant that realisation crystallised in his mind, and he knew.

She nodded. 'Congratulations. ''That would mean'' exactly that.'

He wheeled away, his hands releasing her from their iron grip so suddenly she had to fight at first to find her balance.

'So you're pregnant!'

Her confidence evaporated as she stared at his back, at the broad sweep of his shoulders now turned away from her. She couldn't blame him for the ac-cusatory tone or for his reaction. After all, she'd been the one to claim she was safe. 'Apparently so. The scan is to check that everything is progressing okay.' He didn't move and painful protests from her swollen bladder spurred her into action. 'Look, I know it's a bit much to absorb, but I really should get to my appointment.'

She was pregnant. *Dio*. What timing! He'd tried to ignore the dreams that had dogged him ever since that night in Paris. He'd thought he'd forget, he'd thought his memories would fade and die in the harsh light of her cold departure. But something had happened that night to him and the memories wouldn't fade. Instead they had taunted him, becoming more vivid, more demanding as the weeks had gone by.

And finally a chance comment from a colleague, no more than a mere mention during a case that the International Bureau of Women's headquarters was right here in New York, and instinctively he'd known that this must have been where she'd come. All this time she'd been living in the same city and he'd had no idea.

Then the thought of being so close to her had driven his dreams to new heights, his needs to new levels. So why fight it? Why couldn't they see each other again? There was no rule that said they shouldn't.

And now, when he'd finally managed to track her down, it was all too late!

It was bad enough when he'd merely thought she was just planning on meeting someone. The possessive urge he'd had to physically restrain her from going had taken him by surprise. Her taunt about taking off her clothes had set his brain searing to white-hot mode. But then why wouldn't it? In all the weeks since he'd seen her, not once had he imagined her in someone else's arms—*in someone else's bed*—and the knowledge that she could turn over her lovers so quickly had hit him like a blow to the gut.

But it was worse than that.

She was pregnant. Having someone else's baby. And he could see her now with that child, maybe a little girl tugging on her mother's skirt, with soft wavy hair and green eyes just like her mother's…

The concept left him with a very bad taste in his mouth. Helene sure hadn't been wasting her time in New York as he had, that was a certainty.

'Paolo? I'm late for my appointment.'

He spun around, exhaling a breath that said it all as he strode past her into the lobby. He had something that he'd left off doing and there was no time like the present.

'Then don't let me keep you. I'll see myself out.'

He bypassed the lifts and strode straight for the fire escape. He wasn't in the mood to wait for anything.

'Paolo?'

The round English way she said his name carried softly down the hall. He stopped, his hand poised over the stairwell door handle. He looked over his shoulder to see her still framed in the doorway, much as she'd been when she'd first opened it, except her features now appeared more bewildered than shocked.

'Yes?' he asked her.

'You're not coming with me?'

Come with her? She had to be kidding. Hadn't that just been part of her game?

'Why should I?' he said, looking to turn the words

that had seared so deep back onto her. 'Just so I can see you take your clothes off for another man?'

Her spine must have stiffened then, to add so many apparent inches to her height, because her whole bearing suddenly seemed different—more aggressive, more challenging—her eyes cold and frosty.

'Up to you. I don't really care,' she said in a tone that made it abundantly clear that she did. 'I just thought that, seeing as you were here, you'd want to come along.'

He felt his eyes narrow even as his grip tightened on the fire-escape door handle. He should walk out now, leave Helene and her mess and any fantasies he'd had of looking up a woman he'd had trouble forgetting. But something else was happening here, something unsettling and disturbing that turned the air to crackling between them. He couldn't leave, not yet.

'Give me one good reason why,' he said when he could stand the frigid silence no longer.

She looked at him for a few seconds more without answering, her green eyes almost too large in her otherwise perfect face.

'Because it's your baby, Paolo. You're my baby's father.'

CHAPTER FOUR

THE lift doors pinged open between them, an incongruously cheerful sound in the otherwise tinder-dry atmosphere. A couple, a mother and daughter carrying numerous shopping bags, spilled out, their bright chatter halting as they stepped into the hallway and took in the scene—the woman standing rigid at the door; the man, his expression grim, poised to leave via the stairs—before they both bolted for the sanctuary of their apartment.

A second later Paolo crossed to Helene's door and bundled her inside.

'What do you mean?' he demanded, his tone brusque, his manner aggressive.

She pushed away his hands from her arms, her eyes blazing. 'What is there not to understand? I'm having your baby.'

'You're lying!'

'Excuse me? I think I'd be in a better position to know who the father is than you are.'

'How can you be sure it's mine?'

'We had sex, Paolo. I believe that's usually a reasonable indication where conception results.'

'That doesn't answer my question. How do I know I'm the only one?'

She sucked in a furious breath. 'What are you implying—that I sleep around? What kind of woman do you think I am?'

'Based on my limited experience of you—what do you expect me to think?'

Fury mounted within her. 'It's *your* child, Paolo,' she heaved through gritted teeth. 'You'd better get used to the idea, because it's the truth.'

'And it never occurred to you to let me in on "the truth" until I just happened to drop by? How convenient was that? What's the problem? Are you so desperate to pin this baby on someone you took the first guy who walked through the door?'

'No! It's not like that. This is your baby. Yours!'

'So when were you going to tell me? We spent the night together nearly three months ago. When were you going to let me in on the big secret? Or were you hoping to keep it a secret? To shut me out!'

'Why would I do that?'

'Because you couldn't wait to get away from me that night in Paris. You slunk off without a word, without an address or contact number. You never wanted to see me again and this baby, if it is mine, would make no difference to you.'

She shook her head. 'No. I only just found out myself. I had no idea until yesterday. And I was going to tell you anyway, but not until after the scan.'

'You expect me to believe that?'

'It's the truth,' she said flatly. 'Take it or leave it.'

He strode to the windows, his hand raking through his hair.

'I don't understand how this could have happened,' he said. 'You told me you were protected.'

'I know.' Her voice faltered. 'I thought I was safe.'

'You *thought* you were!'

'Hey, you didn't even bother to ask until after we'd

made love the first time. And I didn't see you break-ing out the condoms!'

'Because you said you were safe!'

'I'm sorry. I made a mistake.'

'That's one hell of a mistake!'

'You're dead right. And I'm beginning to think it was neither my first nor my biggest mistake that night.'

She hitched her bag higher up her shoulder. 'I have to go now. So if you'll excuse me.'

She went to move past him, but his hand seized upon her forearm, locking her to the spot.

'Not so fast.' His eyes bored into hers, as hard and unforgiving as granite, 'If this is my baby—'

'It *is* your baby! There is no doubt of that. I can only pray it doesn't take after you.'

He blinked at her comment, slow and hard, the lines of his face rigid. 'Then I'm coming with you.'

'You know,' she said, 'I thought I was doing the right thing, but I really wish I hadn't told you. I wish I'd let you walk down those stairs and out of my life like you wanted to when you thought I must have been fooling around with someone else. Because right now I don't want to have a thing to do with you. And I certainly don't want you coming with me.'

'Too late,' he said, marching her towards the lifts. 'If you want to turn my life upside down with news like this, then you can expect me to hang around and deal with it.'

He was still holding onto her when they reached the lobby. The doorman snapped to attention as soon as they appeared. 'Winston,' Paolo ordered before she'd had a chance to open her mouth, 'we need a taxi. Ms Grainger has the address.'

'Yessir, Mr Mancini. A pleasure to help you.'

She didn't have time to ask him what was going on. Within a few seconds Winston had a taxi pulling into the kerb. 'A real pleasure, Mr Mancini, Ms Grainger. You look after that grandson of mine—he's going to make a fine lawyer one day.'

'I know,' Paolo said, slipping the man a tip, no doubt not the first for the day. 'He's one of our most promising recruits.'

Once in the cab he finally released his grip on her arm. She rubbed the place where his hand had branded her.

'I wondered how you'd made it past Security.'

He gave a nonchalant flick of his head, fixing his gaze out of the window on the passing traffic. 'I would have found a way.'

Somehow she didn't doubt it. It was the second time he'd bypassed Security to get directly to her door. What would it take if she really wanted to keep him out of her life?

Paolo remained sullen and silent the entire journey while she sat alongside him, her teeth troubling her bottom lip. Her biggest problem an hour ago had been making it to the clinic with her bladder intact. That short-term concern faded to insignificance, though, against her worries as to how Paolo would react. What would he expect? What would he demand? It was difficult enough coming to terms with the idea she was going to have a child without the added complication of not knowing how he stood on the issue. He wanted family, she knew that much. But that hardly meant he wanted an illegitimate child with the woman he'd just divorced.

'You don't need to come in with me,' she said, clambering awkwardly out of the cab when they'd pulled up outside the clinic. 'Why don't you wait for me out here?'

'No way,' he snapped, alighting and taking hold of her arm again. 'I'm coming with you.'

She tilted her chin, looking up at him, the sun behind his head turning his features dark and unreadable although she could tell he was furious. 'I'll let you know the results,' she insisted.

'I want to hear it firsthand. I have a couple of questions I wouldn't mind asking myself.'

Inwardly she groaned, having no doubt that his first question would be aimed squarely at establishing whether he could be the father. Why the hell had she asked him to come? She didn't want the first glimpse of her baby to be marred by the presence of someone determined to turn the proceedings into a battleground, father or no.

He tugged on her arm, ushering her towards the main entrance, and something inside her snapped. She wrenched her arm from his grip.

'You don't have to manhandle me. I can make it inside on my own. I'm not planning on making a break for it.'

His sun-drenched presence blasted pure heat back at her, but he said nothing, just turned and took the steps two at a time. She followed more slowly, using the handrail to help haul herself up. Not too much longer, she told herself resolutely, and she could rid herself of this pressing urge.

She reached the doors only to find Paolo standing in front waiting for her. *If only he were going to be as easy to dispense with.*

'What's wrong?' he asked her, for the first time a hint of concern edging his words. 'You look like you're in pain.'

'I *am* in pain!'

'Why? What's wrong?' he said. 'Do you need a doctor?'

She pulled herself up straight, wishing he would get out of the way so she could just get inside. 'After holding onto a litre of water for the last hour it's not exactly a doctor I need right now.' She pushed past him, trying unsuccessfully not to breathe in the spice of his cologne, the masculine essence of him. 'If you'll excuse me.'

He wouldn't let her check in. Instead he started barking orders for her immediate attention that had her cringing. He got results, though, as receptionists and orderlies rushed to meet his demands. The wheelchair, though, was the final straw.

'I don't need a wheelchair!' she said to anyone who would listen. Nobody did. They were all too busy taking orders from Paolo.

She was whisked away to a cubicle and allowed to change into a robe in peace before the radiographer collected her. Paolo tried to follow.

'I'm afraid not,' the radiographer said, barring his way into the examination room. 'I'll let you in once I know everything is all right.'

'What do you mean?' he demanded. 'Why shouldn't it be all right?'

'It's routine. It's nothing to worry about.'

'But what could be wrong?'

Helene took in a calming breath. 'I've had some bleeding. The doctor doesn't think it's a problem, but they just need to confirm the pregnancy is progressing normally first.'

'That's right,' the radiographer agreed, 'and as soon as we know that, then I'll invite you to come and see the images. So if you'll excuse us?'

Paolo wheeled away, his features clearly showing his resentment at being shut out of what he considered something he had more of a stake in than a man merely operating a machine.

'First baby?' the radiographer inquired, making idle chatter as he got her settled on the bed and ready for the scan. 'Dad seems to be a bit strung out.'

Strung out probably didn't come close to how Paolo was feeling right now. She'd had a day to come to terms with her new state and it was still a struggle. Paolo hadn't had an hour.

'He's got a lot on his mind,' she replied noncommittally.

Ten minutes later the radiographer opened the door. Paolo burst into the room like a rodeo bull on steroids, powerful and angry and ready to take on all comers. It didn't take much to imagine steam coming from his flaring nostrils.

'What news?'

The radiographer recoiled, resuming his seat and angling the screen towards them.

'See for yourself.' He placed the sensor back on her abdomen and slid it over the skin.

Paolo knew he was supposed to be watching the screen, but somehow the thought of someone else touching Helene's bare flesh, even if indirectly, set his blood to boiling point and it was impossible to drag his eyes away.

There was something on her skin, something slippery that allowed the instrument to slide across the surface and gave her creamy flesh a satiny gloss. His gut clenched as he remembered. He'd felt that skin, pressed up against his own, he'd tasted every square inch of her and had thought about tasting more every night since then.

As he wanted her now. Even though she was pregnant, possibly with his own child, one snatch of skin and he wanted her more than ever.

'There's your baby.'

The radiographer's words sliced through his thoughts and desires and finally he turned his attention to the image on the screen. He felt his gaze focus more intently. It was amazing, just so incredibly clear, lying with legs crossed, a hand clearly resting by its cheek. And possibly…

'It's incredible,' Helene said.

'How many weeks along is it?' he demanded, holding his breath.

'Well,' the radiographer said, oblivious to the atmosphere in the room while busy manipulating the monitor to get an even sharper image, 'the measurements I took will be more accurate, but I'd hazard a guess that this little one is about twelve weeks along. Does that sound about right to you?'

'That's right.' He saw Helene mouth the words, but he heard nothing but the tidal wave of blood that crashed through his senses.

It was his child. It had to be. The tiny creature with

the transparent legs, the tiny fingers and toes and the huge shadowy eyes was his baby!

'What's that?' he asked, pointing to a flickering shape on the screen.

The radiographer checked where Paolo was indicating. 'Ah, that's your baby's heart.'

'*Dio,*' he said, in awe and wonderment. His child's heart. Beating and pulsing with life already. It was almost too much to comprehend.

Someone was talking, but it was too unimportant compared to the new life he was witnessing on the screen.

'Mr Grainger, would you like to take a photograph of the baby home?'

'Oh, no,' Helene said. 'We're not mar—'

'What *my wife* means,' Paolo said, cutting her off mid-stream, and patting her on the hands affectionately, 'is that she kept her maiden name when we married. My name is Mancini. Isn't that right, darling?'

'What did you mean back there?' Helene asked once they were back at her apartment. 'Why the pretence that we were man and wife?'

'It's no pretence,' he said. 'We've been married for years.'

'But the divorce? I signed those papers months ago. It should be through by now.'

'It would have been.' He shrugged.

'What do you mean?' she insisted. 'What are you saying? You *did* lodge those papers, didn't you?'

The silence stretched out between them and yet Paolo made no attempt to ease the mounting tension.

She shook her head, scarcely able to believe the truth his reticence had confirmed.

'You didn't lodge them. Why on earth not?'

His eyes surveyed her coldly and she wondered why. It wasn't as if the divorce had been her idea. She hadn't been the one pounding on his door in the middle of the night to wind up their marriage.

'I didn't have time. I had to come back to the States and finish off a case.'

'So, that means—technically—we're still married?'

'Technically, yes.'

She crossed to the window, gazing out over the treetops to the buildings beyond.

Still married. And yet he'd seemed in such a desperate rush to be done with her.

She licked her lips. 'So when are you planning on lodging the papers?'

People were rushing along the pavement below, either swinging briefcases or shopping bags or jumping in and out of the never-ending sea of yellow taxis. People were in a hurry to go somewhere.

Yet inside her temporary home the world seemed to have slowed down as time strung out between them. She knew when he moved in close behind her, but she sensed his presence rather than heard his hushed footfall on the carpeted floor.

She found his reflection in the glass, saw his hands hesitate on their way to her shoulders and fall away again.

'What are your plans?' he asked.

She spun around, taken aback by the question. 'What do you mean?'

'Are you giving up your job?'

'Why would I do that? I love my job.'

'You are planning on having this baby?' His words were framed as a question, but his tone carried a thinly veiled message. There was only one answer as far as Paolo was concerned. Well, so be it, but why did he have to be so convinced that she would not do the right thing by her child?

'First you believe me capable of flitting from bed to bed with any number of men upon whom I can pin my baby, and then you seem to think I could destroy the incredible brand new life that we both witnessed today.

'You saw it, Paolo, I know you did. This baby isn't some vague concept, it's a life, with a heart and brain and fingers and toes. How could you even think I could try to undo what we've created, even if by accident?' She took a deep breath, letting it out slowly. 'You obviously have a very low opinion of me.'

He brushed her protest aside with the wave of one hand. 'But for all that you still intend to work.'

'For as long as I can, yes.'

'What about the baby?'

She moved to the other side of the room before turning to face him. She needed to put distance between them to dilute his impact. 'I'm pregnant, Paolo. I'm not ill. There's no reason I can't work till I'm seven or eight months pregnant. Lots of women do.'

'Not when they're having my child, they don't!'

'Oh? And exactly how many women are we talking about?'

As soon as she'd let the words go she realised how stupid they sounded. He hadn't had a chance to have children because he'd never had a chance to commit to anyone—not while he'd been married to her and protecting her from Khaled. She dropped her face in her hands and breathed deep before waving away her comment with one hand.

'I didn't mean that, Paolo. I'm sorry. But, honestly, I'll be fine.'

'What about the problems you mentioned—the bleeding?'

'It shouldn't be a problem. Today's scan showed everything was normal. You saw the doctor's report—he thinks it was probably just due to hormonal fluctuations. So there's no reason for me to stop working just yet.'

'And what about when the baby comes? Then what will you do in your apartment all by yourself?'

She turned away, searching for answers in the plate-glass windows. 'I... I don't know—take leave— I haven't had time to think about it. I'll work something out, though.'

'Then don't bother,' he said emphatically. 'I have already come up with a solution.'

Cold tentacles of dread clutched at her insides and squeezed tight. He sounded much too sure—much too confident for her liking—and she felt her handle on the situation slipping away.

'I'm certainly willing to hear your input,' she maintained shakily. 'This baby belongs to both of us. There's no reason why we can't work something out together.'

'There's no need. I have the only practical solution.'

'What do you mean?'

'You will come and live with me in my villa in

Milan. I have almost concluded this case; it's time I was returning home. And you will have everything you need. I will look after you and the baby.'

'But, Paolo, that's not practical. I live in Paris. And our divorce will be through ten minutes after you lodge those papers.'

'Then I simply won't lodge them,' he said.

'Why?' she asked. 'What do you mean?'

He moved closer until he was standing directly in front of her, his mouth tilted in victory, his dark chocolate eyes so satisfied they should have been tinged with cream. Then he reached up one hand to grace her cheek.

'It's quite simple,' he said, so close that his breath fanned softly against her face. 'As far as the law is concerned, we're married. And,' he said, after giving her just a moment to assimilate that fact, 'for the time being, we're going to stay married.'

CHAPTER FIVE

'I DON'T understand,' Helene said, shaking her head against the palm of Paolo's hand, trying to suppress the flare of hope that sparked into life inside her, battling to make sense of his unexpected announcement. 'You initiated this divorce. Now you're saying you've changed your mind?'

'Now we have someone else to consider. I don't want my child to be considered illegitimate. We should stay married, at least until the baby is born.'

It took only a second for it to sink in. His sudden interest in staying married had nothing to do with her. He was protecting the child. It wasn't that he wanted to divorce her any less. It wasn't his intention that had changed, merely the timing.

She clamped down on a dank bubble of disappointment. For while logic told her that of course that was what he'd meant, irrationally part of her wished he'd been having second thoughts for an entirely different reason, such as whatever had brought him to her door today in the first place.

'What are you thinking?'

His question snapped her attention back to him. 'I'm thinking you're expecting a lot to ask me to give up my life in Paris to come and stay with you, just because I'm pregnant.'

One eyebrow arched high as his head tilted. 'And

it wasn't asking me a lot to marry you twelve years ago to save you from Khaled?'

'Don't hit me with the guilt thing. It's hardly the same thing. You continued with your life. I didn't expect you to live with me.'

'It's very much the same thing. I did something for you—for twelve years. Don't you think there were things I gave up, that I might have done, if not for my marriage to you?'

Oh, God, she thought, jamming her eyes shut. Of course he had. He'd given up the chance to marry Sapphire, the woman he loved, before she was stolen away from him.

She'd cost him his lover and his future and yet now she was acting as if she were the victim. And it wasn't as if he'd asked for this baby. They'd both known the risks and she'd guaranteed him there was none. She could hardly take the higher moral ground.

'I'm sorry,' she said, knowing her words were painfully inadequate, 'I didn't mean—'

'So now you do something for me. And for our child.' His eyes glinted dangerously. 'And in six months, when our child has been delivered, you can still have your divorce.'

The word hissed through his teeth like a curse and she shuddered.

'And if I don't want to give up my job?' she said, trying to infuse a degree of confidence into her voice. 'If I don't want to come to Milan?'

'Then I'll sue for sole custody and you'll lose the child altogether.'

She didn't doubt it. Even as the cold fingers of his control crawled down her spine she knew it was true.

With the resources of his legal practice and his family's wealth behind him, she wouldn't stand a chance, even as the child's biological mother. But could he be that ruthless?

'You wouldn't deprive me of my child!'

He held up one hand to silence her. 'It needn't come to that. All we have to do is to give the impression that we are a family. Surely you can do that until the baby arrives?'

A family. The word seemed almost foreign to her now. Long ago she'd thought she'd been part of a family, but those ideas had been shot to pieces when her father's wishes for her marriage to Khaled had been stymied. Then she'd realised she wasn't part of a family at all, rather she was part of their assets, her life played out as if in a shop window, ready to be sold off to the customer who paid the highest price. And since then she'd been alone for such a long time.

Yet the concept of family tugged at her senses in a way that drew her inexorably to his proposal.

'You want us to act like a real family—why?'

'My mother is getting older. She wants to see me married and settled down. She wants more grandchildren. I can now give her one but her joy will be nothing compared to that she would get if she thought I was married.'

'And—after the baby is born?'

Her heart hammered loud in her chest. This was her moment of truth. Surely he would not insist she leave her newborn child and return to Paris. Surely he could not expect any mother to do such a thing.

'*Sì*,' he acknowledged with a nod, 'she would be disappointed that the marriage did not last. But by then she would have her grandchild to dote upon. The pain would soon pass.'

Her breath caught in her throat. *What of her pain?* Her life seemed to be turning into a series of rejections from Paolo. How much more could she bear? The wedding night and his desperate late-night rush to have her complete the divorce papers—if those occasions hadn't been rejection enough, now he was planning to dispense with her again just as soon as her baby was delivered.

'And when would I be able to see my child?'

'We would arrange visiting rights, as do other divorced couples.'

'But you would expect custody.'

He shrugged. 'Of course. Besides, a child will only stifle your career. I know you care too much for that to happen.'

'You make it sound like I would neglect my own child and yet your career is not something you can toss aside either.'

'But you are alone. Who would look after the baby when you are at work?'

'There are childcare places—nannies—'

'I will not have my child taken care of by strangers! In Milan the child will have family, my mother, its cousins, when I am not able to be there. Can you not see that this will be better for the child?'

'You don't seem to give me much choice.'

'You have no choice. This is the best possible arrangement.'

'No! It might be for you, but not for me or the child.'

'For all of us! Look at it this way,' he said. 'For

twelve years I put up with a marriage of convenience. All I'm asking of you is a fraction of that. Six months in a family of convenience. Six months compared to twelve years—surely that's not too much to ask?'

It was way too much to ask. The closer it came to their departure day, the more convinced of that she was. He'd organised her flights, her removal from her apartment and already he'd teed up appointments with specialists for her the moment they arrived back in Milan. He'd left her nothing to do but to sort out her personal effects here in her apartment prior to packing.

Her arms full of books she'd collected during her stay, she paused on her way to the packing box and gazed out over the park.

He'd done everything, even overseeing her application to take extended leave without pay from her work. He was taking no chances that she'd change her mind about not working once she returned to Europe.

He'd taken over her life.

In two days they would leave for Milan where she would be expected to live in the Mancini villa for the next six months, pretending to be Paolo's whirlwind wife. His *real* wife, not just his wife on paper.

She wasn't sure if she could do it. She wasn't even sure if she liked him any more. Gone was the man who'd turned up at her apartment that night, leaving in place an angry stranger who held her responsible for everything that had gone wrong in his life, from the loss of Sapphire to her unplanned pregnancy.

Well, maybe she was and maybe living in close proximity to Paolo for six months was her penance.

No, penance was way too easy, she decided, dropping the books into the box. Hers was a life sentence.

She moved into the bedroom and was putting away some earrings from her dresser when she found it. In the bottom corner of her small *cloisonné* jewellery box she'd had since a child was the ring Paolo had given her on their wedding day. Paolo's signet ring.

She slipped it on and watched as its square ebony face immediately fell to the back of her finger. She smiled. It was way too big for her. It always had been. They'd both stressed so much about escaping from her family and getting married as soon as they could that they'd completely forgotten they needed a ring.

When the registrar had asked for it during the brief ceremony there'd been a hushed silence, stunned looks and a scramble to find something, anything, that would do the job. Paolo had finally wrenched off his signet ring and placed the warm metal on her finger, holding her fingers together so that it couldn't slip around.

She held her hand up now, feeling the weight of the chunky ring on her fingers. After the wedding she'd tried to give it back, but he'd told her it was hers and she'd treasured it, wearing it on her thumb and holding it close to her heart at night. Only later, after one scare where she'd thought she'd lost it that had had her searching her room for days, she'd relegated it to the safety of her jewellery box.

Sighing, she slipped the ring off and placed it back in the box. It was a memento of a different time, a time long gone, when Paolo had been her knight in shining armour, saving her from a forced marriage to a man for whom she could feel nothing but hate.

But now Paolo was calling in the debt. No longer her saviour. This time he was her nemesis, forcing her into yet another arranged marriage.

A key turned in her lock and she gritted her teeth. Winston had organised a key for Paolo without blinking, obviously assuming she wouldn't object. But then, why wouldn't he think that? As far as she could see, nobody, but nobody, said no to Paolo Mancini.

Then he was standing in the doorway, larger than life, his height and his shoulders blocking out the light pouring through the windows behind him.

'I wish you wouldn't do that,' she said, assigning the small jewellery box to the pile designated for her carry-on luggage.

'Do what?'

'Let yourself in. You could knock.'

'What if something was wrong with you? What if you couldn't answer the door? You might be grateful for my attention then.'

'*Nothing* is going to happen. Don't you understand?'

'You're pregnant. You don't know that.'

'Listen, Paolo. Millions of women all over the world have babies every year without any worries at all.'

'And some don't. I don't see the point in taking any chances.'

She sighed, long and hard. There was no point arguing with him. He'd made up his mind that she was the least qualified to look after her own pregnancy. She was hardly going to convince him otherwise.

He strode to her wardrobe, checking the contents. 'You have much to do still.'

'It won't take long.'

'No, I'll get someone.'

Before she could protest he'd whipped out his cell-phone and barked some orders as all the while her anger grew.

'You don't have to run my life, you know.'

'You're too slow. Besides, I want you to come with me. We have some business to attend to. This can all be handled while we're gone.'

'What business?'

'You'll see. Get your coat. I don't want you catching a chill.'

She brushed his order aside as she headed for the door, scooping up her bag on the way. She'd been out earlier, and in a mid-sleeved top and low-cut trousers she'd been more than adequately dressed for the day. 'I won't need it,' she said. 'It's a beautiful day—'

'Get your coat!'

She pursed her lips, forcing them to remain closed when all she wanted to do was to yell at him to get out of her life and leave her alone.

How could she ever have imagined she loved him? How could she have harboured secret hopes and dreams about him ever since that night in Paris? Not even the prospect of them having created a new life warmed him. He'd sucked out every last shred of joy she should have been feeling about having this child, just as he was sucking her life dry.

'Where are we going?' she asked at last when Winston had seen them into a cab.

'It's not far,' he said.

They turned left along Fifty-Ninth Street, past the drink vans and stalls lining the southern wall of Central Park and then into Fifth Avenue before coming to a stop.

'We're here?' she said. 'We could have walked.'

'I don't want you taking any unnecessary risks,' he said, ushering her out after paying the driver.

'Walking a kilometre or so hardly constitutes a risk.'

But he wasn't listening. Already he was shepherding her towards the imposing sandstone building. The flags caught her eye, flapping in the breeze over her head either side of the door. Then the name struck her. *Tiffany & Co.*

'What are we doing here?' she asked.

'You need something to look married. My mother will expect it.'

Look married? Fat chance. Hadn't it occurred to him that no ring in the world was going to convince anybody? That it would take more than just a gold band on her finger to give the impression they were a loving couple?

'I don't get this,' she said as, with one arm around her shoulders and the other holding her hand, he propelled her into the building. 'Do you really think that a lump of gold is going to magically transform us into the perfect couple?'

He snorted his disapproval as he steered her through the ground-floor shoppers.

Maybe that was what he wanted, though. Maybe

he wanted them to look unhappy. The long-suffering husband, the petulant wife. She could almost hear him bewailing his misfortune already—no wonder the marriage had come to a sticky end!

They must have been expected. After a word they were whisked away into a tasteful private consultation room and it seemed the riches of the world were on display before them.

'What style of engagement ring were you after, Ms Grainger?' the consultant asked when they were settled.

'Oh,' she said, taken aback that she was allowed to even have any say in the issue. Given Paolo's attitude of late, it was amazing he hadn't just had something delivered.

But she certainly didn't need an engagement ring. They'd never been engaged. Why add unnecessary expense to the deception? 'Just a wedding band will be fine.' After all, they had been married. Were married still.

Without moving his face the consultant flicked his eyes to Paolo.

'My fiancée is too unassuming,' he said. 'Of course she must have an engagement ring.' He looked down at the display, pointing one out to her. 'What about something like this?'

She suppressed a gasp when she saw where he was indicating. It was simply beautiful. One large diamond flanked by two almost as large that would make stunning solitaires by themselves. Together in their white gold setting they were just dazzling with brilliance. No doubt the dollars would be equally dazzling.

'I don't think so,' she said. 'Maybe something more simple.'

'Try it on,' he insisted, and the consultant immediately complied by removing the ring from the display and sliding it on her finger before she could object.

It was stunning, sparking light with every move of her hand. But a ring like that should be worn by a woman in love, given to her by the man in love with her. It didn't belong on the hand of a woman like her, a woman expected to live a lie for the next six months.

'I don't think so,' she said, with a tinge of regret as she took one final look. 'What else—'

'No,' Paolo said. 'We'll take that one. And a band to go with it.'

'You can't!' she protested.

'It's decided,' he said, brushing away her protests.

The consultant was away processing the transaction before a thought occurred to her.

'You're not getting a ring for yourself?'

He stood up.

'It's hardly necessary,' he said dismissively before striding his way across the room.

Of course it wasn't necessary. It was hardly necessary to weigh her down with what amounted to several carats either, but that hadn't stopped him. Yet he himself wouldn't stoop to wearing a ring that said they were in some way linked. Clearly he wanted nothing that reminded him of their marriage.

In a surge of frustration she headed for the opposite side of the room, barely registering the contents of the display cabinets despite their inherent beauty and style. Until a flash of colour caught her eye.

The rich red crystal was formed into a stylised heart shape, its softly rounded contours and lush Elsa Peretti design turning its colour anywhere from neon red to dark shadow as her eyes changed angles over it. It was so simple and yet so wonderfully evocative, probably one of the cheapest things in the store, but it was impossible to drag her eyes away.

Across the room Paolo knew he was better off staying right away from her. So long as he maintained his distance he had a chance of controlling the desire that burned inside, the need to possess her.

She was standing over the display case, totally absorbed in whatever was held there, and his eyes relished the opportunity to drink in her curves. He approved of the way the pregnancy was already making her look, her body subtly changing, her breasts heavier and rounder than they'd been. He wanted to peel her top from her right then and there and let them fall, plump and full, into his hands. He wanted to fill his mouth with their firm peaks.

He swallowed back a groan. The hunger for her was back, more than ever, the shock at finding out she was carrying his child a mere blip in his desire.

But he would wait. He would do nothing yet, not until the doctor gave the all-clear and he was sure he could not harm the baby. Then he would have six months with her in his villa, six months where she would be his, in body as well as in name.

He drew closer, telling himself he was only curious about whatever it was that had so captivated her, moving silently over the signature carpet. He breathed in a hint of her scent, the fresh smell of her hair, and he longed to wind it in his hands and pull her mouth to his once again. Instead he forced his gaze lower, down into the display case and whatever it was she was so taken by.

It was a paperweight, that was all, although there was something about it, something intriguing…

Then it hit him and he remembered—the scan, the transparent flesh, the easily recognisable bone structure from its corded spine to its minuscule toes, and the most amazing thing of all—the shadowed trace of a tiny heart beating.

His baby's heart.

'Il cuore del mio bambino,' he said, his breath stirring the feathered ends of her hair.

She jumped a little, turning her face over her shoulder, her lips parted, her eyes widening when she noticed how close he was. And for the first time he noticed the dark smudges under her eyes, the hint of strain stretching tight the muscles in her cheeks, and he felt his own brow pull into a frown. But before he could say anything the assistant signalled he was ready.

Without uttering a word, he peeled away from her, leaving her standing there while he concluded the transaction.

Helene struggled to catch her breath. He'd been so close. *Too close.* And he'd looked at her in a way she hadn't seen for days, his dark eyes steamed with desire. In a way that had brought back a night of passion in a Paris flat and the fires that had raged between them. Lately his eyes had been filled more with hostility and anger and an icy coldness that had frozen her spirit. The sudden thaw had taken her unawares.

What was he thinking about?

She huffed in a breath, hugging her sides and wishing he'd maintained his steely demeanour. If he was expecting her to walk out after six months, the last thing she wanted was a rekindling of the kind of fires that had already burned between them. For him it was obviously just physical. But for her it would be much more. The cost would be too great.

She wanted him to hate her. She needed to be able to hate him in return. Only then would she be able to walk out of this arrangement with her pride intact. It was going to be devastating enough as it was, given that she was expected to leave her baby behind. Her breath lurched as every muscle inside her clenched.

How the hell was she supposed to cope with that?

He couldn't make her do it. No one could expect her to just give birth and walk away, to relegate all maternal responsibilities to someone else. It wasn't right. It wasn't human.

She blinked as he shoved her coat towards her. Blankly she took it, turning toward the lifts. So he was finished. The deal was done. Signora Mancini would no doubt be suitably impressed by the glittering armoury of jewels he'd bestowed upon his 'wife'.

Similarly she'd be heart broken when said wife left, leaving a newborn baby in the care of its father.

And suddenly the reason for Paolo's easy extravagance hit home. Doubtless he'd insist she take the diamonds with her.

Her damnation in his family's eyes would be complete.

Such a generous husband.

Such a selfish and greedy wife.

Bile squeezed up in her throat as he ushered her to the lifts. She didn't want the rings. She couldn't wear them. She had one wedding ring already and it had been all she'd needed for all these years. Maybe it was worthless, compared to the dazzlers he'd bought today, but at least that one had been honestly given, in the spirit of the moment, something that had cost him a part of himself rather than meaningless dollars.

They reached the ground floor and she launched herself for the doorway to the outside as if it were a life-saver.

'Stop!' Out on the street he lunged for her arm, pulling her around. 'Stop!'

'No,' she said, pulling in the other direction, knowing the last thing she needed right now was to be cooped up in an enclosed space yet again with Paolo. What she needed was room to move, and air, and freedom. She yanked her arm free and crossed both in front of her. 'I need to walk.'

She headed in the direction of the park, not caring whether or not he followed. But of course he did. With a sharp intake of air, she reminded herself that his reaction was the only one she could have expected.

He was hardly about to let her go, not with his child on board.

Within a few metres he fell into a rhythm alongside her, matching her pace easily, his long legs making her naturally shorter steps look all the more hurried and desperate.

'Where do you think you're going?' he demanded.

'Anywhere you're not,' she snapped, without looking over at him, making an unheralded pitch towards Fifty-Ninth Street.

She knew she wouldn't get away. There was no hope of that. But just the momentary charge from having him following her, going where she wanted to go, after his stultifying presence the last few weeks— it was incredibly liberating.

'I'll get a cab.'

'You do that,' she said. 'I'm walking.'

She pushed her way through the ambling tourist traffic along the south-eastern boundary of Central Park, where the earthy smell of horses overtook the otherwise inescapable smells of the city. Brightly adorned carriages lined the road and lyrical Irish voices chatted amongst themselves or soothed their patient animals.

He looked more dominating than usual here, she thought, swinging her glance sideways, watching him striding purposefully along in his Armani suit amidst the camera-wielding tourists and street vendors. Totally out of place and yet still so supreme. But then it wouldn't matter where he was. The man was made to be noticed.

She drew closer to the head of the queue of carriages, feeling herself soothed with every step by the rhythmic clomp of hooves and the creak of wheels setting off with another load of sightseers for a tour around the park.

A sudden urge bit deep. She'd never once had the opportunity to give in to her desire for a circuit around the park and tomorrow they would leave.

A glimpse across to the man at her side told her

Paolo probably hadn't even registered there were horses here, his hooded gaze focused on the path directly ahead, his mind no doubt working on the next step in his plan to secure her child.

The driver of the lead carriage saw them coming. He stepped out to greet them, his satin vest glossy in the afternoon sun.

'Sir,' he said in his Emerald Isle brogue, 'would you like to take the beautiful lady for a spin around the park?'

But it was Helene who stopped and smiled.

'Thank you,' she said without hesitation. 'I believe he would.'

She allowed the driver to hand her up into the carriage and when she turned it was to see Paolo's brows drawn together, his expression quizzical as he gazed up at her. Pleasure zipped through her. It was exhilarating catching him unawares. He was so used to calling the shots.

'I thought you wanted exercise.'

'So I'm exercising my fun muscles. Climb aboard,' she invited. 'Yours could definitely do with a workout.'

A burst of laughter followed her challenge, but it didn't come from Paolo. 'I've a feelin' you might have met your match in your young lady,' the driver said with a wink.

She allowed herself a smile as Paolo said nothing, unbuttoning his jacket while sinking grim-faced into the plush upholstered seat alongside her, the driver meanwhile climbing up in front and collecting up the reins.

He flicked them twice. 'Gee up,' he said and the

powerful Clydesdale horse set off. The carriage lurched into action before settling into a smooth ride as they entered the park through the wide gates.

The city melted away behind them as they cruised along the shaded avenue, the towers and buildings soon replaced by massive trees and wall-to-wall greenery, the permanent traffic noises muted by the sound of birds, the splash of water and the lilting rendition of an Irish ballad. Red squirrels darted between the trees and the sunlight made crazy patterns through the foliage.

Despite Paolo's presence, she found herself relaxing for the first time since she'd discovered the pregnancy. She closed her eyes and leant back, breathing in deeply and enjoying the gentle rocking rhythm of the carriage. It was good to be outside. It was good to have a chance to think.

'We have some matters to discuss.' Paolo's rich tones permeated her consciousness, but she refused to let his words disturb her reverie.

'Go ahead,' she said, still not opening her eyes, 'if you must.'

'It would be more private in your apartment.'

She snapped her eyes open, saw him weighing up their proximity to the driver.

'Not if the minions you've organised to pack my gear are there, it won't be. The driver is singing; he can't hear you. So long as you don't shout at me, that is.'

For a second his eyes sparked displeasure and the muscles in his jaw clenched and she could see he'd like nothing more than to shout at her right now. But then he blinked and took a deep breath, eventually turning side on to face her and sliding one arm along the back of the seat.

'I telephoned my mother to let her know to expect us. I told her about the baby.'

'How did she take it?'

His head tilted. 'Naturally she's excited, although she would have preferred it if we'd been married before the baby came along.'

'I thought we *were* married.'

'There's no point telling anyone about that, let alone my mother. I said we were married on impulse a week ago in a register office here in New York.'

'So now she thinks that I was careless enough to get pregnant and you decided to marry me just to do the honourable thing?'

'Isn't that more or less how it is?'

'No!' She could see the case building up against her. The inconvenient circumstances of their quick marriage, the woman he'd done the right thing by marrying and taking for his own, the woman who would betray him and walk away from her child with a handful of diamonds.

'She wanted to have another ceremony, a blessing, performed in Milan, but I told her to wait until after the baby as you were worried about your figure.'

'Oh, lovely, thank you.' She leaned back against the seat, pressing her eyes shut as mentally she added vanity to the list of her transgressions. But what did she expect? There was no way that Paolo was going to admit to his mother that a blessing didn't suit him given his intention to dispose of his temporary wife the first chance he got.

'Is there anything else I should know?'

For a moment all she heard was the clop of the horse's hooves and the quiet croon of the driver.

'I told her that you were a very beautiful woman.'

Just vain, greedy and selfish. She took a deep breath. If his comment was supposed to be some sort of compliment it hardly made up for the faults he'd already attributed to her in abundance. 'I'm not sure I can go through with this,' she whispered, looking up into the treetops for solace, her earlier feelings of peace and serenity shattered.

'You will go through with this.' He took her chin in one hand, steering her face around to face his. 'Because you owe me. You know you do.'

She swallowed as dark eyes held her own and she knew that what he said was true. He'd put aside any hope of having a family for years while he'd honoured his promise to her. Now he was calling in the debt. Now he was exacting repayment. Okay, so she owed him, but did he have to take over her life as if he owned it? Did he have to take over their child as though it were his alone?

She looked into his eyes, searching for reason, praying for understanding. Couldn't he see that he was asking too much?

But his gaze failed to offer her answers; instead it seemed to be seeking answers of its own. The place where his hand touched her chin prickled with awareness as his fingers shifted subtly over her skin. The lashes framing his eyes suddenly seemed darker, his gaze a heated caress that whispered over her skin, and she knew instinctively by the way her body reacted that he was thinking about a night they'd shared in Paris those few months ago.

Then conflict and confusion muddied their dark depths and he broke his gaze away, dropping his hand and sweeping it back through his hair. Embarrassed, she turned away to look out of the carriage, feigning interest in the view and feeling strangely let down.

He coughed, low and rough, and she got the impression he was clearing his mind of the unwelcome images as much as clearing his throat.

'Apart from my mother,' he said after a few awkward moments, 'you will meet my younger sister, Maria, and her husband, Carlo. They have two small children.'

She looked back over at him. 'And your father?'

'He's dead.'

His flat response was clearly designed to be a full stop to the topic. She studied his face and the fierce set of his chin and thought about pressing him for more details. After all, they really knew so little about each other when they were supposed to be happy newly-weds—surely it would be normal to know more of his family history? But his eyes looked so pained and ill at ease that she desisted. It was obviously not a topic that he wanted her to pursue.

'I'm sorry,' she said.

His jaw clenched. 'It is my mother who I am concerned about right now. She is not happy about missing our so-called wedding.'

'That's hardly surprising,' she offered, happy to go with the change of topic. 'Who would want to miss their child's wedding?'

Other than her own parents, of course.

She looked down at the fingers tangled together in her lap and wished so much that things had worked out differently. As far as her parents were concerned she didn't exist any more. Had never existed. They would never know that she was a mother, that they had a grandchild.

A choking feeling grabbed her throat as tears pricked her eyes, threatening to unleash themselves and spill over. She blinked rapidly, struggling to keep them at bay.

Damn! She pulled a tissue from a pocket and pressed it to her nose, squeezing tightly. She hadn't thought about her parents for ages, much less made herself cry over them. This pregnancy was turning her emotions upside down. In the space of a few hours she'd gone from anger to light-heartedness and all stops in between and now she was plunging headlong into the depths of gloom.

'Are you going to tell your parents about the baby?'

She swung her head around. Did he know what she was thinking?

'I can't see the point. They haven't bothered to contact me in twelve years.'

'But it's their grandchild. Surely they have a right to know.'

She wanted to agree with him, but she couldn't bring herself to do it. 'Maybe. In a perfect world. But family obviously isn't as important as the bottom line where I come from. As far as my family is concerned, I cost them, so now I'm paying the consequences for my actions.'

'Your father was wrong to treat you like that, like some kind of asset only there to produce him a return. He was expecting too much.'

The irony wasn't lost on her.

'Oh, and you're not?' But this was about her parents. She shook her head and continued. 'Look, it doesn't matter. It amounts to the same thing. And if I told them about the baby and they didn't want to know, I'd hate myself for letting them know I cared enough to tell them and giving them the opportunity for rejecting me once again.'

'They should care,' he said solemnly.

'That may be true,' she agreed. 'Although, let's face it, even if they did and were happy about it, is there any chance they'd get to see their grandchild? It sounds to me like you've got the access situation all tied up.'

She noticed the spike of anger in his eyes and was surprised. She hadn't meant to go on the attack, but it was a fair point. There was little incentive she'd want her parents to know anyway, given their predilection for treating children as something that could be bartered or traded like a business asset, but that didn't mean she had to defend Paolo's actions.

As it was, he'd arranged everything to suit himself, without regard for her feelings or even for the child that would be forced to grow up separated from its mother.

'You resent me for wanting the best for this child,' he said.

'And don't you think I do?'

'You'll always be this baby's mother. No one is denying that.'

'But you expect to keep the child with you. You won't let me take it.'

'That's out of the question,' he hissed, his voice

tight and tense and inviting no argument. 'The baby will stay with me.'

The baby—but not her. He couldn't have said it any clearer painted in the sky in letters sixty feet high. The meaning would be the same. He expected her to go and he expected her to leave her child with him when she did.

She turned her face away, her knuckles aching from pressing her fingers into her palms. She wanted to cry. She wanted to scream. She wanted to jump up and down and make him see that what he was doing was simply wrong and that she wanted no part of it.

But that way wouldn't work with him. He was used to arguing with the best people in the legal fraternity. There was no way she would sway him with her simple words or raw emotion.

She would have to come up with some way that would make him see that she deserved one heck of a lot more than being put out to pasture once she'd delivered his child, something that would change his mind about making her leave.

The carriage pulled out of the shadowed park and onto the shoulder and she blinked with the sudden change of light.

'Helene,' he said, 'I want you to have this.'

He pulled a neat blue box tied with a white ribbon from his jacket pocket. She shook her head and pulled away. The rings could wait. She could put them on the minute before they arrived at the villa for all the good they would do her. 'Maybe later,' she said, looking away again.

'No,' he urged. 'Take it.'

He pushed it into her uncooperative hands and she

stared down at it for a while. As soon as she put on
these rings she would be accepting the fate he had
decided for her. She would be acceding to his plans.
She wasn't ready for that yet.

'Open it!'

She blinked, her senses snapping to attention with
his abrupt command. Yet his dark eyes spoke to her
on a different level. They contained no anger. Instead
they encouraged her to do as he asked, beseeching
her to trust him.

Reluctantly she took one end of the immaculate
ribbon tie and tugged, letting the bow fall apart. She
slid the ribbon off and lifted off the lid. Thick tissue
paper covered whatever was inside. She looked up at
him, questioning, but his eyes gave no answers, instead urging her on.

She peeled back the thick layers of tissue and
gasped.

The paperweight!

The heart-shaped crystal glowed blood red against
its white-tissue background, the natural light heightening its lustre while at the same time accentuating
its shadows. She lifted it from the box, feeling its
smooth weight in her hands, running her fingers over
its sensually rounded surface. It was the most beautiful thing anyone had ever given her.

And Paolo had been the one to give it to her.

She smiled and lifted it with both hands, holding it
close to her chest. 'Thank you,' she said. 'It's beautiful.'

The sides of his mouth turned up and he nodded.
'*Buono,*' he said. 'I'm glad.'

And it seemed the most natural thing in the world

then, with his eyes, rich and warm, looking down on her, to reach up and kiss his cheek, an innocent gesture of thanks. Except that at the last second he moved and it wasn't his cheek her lips found under them, but his mouth, warm and supple and electric.

The carriage rocked to a standstill, breaking them apart, and she looked around, dazed. They were back in the queue of horses alongside the kerb, their ride over.

The driver stashed the reins and jumped down, pulling open the carriage door and smiling up at them both.

'Well, how did you enjoy that?'

She smiled a little self-consciously in return, replacing the paperweight into its box before taking his proffered hand. 'Thank you, that was wonderful. Something I've always wanted to do.'

'Ah, there's a certain magic about it,' he said, tipping his head to his finger as he helped her down.

CHAPTER SIX

His mother was waiting for them. The moment the car pulled up outside the columned portico of the gracious villa the front door swung open and an elegantly dressed woman appeared on the top step. Helene twisted the unfamiliar rings on her finger, drawing in a fortifying breath as she registered the resemblance immediately.

It had to be Carmela Mancini. Paolo's mother. Even though the woman's build was tiny when compared to his powerful frame, they shared the same luscious dark eyes, framed with the same thick lashes.

'*Casa benvenuta,*' she said, her generous mouth smiling as her arms stretched out in greeting. 'Welcome to you both.'

'*Mamma,*' Paolo said, bestowing a kiss on each cheek, 'this is Helene.'

'It's a pleasure to meet you, Signora Mancini.'

The older woman took Helene's hands in her own and squeezed them tight, her eyes narrowing, evaluating even as her smile genuinely bid her welcome.

'So this is the woman who has finally turned my son from a bachelor into a family man.' She nodded. 'I can see why he would be so impatient to marry you even though—' she winked at Helene, her smile broadening as her nod turned into a shake '—I cannot believe my thoughtless son would not even allow his poor mother to be there for the wedding.'

'*Mamma!*' Paolo scolded.

Helene knew she was only half joking. She would have to be made of iron not to have been hurt by her exclusion from the wedding Paolo claimed had been performed in New York. In normal circumstances a wedding would be a celebration for the entire family, not something to where the bride and groom sloped away as if ashamed.

'I'm sorry it happened the way it did, Signora Mancini,' she said sincerely, 'but it was all such a rush.'

That much at least was the truth.

'I understand.' Carmela stroked the younger woman's hands before slipping her arm under Helene's and tugging her towards the house. 'I was once young and impetuous. And, of course, I forgive you, given that you have brought me such wonderful news. It is much too long since we have had a *bambino* in the house. Maria's two children are growing up too fast.' She turned to Paolo misty-eyed, touching his cheek. 'Your father would be so proud of you, I know.'

She sucked in a deep breath and blinked her eyes rapidly, smiling to cover her brief display of weakness.

'But you must both be tired after your long journey. Come inside and rest.'

Helene allowed herself to be led inside the house, feeling as if she'd just passed some sort of test. Carmela had been searching for something in her face, she was sure of it. And she didn't seem half as protective of her son or unwelcoming of her as she'd expected. Was his mother just so happy to see her son married that she was prepared to overlook the rushed circumstances of their marriage or did she suspect that things were not quite how Paolo had explained?

Whatever, it was a welcome surprise for her Milan homecoming. It was clear already that they would get along.

She looked over his mother's dark head across to him, smiling, wondering if he was as relieved as she was with how the introduction had gone, but when her eye caught his she was just about stopped in her tracks. Because it wasn't pleasure she saw there. There was none of the relief she was feeling, none of the satisfaction. Instead every angle and plane of his face was set to accentuate the message coming from his eyes. Anger.

She turned her face away. What had she done now?

She hadn't even made it under the covers. She'd clearly been so tired she'd just taken off her jacket and kicked off her shoes, leaned back into the pillows and fallen fast asleep. And she'd even chosen the smallest bedroom in their allotted suite to do it. She'd gone up to bed hours before him and when he'd finally left to join her he hadn't found her in the suite's main bedroom at all. Instead, here she was, tucked away like some nanny or maid in one of the minor bedrooms.

Was she hiding from him? Was she so anxious to avoid him that she thought she could evade his reach for the next six months by choosing another bedroom from his?

Not a chance.

He looked down at her, her face at rest, her mouth

slightly open, her hair floating out around her head on the pillow.

He reached out one hand, tracing the tips of his fingers over one coiling loop. So soft. He remembered how it felt against his face, its heavy weight smelling of fruit and summer, and he longed to bury his face in it again.

And he would, just as soon as the doctors assured him it was all right. He pulled his hand away, taking in the rest of her, still dressed in her knitted top and fitted trousers.

She couldn't sleep like this, fully clothed on top of the bed. And if he was going to get her under the covers... Blood crashed loud in his ears at his next thought.

He would have to undress her.

For months he'd thought about doing just that. And yet now the opportunity had presented her to him on a plate, he could do nothing more than that. Tomorrow she would see the doctor. Tomorrow he would know. Until then he would have to wait. But that didn't have to stop him from wanting to make her more comfortable.

She would probably stir anyway while he slipped off her clothes. That was a risk he was prepared to take. She looked so deeply asleep it would be cruel to wake her just to make her get changed for bed. And it wouldn't take him long.

He pulled down the covers on the other side of the bed so it was ready for her, then he knelt down alongside and, watching her shuttered eyes for any flickering movements, took hold of the tab on the side closure of her trousers. Holding his breath, he eased down the zipper. Her slow, even breathing hitched only the slightest amount and she moved a fraction, just enough to make the sides of the opening pull apart. A tiny sliver of creamy skin down to her thigh, punctuated by a mere ribbon of lace, met his gaze and he swallowed, suddenly aware of his parched throat.

The dream was back. The dream she'd had time and again since that night in Paris, and this time it felt more real than ever. But this time she was determined her night-time lover wouldn't escape with the dawn light, except she was so tired, her limbs too heavy to lift, and her spirit only too willing to accept the ministrations that soothed and massaged and comforted.

She felt his hands at her waist, peeling away her clothes and easing her to one side so they would slide right off. The air was cool against her legs until she felt his hand, lightly skimming the surface of her skin from her waist right down to her toes, and warmth bloomed under his touch.

His hands scooped under her top, rising up under her arms. She dropped an elbow and he slipped off first one sleeve, then the other. Like a breath of wind she felt the garment lifted over her head and eased away. Fingers traced the lines of her ribs, circling her waist, rounding her back, a massage that simultaneously soothed and stimulated.

She wanted to reach for him; she wanted to hold him in her arms and pull him to her for a kiss. But her arms were so heavy, so lethargic. And she knew that there was no one there and that if she reached for him her dream lover would disappear and she would be left cheated once again.

The clip on her bra dissolved and the straps slid free from her shoulders and for the first time she was sure she heard her dream lover groan. Even in her dream she tingled with anticipation. He wanted her.

Heat focused in her breasts, warmed by a gentle breath—his breath—fanning gently against her peaking flesh. Then his mouth was on her, the soft touch of his lips, the gentle lap of his tongue, to first one nipple, then the other. She arched her back, wanting it to go on; she wanted more of the delicious sensations; she ached for them. But when his lips met her again it was at the skin of her belly, his mouth brushing over the surface in little more than a heated breath. Then his hands were on her thighs, his beautiful long-fingered hands stroking her legs, lower and lower and taking her last remaining garment with them.

She sighed. He could take her now and her dream would be complete. Yet there was nothing more, and she drifted between sleep and dreams and unreality amidst wishes that real life could be so perfect, so gentle and blameless.

Only vaguely she was aware of the sensation of being moved, but she was soon so comfortable, so warmly wrapped in his arms, that it didn't matter.

Her breathing was slow and even again, signalling a return to deep sleep. He envied her. He'd be lucky to sleep at all tonight. The way her body curved luxuriously against his, the neat way she pressed into him in all the right places, the way her natural scent and the fresh smell of her hair coiled into his senses, it was probably madness to hold her this close when his need was so great.

But it had been so long and the torture was worth it to have her in his arms at last.

Even in sleep she'd been so responsive. For a while he'd thought she'd woken, his movements too disturbing, and her flesh so eager, but her tiny sighs were like someone sleep-talking, the breathful murmurs of one in a dream state.

Next time, he promised himself, she would be fully awake. Then she would know it was him and not some fantasy. She would watch him as he made love to her. He wanted her eyes open. He wanted to look into their cool green depths when he entered her. He wanted to see them explode when she came apart in his arms.

He sighed, praying as he clamped his eyes shut that the doctor would have good news for him when he took Helene in to see him in the morning. Until such time as he had the go-ahead to assuage this throbbing need, he would have to ignore it. He could stand one night of torture if he had six months of hot nights to look forward to.

But would six months be enough?

He shoved the thought back from where it had come. It would have to be.

He would make sure it was.

Helene drifted in and out of sleep, coming ever closer to waking before briefly slipping back into her comfortable dream state, easing herself into wakefulness like the tide creeping further up the shore with every lapping wave. Warmth surrounded her, encased her—pinned her down.

Her eyes opened suddenly at the unfamiliar weight, blinking, focusing on the grey light of a room laser-lit with tiny needles of light that eluded the otherwise blackout curtains. Holding her breath, she heard the unmistakable sound of someone breathing behind her.

Paolo.

She tensed and the arm over her shifted slightly, curled fingers brushing against her naked skin.

Naked?

Her senses kick-started into life. She couldn't remember getting into bed, let alone taking her clothes off. And she definitely had no recollection of Paolo joining her.

A wave of panic prickled over her. What else didn't she remember?

Snatches of a dream swirled around in her mind. Like random snapshots from a scene they teased her, refusing to come to order, making no sense. She'd dreamed of Paolo again, only this time it had seemed so real. Snippets of sensation came back to her—her clothes peeling away, a gentle hand gliding over her skin, a warm mouth at her breast.

And like a bolt of electricity, it hit her. She hadn't been dreaming at all. But what concerned her the most was what she couldn't remember. What else had he done? Her mind rewound her dreams in a desperate search for answers. Surely she would remember if he had made love to her? And yet there was nothing, no memory, no musky scent of lovemaking, no physical reminders of any kind.

So why was he here?

Nothing made sense.

He hadn't touched her since his reappearance in New York. And while his control over her life had become an all-pervasive thing, he'd kept his distance from her physically, his eyes only once or twice betraying a hint of memory as to what had happened between them. Which made perfect sense. That night in Paris had been an aberration for them both. He saw her only as a vessel for his baby. An incubator.

An incubator destined for the scrap heap as soon as this child was born.

So what was he doing in her bed now? What did it mean?

And why was every cell of her body on high alert? The skin under his arm tingled, setting off charges that sent out sparks like the sparklers she remembered holding as a child on Guy Fawkes night. Only these sparks relayed through her body, making every part of her exquisitely aware of his naked proximity.

His heat warmed the bed, his heat seeped under her skin, warming her blood.

He shifted alongside her and she held her breath, wondering how she was going to edge out from under his arm without disturbing him further and where she might find her robe when she managed to escape.

His hand slid over her waist, his fingers spreading over the swell of her hip, squeezing slightly, and she jumped involuntarily.

'You slept a long time,' he said. 'You must have been very tired.'

His voice was pure early-morning husky and its throaty edge snagged into her feminine senses like a dose of pure testosterone. She didn't have to turn over to know how he would look; his voice carried with it the visual. His dark eyes would be hooded, slumberous, and his jaw would be shadowed with stubble.

She knew *exactly* how he would look.

All masculine.

Incredibly sexy.

And way too dangerous.

'What happened to my clothes?' she asked, without lifting her head from the pillow and trying to sound as if it was the first thing she said every morning when there was a man in her bed who hadn't been there the night before. 'Who undressed me?'

'I did,' he responded. 'Is that a problem?'

She licked her lips. 'What do you think?' she said, realising her attempt to put him on the defensive had failed miserably and wishing she'd never asked the question at all.

His hand slipped away as the bed moved and she sensed him rise up on one elbow. 'Look at me,' he said.

Wavering, she hesitated. 'Why?'

'Just look at me.'

Keeping the bedclothes tightly wrapped around her, she eased herself over until she was facing him. He looked just how she'd imagined, except his shadowed jaw was set and tight, his eyes more determined than ever.

'You have no need of all this,' he said, indicating the tangle of bedclothes pulled up tight. 'I've seen it all before. And I saw everything last night. You have no secrets from me.'

Heat flooded her cheeks. 'What gives you the right?'

'I am your husband!'

'That's a joke!' But she couldn't argue with him lying down. Pulling the covers with her, she backed herself up against the headboard.

'You're my gatekeeper. You're my jailer. You've locked me up here until I deliver you your child. But as for being a husband? I don't think so. I don't think you know the meaning of the word.'

Skin pulled taut over the bones in his face and his nostrils flared over lips drawn tight.

'In the eyes of the law I am your husband and I—'

'Then the law is a joke!'

'Maybe that's true,' he said with barely controlled fury, 'but that doesn't change anything. I am your husband and I will undress you if I see fit.'

'And am I to believe that that's all you did?' She'd said the words before she realised that she'd given too much away. That she'd shown that she even cared.

Something in his eyes flickered, but not with amusement, despite the curved set of his mouth. 'Would it matter?'

'Of course it would matter! I was asleep. You would have been taking advantage of me.'

His eyebrows lifted and this time he did look amused. 'Don't you think it's a little late to be worried about your virtue? Some might even conclude you are the one taking advantage of me. You were the one who claimed to be protected, were you not?'

'It's not like that!' she insisted. 'You didn't even bother to even ask until we'd had sex that first time and it may already have been too late. And I didn't *claim* to be protected. I believed I was safe and that's what I told you. But none of that is relevant anyway. None of that gives you free access to my body now.'

'You didn't seem to object to the prospect of making love with me last night. On the contrary, you seemed quite accommodating.'

'We didn't—'

His eyes told her nothing. They were blank of emotion, dark windows to nowhere.

'Unfortunately not,' he said, turning away. 'We didn't. But you would have. I have no doubt of that.'

'No,' she insisted emphatically, shaking her head, even though the memories of her dream told her she was kidding herself. 'Look, Paolo, this isn't fair. Isn't it enough that you lock me up here until I have your child? I didn't realise you expected to sleep with me as well. I didn't realise you expected...' Her words trailed off.

'We are married,' he said, throwing back the covers and rising from the bed unashamedly naked, 'whether or not I have any concept of what a husband is. And we are good together in bed. We might as well make the most of it while you're here.'

His callous words fell like acid rain on her heart. He couldn't be that insensitive, that cruel. To use her for sex while she was just about his prisoner and then discard her when he had no more use for her? It was too much. It was too hurtful. He couldn't mean it.

She wanted to drag her eyes away from his naked body as he padded across to the adjoining bathroom— it would be some kind of protest at least. It would show she didn't care, that his body held no attraction for her.

But she couldn't. The magic of his predator-like stride, the beauty of his perfect form, the sheer size of that which made him man—there was no dragging her eyes away, just as she knew there was no denying the fundamental truth of what he'd said.

They had been good together.

They could be again.

But why should it be only on his terms?

She gulped in air as an idea formed in her mind. Maybe there *was* a way to make this work, to bring Paolo closer to her.

Maybe she didn't have to fight him.

Resolve flowed through her veins, warm and reassuring and edged with hope. He didn't have any concept of what he was letting himself in for. He had no idea of the tool he'd just handed her.

Because what he wanted from her, she could use to reach him.

She'd reached him that night in Paris; there was no doubt of that. Otherwise he'd never have bothered to look her up when he was in New York. That first night together in her apartment he'd been in torment, suffering the loss of Sapphy, battling his feelings of guilt, and she'd shared in that pain, and together they'd found a way of dealing with it, a way of blotting it out, at least temporarily.

And now they had more than just a tired wedding contract to bind them together. Now they'd created a life. A child's life.

So could she reach him again? Could their love-making make a difference to his attitude?

It had to. Because the man she knew as Paolo couldn't be gone. He'd saved her from a marriage against her will; he'd stood up to one of the most powerful men in the oil world for her, and there was no way he could have changed that much. Because he was a man of integrity, a man who held intense passion for wanting what was right.

That Paolo might be hard to find right now, he might be elusive, but he was still there, buried somewhere beneath the layers of hurt and loss. He had to be.

And maybe, just maybe, if she could find a way to uncover the real Paolo, there was a chance for them all.

CHAPTER SEVEN

THE sound of children's laughter greeted them on their return from the clinic, signalling the arrival of Paolo's sister, Maria, her husband and two children for lunch. Carmela had apparently planned quite a feast and already fabulous aromas were wafting from the large kitchen.

Carmela rushed out and greeted them, asking after the baby in a torrent of kisses and words.

'Buono,' Paolo answered for her as he embraced his mother. 'Things could not be better.'

Helene stole a glance at him. He'd pointedly asked the doctor when it would be safe for them to resume sexual relations despite Helene's obvious embarrassment at his line of questioning. His control last night had suddenly made sense. It wasn't out of concern for her sleeping state that he'd not gone further than he had. He hadn't wanted to harm the baby.

But now that he'd received the answer he'd wanted, how soon before he took advantage of it?

Tonight?

She had to focus on appearing normal, on greeting his younger sister and her husband and their two young children, Vincenzo and Annabella, on listening to what they said and saying the right thing in return. But how could she even pretend to be normal when her body was making preparations for an entirely different kind of celebration?

Paolo swung a giggling Vincenzo up onto his shoulders and looked around, and as his eyes met hers she felt it. Desire reached out from their dark depths, telling her that he was thinking the same thing.

Definitely tonight.

She turned her eyes away, but that didn't stop the heat spiralling deep inside. Despite the harsh words they'd exchanged this morning, it didn't stop the anticipation.

She tried to tell herself that her excitement had something to do with the chance to put her scheme into action, but she knew she was lying. Her excitement had everything to do with knowing that he wanted her—that she wanted him. Her excitement was nothing more than primal.

After lunch Helene found herself banished from the kitchen, ordered to relax by both the Mancini women and the housekeeper. She wandered out to the patio, following the sounds of laughter and happy squeals. Carlo leaned against the balustrade smoking a cigarette, laughing at Paolo on all fours on the grass below offering pony rides to Vincenzo and Annabella in turn.

Vincenzo at four was supremely brave and clearly fancied himself as cowboy. Paolo accommodatingly bucked and reared, giving the boy the ride of his life.

At just two Annabella was more hesitant, and content to let her favourite uncle walk her around the grass.

'He's very good with the children,' Helene said, coming up alongside Carlo.

'Paolo will make a great father,' the handsome Italian said reassuringly. 'For a long time he has seemed like a man who hungered for a family. We thought he might marry before now, but somehow he's never seemed able to take that final step.' He turned to her and smiled. 'Until you came along.'

Helene somehow dredged up her own smile in response before looking away, too uncomfortable to try to respond. They'd all expected Paolo to marry Sapphire. He didn't have to say her name for Helene to know that was whom he was thinking about. They'd been a couple for longer than two years. The gossip columns had had them all but married off. The family must have thought their engagement was imminent, and then Sapphire was gone and suddenly a pregnant Helene was on the scene, the new Signora Paolo Mancini.

None of them had any idea of the truth, of the real reason why he'd never married Sapphire or anyone else, why he'd never started a family earlier. Helene had made that impossible.

Would his family resent her for what she'd cost him, the same way Paolo did? Would they support him in his plan to keep the child and set her adrift because of it?

Maybe they would. Unlike her own circumstances, family for the Mancini's seemed paramount. The feeling she had with them was like being wrapped in a giant, soft duvet, surrounded by security, cheered by warmth. But then, if they learned that she'd caused him such long-term heartache—maybe they would think she deserved all he gave her.

She shivered.

'You should relax,' Carlo said, obviously sensing something in her face and drawing his own conclusions. 'Yes, the news of your marriage and the baby was sudden and took us all by surprise, but it is good news for the family and very good news for Paolo. He looks happier than I've seen him in years.'

He did? She looked over to where Paolo had collapsed onto his back on the lawn, the two children climbing and tumbling over him, his rich, deep laughter ringing out between the giggles and squeals, and her heart squeezed tight.

In a year or two their own child might be doing the same thing, playing rough-house with his or her *papà* on the lawn. Would she be here to see it? To witness her child's delight?

She wanted so much to be. Why should he be so anxious to be rid of her? There was still so much she didn't understand about him.

'What happened to Paolo's father?' she asked at last. 'Paolo won't talk about him and I don't feel I can ask Maria or her mother.'

Carlo dragged deeply on his cigarette before flicking it into a nearby ashtray. 'No. They feel his loss greatly still. He died just before Vincenzo was born. We named him for his grandfather.'

'What happened?'

'He had cancer, very seriously. He had operations to remove the malignancy; he had chemotherapy and then radiotherapy. It was one thing after another and then the process started again. He was sick for many years, fighting the disease, Carmela by his side tirelessly supporting him. It was a very difficult time.'

'But ultimately it killed him?'

He leaned down, resting his arms on the balustrade as he watched Paolo with the children. 'Not at all.

After years of struggle he finally beat the disease. The doctors announced he was in remission. Everyone was very excited. The whole family was here to celebrate, cousins, uncles, friends, friends of friends. Paolo flew back from a case he was working on in Germany specially to be part of the celebration.'

He paused and she waited, knowing in her heart that this story did not have the happy ending one would normally associate with overcoming such a heinous disease, not wanting to hear what he had to say next, but knowing that she must.

'Paolo never got to see his father. After spending years overcoming the disease and winning back his life, Vincenzo lost it in a fraction of a second on the *autostrada*. An out-of-control truck hit his car. He didn't stand a chance.'

'Oh, my God,' she said, horrified. 'How terrible for Vincenzo, for everyone.'

'It was worst for Paolo,' Carlo continued. 'His father had planned on surprising him by showing him how much he'd recovered. He was on his way to collect him from the airport when the accident happened.'

She shuddered. It was too horrible to imagine. What should have been a happy homecoming had turned into a shocking tragedy.

Carlo shrugged, crossing his arms as he leaned back on the balustrade, though she could see the harsh lines in his face as he remembered that time. It was clear Vincenzo's death had exacted a terrible toll on the entire family, even for those not directly related by blood.

'Paolo took it badly. They'd always been close, but

now he felt cheated. Just when he was about to have his father back, he was stolen away. Of course he blamed himself. If his father hadn't been driving to collect him, then the accident would never have happened.'

Stolen!

Her blood ground to an icy halt as suddenly everything that was happening made sense. He'd lost his father, stolen from him in the blink of an eye when he'd fought and won the battle to defeat the cancer that had ravaged him.

Barely over that and he'd lost Sapphire, stolen by Khaled, the man who had sworn revenge against him for marrying Helene.

It all made such perfect and ghastly sense.

He'd lost his father and then he'd lost his lover in short order. No wonder he was so determined not to lose his child. No wonder he was so desperate to control her life.

He was a man who had lost far too much already.

Could she really make up for any of that in just a few short months? Would she really be able to give him something back that would help ease all that he had lost and all that she had cost him?

She wanted to try.

She needed to try.

The future of all of them depended on it.

Paolo stood up, a child held in each arm, telling them in their own language that they had worn him out and that he was taking them to their *papà*. But as he looked up towards the balcony it wasn't his brother-in-law his eyes snagged on.

She stood there leaning against the balustrade, her

wavy hair turned to spun gold by the sunlight, the skirt of her short dress floating around her legs. Like a fair-skinned goddess, a bright light amongst his dark-haired, olive-skinned family. She'd been watching him, her green eyes layered with emotions he couldn't guess at. What was she thinking? Why was she watching him?

Need stirred inside him at the vision she made, need that had been making itself felt ever since seeing the specialist that morning. Even the pranks and energy of two small children could not quell the rush of blood he felt at every thought of what he was going to do tonight—at the thought of what he was hungry enough to do right now.

But she'd been so angry this morning, so outraged at the prospect that they should share a bed for more than just sleep, that there was little chance she would be waiting for the same opportunity he was. And yet there was something about the way she looked— something that told him that she wanted more than to argue with him right now.

The pale skin at her throat begged to be kissed, the soft, taunting fabric of her skirt pleaded to be pushed aside so his hands could sweep upwards over the smooth skin of her thighs, to where her liquid heat could wrap itself around him and he could bury himself deep inside her. And the way she was looking at him…

Carlo's voice intruded on his thoughts. The children in his arms were squirming for release.

'Paolo,' he said, laughing, as if this wasn't the first time he'd tried to get his attention. 'Let the children down. *Nonna* has *gelati* for them.'

'Gelati!' they squealed as one. He set them down and they took off into the house, Vincenzo going like a rocket, Annabella toddling along behind with her father as fast as her short legs would allow.

He watched them go before he looked back at Helene. Without saying a word he devoured the few short steps leading up to the patio to where she stood, following his progress through eyes that were slightly lowered, the fingers of one hand toying with her necklace.

He lowered himself the few inches to the balustrade alongside her so that they were almost eye to eye. Her lips parted slightly and he watched the pink tip of her tongue appear then retract, leaving a film of moisture over her top lip. He wished he could have thought of something appropriate to say, but he couldn't speak, couldn't find the words, when all he wanted was to mimic the action of her tongue and moisten her lips himself.

'They're beautiful children,' she said after a little while. 'And they obviously love their *gelati.*'

'All children love ice cream,' he said. 'Do you want some? I'm sure *Nonna* has enough for an entire army of Mancini adults as well as children.'

She shook her head, making the soft, waving tendrils around her face bounce and spring, as if they had a life of their own.

'No,' she said on a breath. 'Do you?'

He reached out a hand and tucked one of the loose tendrils behind her ear. He saw her sharp intake of breath, he witnessed the movement in her throat when she swallowed, but he didn't take his hand away. He left it there, his fingers gently stroking the downy softness of the curve of her ear.

'What I want right now isn't ice cream.'

Her eyes slid sideways to meet his. 'What…? What do…?' She stopped and looked away, as if uncertainty had eaten her words.

'What do I want?' he prompted. His hand slid through her heavy hair, weaving his fingers around and between and dragging the thick streams of hair, exerting just enough pressure to turn her head towards his.

Her eyes dropped to his lips—uncertain, then expectant—and he smiled.

She had to know what he wanted, but that still wasn't going to stop him telling her. With both hands he drew her around, hauling her in closer to him. And when his lips were but a fraction away from hers, when he could feel her warm breath mingling with his, her soft breath on his skin, her soft hair curling into his cheek, he told her.

'I want you.'

CHAPTER EIGHT

PAOLO felt the shudder move through her as his lips meshed with Helene's, supple and pliant and slightly parted, as if she was ready. As if she was anticipating his kiss. And that knowledge fuelled his desire. He breathed her in, her taste and scent tangling together with warmth and need, and he steered her closer, drawing her in between his legs as his kiss deepened.

Her mouth opened at his coaxing and the liquid heat of her welcomed him inside. She tasted so sweet, so compulsively addictive, and his thoughts turned to hopes of another invitation, a deeper taste of heaven that beckoned as he held her so close against his aching hardness that she could not mistake his intention.

She didn't, if her subtle movements were any indication, her hips between his thighs, her breasts firm where they brushed against his chest. But, whilst subtle, their effect on his body was anything but. Every pulse of her body, every tiny shift in her position was enough to make him want to act on his desires.

His hands ached to pull up the skirt of her dress and clamp down on her bare flesh; his mouth yearned to seek the hard points of her breasts that butted into his chest and drag them into his mouth. But this was not the place. As much as he wanted to keep going, as much as he wanted to follow this beginning to its logical conclusion, they couldn't stay here. Any moment the children could return.

On a ragged breath he dragged his mouth from hers.

Her eyes were bright and luminous, her lips plumped and lush, and it was anguish to tear himself away.

'Did you have plans for this afternoon?' he asked, knowing he'd never make it if he had to wait until tonight.

The green lights in her eyes sparked with passion. 'I do now.'

His growl was tinged with victory as he swung her into his arms, his mouth meeting hers once more in a silencing kiss. Her weight was nothing in his arms. She curved against him, not fighting, her limbs settled around him like liquid, her breasts crushed into his chest.

As soon as they were alone he would pull back the fabric that covered them. He longed to fill his hands with their weight. He longed to take their pebbled peaks in his mouth once more. Last night had been a taste. Today would be the feast.

Footprints alerted him to the fact they weren't alone and he cursed that he hadn't already made his escape. He lifted his head to see two small children, their chocolate-smeared faces seriously studying whatever he was doing with their new aunt.

Helene turned her head at the intrusion, and smiled when she saw their faces, her lilting laughter nowhere near soothing the raw edge of his desire. She straightened up in his arms, gesturing that he should let her down. Slowly, reluctantly, he complied, allowing her legs to slide gently to the ground. But he maintained his proprietary hold on her shoulders.

'What are they saying?' she asked Paolo, after Vincenzo junior had rattled off something, promising herself she would start to work on her Italian as soon as possible so she could better communicate with them all.

Paolo sighed. 'I promised to take them swimming in the pool after lunch. I had forgotten.'

The two children looked so hopeful and yet so forlorn that their uncle might have changed his mind.

'Then you must. Come on. Last one in is a rotten egg.'

They didn't understand her words, but it didn't matter because they picked up on her enthusiasm. In a few minutes they were all changed and splashing together in the crystal-clear water of a pool set skilfully into part of the terrace where the land sloped away, providing views over the surrounding countryside that seemed to go for ever.

Annabella sat in a blow-up duck, floating and kicking herself along happily on the surface. The young Vincenzo was eager to display his already advanced swimming skills and challenged anyone and everyone to a race.

They spent a good hour in the pool with them both. Afterwards Carmela came with refreshments and Helene dried off in a lounger with her, taking in the view over the landscape spread out beyond, while Maria took her worn-out daughter off for a bath, Vincenzo following reluctantly on their heels.

She sipped on her ice, watching Paolo churning up and down the now-quiet pool, his gleaming muscles pumping hard, water alternately sliding over and then sluicing off his streamlined body as his arms powered through the water. She'd lost count of the number of laps he'd completed of the long pool, but he must have swum kilometres already and still he showed no signs of easing off.

Carmela offered the jug of soda and she held out her glass for a refill.

'It seems my son has the devil at his heels,' the older woman said. 'Even when he relaxes he seems driven.'

Helene looked over at her, wondering if there was more to her words than first appeared, but Carmela was contemplating the contents of her glass, swirling the icy mixture around.

'I notice he plays to win,' Helene offered. 'Whatever he does.'

The older woman nodded. 'That's so true. In that way he's very much like his father was. There was nothing his father couldn't do once he set his mind to it…' She looked away, over into the distance, and Helene knew that she was thinking that all the determination in the world hadn't been able to save him from such a pointless death.

'You must miss him terribly.'

She nodded and turned her head back, her eyes sheened with moisture. 'I feel bad that he's missed out on meeting his grandchildren. He was so looking forward to Maria's first child. I know he would have loved them all so much.'

Carmela took a sip in the ensuing silence, visibly collecting herself. 'But it's the present we have to focus on and we have so much to look forward to now.' She reached across and took Helene's hand. 'I'm so glad that Paolo has found you. He seemed so lost for so long—so unsure of his place in the world even as he was making a success of it.'

She smiled and squeezed her hand. Helene battled to return the gesture, the enormity of what she'd cost Paolo only now sinking in, when she had the chance to hear from his family how twelve years of being tied to her had affected him. It was more than just the cost of losing him Sapphire; it was what he had been denied all that time, the uncertainty, the inability to make his own life.

And he'd done that for her. For a promise made when he'd been barely twenty years old. And he'd stuck by that promise no matter what it had cost him.

'Your son is a good man, Carmela.'

'I know. And I know you will make him very happy. A child is just what he needs to give his life focus.'

They both turned back to watch Paolo, still churning through the water, his body sleek and arrow-straight. Helene couldn't look at him without thinking about what they might have been doing if they hadn't been interrupted with this swimming session.

All that energy, all that intensity… His long arms, those strong legs would be right now tangled with hers. Those narrow hips, now encased so enticingly in black trunks, could be pressing against her, his endless power surging into her.

Despite the warmth of the afternoon sun she shivered involuntarily, aware of nerve endings under her blue and white patterned one-piece prickling into awareness again.

Oh, Lord, she only had to look at him to get ideas.

'What about your parents, Helene? Are they excited? I hope they're not too disappointed that we've stolen you away to live with us.'

She blinked and stared at her glass, thinking that the ice came a poor second to the subject of her parents for cooling her heated thoughts.

'I'm not sure they'd even care,' she began, then wondered how to finish when she noticed Carmela's look of shock. 'My parents have had nothing to do with me since I was seventeen.'

'Oh, but that is terrible. How could they do such a thing to you? And how could they not want to know about such a wonderful thing?'

'Carmela,' she said, trying to calm the older woman, 'it's okay, really. I disagreed with something they wanted me to do and—'

'What did they want you to do?' she demanded.

'They arranged for me to marry the son of a business partner of my father's as part of their deal. I refused.' She hesitated, wondering how much she could tell, but there was no need to bring Paolo into this. It was not her place to reveal his truth. 'So I ran away.'

'Oh, but of course you did!' Carmela sighed, reaching over to stroke Helene's hand. 'So you have no family in England? No family anywhere?'

Her teeth bit down on the inside of her lip as she shook her head.

'Then it is right that you are here. We will look after you.' She moved across to embrace the younger woman. 'This is your home now. We are your family.'

Tears pricked at her eyes and she smiled, warmth filling her heart. 'Thank you,' she whispered as she hugged the woman back, trying to force away the tightness in her throat. She'd always managed by herself; she'd made a success of her life by herself; she'd told herself time and again that she needed no one. And yet Carmela's generous words touched her on a level she'd thought long dead.

To belong to a family—a real family. It was more than she could ever have hoped. Paolo's plans for her might not be long-term, her own plans to win him might not be successful, but she had been welcomed into this family and it felt so good.

'You don't know how much that means to me.'

Carmela patted her on the back. 'It's an honour to have you as part of our family. Now I'm going inside to check if Maria needs help with the children.'

'Can I do anything?'

'No,' she said, urging her to stay seated when she'd tried to rise. 'We promised the children a visit to the market. You stay and relax, but make sure you take care—your skin is far too precious for our sun.' She gave her a quick kiss on the cheek and a promise to be back later that afternoon before heading off towards the house.

'That sounded cosy.'

His voice sliced through her warm feelings like a scythe. Paolo was standing at the shallow end of the pool, water running from his gleaming body in rivulets. He tossed back his head, flicking the moisture from his dark hair in drops that shone like jewels in the sun while his hand followed the action, raking back his sodden hair into some sort of order. If he was breathless from his exertions, the gentle rise and fall of his glimmering chest gave no indication.

She swallowed. She had no idea how much he'd heard, but she was damned sure she'd said nothing that he could be angry about.

'Your mother is very kind.'

'Don't get too close to her. I don't want her hurt.'

With a push he hoisted himself straight out of the pool and onto his feet.

'How would I hurt her?'

'When you leave.'

When she left. Of course. After Carmela's warm words, Paolo's reminder came like a dose of ice.

'I see,' she said, sitting up in her chair as pieces of the puzzle fell into place. 'That's what that dark look was yesterday when we arrived—you were warning me off. You don't want me getting too friendly with your mother.'

'Exactly,' he said, picking up a towel to blot his face.

'So I take it you'd rather I was rude to your mother—that way she'll be happy when I leave. Is that it?'

'Don't be ridiculous,' he said, tossing the towel away. 'Just keep your distance.'

'Which was no doubt your cunning reason for bringing me here, I guess,' she said, her voice heavily laced with sarcasm. 'So I could keep my distance. Who would have picked that?'

She stood up to move away from the chair, but her path was blocked by six feet two of scowling Italian testosterone.

'I brought you here to look after you,' he thundered, his eyes blazing fury, the tendons in his neck stretched tight.

She stared up into his face with a look that would ensure he was one hundred per cent aware of her own anger.

'Then you needn't have bothered,' she said, her teeth barely parting as she let the words fly, 'because I'm perfectly capable of looking after myself.'

Before he had a chance to respond, before waiting for his reaction, she'd stepped around him and dived headlong into the pool. The water hit her like a rush, but it would take more than a drop in the temperature to cool her anger. Paolo wasn't the only one who could take his frustrations out with laps. She started striking out, building up a rhythm, blocking out everything but the feel of propelling herself through the water.

Again and again she turned, lap after lap, revelling in the feeling of moving through a different medium. If only she could negotiate a route as easily through the hazardous depths that made up Paolo. But unlike the pristine water of the pool there was nothing at all clear about him. His emotional landscape was murky and filled with snags that threatened to pull her down whenever she thought she was making progress.

She kept on, ignoring the heavy burn in her arms, forcing them to work, and counting down the strokes until the wall and her next turn.

Except this time something was blocking her way. She saw his legs in front of her, planted wide on the pool's tiled floor. Without breaking her stroke she changed direction to move around the obstacle. Suddenly a hand snared her wrist and stopped her dead. She came up spluttering, trying to wrest her hand away.

'Let me go!' She wanted to shout, but the necessary breath just wasn't there and her words came out a gasping cry of desperation.

'Stop fighting,' he ordered. 'Calm down.'

Now he had both her wrists and there was no way she was calming anywhere. It didn't help that her muscles felt like jelly after her exertions, and without the water to support her she doubted she'd even be able to stand.

'What do you think you're doing?'

'I'm telling you to stop.'

'I don't take orders from you. Let me go!'

She twisted one of her slippery wrists out of his grasp and thrashed out at him, but he moved and her fist slammed into water sending the splash high into his face. Within a second he'd snared the free wrist again. Frantically she bucked against his grip. 'Who the hell do you think you are?' she demanded.

'What are you trying to do? Wear yourself out?'

'Don't pretend to care about me. I know that's a lie.'

'Someone has to look after you.'

'You couldn't give a damn about me!' She spat out the words like machine-gun fire as she fought to free her arms. But this time his grip wasn't giving way; if anything it was edging her towards him, closer to his wall of chest, and he was moving, circling around so that it was becoming more and more difficult to keep herself braced on her feet. She shifted her stance, fighting for purchase as the water swirled between them, trying to maintain her distance from his muscled body.

'You only brought me here so you could control

this pregnancy. You don't really want me here and you don't want me getting close to your family. All I am to you is a walking incubator. All you want is this baby!'

'That's where you're wrong.'

'Admit it! It's the truth.'

'You know that's not the whole story,' he said, ceasing his fight, his voice suddenly low and even. 'You know that's not the only reason I want you here.'

She blinked in the sudden stillness, as if taken aback by his sudden change of direction, her eyes wide and questioning.

'You know I want you for much more than that.'

Through parted lips her breathing came fast and shallow as she recovered from both her swimming and the torrent of arguments that had ensued. And maybe they weren't the only reasons. Below her Lycra swimsuit her chest rose and fell rapidly, forcing the clearly outlined shape of her breasts and the peaks of her nipples to his attention. Despite the cool water he felt his own internal heat rising.

He smiled and nodded his head a fraction. 'I see we're on the same wavelength.'

He let go her wrists as his arms circled her hips, taking advantage of her stunned silence to haul her in closer to him.

Her hands braced against his shoulders, her hair curled unchecked, a wild frame around her face where her lips waited, full and quivering.

'Paolo,' she said on a whisper, her voice somewhere between a question and a warning. 'Paolo.'

CHAPTER NINE

Dio! Paolo sucked in a breath. What her voice did to him! It seemed to reach inside and curl its way into his deepest places. He pulled Helene closer against him and it was her turn to gasp when their bodies collided, his hands lifting her higher so that her hips lined up with his and there could be no mistaking his intent.

One hand cemented her to him while the other travelled languorously up the length of her back, to curve around the column of her neck. He felt her skin, moist and supple; he felt the firm press of her body against his; he felt the beat of her heart through his fingertips on her throat. He groaned. It wasn't enough. There was so much more he ached to feel.

He slanted his mouth and meshed his lips with hers. She tasted slightly salty from the pool, and lush and warm, like a siren should taste. She'd coaxed him into the pool as surely as if she'd sat on a rock and sung magic to him, her feminine form a magnet for his eyes, her cool indifference a calculated provocation.

Her mouth opened, blossoming under his, letting him taste more of her, possessing her mouth. As she leant into the kiss her shoulders melted against him and with no difficulty he swept aside the straps of her swimsuit.

Her head pulled out of the kiss despite his resistance. He couldn't lose her now, not when he was so close. Already his plans to have her again had been delayed. If it wasn't enough that he'd had to wait the weeks it took to have the doctor's go-ahead, even today he'd had to grit his teeth against the demands of his family when all he wanted to do was have her alone.

And now he did, there was no way he wanted to stop.

Her eyes looked nervously around, darting from side to side. 'Your family—the children…'

He could have howled with relief. 'Carlo drove them all into town. They won't be back for hours.'

Her focus settled back on him, the green of her eyes reflecting facets of gold in the light that echoed the sun-kissed streaks in her hair. He removed her hands from his shoulders and slipped her one-piece straps down over them. Then he lifted each hand and, without taking his eyes from hers, kissed it solemnly before replacing it around his neck.

'You are so beautiful,' he said. 'You know, I have dreamed of this ever since that night in Paris.'

Her eyes widened, her breath barely a whisper as she gazed up at him.

'Make love with me, Helene.'

For a moment she didn't move, only the staccato pulse in her throat betraying whatever was going on inside her head. Then she tightened the grip around his neck, pulling herself up higher until her lips could reach his, and this time it was her lips issuing the invitation, her tongue seeking entry into his mouth.

He had no intentions of declining. Exhilaration surged in his veins as her passion was given free reign, welcoming his efforts and matching them. They slid into the water, tumbling and rolling under the surface, their mouths locked in a kiss that defied their need to breathe, her hair drifting around them like a sensual cloud.

Then together they broke the surface, gasping for oxygen to further fuel the blaze they had started. This was the woman he knew from Paris; this was what he'd hungered for ever since.

His hands peeled away the rest of her swimsuit and revelled in the touch of her exposed flesh, cupping her breasts, skimming down the curve of her waist to the flare of her hips and her neatly rounded behind. Every part of her was perfect. Every part of her would be his.

Was his.

Heat pooled in his loins and he shucked off his trunks in record time. He angled her into the steps, drifting her back against their support, bracing her in his arms to cushion her skin. Then his mouth could no longer resist what his hands had been rediscovering. Almost reluctantly he dragged his mouth from hers, trailing kisses down the line of her throat and chest, to where the peaks of her breasts broke the surface like sleek white islands, firm and inviting and glossed with moisture.

With a low growl he took the tight bud of one ripe breast into his mouth. He heard her inward rush of air, he felt her body meld to his nuzzling movements and felt himself react in turn.

Her fingers raked the skin at his back and lower, her touch an incendiary to his desire. The arch of her back, the thrust of her hips, everything was right, everything was perfect. Her need fed into his own.

He lifted his mouth and found her other breast, drawing it into his mouth, rolling the rigid peak with his tongue, suckling gently on the tip. He wanted to taste more of her, all of her, but, as on that night in Paris, there was a more pressing compulsion, a more urgent need.

His mouth found hers again, hot and waiting and expectant, the water between them eliminated in a rush in the press of their bodies. She shifted to accommodate him and he slid between her cream-skinned thighs to somewhere he'd longed to be for months. And he wanted to take his time, he wanted to spin out this moment, but there was no way he could, not with her in his arms, in this place where soon they would be joined.

And then anticipation became reality. He entered her slowly at first, testing, teasing, driving them both insane with primitive need before he filled that need with one single, slick thrust that stopped the world as every cell in his body focused on their union. Her muscles tightened around him, welcoming, coaxing as every sensation seemed magnified. He felt her cool skin and her liquid heat; he felt the gentle lap of water at their sides; he saw her hair fanning out like a golden mantilla around her head, he heard his name on her breath.

And as he began to move she responded, their movements a choreographed dance older than time, a rhythm governed by the cosmos.

They took each other there, to the sun and the stars. He felt her come apart with his final thrust, he felt her shatter in his arms and that was all he needed to know as he went with her over the brink.

* * *

The bright afternoon had long turned into the dusky tones of evening before they stirred. They'd moved from the pool eventually, when their breathing had been under control and when their limbs had been able to support them once more, and made it to the showers and then to the master bedroom in their suite. At each stop they had given in to the temptation to make love, as if making up for the months they'd wasted.

She lay with her head on his arm, his face so close to hers that his warm breath skimmed over her like a balm, the heat from his body a glow, filtering its way through her like a heated massage.

He was the most wonderful lover, strong, considerate—she hugged herself with a smile—*insatiable*.

Every muscle hummed with the after-effects of their lovemaking, every part of her had been made love to, felt loved.

She looked up at him, his lids closed, his breath even and steady. He wasn't asleep, she knew, simply dozing as she had been, enjoying the brief peace, the time between sessions. Because they would make love again—she knew it.

But it was more than that. She'd hoped there was a chance to get through to him, to make him realise that she had more to offer him than just a child, that she could be more to him than just a temporary wife. And after today she knew there was that chance.

He hadn't made love to her like a stranger, like a person who meant nothing. There was no way that was possible.

Reaching up, she lightly touched her lips to the corner of his mouth. 'Thank you,' she whispered.

Without opening his eyes, he turned his lips into a lazy smile. 'What was that for?'

'Just…everything,' she said, nestling down again into the crook of his shoulder.

He lifted his head then, rolling her back along his arm and looking down into her face, with his free hand smoothing away the loose drifts of her hair. There were questions in his eyes, then a sudden narrowing.

'Are you all right?'

She blinked. 'I'm fine.'

'I haven't hurt you, or…?'

'Or the baby?' She finished his question for him, feeling her warm inner glow dissipate in the cold reality of his primary concern. But then, she'd known this wasn't a one-shot deal—that she couldn't expect to bring him around to wanting her in just one day. As it was, she hoped six months would be long enough.

'We haven't hurt the baby,' she said. 'I'm sure of it.'

'Then why do you suddenly seem so sad?'

She forced a smile and a low laugh. 'Maybe you just wore me out.'

This time the smile on his face looked positively smug. 'Does that mean you've had enough?'

'Oh, no.' She smiled back, her eyes issuing their own challenge. 'Not a chance.'

'Good,' he announced. 'Because I'm not finished with you yet. Not by a long way.'

He rolled her back over so that now she was sitting

astride him, the evidence of his endless stamina yet again making its presence felt between them.

She swallowed back on a sudden urge of heat as he reached up and took the weight of her breasts in his hands.

'You don't think we should be going down and joining the others?'

'We'll go down,' he said, lifting himself up to take one already tightening peak in his mouth. 'Eventually.'

Paolo's desire showed no signs of waning over the following few days. To all the world they must have looked like true newly-weds, his touch never straying far from her, his eyes always seeking her out across a room. The tension he'd displayed in New York had gone and he actually seemed happier.

He even started drawing her into conversations in the evening when sitting with his mother after dinner.

She'd held back at first, reluctant to contribute to the conversation if it meant incurring his wrath for somehow trying to ingratiate herself with his mother, but he'd insisted on her opinions and their discussions had become a nightly ritual.

During the days he explored the countryside with her. He took her into Milan and showed her around his city like the proud countryman he was. They spent hours in the magnificent Duomo in Milan's central square and she marvelled at the intricate Gothic architecture that had taken five centuries to complete, with its stunning stained-glass windows and thousands of statues. From the roof terraces all of Milan seemed to stretch out before them in a breathtaking view that ended on the nearby snow-capped Bergamo Alps.

Together they toured through the renaissance glory of the Castello Sforzesco and the museums and collections it housed before wandering aimlessly along the streets arm in arm, stopping for pastries and coffee along the way. It was only when they reached the Via Monte Napoleone that Paolo's demeanour suddenly changed and tightness once again pulled the skin of his face achingly tight.

She didn't have to ask. The shopfront heralded the name of its designer in large letters. Bacelli. They were deep in the heartland of fashion design and this was the salon where Sapphire had once worked.

Her heart constricted. She'd known it would take more than sex to make him forget about the pain of losing Sapphire and be willing to accept Helene herself in her place as his life partner. But as the days had passed she'd convinced herself she was making progress. Now just one look at his anguished face told her she had such a long way to go.

'You miss her very much,' she offered as he hustled her past.

He looked down at her, clearly taken aback that she had any concept of what he was thinking. 'I failed her. I as good as delivered her to him on a plate. I can never forgive myself for that.'

His eyes were empty and devoid of hope, open wounds to his hurt, and pain tore through her like a thunderbolt. If he would never forgive himself, how then could he ever forgive her?

That night their lovemaking was different. More tender, more poignant, as if tinged with regret and sorrow for all that had been lost, for all that had been wasted.

She wanted to soothe him with her love, to reach out and absolve him of his guilt and his pain, but he didn't want her love. He never had. The woman he loved, the woman whose love he wanted, was gone, lost to him, and Helene was the one to blame.

So she gave the only thing left to her that he could use—her body—and as he launched himself with her into the abyss she hoped it was enough to keep him.

CHAPTER TEN

'YOU look happy.'

Helene felt Paolo's hands circle her waist and reel her in, his touch drawing her like a magnet. She drew her eyes from the blue waters of the lake and looked back at him. Dressed in his fine Italian knit shirt and dark trousers with the light breeze tugging at the hair at his collar, he looked so good she felt an insane burst of pride.

He might not be hers, but she was with him, and that was enough to draw looks of envy from passing women. Who could blame them?

'How could I not be in a place such as this?'

They both looked out over the view. He'd brought her to Lake Como, just a short journey from his family's villa outside bustling Milan, yet a complete world away from the frenetic pace of the city.

They journeyed around the lake, stopping in the town of Como to take in the view from the Piazza Cavour, and it was another breathtaking view. Ancient villages clung to steep hillsides that plunged into the jewel-like waters of the lake. Lush Mediterranean foliage vied for attention with alpine peaks.

The overall effect was one of tranquillity and peace and it was impossible not to feel good. But there was more to it than that. The past few days he'd made her feel more and more special. Their lovemaking had become more tender, less rushed, and there were times when she thought he must be starting to love her, even just a little.

He spun her around to face him and she caught something fleeting momentarily shadowing his eyes. 'Come,' he said, with his hand at her shoulder. 'Let's find somewhere to eat. We need to talk.'

Apprehension put a sudden halt to her good feelings. They'd been talking for days with hardly an argument between them. Why the cloak of seriousness now?

'About what?' she asked, doing her best to keep her voice light.

Without answering he found them an isolated table at a local trattoria and reeled off an order in Italian before sending the waiter scurrying away.

'What is it you want to talk about?' she prompted.

He leaned back in his chair, his legs stretched in front, his arms wide, and she gained the distinct impression she wasn't about to hear good news.

'The case I was working on in New York—there have been complications—an appeal.' He paused. 'I need to cut short my leave and return to work on the case.'

'But it's your firm! You're the senior partner. Can't they find someone else?'

'There is no one else. I know the case better than anyone. I can't let them down now. We're too close.'

'But you will be working from the Milan office?'

His eyes remained on hers, but there was none of the assurance she wanted. 'Then...?'

'There are times I will have to be in New York. It

is unavoidable. But I will spend as much time as possible based in Milan.'

'I see.' The words were clipped and sharp and she'd meant them to sound that way.

His jaw shifted sideways. 'What do you "see"?'

'That you can't stand the thought of someone else heading your case. That you're too much of a control freak to let go.'

His sigh was long and spoke volumes as he sat forward in his chair. 'I was hoping you might understand.'

'Of course I understand. You're following a time-honoured tradition, after all.'

His frown joined his heavy brows together. 'Now what are you talking about?'

'It's how every good caveman is supposed to act. First you drag the woman back to your cave to bear your offspring and then you leave her there while you go out slaying dinosaurs.'

'Don't be so melodramatic!'

'I don't believe you're going to do this! You ripped me out of my life and brought me here so you could control me, and now you're taking off for New York again. I don't get it. Are the fees worth that much to you that you can't trust someone else with the case?'

Cold fury tightened the skin of his face and the set of his jaw as he regarded her silently.

She'd made him angry again. What did he expect? But he had no idea what he was really costing her. Because if her plan to make him love her was to have any chance at all, she needed him to be here, she needed to be able to show him how good things could be between them. It was clear that already he'd mellowed these past few days. She was making progress, but she couldn't if he was in New York. They would never bridge their differences that way.

'Maybe I should come with you?' It was the perfect solution. He might have to work long hours, but at least they would have some time together.

'No,' he said, dashing her hopes emphatically. 'You will be better off here.'

'Then what am I supposed to do while you're off lighting up the legal world?'

'Enjoy yourself. Relax.'

'And after I've filed my nails and washed my hair?'

'I am offering you luxury on a plate and you find fault? I'm saying you can spend your days how you see fit—go shopping, visit the sights, laze by the pool if you choose. There are plenty of others who would jump at the chance for such a lifestyle.'

'I can spend my days how I see fit?' Her ears had pricked up with this comment. 'Then I have a better idea,' she said, suddenly leaning forward in her chair. 'I could do project work here, in Milan, for the IBW. There's no need for me to go near an office. I can set something up at the villa, turn one of the smaller bedrooms into an office and have the Bureau send work to me online—'

'No!'

His sharp retort threw her back in her seat. 'But—'

'You do not have to work.'

'I like to work. I'm good at my job—it's important to me.'

'I will not have you working. That was not part of our arrangement.'

'"Our arrangement"? This was never *our* arrangement. It was always what you wanted; you never once considered me.'

'Nevertheless, you will not work.'

'But you'll be working! Why shouldn't I do the same?'

He waved aside her protests with a flick of one wrist. 'It's not an issue we need to discuss.'

'Oh, yes, it damn well is!' Harsh and bitter fury ran in her veins. It was her father again, telling her how to run her life, telling her what she could and couldn't do. 'I need to do something. Maybe my work doesn't seem as earth-shattering as your big-bucks legal business, but the IBW does make a difference to women's lives all over the world and especially in Third World countries. Why shouldn't I be able to keep working while I'm here? What is your problem? Don't you have enough money already?'

His olive skin darkened, a tell-tale pulse at his temple betraying his anger. 'Forget about your job. Right now this baby is your first responsibility.'

She turned away from him, too angry to look in his direction, and wondering if she was ever going to get through to him. But there were no answers in the lively clatter of the restaurant, no solutions that could be plucked out of the air, and she knew in the end she had to face him. 'I want to know,' she said, turning back, 'if you are going to try and control this baby's life like you control mine. Are you going to push it around and tell it what to do? Are you going to make all its decisions for it? Because I feel sorry for the poor child already. You sometimes make me wish there was no baby.'

'I will not let you speak about our child in such a way!'

His words were quietly spoken but intensely felt and she reeled back with their force. Did he think she was wishing away her child? How could he?

Her hand flattened down low on her belly, below where her waist was just starting to noticeably thicken. He might want to run this child's life, but it was still her child—would always be her child, and she would love it for ever.

'I didn't mean…'

'It's too late to wish this all away,' he hissed, cutting her off. 'There is a baby and we're all living with the consequences.'

Aren't we just? she thought mutinously as the waiter arrived with their meals.

'Now that that's settled,' he said, after the waiter had filled their water goblets and departed, 'there's something else I want to discuss with you.'

'It's far from settled, Paolo,' she said, her voice even and firm. 'If you are away in New York, I fail to see how you can stop me working. Besides which, it's the only way I'm going to be able to keep in touch with what's happening at the Bureau. Otherwise I'm going to be hopelessly out of touch with my projects when I go back next year.'

The look he gave her was pure basalt, shiny and hard and the product of some of the world's greatest heat.

'That's what I wanted to talk to you about,' he said. 'You're not going back.'

CHAPTER ELEVEN

'WHAT do you mean?'

'There is no reason for you to go back.'

'But my job...'

'There is a more important job for you here. You will have a child to take care of.'

Helene's heart lurched in a way that sent hope unfurling cautiously within her. But she'd had her hopes raised before, only to be dashed again, and she couldn't let herself get on that emotional roller coaster again.

'You—you want me to stay?' It was almost impossible to get the words out. And it was inconceivable that Paolo's stance would have softened to such an extent that he had changed his mind about her leaving—particularly given the heated discussion of the last five minutes.

'It seems to me,' he started, wishing he'd gone about today's topics entirely differently. He'd known she wouldn't be happy about giving up her work, so why had he mentioned his need to go back to work first? It had only aggravated the situation with her when he needed her to put the baby first if she was to accede to his plan. 'That there's no reason for you to go back to Paris once the child is born.'

Her heart thumped so loud in her chest her words almost tripped over it. 'And...why is that?'

'The child will need you—you should breast-feed.

141

Carmela said so, and Maria, that it is best for the baby.'

'*They* said so.'

Her tone offered him little encouragement, but he wasn't about to give up now.

'You have something against breast-feeding?'

'I never said that.'

He surveyed her face, searching for the truth behind her glinting green eyes and her cool words, but unable to shake the visions that had plagued him ever since his mother had asked him if Helene would feed the baby herself.

Their baby, suckling at Helene's creamy breast, its lips attached firmly to her nipple.

He wanted to see it.

And it made him burn in ways he'd never before imagined. It wasn't about sex, which had surprised him. It was more a strange pull, or an instinctive knowledge that this would be a good thing. The right thing.

He swallowed, dragging his thoughts back to the present. He had to convince her to stay first.

'You do want the best for our child.'

'Of course I do. I have all along.'

'Then stay, and look after the child.'

Her eyes swirled with uncertainty as tiny creases marred the perfect bridge of her nose. What was she thinking? Was she weighing up the baby with her job?

'How long exactly would you require me to breast-feed?'

His jaw clenched, jamming his back teeth together. He was right. Already she was calculating how long she could be away from her work, how far she could extend her leave without jeopardising her position. He blew out on a long breath and recognised his disappointment. Knowing that he was so right about her wasn't the least bit satisfying.

He ran one hand back through his hair.

'Carmela is genuinely fond of you, as are all the family. Already she's grown used to having you around. She would be devastated were you to leave to return to Paris.'

'You told me in New York that she'd get over me.'

He nodded his acknowledgement. 'Even so, it would be hard for her. And for the children. Already they love you as their aunty. Is there any reason to disappoint them?'

Her eyes considered him critically. 'And staying longer will make it easier on them? I don't understand what you're saying, Paolo. What exactly are you proposing? I think you should spell it out.'

'It's quite simple. My family believes we're man and wife and has accepted you into the family. On top of that our first child is due before Christmas.'

'Hang on,' she said, holding up her hand. 'You said "first child".'

Silence slid open between them like a chasm.

'Exactly,' he said at last. 'Whether we like it or not, we're already bound together by this child. Why then shouldn't we use it to our advantage? I want more children.' He shrugged. 'My family likes you. So why shouldn't we stay together? Why shouldn't I have those children with you?'

As little about proposals as Helene knew, she was pretty sure they were supposed to sound warm, and not like something that came gift-wrapped in ice crystals. And yet she must be insane even to hesitate. This was the very thing she'd wanted and hoped would happen, that he would relent from his determination to be done with her as soon as the child was born and ask her to stay with him and the baby. This was exactly what she'd hoped for.

Except, the way she'd planned it, it wasn't intended to be based on her child-rearing capacities, or be done to ensure the minimum of disruption to his family. Her plan had been predicated on him asking her to stay because he would suddenly realise that he wanted her.

That he loved her.

'Let me get this straight,' she started. 'You want to keep this arrangement between us going?'

'It makes sense. The baby will have two parents to grow up with, maybe even brothers and sisters in the future.'

'And you think that would work?'

'Why not? Over the last few weeks you've been happy enough, haven't you? And we've proven how compatible we are.'

'Compatibility in bed is hardly the basis for a permanent relationship.'

'It counts for a lot. Most couples don't have half of what we share.'

Maybe that was true, but didn't he feel anything for her at all? Didn't he want her to stay for what she could give him, and not just for the baby and his family?

She had to know. 'And what about love? Where does that come into it?'

There, she'd said it. She held her breath, not knowing where it would lead—she had no idea how she could confess her love for him even if he demanded to know the truth—but the question was out there between them.

He pushed his barely touched dish away, brushing the napkin across his lips.

'We both know why we're here,' he said. 'If it weren't for this baby, then you would be back in Paris and I would probably never have left New York. I think we both have to be realistic. This isn't a normal marriage by any stretch of the imagination, but I'm prepared to live with that. The question is, are you?'

If it weren't for this baby. Her mind was numb and reeling as his phrases played over and over in her head. *Whether we like it or not, we're already bound together by this child.*

There was no question of him liking it, none at all. That much at least was clear. Without this baby they wouldn't be together at all. It was as simple as that.

Her throat tightened, tinder dry, making it impossible to swallow and yet her glass was near empty. Their heated discussion had turned any lubricating effects of the water to dust.

'So, what's in it for me? Apart from the regular sex, I mean.' She threw out the challenge even while part of her screamed at her to hurl her agreement at him before he changed his mind. After all, she could have him, she could have their child—their children—and she would belong, really belong, in a family for the first time in her life.

She could have exactly what she wanted.

But it wasn't *how* she wanted it.

And it wasn't enough.

His eyes glinted pure heat while a muscle twitched threateningly in his cheek.

He was angry. Good, so the hell was she. She wasn't in the mood to stop now.

'And all it will cost me is to give up my job, my apartment and basically my life. Tell me, Paolo, what are *you* giving up in return for this cosy relationship of sex on tap and a ready incubator for your children?'

By the way his mouth was set, she could tell that his jaws were all but cemented together.

'I seem to have made a mistake.' The words hissed through his teeth. 'I thought this is what you'd want.'

Nerve connections snapped in her brain. 'You *thought* this is what I'd want!' She shook her head. 'I don't understand. What gives you the right to decide or even to think you know what's best for me? Didn't it ever occur to you that I might have an idea of what I might like myself? Who do you think you are—my father?'

He sat bolt upright. 'What are you saying?'

'He had plans for me as well. He never asked me what I wanted either.'

'I saved you from your father!'

'I thought you did—at the time. But now you're doing the exact same thing—telling me what I can and can't do. I thought I was free from having a control freak run my life—and for twelve liberated years I was. Then you had to come back.'

She gasped for air, letting him work out the rest.

Her breathing was fast and furious, her cheeks so hot that it was clear her anger had translated into more than harsh words.

He said nothing as the pulse in his temple worked overtime. Instead he glanced down at his watch and lifted himself out of his chair with a sharp exhalation of air. 'It's time we were getting back.'

Without waiting for her, he thrust some notes into the waiter's hands and strode from the restaurant.

Neither spoke on the way back to the villa, but the way he drove told her exactly how he felt. He handled the Ferrari like an extension of himself, powering confidently through the curves, eating up the bitumen with a controlled determination. The car did exactly what he wanted. No wonder he liked it.

She was glad for the silence. Their argument and the sun had left her with a niggling headache. He pulled up in the courtyard, stopping long enough to see her out of the car before disappearing abruptly into the house.

'How did you like the lake?' called Carmela from the garden, wandering over towards the car. Even in gardening clothes and with a wisp of her strong hair escaped from the clasp holding it behind, Paolo's mother looked cool and elegant.

'Just beautiful,' replied Helene, smiling as she accepted the older woman's arm in hers. 'I didn't realise how perfect it was. You're lucky to have it so close.'

'Oh, where's Paolo?' Carmela asked, looking around. 'I thought we might all have coffee together.' Then she waved the hand holding her gardening gloves. 'Of course, he will be in a hurry to get organised, no doubt. It's a shame he must leave so soon.'

'So soon?'

Carmela stopped and turned to her, frowning slightly. 'He did tell you about the New York trip? He's leaving tonight.'

'Oh, yes,' Helene said, trying to cover up the fact that he was leaving so soon was news. 'Of course.'

Helene headed for their suite to find Paolo. She had an apology to make and she wasn't looking forward to it, not after the day they'd had. She entered their bedroom, spying an open suitcase on the ancient blanket box at the end of their bed.

Paolo emerged from the walk-in wardrobe carrying shirts and a handful of silk ties. He took one look at her standing by the door before continuing directly to the suitcase, dropping in the ties and removing the hangers. His easy disregard of her was like a slap in the face.

'Why didn't you tell me you were leaving so soon?'

'Would it have mattered?'

His words sliced through her. It did matter, more than he knew. 'How long will you be gone?'

He folded the shirts loosely and stacked them in before returning to the wardrobe.

'A week, maybe two.'

Her heart squeezed tight. She didn't want him to go for a minute. She wanted to be with him. She loved curling into him at night after they'd made love and having his hands stroke her to sleep. After years of sleeping alone she had no desire to rush back to it.

'Your mother and I had a long chat.'

Her words were met with stony silence and she gulped in a breath, looking for strength. She waited for him to re-enter the room before she continued. 'She said this case you're working on is all *pro bono* work—that you and the firm receive no money. That you're providing your services free of charge.'

'That's right,' he said, shrugging. 'What of it?'

'I said some things—about you not taking on the case because you didn't need any more money. I want to apologise. I had no idea.'

He held his hands wide open after dropping a silk robe and some trunks on top of the shirts.

'But you're right. I don't need the money.'

'You're not making this any easier for me,' she accused.

'You have such a low opinion of me, why should that come as a surprise?'

'Well, I just wanted to let you know that I'm sorry.' Given the circumstances it sounded painfully inadequate. Carmela had spent the time it took to serve the coffee to fill her in on the class action his firm was fighting against a cartel of powerful pharmaceutical companies across three continents. She'd known the basic details from the reports in the papers, but she'd had no idea of the details or that without Paolo's firm's intervention the case, and with it any chance of compensation for ongoing medical costs for the child victims, would have been lost months ago.

In so many ways it echoed the work she did providing education programmes for women and children in Third World countries, work of which she was immensely proud.

'I knew you were working on a major case and yet I had no concept as to how important it was.'

One hand still arranging the things in his case, he angled his head over his shoulder and looked at her properly for the first time, one eyebrow arched speculatively. 'And if I was doing it for the money, it wouldn't be important? I'm afraid I don't understand your concept of importance, Helene. For instance, what is it that makes you believe your work is more important than having this child?'

'That's not true! I don't.'

He turned fully. 'Then why are you so determined to return to Paris and go on with your life as if this child had never been conceived?'

'I've never said that. You were the one who engineered that outcome!'

He uttered a torrent of Italian expletives, his hands palm up in the air between them. 'What was all that about earlier today, then? You made it perfectly obvious that your choice was to return to work rather than raise this child.'

'Choice? I don't remember discussing anything to do with making a choice, or even being given one. You told me what you'd decided and you expected me to fall in with your plans exactly as you've been doing ever since you reappeared in my life. So don't talk to me about what I have chosen to do—you're the least qualified person in the world to do that. You've never even bothered to consult me on the topic.'

He'd never thought of green as a hot colour, but

the way her eyes were flashing right now told him a different story. They pierced like lasers, while her cheeks betrayed her inner heat with colour, her chest by the way it rose and fell so dramatically.

He hauled in a breath as his body stirred. There was an energy about her tonight, a passion that fired his own desires. She was so beautiful, but angry like this she was magnificent. He watched the heated rise and fall of her chest and almost groaned.

He would miss those breasts. He would miss the way they responded in his mouth. He would miss the way they tasted.

He would miss all of her.

Right now he didn't want her angry. He wanted her chest to be heaving for an entirely different reason. Before he left he would have to have her.

Dredging up a laugh to break the mounting tension in the room, he put his hands on her shoulders. 'You are taking things too much to heart. My sister warned me that pregnant women are sometimes emotional. I should have remembered that today. I could have saved you both an outburst and an apology.'

'No!' She lifted her arms and broke his grip, spinning away across the room. 'Don't patronise me. This has nothing to do with me being pregnant!'

'Then tell me,' he invited soothingly, moving ever closer to her, slipping one hand around her neck. 'What is it about?'

His change of tone had caught her unawares. Her eyes seemed suddenly too big for her face, her skin now so pale it looked almost translucent, her breathing still choppy but now holding an edge, betraying an inner turmoil of a different kind.

'It's about me making my own decisions,' she said softly, her head leaning towards the warmth of his hand even though he saw the battle going on in her eyes not to.

'And I don't let you.' His other hand followed the lead of the first and he just rested his forearms on her shoulders, stroking the nape of her neck with his fingertips.

Her eyelids closed. 'No. You expect me to act like your precious Ferrari.'

'I do?'

He drew closer, his lips brushing her brow, his fingers laced through her hair.

'You do! You steer left, the car goes left. You steer right, the car goes right.'

'What can I say?' he asked, sliding his arms down her back and easing her towards him in the process. 'It's a car.'

'But I'm not. And yet you expect to steer me exactly the same way.' She gasped as his hands found their way under her ruffled skirt and slipped under the edge of her brief panties.

He covered her gasp with his mouth, softly pressing his lips over hers so that when she breathed in she would breathe his scent before he lifted his lips away.

Her hands lifted to his shoulders and she clung to him as if she would otherwise fall. Her eyes looked up at him, openly curious as her tongue found her lips. 'Your problem is you don't like it when I don't want to be driven. You can't accept that sometimes I want to be in the driver's seat. That I'm more than qualified to drive.'

He lowered his mouth to her throat while insinuating his fingers through the spring of her curls, gently opening her to his touch only to be welcomed by her slick, wet heat.

'*Dio,*' he uttered, 'I have a problem.'

'You agree?' Her voice caught as his fingers circled the sensitive flesh.

'I have never known anyone who makes me feel so inadequate. I have no control where you are concerned. Wanting you is *driving* me crazy.'

Her flesh was growing moister, her words breathier. 'You know that's not what I meant.'

'But it is true. And I am leaving it up to you.' Slowly, reluctantly, he withdrew his hand and lifted her two hands away from his shoulders. Her eyes looked dazed and she blinked, unsteady with his sudden loss of support. 'What do you want? I am giving you the choice whether or not we make love now. You decide.'

Already her body was humming from his sensual touch, her breathing shallow in anticipation of that place where only he could take her. Already she could feel her body preparing itself for sex, nerve endings alive and receptive. So what kind of choice was he giving her? No choice at all.

But he thought he had her. He thought she was so far gone she was his for the taking. Desire reached out from his dark, confident eyes, coiling around her as he waited. But it wasn't the kind of choice she needed, even if it took her every shred of self-control she had.

She let him stand there, watching her, and then slowly, sensually she slid her hands until they crossed over at the hem of her top as if she were going to peel it off. His eyes followed every tiny movement so that she recognised the very moment his pupils dilated as he took the gesture for compliance, noticed his rapid intake of air and the twitch of the muscle in his jaw as he silently urged her on. She read hunger in his eyes, she could taste his anticipation.

'Actually,' she said, rearranging her hands into an innocent clasp in front of her, 'given that you're going to leave so soon, it's probably not a good idea to interrupt your packing.'

His nostrils flared, his eyes widened with disbelief on reflex. 'You're saying no?'

It was her turn to raise one eyebrow at him. 'Unless you really want to?'

They never made it to the bed, not the first time at least. He took her there, passionately, desperately, right where she was, her legs drawn up tightly around him, and only when the last shuddering waves rocked through her and her legs slid down to find support did they collapse together onto the bed so that he could make love to her all over again.

It was some time before they moved. 'I have to leave now,' he whispered in her ear, kissing her lightly. She must have dozed while he'd showered and changed. 'My car will be here shortly.'

Heaviness filled her muscles and the shadow of a headache from her day at the lake had built to something more. Even the afterglow she was used to feeling low down after orgasm had staled into something more like an insistent ache. A sudden moment of panic gripped her and she sat up. 'I don't want you to go.'

'I have to go,' he said. 'But what we talked about at lunch—' He dipped his head in a nod. 'You were right. I didn't ever ask you what you wanted. But I know we can build a family around this child.' He kissed her again lightly on the lips, picked up his jacket and suitcase and headed for the door.

Her heart hammered loud in her chest. Should she tell him now before he went away? Tell him the truth—tell him that she loved him and she would stay with him for ever, on whatever terms? Her lips fought to frame the words.

'Paolo.' Even as her teeth dragged over her bottom lip she knew that she couldn't. He couldn't love her— not if he was leaving her so suddenly this way. The last thing he'd want to hear right now was her telling him that she loved him. He'd never believe her now.

But she couldn't let him go entirely without him giving her something, a kernel of hope, something for her to hold onto. 'I need to ask something before you go.'

'What?'

'I know this child is very important to you and I understand that. It's very important to me too. But I need to know…' She hesitated in the silence while he waited. 'I need to know if I'm important to you too.'

His eyes narrowed immediately, creasing at the sides as if the question was all too easy. 'After what we just shared you have to ask? But of course you're important to me. Apart from the sex, you're carrying my child.'

The pain woke her from a fitful sleep. Sharp spasms racked her insides, the cramps acute, and for a few minutes she desperately feared the worst. But then the sickness rose in her throat and it was almost with relief that she staggered to the bathroom. It *had* to be food poisoning, even though she knew she'd barely touched her lunch and hadn't felt like dinner.

It just had to be.

CHAPTER TWELVE

THE cab topped the small rise and the outline of New York City appeared on the skyline before them. Yet today Paolo felt none of the excitement he usually did *en route* from the airport, no anticipation of the battle to come, none of his usual hunger to win.

Instead his thoughts centred squarely on home. Leaving had been one of the hardest things he'd done in a long time and that in itself was a surprise. But the fact he'd been unable to shift his thoughts and focus on the brief in front of him all throughout the long flight was even more unsettling.

But it was hardly home he was thinking about—it was Helene. He'd never been so wholly distracted by thoughts of anyone before. Even the guilt following Sapphy's sudden marriage to Sheikh Khaled Al-Ateeq, both the guilt that he hadn't been honest enough with her to prevent her from going to Jebbai in the first place and guilt that his inability to do so had resulted in a marriage borne out of revenge, didn't come close to what he was feeling now.

It was Helene and her compassion one night in Paris that had got him through that time and it was Helene and the look on her face just before he'd walked out of their room that haunted him now. She'd looked so fragile, so sad. Why should she be sad?

She'd asked him what she meant to him and he'd told her exactly how important she was to him. Yet her face had fallen, her eyes had grown more crystalline. Had she been expecting something different? Something more?

A sudden memory collided into his thoughts like an express train. There was only one thing more.

'What about love?' she'd asked him at lunch, and he'd answered her honestly. But to then ask him whether or not she was important to him—was that what she'd been leading up to? Had she wanted him to say that he loved her?

It made no sense. She was the one who wanted out of their relationship, after all. She was the one who wanted to get back to Paris and resume her precious career as soon as possible, even sooner if he would let her run a home office from the villa. She was the one who kept denying him at every turn. Those things were hardly the actions of someone in love.

No, he decided, their relationship was purely physical. They shared great sex and a growing baby. That should be enough for anyone.

Traffic was heavy and it was taking for ever to get to his hotel, so he requested the taxi driver to drop him off near the office. He'd got nothing done on the plane and he would probably end up wasting everyone's time because of it, but at least there he might be able to focus on the case.

By the time he'd checked into the hotel he'd been awake for more hours than he cared to think about, but at least finally he'd made some progress. Tomorrow he could start to assemble the team.

'Oh, and there's a message for you, sir.' The concierge handed him his room card in a small folder together with an envelope.

His mind in autopilot during the formalities, Paolo scooped them both up in one hand and headed for the lifts. Only after he'd discarded his bag and jacket and poured himself a slug of scotch did he notice the envelope on the credenza where he'd tossed it upon entering the room. He tore it open and froze. The message from his mother was chillingly brief.

'Urgent. Call home immediately.'

Helene!

It was insane—in his mind he recognised the emergency could involve any one of his family or anything and yet in his heart he knew instinctively that it had to be Helene and that she was in danger.

Panic gripped him as he battled with the phone for an international connection. He couldn't bear it if she was hurt—or worse. Nothing must happen to her. She was part of him now, a part he never intended to lose.

He'd misdialled the number for the second time when it hit him. He hadn't given a thought to their child—Helene had been his first and only concern. The truth slammed his heart against his chest wall as the one thing he'd thought not possible screamed out its truth.

He loved her.

Fear lurched inside him. The truth was staggering in itself, but it was the implications that made him reel, made him throw his hand to his forehead as the ramifications of his discovery hit home.

He'd told Helene that all she meant to him was nothing more than good sex and as the mother of his child. He'd as good as told her that that was all there could ever be. And he'd thought he was doing the right thing—but when he recalled her eyes, so lost and hurting as he'd turned and walked away...

Dio! He was half a world away and he loved her and she didn't know and if anything happened to her...

Frantically he stabbed at the buttons of the phone and after an interminable wait for a connection he made it through at last. The housekeeper answered on the third ring despite it being something like five a.m. her time. She promptly burst into tears amidst a torrent of impassioned words, but in a few short seconds his worst fears were realised.

His blood turned to ice.

Helene was in hospital.

And she'd lost the baby.

She was empty inside, empty of the new life she'd nurtured in her body these past seventeen weeks, empty of her hopes and dreams for the future—a future that now stretched out as bleak and barren as she felt within.

No baby. No precious child to hold in her arms, no tiny fingers to cling to her own, no sweet features to soothe into sleep.

She couldn't stay at the villa. She'd checked herself out of hospital saying she'd be better off in her own bed, but there was no reason to stay. There was no point pretending any more.

She'd lost his child.

He didn't want her love.

There was nothing she could offer Paolo now.

Another wave of grief washed over her, filling the yawning spaces inside with pain and hurt.

She'd wanted this child so much! Whatever custodial or living arrangements Paolo and she had eventually settled upon wouldn't have mattered in the end. This would have been her child and she would have loved it and nurtured it regardless. She would have showered upon it all the love that she had been denied her entire life. Whatever else might have happened, her baby would always have had a mother.

But now there was no chance to be that mother.

Now she had nothing.

No baby, no future, no hope that Paolo would want her.

She clasped her hands protectively low over her stomach—she couldn't stop herself—even though she knew there was no point and that it was too late. There was no child any more.

It was too hard to accept. Being told she was pregnant had been a struggle to accept, certainly, but the knowledge that she was no longer with child was any number of times more impossible to come to terms with. Even when she'd felt that one godawful paroxysm that had left her feeling as if it had torn her apart inside, she'd been in denial. It hadn't been until the warm swell of moisture and the trickle down her thigh that she'd known there was no point kidding herself any more.

She sucked in a breath of air as she did a mental stocktake of what she'd need. The doctors and Carmela had ordered her to stay in bed and rest, but she was sick of the inactivity, sick of thinking endlessly about what might have gone wrong. Thinking about what she must have done wrong.

So instead, she moved about the room, packing only what she could carry in a small overnight bag. She'd get a taxi to pick her up. They could send the rest of her gear on, but she had to leave now, before he arrived.

Because there was no way she could face him.

She'd lost him his child and there was no way he would ever forgive her. And she couldn't face another scene, not now. Besides which, there was no point.

There was no reason now to continue their farce of a marriage, no tie to bind them together and certainly no reason to imagine he'd want to stand by his offer of making a family together. She'd let him down, and the sooner she removed herself from his life, the sooner he could find himself a real wife. The sooner he could find someone he loved.

She picked up a few items from her dressing table, her eyes falling on the crystal heart paperweight that he'd bought her in New York. She picked it up, feeling its cool weight in her hands. Her own heart squeezed tight when she remembered the day he'd bought it. He'd been so controlling, insisting on spending a fortune on rings when the last thing she felt like was a bride, and then he'd surprised her completely by gifting her the heart. And she'd thought— she'd hoped—that maybe they could make this work. But it would never work. There was too much history between them, too little love.

At long last he could get on with lodging the paperwork they'd both signed and made ready for their divorce months ago. At last he'd be free of her. The inconvenience was over, the lies and the deceit needed no longer.

Reluctantly she replaced the paperweight on the table, tracing her fingers around its sculpted sides. She didn't want any tender reminders of this time that might cause her to regret what she was doing. She *was* doing the right thing. She had no choice. Now that she was no longer bearing his child he didn't need her any more. He wouldn't want her to stay.

And she had to get out before he asked her to leave.

She removed her rings, the plain white-gold wedding band and the stunning three-diamond engagement ring he'd insisted she have. The skin underneath looked pale after the Italian sunshine and she rubbed absently at the mark as if she could somehow eradicate the past few months by removing all trace of it. Then she put the rings down alongside the heart. Whatever they thought of her after her departure, it wasn't going to be that she was a bloodsucking witch, out for anything she could get.

A sob lodged in her throat when she thought of what she was about to do, leaving Carmela without a word. It wasn't right, but she knew that if she tried to say goodbye the older woman would make her stay and face Paolo and there was no way she could cope with that. Carmela didn't understand because she didn't know the truth, and this was hardly the time to tell her.

Her minimalist packing completed, she propped up a letter she'd written for Paolo alongside the rings and the heart before taking one more look around the room where she'd been so happy with Paolo, in bed at least. She had some good memories—great memories—to take away with her. She'd seen both tenderness and passion, felt his gentle hands and his surging power, tasted his liquid mouth and his velvet heat.

But it was time to order her taxi and leave. She picked up the telephone at exactly the same time it started to ring.

She froze. She'd picked up on an incoming call. What if it was Paolo calling? What would she say?

Her heart hammering, she put the receiver up to her ear, but it was a woman's voice that met her silence—her Italian fluent yet with a trace of an accent. She recognised Paolo's name and blinked.

'I'm sorry,' she said in English, without the energy to try to respond in her faltering Italian. 'I'm afraid Paolo is unavailable just at the moment. Can I help you?'

Her earlier silence was now mirrored at the other end.

'Is that…Helene?'

She couldn't speak. Why would this stranger be calling Paolo on his unlisted family home number, for a start, let alone know about her? There was only one person this could be…

'Who's calling, please?' she managed to get out, doing her best to sound calm and professional even while her fingers clawed white-knuckled on the receiver and her pulse thrummed loud in her ears.

'It's Sapphire Clem— I mean…' She laughed a little as if a little nervous, a little uncertain. 'I mean— just Sapphy. I'm an old friend of Paolo's and I need to talk to him.'

Oh, God. Helene closed her eyes, her free arm

steadying her against the table, wishing she had already left.

Suddenly the accent made sense. It belonged to Sapphire Clemenger, the fashion designer he would have married if not for the small complication that he'd already been married to Helene, and the woman Paolo loved.

But how did Sapphire know about Helene?

And why was she calling Paolo now?

Unless she needed help to escape from Khaled? And who else would she call but the man she should have been with?

New resolve gripped her. This was Helene's chance to make up for the mess she'd created over twelve years ago. Now she could finally put things to right between Paolo and Sapphire. They deserved every chance to be together. They deserved to be happy.

'I'm sorry,' she said at last. 'Paolo won't be home until later, so if you'd like to call again?'

'I won't have a chance,' Sapphire responded. 'I'm about to board my flight to Milan. But it's great to hear that he'll be there. Please let him know I'm on my way.'

Helene put the receiver down, resting both hands on the phone as she took some welcome deep breaths. It was good that Sapphire was coming. It was right. A tear rolled down her cheek. Even though her own heart was broken, there was no need for Paolo to go without happiness. After all he'd done for her, the years he'd wasted on her behalf, he deserved his chance to love.

She picked up the receiver again, ordered a taxi in

her stammering Italian and, after seizing a stack of tissues to mop up her leaking eyes, quietly exited the house to wait.

She was gone. For the second time she'd left him, leaving only a few written lines in her wake. Guilt that he should have been here with her, guilt that somehow he was responsible for what had happened by his persistent lovemaking—all his guilt evaporated as his eyes slid over the contents of the brief note yet again.

Paolo,
I couldn't stay after what's happened. I'm so sorry about the baby. I know what having a child meant to you, but maybe this way is for the best.
Now there is no need to pretend any longer.
Thank you so much for rescuing me so long ago and for standing by me all these years. I'm sorry that I couldn't repay you in a better way—you deserve much more.
Goodbye,
Helene

Paolo threw back his head and roared, his cry a rough animal mix of anguish, despair and heated fury. How dared she say that this was for the best?

His child was dead! How could such a tragedy ever be for the best?

It might be for her. She'd wanted out of their arrangement as soon as she could, wanting out of any chance of a life with him, wanting to return to her neat life and her perfect career. A miscarriage must have suited her perfectly.

And he'd imagined she loved him! He'd even convinced himself that he loved her. He must have been insane.

She couldn't wait to get out of here. She couldn't wait to get away from him.

So much for love.

CHAPTER THIRTEEN

SHE'D been kidding herself. Helene tossed the last of her laundry into the machine and followed it with an unusually reckless dose of powder. She'd thought when she'd left the villa that she was leaving behind all trace of Paolo and what had happened between them, but even her apartment was full of memories.

Nowhere provided the sanctuary she needed. His presence was right through the place—from the reception room where he'd studied the items on her mantelpiece with such apparent fascination before their torrid lovemaking, to the bedroom where even now she imagined she could smell his scent on the sheets alongside her.

Everywhere held memories of him and every part of her empty life threw into sharp relief exactly how much she'd lost.

Everything.

But the very worst part of it all was knowing that she'd made the right decision. It was two weeks since she'd returned from Milan and there'd been no word from him, no effort to get in touch. She hadn't expected him to follow her, yet the fact that he hadn't made the slightest attempt to contact her simply confirmed the correctness of her actions. She'd done the right thing for both of them by leaving.

If only she felt better about it. It was one thing to want Paolo to be happy, but another thing entirely to know that he had so easily let her go. It stung. Though what had she expected? She'd just about set him up with his former lover.

She punched at the washing-machine buttons with much more force than strictly necessary before swiping from her face the strands of hair that had worked loose from her pony-tail. There was no point thinking about what might have happened between Paolo and Sapphire after she'd left. No point at all torturing herself and imagining them together. She just had to get over it.

Noises from outside her door jagged into her thoughts, jerking her head around—voices on the stairs, on the landing outside, then the sound of the neighbour's door closing before the empty resumption of quiet—and she sighed. How long would it be before she didn't jump every time she heard a footfall on the stairs, or freeze when the telephone rang? How long would it take before she felt normal again?

Another door banged shut and someone tapped on her door. She tried to extinguish the spark of hope that flickered into life as she walked towards the door, telling herself it was no doubt Eugene back from shopping with a slice of Brie or a croissant for her. But the spark raged into a firestorm when she looked through the peep-hole and saw who was standing on the other side.

Paolo.

A tidal wave of conflicting emotions crashed over her, a mess of rippling sensations assailing her senses, all conspiring to take her breath away. She clutched her hands to her chest and felt her panicked heartbeat racing beneath as she fought for air.

He was here. And just like the first time he'd appeared on her doorstep his dark eyes looked wild, his face strained and tense. Would his message this time be the same? Was that why he'd come, to deliver in person the final blow to their marriage? Was he taking the opportunity to put into words what his two weeks of failing to contact her had made plain?

She pulled open the door and reminded herself to breathe.

For a second it was almost tenderness she thought she saw in his eyes, but then he blinked and they narrowed and any tenderness slid straight off their glinting, rock-hard surface. 'You've got some explaining to do,' he said as he pushed past her into the apartment.

There was little she could do but follow him, her skin tingling where he'd brushed by, her senses reeling in the wake of his familiar scent, her late-night dreams and memories inadequate preparation for the sheer physical impact of the man.

'Why did you leave?' he demanded, his hands on his hips.

He wasn't wasting any time on pleasantries. He hadn't even bothered to sit down before he'd turned and fired the question off like a salvo. So that was how it was going to be. She pulled her loosened hair back tightly behind her ears and crossed her arms.

'I couldn't stay.'

'You mean you couldn't wait to get away.'

'It wasn't like that—'

'No? So you're not already back at work, then?'

She dropped her eyes and looked away. The doctor had pronounced her fit and she'd started back two days ago. It wasn't that she was desperate to get back, despite what Paolo thought—it had just seemed a much healthier option than moping around the apartment feeling sorry for herself.

'You couldn't wait to go back to your precious job.' He spat the words out like bullets.

'And what was I supposed to do?' she retaliated, throwing her arms out wide. 'Hang around and wait for you to arrive so you could push me around again? No, thanks, I've had enough of being pushed around for one lifetime.'

'You were supposed to be resting at the villa, not running away.'

'Who said I was running?' She hadn't been running. It had been more like a tactical withdrawal. She'd got herself out of his life before he'd thrown her out.

'You've been running all your life. Running away from your father, running away without a word the night we spent together here in this very apartment. And you're still running. You stole away from the villa like a thief.'

'And who wouldn't leave in the circumstances?'

'Any normal person! You'd just lost a baby—remember? Or were you so keen to get back to work that a mere miscarriage was too insignificant a detail to register with you?'

The cold shock of his words came with an acid burn.

'How *dare* you say that? How could I forget? I was the one who was there. It was me who felt the pain. It was me who felt my baby tearing itself free from my womb—'

Her voice cracked on the last word and she spun around, battling to regain some sort of control after her impassioned outburst.

But she didn't have a chance before his hands were on her shoulders. 'I'm sorry,' he said, turning her around to face him. 'I didn't mean that. I didn't come here today to upset you.'

'Then don't you ever say that losing our baby didn't mean anything to me. You have no idea how much I wanted that child, how much I wanted it all to turn out perfectly.' Her lip quivered. 'But it didn't. It all went wrong. I lost my baby.'

He pulled her into his arms as the bubble in her throat became a sob, opening the floodgates to her grief. 'Our baby,' he said. '*We* lost *our* baby.'

He held her tight as she cried, really cried. For two weeks she'd held herself together, defying the tears, refusing to dwell on her loss, but there was no stopping them now.

'I'm sorry,' he said, stroking her head. 'I should have been there with you.'

She sniffed, lifting her head away at last and wiping the liquid tracks of tears from her face. 'It doesn't matter now. There's nothing you could have done.'

'I should never have left you,' he insisted. 'It must have been terrifying. My mother said you were in a lot of pain.'

Reluctantly she thought back to that awful night. There had been pain, and plenty of it, and yet it wasn't the pain that was foremost in her memories of that time. 'The worst pain,' she said softly, 'was knowing there was nothing I could do. The worst pain was knowing there was no hope for our child—no chance for it at all.'

He pulled her back in close and wrapped her securely in his arms again. She met his broad chest and inhaled deeply, revelling in the feel of the muscled wall of his chest against her cheek and the musky tones of his masculine scent. She'd missed him so much and yet he hadn't bothered to follow her here until now. If he'd really wanted to be with her, to console her and share in her grief, he'd had plenty of time before now.

She eased herself out of his arms, needing to show him how strong she was, that she could cope, so that when he left her again to go back to Sapphire he would never suspect the truth. He would never know that she loved him.

'I'm sorry,' she said with a shrug, recognising the pain in his eyes because it so closely matched her own. He'd lost his child and he looked just as confused, just as bereft. 'I don't even know why it happened.'

'I made love to you before I left,' he said. 'Could I have hurt you? Was I to blame?'

His features looked so anguished that for a moment she wanted to take his face in her hands and kiss his torment away. He wasn't blaming her! It was the last thing she'd expected. She smiled a little and shook her head.

'Not a chance. The doctors said that sometimes these things just happen. They assured me that it's nothing to do with anything either of us did.'

'There must be a reason.'

She sighed, rubbing her hands together for the sake

of doing something. 'I've been thinking about that. Maybe our baby knew that things weren't right between us. Maybe somehow it didn't want to be born to people that weren't entirely happy about having it.'

'I wanted this child!'

She held up a hand to stop him. 'And you don't think I did? Of course I wanted it! But neither of us was particularly happy about the circumstances of its conception. Neither of us was happy about being forced together the way we were. We both wanted this child, certainly, but maybe—and it probably sounds crazy—but maybe, the baby just didn't want us.'

Her teeth sank down on her bottom lip and pressed tight, hoping the pain would take away another.

'That is crazy.'

'I know, but have you got a better theory? Who would want to be born into a family with so much heartache, into a relationship built on deception? You could hardly blame a child for not wanting to get tangled up in our mess.'

He shook his head, making sweeping arcs of denial with his arms as he strode around the room. She watched his progress, feeling his pain, understanding his anguish. Just as on the night he'd turned up on her doorstep four months ago, he seemed suddenly uncertain of his place in life, his natural arrogance tempered by his innate humanity. She could see the battle for understanding going on behind his weary eyes. She could feel his internal struggle.

But how could you understand something that made no sense? How could you unravel a fathomless mystery?

After a time he stopped pacing and reached a hand into the pocket of his jacket.

'I had your belongings packed, but I wanted to bring you something.' For a moment she thought he must mean her rings. He held out his hand, palm down, and she placed her hand under his, expecting something small, and so totally unprepared for the weight when he dropped the object into her hands that she almost let it spill out of her hands onto the carpet. She pulled it in close and looked down at it, her fingers curling around the edges as she studied its ruby depths.

'Why did you leave it behind?' he asked.

'I couldn't bear to take it,' she replied honestly, two fat tears rolling silently down her cheeks as she remembered the scan, the transparent flesh, the tiny beating heart. 'I was too raw and it reminded me of something much, much too special.'

He nodded, coming closer to look at it in her hands. 'The first time I saw it in the display cabinet, it made me think of the scan—'

She looked up at him, blinking away the moisture in her eyes only to notice the sheen in his. He'd seen their baby's heart in the simple paperweight too?

'Why are you here?' she asked hesitantly. She didn't know why she should feel hope, except that this wasn't turning out to be the blamefest she'd expected from Paolo's visit. 'You didn't come just to bring me this.'

'No.' He sucked in a burst of air and expelled it in a rush. 'I didn't.'

She waited, her hands squeezing the crystal heart as if it might lend her some of its cool, hard strength.

'I've lodged the papers to finalise our divorce.'

CHAPTER FOURTEEN

THE oxygen was sucked from the room, the ticking clock the only sound in the vacuum of Helene's world.

'Ah. I see.' How not to sound disappointed when the bottom was dropping out of her world? She'd known this was going to happen, had suspected the wheels were already well and truly in motion. But still, Paolo's words were final confirmation that he was happy to let her go, that, now the child they'd both had a part in making was lost, he had no further need for her.

She sat down on her settee, feigning interest in placing the crystal heart down on the coffee-table in just the right position. 'Of course, I expected as much. I know it's taken much longer than what we ever anticipated.' She tried to laugh, but the sound came out broken and flat. 'Who would ever have imagined our rushed marriage would have lasted so long? At last now you can finally be free.'

A muscle twitched in his jaw. 'If everything goes to plan, I'm not planning on being free for long.'

Prickly fingers skittered down her spine before grabbing hold of her heart and squeezing it tightly. Surely not already? 'I'm afraid I'm not with you.'

'I'm planning to get married again.'

What was left of her heart dropped to her feet. There was only one person he could be marrying. It didn't matter that this was the very thing she'd expected when she'd left, that this was how she'd envisaged their futures working out. Now it was real, it was happening and it hurt so very badly.

'I understand.' The words squeezed out through her teeth. 'How is Sapphire?'

His coal-black lashes tangled together in a blink that seemed to last an eternity. Then they opened to a twitch in his jaw. 'That was you she spoke to when she called the villa? We suspected it must be, but we had no idea when you'd left.'

She nodded. 'I'm sorry, she said to leave you a note. I forgot...'

He considered her response for only a moment. 'It's of no consequence. She's well, as it happens. Better than well. In fact, I've never seen her looking so happy.'

Every word was like a spike to her soul. Every word sealed her fate a little more securely. Paolo would divorce her and marry Sapphy and once more she would be alone.

'I'm so glad,' she lied, determined to put on a brave face. 'You both deserve to be happy after all that's happened. I feel so responsible for the whole mess—you were so right—if it hadn't been for me running from my father and that forced marriage to Khaled, none of this would have happened. So it's right that you two have been able to salvage something from the wreckage. It's good that you can finally be together.'

'Together?' His brows drew close as he frowned. 'What makes you say that?'

'Well, you and Sapphire. I thought that—that you and she…now that you were free…'

'You thought I was planning on marrying Sapphy?'

'Aren't you?'

'She's married already, and she's staying married.'

'But that's to Khaled!'

'I know, it's hard to believe. But like I said, she's the happiest I've ever seen her. She's in love with him, I have no doubt of that.'

'And what about him?'

He nodded. 'I met Khaled. Sapphire brought him with her. She didn't say anything about her plans during her call because she thought I'd refuse to see him.'

Helene shivered, wrapping her arms around herself. It was just as well she'd left the villa. There was no way she could have handled seeing Khaled again, knowing what she'd done all those years ago. Her simple teenage act of defiance had spawned more than a decade of hatred and retribution. Coming on the heels of her miscarriage, even being in the same house with him would have been unbearable.

And yet it must have been almost as difficult for Paolo, if not more so, given that he had lost the woman he loved to him.

'But you saw him?' she asked, her curiosity about the man she had snubbed so long ago intensely aroused, despite the dark place he'd always occupied in her mind. 'I couldn't,' she said with a shiver. 'To hate someone for so long just because he married the woman promised to you first—I don't think I could handle meeting him.'

'I thought the same thing at first. But I finally discovered that there was more to his desire for revenge against me than having lost you. I discovered he held me responsible for the sudden death of his parents and that's what really drove him to do what he did.'

'But that's crazy. Why would he possibly believe you had anything to do with his parents?'

'They died in an avalanche in the Alps. It never occurred to me that it had happened the same day he was supposed to marry you.'

'Oh, my God!' The full ramifications of what he was explaining sank in. 'So they should have been in London attending the wedding and not in the Alps at all? And he held you responsible for that because you married me instead?'

'So it would seem. I'd stolen you away and the wedding plans were aborted. His parents left for the Alps to get over their disappointment. They were killed outright by the avalanche, along with their two companions.'

'How horrible,' she said on a shudder, finally starting to understand what might possibly drive a man to hate so much. 'But he came to Milan with Sapphire? What's changed that he would want to meet with you, after all that's happened?'

'Sapphy's changed him, for a start. It seems that he would never have made any attempt at reconciliation if not for her influence. He really does love her. But that's not all. It seem recent events in Jebbai have thrown doubt on the circumstances of the tragedy. There's a chance the avalanche wasn't an accident at all, that it was triggered by one or both of the companions.'

'Khaled's parents were assassinated?'

'They now suspect that may be true. The companions' daughter was involved in an attempt on Khaled's life recently. They thought initially it was just in retribution for the death of her parents in the avalanche, but now it seems the entire family has been involved in actions against the Sheikhdom all along—a grudge going back generations.'

'So Khaled now knows that you weren't responsible for his parents' deaths.'

He nodded. 'But that's not all. They believe the original plan was to carry out their grisly task at the wedding.' He paused. 'Your wedding with Khaled.'

Her blood turned to ice as she thought about the long guest list her mother had organised and the no doubt packed church. 'It could have been all of us there that day.' She looked up at him as the truth rammed home. 'You saved our lives. All our lives that day—including Khaled's.'

'Ironic, isn't it?' he said with a wry laugh. 'And yet he'd blamed me for stealing his bride and destroying the lives of his parents. When if we hadn't married all those years ago…' His words trailed off. 'Well, we did marry.'

It was impossible to absorb it all. Too much was happening. Too much was changing. She stood up and wandered over to the long window, pulling aside the soft muslin curtain and gazing out over the narrow street outside, the apartment buildings jammed together with their quaint metal balconies, the picture-book roof-line jutting into the summer sky, the people walking down the street. It all looked so perfectly normal. It all looked so perfectly ordinary. And yet she knew things could never be normal or ordinary again. The components of her world had shifted like vast plates moving roughly over each other, altering the connections and changing the relationships for ever.

She turned away from the window, looking back at him. 'I always thought of you as saving me from a fate worse than death, but I never realised how literally true that was. You saved me from more than a forced marriage I never wanted. You actually saved my life by marrying me.'

He held his hands palm up. 'None of it is proven. We can't be sure.'

'I'm sure,' she insisted. 'But I just don't know how I ever am ever going to repay you.'

'I didn't tell you all that so that you would feel you had to repay me. I told you so that you would understand Khaled and see that he is no longer a threat to your happiness.'

She smiled as she moved closer, reaching one tentative hand up to his cheek. 'You have done more for me than any person on this earth. You stepped in when I most needed a friend, when I had lost my family and I was alone and frightened. And you lived with the promise of Khaled's revenge for years because of it.

'I know there's nothing I can offer in return, I know there's no reason for you to have anything to do with me in the future, but if you ever need anything, anything, then please let me know.'

He took her hand in his, holding it against his cheek. 'There is one thing you can do for me,' he said, his voice gravelly and low, his eyes so intense they seemed to pierce into her soul.

'Marry me,' he said. 'Become my wife. Be part of my life for ever.'

She blinked her eyes, but the dream didn't disappear—Paolo was still there and the magic was still fizzing in her veins.

'You can't be serious,' she said. 'We are—*were*—married. You've just lodged the papers for our divorce.'

'No. We had a certificate of marriage, that's all. We were never really married, not properly. I lodged those divorce papers because that marriage never really existed. And I should have lodged them four months ago when you signed them but I couldn't bring myself to do it. I couldn't take that last step to sever the ties we'd created back then, especially after that night together with you.'

'You told me you didn't have time to lodge them.'

'I know. Because I could hardly tell you the truth. That night we shared was special for me. I wasn't prepared to let you go so easily after that. I used the fact we were still married to force you into coming back to Milan, even though it was clear you wanted to be rid of me.'

'What do you mean—it was clear?'

'You signed those papers and left them where I couldn't miss them. They could have waited. There was no rush.'

'Oh, Paolo! But when you turned up looking so desperate, I thought that's exactly what you wanted—to be free of me for ever. I'd already taken up enough of your life.'

He took her hands and kissed them. 'It will never be enough,' he said. 'But I want the chance to start again with you, Helene. I want a real marriage. And this is the hardest thing of all for me, but this time I won't tell you what to do and I won't force you into anything. This time it's your choice. This time you get to decide.'

There was no way she couldn't smile. There was no way her smile wouldn't light up a darkened room, she felt so happy. 'I can't believe this is happening. I thought you were angry with me. When you didn't contact me here I thought you never wanted to see me again—'

He took her hands in his. 'I'm so sorry I let you think that. When I discovered you'd gone I went crazy. I was angry that our child was gone—so damned angry that you'd left that I couldn't think straight. My mother, my sister, even Sapphy—they all urged me to go after you immediately, but I thought I could forget you.'

He took a deep breath before continuing. 'Except as the days went by I realised what made me the angriest—it was because I'd lost you without ever telling you how much you meant to me. It was because if I didn't go after you I'd never get the chance to tell you, and, no matter what your reaction, I had to try.'

She swallowed, terrified that he wasn't going to say what she so wanted to hear.

'I'd fallen in love with you, Helene. I tried to suppress it; I tried to bury it under my anger and grief, I tried to think that you meant only sex and a child to me, but the truth wouldn't be denied. And I know that you have plenty of reasons to say no, but I'm asking you—begging you to say yes. Please marry me. Give us the chance to start again. Because there's no way I can live without you. I love you.'

He loved her? Elation pumped through her veins. It hardly seemed possible—she was hearing the words she'd longed to hear from the man she had loved for what seemed like for ever. And he was asking her to marry him. *Really* marry him.

'Yes,' she said, watching her own delight mirrored as his face lit up at her simple word. 'Yes, I will marry you. Yes, I love you. Yes! Yes! Yes!'

Laughing, she threw her arms around his neck as he swept her up, whirling her around in his arms as his lips met hers in a hungry kiss that spoke of their weeks of separation and their commitment to a long future together.

Breathless, he pulled his head away at last. 'You love me? You said you loved me.'

'You crazy man,' she said. 'I was in love with you the first time I married you. And this time I love you even more.'

'I had no idea,' he said, his eyes wide, searching her face.

'Wait,' she said as inspiration hit. 'I'll be right back.' She left him there behind her, a look of wonderment on his face, while she disappeared into her room. In thirty seconds she was back.

'I've always loved you, Paolo,' she said, taking his hand and sliding the ring on. 'This is a token of my love. All those years of separation I tried to forget you, but it didn't happen. I could get on with my life, but I couldn't get you out of my heart.'

His light frown turned to amazement when he recognised his old signet ring. 'You've had this all that time?'

'All that time.' She smiled. 'I've treasured it and now I want you to have it and wear it as a sign of how far we've come, as confirmation of my undying love for you.'

He shook his head as if it was all too much to take in, then his features edged into a frown.

'What is it?' she asked.

He smiled. 'Something Sapphy said to me when she came to the villa. She said that all the time she was with me she sensed there was always a part of me that would never be hers, that it always seemed as if there was something holding me back.'

'But you couldn't commit to her. Not when you were already married.'

'No,' he said, 'it was more than that and Sapphy recognised it and I've only just realised that what she said was right. Because a piece of paper would never have been enough to stop me giving my heart and soul to her if it had been free to give. It would never have stopped me loving her. But it did. Because someone already had my heart.' He touched his index finger to the tip of her nose. 'You.'

He'd loved her all that time? It was more than a dream. It was a fantasy come to life and she never wanted it to end.

'Are you telling me that you loved me all those years ago?'

'I think I must have. I didn't want Khaled to have you; I know that. Why would I have married you if I didn't love you?'

'But we never... I mean, you wouldn't—'

'I must have been mad. But I didn't want to take advantage of you that night. I didn't want you to think I would expect sex for payment for what I'd done when I wasn't entirely sure of my motives.'

'You have to be kidding me. You loved me all that time and you've only just realised it now?'

'Guilty,' he said, drawing her close to him again, nuzzling the skin below her ear.

'Then I'd say we have a few years of loving to make up for.'

He pulled back and looked at her, his mouth curved up into a sexy smile, his eyes glinting with resolve, and one look at his lips told her he was going to kiss her, and that he was going to be kissing her for a long, long time to come.

Then his mouth dipped down to hers, his lips a mere breath away. 'So when do we start?'